A TASTE OF PASSION

Michael stood up and walked toward Chantel. He took her hand and kissed it. It was soft and smelled sweet. "Join me for dinner," he said, looking into her dark eyes.

"I would like that," she whispered.

They dined on soup made with black beans, a main course of *petits pois* with sausage and rice, a side dish of stuffed mushrooms, and a dessert of forbidden fruit. Each dish was flavored to perfection, a treat for all the senses—as was, he thought, his dining partner.

Chantel finished her dollop of forbidden fruit and smiled. "You cannot still be hungry."

Michael looked into Chantel's dark eyes. He felt drawn into them. Again his mouth went dry. All his instincts told him to seize her and kiss her, to hold her close. He reached across the white tablecloth and took her hand in his. She stared back at him, her lips slightly parted. Was he mistaken? Or did she desire him as much as he desired her?

"I think of you all the time," Michael confessed. "You fill my dreams." Then he stood up and walked around the tiny table, pulling her up and into his arms. He bent down and kissed her. He kissed her softly at first, then with more pressure.

Chantel shuddered against him, but she did not push him away. . . .

—from "A Taste of Fire" by Joyce Carlow

BOOK YOUR PLACE ON OUR WEBSITE AND MAKE THE READING CONNECTION!

We've created a customized website just for our very special readers, where you can get the inside scoop on everything that's going on with Zebra, Pinnacle and Kensington books.

When you come online, you'll have the exciting opportunity to:

- View covers of upcoming books
- Read sample chapters
- Learn about our future publishing schedule (listed by publication month *and author*)
- Find out when your favorite authors will be visiting a city near you
- Search for and order backlist books from our online catalog
- Check out author bios and background information
- Send e-mail to your favorite authors
- Meet the Kensington staff online
- Join us in weekly chats with authors, readers and other guests
- Get writing guidelines
- AND MUCH MORE!

SINFULLY DELICIOUS

Joyce Carlow
Julia Hanlon
Jean Wilson

Zebra Books
Kensington Publishing Corp.

http://www.zebrabooks.com

CONTENTS

A TASTE OF FIRE

Joyce Carlow

CHAPTER ONE

New Orleans
September, 1803

The sun filtered through the windows and fell on the tile floor of the garden room. The pattern of the shadow reflected the wrought-iron curlicues that decorated the windows as well as the balcony below them. This garden room was filled with bright tropical flowering plants and assorted potted greenery. The colors were wonderful, but the visual sense was not the only sense to be experienced. The room was also filled with the scent of the many spices that were grown in large wooden containers.

There were only two chairs in the garden room, both made of woven bamboo and purchased from a sea captain who had traded in the Orient. This large, sunny room was Marie Dumont's favorite, and more often than not, she spent her mornings in it, tending her plants. But this morning she was conducting an interview.

Marie Dumont studied Chantel Boudreau carefully. She had

learned over the years that it was bad business to hire someone without properly knowing them and understanding their motives for wanting a position. One did not become the most powerful woman in the Louisiana Territory without an innate understanding of human nature; still, she deemed it important to supplement intuitive feelings with facts.

Marie acknowledged that this Chantel Boudreau who sat across from her was an extraordinarily beautiful young woman. She had a wealth of thick, curly brown hair that fell in ringlets down her back. Her large, dark eyes were fringed with long eyelashes; her full lips held a certain sensuous promise, and she possessed a figure most women worked hard to achieve. Her waist was tiny, her hips round, her young breasts full and high. This was a young woman who had never had children, and perhaps, Marie thought, she had never even had a lover, though considering her fine looks, that seemed unlikely.

This Chantel's personality was interesting too. She was in some ways shy while in others she appeared outspoken, capable of asking for what she wanted, of expressing herself. She was well spoken, though she spoke English with a heavy Cajun accent. That she spoke English at all was, naturally, an asset. In any case, most of the European men who frequented Marie's hotel preferred women who spoke French. They thought of it as the language of romance and considered it exotic.

"You are most certainly beautiful enough to become one of my young women. And I must say you appear intelligent as well."

Chantel lifted her eyebrow disdainfully. "That is not what I had in mind," she answered firmly.

Did this soi-disant Queen of New Orleans really think she wanted to become one of her "ladies?" Chantel wondered. Not that the women who worked for Marie Dumont were considered common prostitutes. Far from it, they were respected for their beauty and their varied talents. It was common knowledge that many of them had ultimately married men of great wealth and become nothing less than belles of New Orleans society.

But that was not what she wanted; it was not the reason she had come to this hotel that belonged to Marie Dumont. She had no intention of selling her body, even though she absolutely had to find a way to support herself. Young women without family or husbands always had a difficult time, and it was worse when you were even passably attractive because men always made the assumption that you were available for a price. Chantel well knew how careful she had to be, how serious she had to remain, and how hard she would have to work to impress Marie Dumont. Marie Dumont was one of the few persons who offered jobs to young women. She was wealthy and influential and she ran several businesses in addition to her hotel.

Marie Dumont's expression did not change. "To work in another capacity you would have to exhibit some unusual talent. My shop does not require further hairdressers, and though I do have a need for seamstresses, you would have to be very quick with your fingers indeed."

"Madame, I am a chef, a master of most unusual cuisine."

At her disclosure, Marie's expression did indeed change. "A chef? Unusual cuisine? Exactly what is unusual about it?"

"Madame, you have a hotel and that hotel has dining facilities."

Marie tossed her head. "It is said that we already serve the best food in New Orleans."

"Oh, madame, hear me out. Your food may be excellent, but it does not enhance—or perhaps I should say compliment—your other business."

"And to which business do you refer?" Marie asked. Yes, this young woman was intriguing. *She has succeeded in making me curious,* Marie thought.

"The business of love, madame. I am a master of love-inspiring cuisine, of erotic cookery, and of aphrodisiacs. My creations are sometimes—shall I say suggestive? Other dishes are prepared with certain herbs and spices that fire desire. I could provide love-inspiring dinners for both your ladies and the men who visit them. Intimate dinners, which will result in a night of wild, unbridled lovemaking. Men will pay you well for this service. I have been told that Paris has many such places.''

"This is an interesting proposition," Marie replied thoughtfully. "At least it is original."

"You would be the only innkeeper in all of Louisiana, perhaps all of North America, to have an establishment which offers this—full service.''

"I am myself quite accomplished in the art of spells and magic love potions," Marie said, smiling. "Exactly how is what you offer me different?''

An understatement, Chantel thought. Marie Dumont was often called a witch, and she was most certainly the mistress of spells and potions. She was a stunning woman, a quadroon whose African, French, Indian, and Spanish heritage combined to create her great beauty.

Chantel could not guess Marie's age and most assuredly Marie kept it a secret. Marie was statuesque, a willowy woman with a sculptured face and golden, almond-shaped eyes. In addition to her mastery of spells, she was a nurse, a couturiere, a coiffeuse, a courtesan, and the Queen of Voodoo. Yes, given Marie's own talents in the matter of spells, Chantel knew she would have to differentiate her own knowledge from that which Marie herself possessed. Marie's was a good question, and one she considered for a moment before she formulated an answer.

"A spell is of the supernatural, while my cuisine is very much of this world," Chantel explained. "The desire for food is an appetite, as is the hunger for love. There are spices and herbs that create wantonness, and there are sights and tastes which are suggestive. Erotic cuisine combines these concepts.''

"Can you design dishes that will have the erotic quality of this flowering rose?" As she spoke, Marie turned in her chair and lightly touched a pale pink rose that grew in the nearby window box.

"Yes, but appearance is only one aspect of my cuisine. The other aspect involves the spices of love.''

Yes, this young woman had a fine idea. But was she the one to carry it out? Was she the mistress of passion-creating cuisine she claimed to be? "I like this idea," Marie said slowly, not wanting to appear too eager. After all, a future employee should not believe herself indispensable. Such an impression would create a demand for far too high a salary.

"I shall need to test your talent," Marie said thoughtfully. "But first, tell me what you expect by way of compensation."

"Madame, I'm without family and I have no desire to sell my body. I want a place to live, enough money to buy clothes, and to live independently, if modestly."

Marie nodded. "If I hire you, you can live here in my hotel. I will pay you enough to satisfy your other needs."

"I must have your promise that no other duties will be expected of me—with your gentlemen clients, I mean."

"I promise, though you should consider it carefully. There is much money to be made. Many opportunities arise."

"No, I wish only to cook."

"Very well, but as I said, I must have a demonstration first."

Chantel smiled with satisfaction. She liked this Marie Dumont. No matter what was said of her, she seemed forthright.

"You must tell me what you have in mind, madame. Then I shall endeavor to satisfy you."

Marie plucked the rose she had been touching and handed it to Chantel, who silently took it and put it in her hair.

"I have a young woman I have taken into my employ," Marie began. "Unlike you, she is willing to make love for money. She is beautiful, but she is stiff—somewhat cold. Let me see, how can I put this? Lise possesses knowledge without passion. She does not give the impression of being desirous. Naturally, my clients want passion. There is a particular gentleman who will pay well for Lise, but I am afraid her coolness will put him off."

"Then arrange an assignation, madame. A private dinner to be served in a bedroom. Is there a way you can observe the results?"

Marie smiled slyly. "But of course. Is tomorrow night too soon?"

"Not at all," Chantel replied. "Shall I prepare a late dinner, say for eleven?"

"Ideal," Marie replied. "Yes, eleven it shall be. And so this will be a true test, I will refrain from casting a spell on either of the parties."

Chantel smiled confidently. There was no doubt in her mind that by day after tomorrow, she would be employed. Yes, the magic of suggestion and the taste of fire would do the trick.

Marie positioned herself by the peephole that gave a good view of the small dining table and the bed. Lise, dressed in a cream-colored diaphanous gown that hid few of her natural charms, sat uneasily across from Monsieur LeBlanc.

Cuisine, Chantel had explained, must appeal to all the senses. "Sight and aroma are as important as taste."

The dishes that were to be served were elegant masterpieces possessing all three elements. But would they warm the cool Lise?

I have certainly done my part, Marie thought. The room she had provided was decorated in bright, bold colors. The bed was huge, canopied and comfortable looking. The small dining table near the bed gleamed with silver and fine china. "The atmosphere is perfect," Marie said to herself.

First, the butler delivered the appetizer. It was a stunning dish consisting of boiled asparagus tips mildly sprinkled with grated cheese and shimmering with melted butter. They stood erect in hollowed-out ripe, red tomatoes. Chantel called this dish "Desirous Asparagus."

"Delicious," Monsieur LeBlanc praised. He lifted one of the tips to Lise's lips and she obligingly nibbled at it, even as her face glowed with the flush of embarrassment. Still, the flush made her even more attractive, and she ate slowly while Monsieur's own enthusiasm clearly rose.

Next came pepper pot soup—"the first taste of fire," Chantel had promised. She did not explain, but as Marie well knew, the effect of hot spices was that of burning—burning desire, no doubt since women who ate hot spices often seemed to want to be touched intimately, and many said that only lovemaking put out the fire they felt.

Next came Creole Filé Gumbo—more burning spices but this time tempered with the innocence of chicken and the soft taste of juicy, plump pink shrimp. The colors of each dish blazed with red and green peppers, with the pink of shellfish, and with white iridescent onions. The aroma of spices filled the room and surrounded the diners.

The dessert was a rum fluff. As Monsieur LeBlanc had fed Lise the appetizer, Lise fed the dessert to Monsieur LeBlanc.

But Lise tipped the spoon ever so slightly and the rum fluff fell on the tops of her breasts.

"Ah, *ma cherie!* You have spilled the fluff! We must not waste it—let me assist you!"

With those words, Monsieur LeBlanc bent over and began to lap the delicious cream from Lise's warm white skin. This seemed to arouse Lise in a way Marie had not previously believed possible. Quite suddenly, Lise bared herself and wantonly rubbed against Monsieur LeBlanc, who cried out with glee and carried her to the bed, where she wrapped herself about him with total abandon and cried out for him.

"What a success!" Marie whispered to herself. She hurried away from her peephole. Chantel was no doubt still in the kitchen and there wasn't a moment to lose. This talent must not escape! Her business could only flourish with such a master of erotic cuisine in her kitchen.

Michael Hamilton stood on the steps of his office and surveyed the sky. Although it was nearly the first of October, it was still unbearably hot and the air was laden with moisture. For days now the sky had been menacing, as dense dark clouds moved in from the Gulf, threatening New Orleans with a down-pour.

When he moved here, Michael Hamilton had hoped that the Faubourg Ste. Marie, which was separated from the Vieux Carré by a wide common, would be cooler. But it was not. In spite of the park that separated the two sections of the city, the one was as hot as the other. Nonetheless, he admitted that a walk through the common, beneath the lacy trees and amid the semi-tropical flowers, was most pleasant.

Not, he thought ruefully, that he had time for such pleasures now or in the near future. His trading business grew more demanding by the day. He found that there were just too many things he had to do himself, duties he was unable to leave to others. He employed a large staff, but the only one he could really count on was René Gaston, his chief assistant, interpreter, and now, good friend.

Business in New Orleans seemed to move slowly; in fact, to his way of thinking everything moved slowly here. All of New Orleans functioned with a kind of maddening easiness. Perhaps it was the temperature. The heat and humidity combined to make him sleepy, and he imagined others suffered from the same malady, although they did not seem to feel guilty about it as he did.

René seemed to have more energy than most, but alas, like so many Cajuns, even René was apparently addicted to late-night dinners and endless affairs of the heart. How often their conversations centered on what René had consumed for dinner the previous night, or a quite detailed description of the woman who had been his companion.

There was no doubt about it. New Orleans was very different from Michael's home, Boston. The two cities were as unalike as night and day and so were the people who inhabited them. By now, it would be cool and crisp at home. Pumpkins and squashes would be dotting farmer's fields and doors would be decorated with gourds of golden yellow and outrageous orange. A cold, white frost would coat the grass in the early morning, the smell of hickory burning would fill the air, and children would ask to buy bags of roasted chestnuts. In Boston, the buildings were made of stone. They were substantial buildings, buildings meant to last for hundreds of years like Greek and Roman temples. Business too was a different matter. It was brisk and a man worked from early morning till nightfall. But none of this was the case in New Orleans. It was unseemly hot and humid, as the fall refused to come and chase the long, hot summer away. The cotton, tobacco, and indigo had yet to be harvested. Winter was a season one spoke of, but no one experienced. At least not winter as he knew it.

For most of the city's inhabitants, work did not begin till mid-morning, it came to an absolute halt in the late afternoon, and by nightfall the lure of music and food brought the apparently indifferent populace alive for hours of revelry.

He shook his head and went back inside to his airless office. He wiped the excess perspiration off his brow and thought, for the hundredth time, that he ought to get away from this place for a short time. His offices took up the downstairs of this somewhat majestic dwelling and he lived upstairs. He worked from early morning till nightfall, and he rarely left Faubourg Ste. Marie. Once he had gone for a boat ride up some bayou, but the romance of the place was lost on him. All he had thought about was the heat, the all-pervading dampness, and the clouds of blood-sucking insects. How did people stand it here? Why had he come here and why did he stay? Why did a talented linguist like René remain? The answer was simple. There was money to be made here. That was what had brought him here and that was what kept him here, that and his own stubbornness. Naturally, he intended to stay no longer than absolutely necessary. He thought about going home night and day and vowed to make as much money as he could so that he could resume his life in Boston in style. But the more his business grew, the more work there was to do.

"Oh, there you are," René said cheerfully. "I was just leaving for a short time."

He did not say he was leaving for the siesta, a kind of afternoon nap that followed lunch, a three-hour rest period in which everyone seemed to indulge.

"You should rest too. You work far too hard."

Michael forced a smile. "I've always worked hard."

"Life is not all work, my friend. I wish you would come with me one night to Vieux Carré. I will take you to a dinner you will not soon forget, and then I'll introduce you to some friendly ladies with whom you can while the night away."

Michael smiled. He could do with a friendly lady and a good meal, but he wanted to finish building the business he had started. He admitted that he was a man who usually got what he wanted and at the moment, he wanted success. René meant well and he was a valuable employee, but he failed to understand that at the moment, Michael's life was his work.

"I really couldn't. I haven't been feeling at all well of late." It was an excuse with more than an element of truth. His head was pounding even now.

"Of course you don't feel well! It is because you never let yourself go! You should come with me and we'll share dinner and some fine wine. In no time you'll forget all your troubles."

"No, thanks anyway." He tried to sound casual. He was aware of the need not to hurt René's feelings. But he did not want to go to Vieux Carré and eat strange food. He knew he would have a headache if he drank wine, and for the moment he had no intention of becoming entangled with some young French girl.

"You're afraid your father will not approve."

Michael shrugged. It was a gesture he had picked up from René. He used it when he didn't know what else to say. He hated it that René had accidentally touched on a truth. His father was a strict man, and even though Michael was of age and this was his own business venture, he did think about his father and how he would react to the easy manner of New Orleans. It was not that he was afraid of his father, only that he was aware of his own conservative tendencies.

René did not press; he waved his hand and laughed. "When you are ready, my friend, Vieux Carré will still be there. It will wait."

Again, Michael wiped perspiration from his brow. There was no use returning to his desk. Everyone else had left for siesta. And he did have a ferocious headache, no doubt caused by the weather. Perhaps, he thought, it wouldn't hurt if he lay down for just a little while.

"Mon Dieu!" René exclaimed. "Michael!"

Michael heard René's voice, but try as he might, he could not open his eyes. His head pounded, he was bathed in perspiration, yet his teeth chattered uncontrollably with cold.

"It's the fever," Anton, Michael's servant, declared darkly. "Everyone who comes here gets it sooner or later. They either die or they recover."

René did not correct Anton's gloomy prediction because he had lived in New Orleans most of his life and he knew Anton was right.

"Better fetch some cold cloths. I'll send for the doctor."

Anton looked at Michael and shook his head. "He is a strong man. I think he will recover if he is treated by a medicine woman."

René frowned. He thought of himself as an educated man and he knew full well that Michael was educated too. But educated or not, Anton was once again right. René himself preferred local medicine women to doctors. But Michael was from the East—from Boston. He would not understand the ways of the local people, the ways of the women who worked their magic spells and provided healing potions. No, Michael would insist on a doctor, even though René felt most doctors were nothing but glorified barbers whose method of treatment was usually bleeding. When he was ill, he usually went to a well-known quadroon woman. She did not believe in bleeding, though she did offer up strange incantations in some African

tongue and insisted on participation in a ritual before giving
her curative potions.

"I believe you're right," René allowed, "but I'll summon
a doctor first. If he's unable to cure Michael, I'll see to fetching
someone who can."

"It might be too late if you wait. Fever takes some men
fast," Anton predicted darkly.

"I'll go for the doctor," René insisted.

Anton turned about and hurried from the room to fetch the
cold cloths.

When René returned with Dr. Williams in tow, Michael's
fever seemed even higher, though Anton had all but covered
him in cold cloths and stood by the bed dabbing Michael's dry
lips with water.

Dr. Williams was relatively new to New Orleans. He was
from Philadelphia, and the epitome of all René had heard about
the inhabitants of the famed city. He was a tall, gaunt man of
few words. In spite of the heat, he dressed in a dark suit and
wore a stiffly starched white shirt and a narrow dark tie. He
spoke without benefit of hand gestures, always appeared to be
disapproving, and was totally unsmiling. True to the tales of
the wily traders of Philadelphia, he negotiated his fee first and
now looked with disdain at his newest patient.

"Take those cloths off him," he said imperiously to Anton.

Anton's expression remained the same, but as René knew
Anton well, he noticed the flicker of dislike and mistrust in
Anton's dark eyes. Michael Hamilton was an outsider too, but
he was a likeable sort and if he disapproved of local customs,
he did not say so or try to force his views on others. He was
also young, young enough to change. But this Dr. Williams
appeared to look down on everyone; he would not change to
suit New Orleans and would try to change New Orleans to suit
him. He was the type to garner resentment wherever he went,

and in little time and with few words, he had managed to make Anton resentful.

Anton removed the cloths, and Dr. Williams carried out a cursory examination.

"It's a fever common to this area," he finally muttered. "I shall bleed him."

Anton threw René a deadly look—a look that as much as said, "don't allow this."

René bit his lip. "Surely that will make him weaker. He will need all his strength to fight the fever."

Dr. Williams clearly did not like his diagnosis or treatment questioned. "Are you too a doctor?" he asked sarcastically.

René bristled. "I am Monsieur Hamilton's personal assistant and translator. I am in charge when he is ill. I brought you here, but on reflection, I don't believe we will require your services."

Dr. Williams scowled. "If this man dies, I shall be forced to tell the authorities that you rejected the treatment of a licensed doctor."

It was something of a hollow threat since the authorities were French and Spanish and many of the Yankees who had come here were not much liked.

"I will follow my own judgment," René said firmly.

"I shall insist on my fee in any case," Dr. Williams retorted.

René reached into his pocket and withdrew the doctor's fee. It was wasted money, but in his heart he felt strongly that bleeding would not help Michael one wit, and that Anton was right. This doctor knew little of the fever that struck those who lived in New Orleans, but those who had survived it knew something of it and both he and Anton had, at one time or another, had it.

René drew in his breath. Michael would probably not approve of his decision, but he knew he must send for his medicine woman. She would know better than to bleed a man with fever and her chants were little enough to put up with given the potency of her medicines.

* * *

The windows of the large hotel kitchen were all open, and the aroma of food drifted on the breeze. Even Marie's mouth watered as Chantel worked her culinary magic.

"More and more of my customers are requesting your services," Marie disclosed as she watched Chantel prepare one of her divine dinners.

"Then this is an arrangement beneficial to us both," Chantel replied.

"It is indeed. Tell me, where did you learn to prepare this love-inspiring cuisine?"

Chantel smiled mysteriously. "Perhaps I was just born knowing it."

Marie laughed lightly. "That I do not believe."

"Then I shall tell you the truth. My knowledge was passed on from generation to generation. My ancestor was from France. I was told she was of the upper class and had been sent to Quebec as a bride for a high-placed government official. In those days, the parties given by the ruling class were lavish affairs. My ancestor was chosen to be this official's bride because of her ability to create meals that were extraordinary. My ancestor—I think she was my great-great-grandmother—intended to return to the French Court with her husband, but war interfered. Her daughter was born in Quebec, and when she was grown she ran away to marry a handsome Acadian. When the British deported the Acadians, my people were sent here. This cooking has been a family secret for generations."

"Ah, yes. You mentioned Paris when you came here. I have made some inquiries and have learned that Parisian restaurants specialize in dining-cum-boudoir suites. We French—you know, of course, that I too have French blood—have a special fondness for all the sensual delights."

Chantel smiled. "I think of my art as culinary seduction."

"You and I are a good business match," Marie said as she

nodded her head. Yes, she thought, Chantel was a real asset to her hotel.

"Madame, I am so sorry to intrude, but there is a male visitor who says he must see you at once." The little maid stood poised in the doorway.

Marie turned around. "Show him to the parlor," she instructed.

René Gaston sat down on the edge of the chaise longue. The parlor was lavishly furnished—at least by local standards. Usually, he went to see Marie Dumont at her small shop just off the town square. But Michael was no better, and this was an urgent visit that could not wait for a day when the shop was open.

He looked up and rose to his feet when the stunning Marie Dumont entered the room. Her almond eyes examined him. "Have we met?" she asked.

"René Gaston is my name. I have, on occasion, come to your shop. I come about medicine—on behalf of my employer, Mr. Michael Hamilton. He is very ill with fever."

Marie lifted her brow and then smiled enigmatically. She made it her business to know who everyone was and how important they were. This Michael Hamilton had been in New Orleans less than six months, but his business was flourishing and he was known to be wealthy in his own right, as well as the son of a wealthy Boston shipowner. He was certainly not a patient she intended to turn down. Still, she did have other commitments, important ones.

"Everyone who comes here gets the fever," she said slowly. "But of course I can help—though I am too busy to come with you. Perhaps I could send my assistant."

"Does your assistant know as much as you do about curative potions?"

"She knows as much as it is necessary for her to know. Please, wait here."

Marie hurried back to the kitchen. After all, Chantel only had to prepare meals on special evenings, usually on the weekends, and then quite late at night. She could most certainly spare the time to see to this Michael Hamilton. She smiled to herself. If what she had heard about this young man were all true, other most desirable results might come of sending Chantel in her place.

"Chantel, I have a proposition for you, one that could earn you some extra money and an introduction to a handsome, powerful young man."

Chantel looked up. "You know my terms, madame. I do not wish to sell my body."

"And I am not suggesting you do so. Is your knowledge of medicine as great as your knowledge of cooking?"

"But of course. Most all of my herbs and spices have medicinal purpose. One does not know one art without knowing the other."

Marie nodded. "How would you treat fever?"

"With cinchona bark—indeed, I have some."

"Then I would send you to tend this wealthy young man in my place. I am expecting the governor this afternoon and cannot possibly be in two places at once. Naturally, you will be well paid."

"Then I shall go, as long as all that is expected of me is nursing."

"That is all—except, of course, you must tell me what transpires."

Chantel nodded. It was good of Marie to offer her this opportunity. One could always use extra money.

"Go to the third floor and enter the first room on the left. You'll find all the medicine you'll need. I shall go to the parlor and tell Monsieur Gaston that you will be along shortly."

"Very good." Chantel wiped her hands and went upstairs. Perhaps, she thought happily, Madame might make a habit of sharing some of her patients. Such a practice could yield considerable money, and it was her desire to save as much as she could, since she intended to own her own restaurant one day.

René had spoken little to Chantel Boudreau on their way across town. The truth was, he found himself a little tongue-tied, and she was not what he had anticipated when Marie said she would send her assistant. He had expected another mysterious voodoo queen, a woman who would use medicine and chants as he knew Marie Dumont did. But this young girl was not a quadroon, nor was she a voodoo queen. She was French, as he was, and she was exquisitely beautiful as well as shy and charming. He almost wished he were ill so she would tend him. She asked questions about Michael—how long had he been ill? How old was he? Where was he from? She had not commented on his answers, but had seemed to file the information away.

"I have never been to Faubourg Ste. Marie," Chantel confessed as he helped her down from the carriage.

"It is a growing community. All the English live and work here. I don't. I only come here to work."

"What do you do?" Chantel asked.

"I am an interpreter. Michael Hamilton runs a trading business. He is most successful."

Chantel nodded and hardly looked around the office. René led her up the winding staircase, down the long hall, and into a large bedroom.

Chantel looked about quickly; then her dark eyes settled on the man who lay in the center of the bed. His eyes were closed and she could see the beads of sweat on his forehead. This was one of the stages of the fever. His temperature would drop soon, but in a few hours it would come back. He would begin to shake and shiver, and then once again he would sweat. If he lived. Many died in the fevered stage when the body temperature could go very high indeed, and when dreams and illusions filled the head.

She moved closer and put her cool hand on his brow. He had thick, dark hair and pale skin. She guessed that most of the time he was clean-shaven because his beard now was only a few days old and took the form of dark stubble which gave him a ruggedly handsome appearance. Vaguely she wondered about a man with a smooth face. Most of the men she knew had beards.

He appeared to be a tall man, and he had muscular arms. At this moment, he was naked to the waist and lay on his stomach. He was indeed handsome, she thought. In fact, he was one of the best-looking men she had ever seen. She wondered what color his eyes were—eyes were important to her. She thought them to be the mirror of the soul.

"I'll send Anton up. He'll bring you anything you need," René said. He half smiled. This Chantel seemed quite enchanted by Michael. She would probably work hard at curing him, if only to get to know him better. And they would be a good match. She was diminutive and truly beautiful, while Michael was tall, strong and rugged looking. What could be more alluring than the sight of a rugged man in need of mothering—ah, no woman could resist! All of a sudden, and for no rational reason, he felt confident of Michael's recovery.

"I'll need very little," Chantel said, turning away from Michael and looking at him. "Some cool, clean water and a cup of tea."

"I don't think he can drink tea," René said quickly.

Chantel laughed musically. "The tea is for me. I will be sitting by his bedside for some hours and will need some refreshment."

René reddened. "Of course. And I will have supper sent up when it is time."

"I would appreciate that. You can leave us now. I must examine my patient."

René left the room and Chantel put her basket of medications down on the table. Then she sat down on the edge of the bed and slowly set about massaging Michael's broad back. As she moved her small, cool hands over his damp flesh, Michael stirred ever so slightly and then turned over, groaning as he did so.

He *was* handsome! His chest was covered with dark hair and, unable to resist, she ran her fingers through it. It was damp and the hairs glistened like grass in the early morning dew.

Chantel stood up and went to her basket. She took out a vial of liquid and returned to the bed just as Anton entered.

"Good, you can help me lift his head," she said as Anton put down his tray.

Obediently he came over and slipped his arm under Michael's head while Chantel pressed the vial of liquid to his lips. He coughed once, but then swallowed the liquid that she administered slowly. When she had finished, Anton laid Michael's head back down. As silently as he had come, he left the room.

Chantel returned to her basket and brought out a thick, creamy salve. She rubbed it onto Michael's chest, then pulled down the sheet to rub it onto his stomach, hips, and legs.

Her mouth opened in surprise and she audibly gasped. His member, which should have lain at rest, was quite the opposite. In her whole life she had never seen a male member in such a condition. It was considerably larger than she expected—at least this one was. She stared for a long minute and then reminded herself that this was her patient, not her lover.

Chantel forced herself to ignore the incredible sight as she continued to rub the salve onto his skin. It would ease the violence of his symptoms and help cool his body even as the bark of the cinchona would help lower his fever.

Michael's eyes opened and he stared up at her uncomprehendingly.

Oh, his eyes were a wonderful color. They were sea-green and Chantel instantly wanted to dive into their depths. *I must stop this. This man is my patient,* she again reminded herself.

Then she thought that she had been working too hard for too long and must be bored. She knew she had never noticed other men the way she noticed this man. "Such wantonness," she whispered to herself. "You would think I had been eating my own seductive dishes."

If this was death, it was more merciful than he had ever dared to dream! Michael turned lethargically and opened his eyes—there was a wondrous, delicate, dark-haired angel caressing him with her cool hands, kneading his flesh as his mother used to knead bread. She had bright, dark eyes and a mass of dark curls. Her skin was as white as cream, her lips full and delicious looking. She leaned over him, and had he been able to lift his arms he could have reached up and caressed her soft, round breasts. An aroma surrounded her, an aroma that made him want to hold her tightly. She smelled of almonds! Yes, her breasts were large dollops of soft cream and she smelled of almonds.

As a child, almonds and cream had been his favorite dessert. Heaven! He was in heaven being tended by a voluptuous celestial who exuded the aroma of a mouthwatering delight! His stoic puritan father was wrong! Heaven was not a place for the righteous. It was a place for the sensuous! Though he was sure he was delirious or dead, he clung to these sensual delights even as they slid to the very edge of his mind, even as he drifted into the unconscious once again, even as his vision of the sweet-smelling angel disappeared.

CHAPTER TWO

Chantel wiped the dark curls from her brow as she stood for a moment looking at her patient. His temperature was normal now, and his breathing was no longer labored. It had been three days since she had come to care for him. But it was mid-week and Marie had no clients who required her services until Friday night. Thus, being away from the hotel caused her no difficulty.

Since her arrival, she had administered cinchona bark every few hours, had massaged Michael Hamilton's fevered body with soothing, cooling creams, and had applied cold compresses when necessary. Anton had brought her meals, and when she slept it was in a comfortable chair near the bed.

Her face knit into a slight frown. He was good-looking, and a part of her wanted to remain till he awakened, so that she might get to know him. But during his delirium, he had spoken several times to someone he called "my angel." Doubtless, she concluded, this meant that he already had a woman to whom he was committed.

"It is for the best," she said aloud as she drew in a deep breath of resignation. Yes, she was just beginning her career, there were many things she wanted to do, and above all she had learned the importance of independence. She was unlike most women. She was on her own with no family to help her. She was in charge of herself, of making her own decisions. She had long ago decided to make herself financially independent first, then to marry—but only if she found the right man, if she could marry for love.

She turned away from the bed. Michael Hamilton was well now, and she would leave instructions with Anton about further doses of the cinchona bark. It was time for her to return to Marie Dumont's hotel, time for her to resume her work as a chef.

She picked up her basket and left the room, closing the door softly behind her.

"Are you leaving, miss?" Anton asked politely when she reached the bottom of the winding staircase.

"Yes. My work is done. Mr. Hamilton will wake up sometime this afternoon. He'll need another two days of rest and some good food. He'll be fine. But you must continue to give a tablespoon of this medication three times a day for the next week." She handed Anton the bottle, and he in turn handed her an envelope.

"Monsieur Gaston left this for you."

She did not have to open it. She knew that inside was the fee Marie had arranged with Monsieur Gaston. Marie would take a small percentage of it, but the rest was hers. "Thank you," she said as she left. The carriage waited outside. It would take her back to the Vieux Carré, away from this handsome stranger and back to the life she had made for herself.

Michael opened his eyes and stared up at the ceiling. A long, jagged crack ran across it. But it was not the crack on which he fixated, it was the memory of his dream—a dream so vivid it had given him actual pleasure.

Naturally, when he was a lad of thirteen and fourteen he had experienced a spate of such dreams, though he told no one about them and indeed could not remember a single one of them. But this dream he had just experienced was like no dream he had ever had before. It was absolutely vivid in its detail. It was not a fevered dream either. He had awoken with his heart beating with excitement, but he was otherwise cool. His fever was gone, his headache had left him, and though he felt a trifle weak, he knew he was better.

He had dreamt of the woman when he was fevered too, but none of those dreams had been like this most recent one. In this most recent dream, her cool hands had caressed him slowly, barely touching him, yet arousing him in a slow and torturous way. Her wondrous hands had never actually touched him intimately, but had instead moved softly on his back, his chest, and his legs. He could still see her in his mind's eye. In his dream she was unclothed, a small yet voluptuous woman with soft, sweet skin.

His vision had plump, snow-white breasts with nut-colored nipples that were hard and firm. Her waist was tiny and her buttocks were like rounded melons, yet they too were as white as snow.

In his dream she had lain across him, and then hovered above him, tempting and torturing him with her closeness. In his dream, he had closed his eyes and lifted his hips to enter her and she had, in turn, had wrapped herself about him, holding him tightly as he held her breasts in his hands.

He trembled slightly. The very thought of his dream was causing him more pleasure.

The abrupt opening of his bedroom door ended it all. He looked up as René came in, a relieved smile covering his friend's face.

"Ah! You are feeling better! I am told your fever is gone and you will be up and around in a few days."

Michael wondered if his face was red. He pushed the last vestiges of his dream from his mind. "I should go back to work now. I have so much to do."

"No, my friend. You will not go back to work now or even tomorrow. The medicine woman who treated you said you were to remain in bed for at least two days. You've had a bout of our famous fever. It's dangerous, my friend. You've survived, but you do need your rest."

"A medicine woman treated me?" He lifted his brow. Could this be the woman in his dreams?

"Yes. I called a doctor first, but he only wanted to bleed you. I know this fever, and the doctor was new to New Orleans and had likely never seen this particular malady before. Bleeding is not the right treatment, so I sent for someone I know and trust."

René did not mention that Marie herself had not come but had, instead, sent another woman.

"What did she do to me?" Michael asked hesitantly. He now wondered how much had been a dream and how much had been reality. Had he actually coupled with this beautiful creature in reality?

"She administered medicine for the fever, and she lowered your fever with cooling creams."

Michael nodded. In all probability his dream was only a dream save for the feeling of her delicate hands on his body. "I do seem well," he allowed, even though he still wondered where reality had ended and his dream begun. René would no doubt think it odd if he asked for a description of the woman who had tended him. He decided to make inquiries about her later and, indeed, to try to find her. Allowing such an experience to remain a mystery would have been far too troubling. It was, after all, common knowledge that most of the women in the Vieux Carré could be had for a price. Yes, he had been without a woman for far too long, and the memory of this woman was nothing short of haunting. It seemed an appropriate time to end his fast; he vowed he would find her and arrange to spend a night making love to her. He said nothing of this plan to René, who would no doubt think he had taken leave of his senses.

"Are you certain I must remain in bed for two days? I've already lost a lot of time. I ought to get back to work."

"Absolutely, my friend. You know, you would not have gotten ill in the first place had you not been working so hard. You have to learn how to enjoy life. You are not really living my friend, you are simply existing."

Michael looked into René's face. It was as if René had read his mind. He did need some recreation, something more regular than his recent vow to find the woman who had tended him and make love to her. "What do you suggest?"

"I suggest a few trips to the Vieux Carré. I suggest you go to a fine restaurant, enjoy a few good meals, and perhaps avail yourself of some of New Orleans' most beautiful women."

Michael grinned. "That is just what I had in mind." He had heard a great deal about the courtesans of New Orleans and he now wondered if all he had heard was true. He hoped it would prove true in at least one case, but still he did not mention his specific plan to René.

Marie Dumont fairly sailed into the kitchen. She wore an elegant multi-colored African headdress and a clinging amber gown. Her long ivory earrings dangled back and forth as she walked, and her shoes clicked on the tile floor.

"Back at work so soon?" Marie asked.

Chantel turned from her mixing bowl and smiled warmly. "Yes, the patient is quite cured."

Marie's expression grew somewhat mischievous. "And is this young businessman as handsome as I have heard?"

Chantel tried to prevent herself from blushing. "He is quite handsome."

"Did you speak with him when he woke up?"

"No. I left before he woke."

Marie shook her head. "You are a young and beautiful woman. He is a handsome, rich young man. I would have thought you might get to know one another. Who can say what might have happened, or what fate might have ordained?''

''I believe he is spoken for. In his fevered sleep he spoke to some woman he called his 'angel'.''

''Perhaps he spoke to you.''

''Oh, no. I think not.''

''You're not at all interested in him?''

''It's more that I don't believe he would be interested in me.''

''You of all people know that attractions work in mysterious ways.''

Chantel laughed and tried to push the memory of the handsome young man from her mind. He was her patient, and it had been wrong of her to look on him lustfully. Most women would not have admitted, even to themselves, that they felt lust. But she knew she did, and she suspected many other women did as well. Certainly Marie was a lustful woman. She was always commenting on the various attributes of young men. If Marie had cared for Michael Hamilton, she would have returned with detailed descriptions of all his masculine qualities. Most certainly she would have commented on his firm buttocks as well as his other more than adequate attributes.

Yes, it was a pity that he seemed to belong to another. But that was that. She reminded herself that she had interests of her own and many things to keep her busy, it was unnecessary to linger on thoughts of her former patient.

''I have an elderly client coming tonight,'' Marie said. ''The woman he has chosen is most experienced, but perhaps he could use some—shall I say, stimulation?''

Chantel smiled. ''I have many stimulating recipes.''

''What do you suggest?''

''Well, long ago when the Spanish claimed Mexico, they found the Aztecs eating *ahuacatl*. I have been told that this fruit, which we call the alligator pear, or avocado, was taken to the court of Louis XIV to help the aging king achieve his desires. It was said that after he began eating it, he impregnated many women."

"And how will you prepare this dish of green pear?"

"With other stimulants. I'll peel it and cut it lengthwise, then I'll hollow out a bit of the center and mix it with a teaspoon of mayonnaise, some chopped chives, a large spoon of walnuts, and a few jet-black olives. I'll fill the cavity with this delicious mixture and place the two halves together. Then it shall be brushed with lemon and served with tiny slivers of oranges."

Marie ran her tongue around her full lips sensuously. "Ah, and that is only the appetizer. My dear girl, you are a jewel! Naturally, I will tell the gentleman in question about the King of France, since we both know the power of suggestion to be as potent as the food presented."

Chantel set about her culinary alchemy. She delighted in her creations and the pleasure they brought. She sighed. How strange her life was! She knew all there was to know about lovemaking, but had never actually allowed anyone to make love to her.

Michael sat at his desk and stared out the window. The long-promised rains had come and gone. Now the sky was a deep blue, and it seemed far less humid. The November sun was bright and the days warm. Had he been home in Boston now, there might even have been snow. But here it was warm, though not as warm as it had been, and the nights, much to his joy, were far cooler.

He turned back to the pile of endless papers on his desk. For the first time, he admitted he was bored. "Yes, I'm bored and restless and I've been so since my recovery," he said aloud to himself. He shook his head. Though he thought of his dream often, he had not kept his promise to himself.

As caught up as he was during the day by his work, at night thoughts of his dream angel still haunted him. When he was

alone and had nothing particular to do, she again crept into his
thoughts.

   He shook his head as if to dispel her image; then he thought
of René's assertion that he should enjoy himself, that he should
venture out of the English section of New Orleans and into the
French section, the Vieux Carré. He wondered if the infamous
area was as licentious as his American compatriots claimed.
Of course, those who said it was licentious were Puritan types
from Massachusetts, men like his father who clearly believed
that a taste of honey could only result in the consumption of
the entire honey pot. It could not be so. René, his assistant,
lived in the Vieux Carré, and he was a sensible sort who worked
hard. Yes, René was no doubt right. He needed some diversion
and had put it off far too long. He had been drawn back into
work quickly and completely, and once again he had put off
all entertainments. But now, he acknowledged, he had finished
everything and had a little spare time. Now was the time for
him to find some pleasure and test all that he had heard about
the Vieux Carré.

   Michael lifted the little silver bell on the corner of his desk
to summon Anton. He decided to order a carriage for nine, the
hour at which he had been told the night life in the Vieux Carré
began. Anton would surely know where he might find a good
restaurant.

   The carriage clambered through the common and then
entered the narrow streets of the Vieux Carré. He had seen the
Vieux Carré many times when he was on his way to the docks,
and it was far different from the area in which he lived. The
houses were all attached, as indeed many of Boston's houses
were attached. But these homes were not stone and brick; they
were built of stucco and painted unusual colors. Most were
white, but there were also pink and light-green houses. They
all had wrought-iron outside staircases and balconies that over-

hung the street. Flowers swung from the balconies in baskets, and the heady smell of spices emanated from every doorway.

Michael decided to ask his driver a question which had troubled him since he had come to New Orleans. "Why are these houses built so?" he asked. "Surely the staircases would be better on the inside."

The driver laughed. "But more heavily taxed. Under French law, a building with stairs on the outside is taxed less than one with the stairs on the inside."

Michael shook his head. The ways of the French were strange indeed.

"I want to go to a good restaurant," he said.

"So your manservant said. I shall take you to a famous hotel. It is said that the cuisine is the best in all of New Orleans."

Michael nodded and continued to look out the window. At length the carriage turned again and came to a clattering halt in front of a three-story pink stucco building. Like the others, it had narrow, winding stairs in the front and tiers of tiny balconies laden with flowers.

"Please return at midnight," Michael requested.

The driver lifted his thick brow. "That would be very early, sir."

"I am only having dinner," Michael protested. Doubtless the driver thought he intended availing himself of some woman, but that was not the case. He had already decided to simply make some inquiries and to find out more about the area and the people who inhabited it. There would be time for women later.

"It would still be early. A meal here is a work of art. Its serving takes many hours."

Michael sighed and wondered if he had made the right decision coming here. "Very well, come at one-thirty then."

The driver smiled back at him. "I'll be here, and if you decide to stay later or through the night, I'll come back in the morning."

Michael knew that wouldn't be the case.

* * *

The woman who greeted him was tall and slender, with high cheekbones and slightly slanted golden eyes. She was no doubt in her forties, but she was beautiful still in a strange, exotic way.

"You must be Monsieur Michael Hamilton," she said, looking into his eyes steadily.

He was quite sure that the surprise showed on his face. He had, after all, made no reservation. He had, in fact, told no one he was coming.

"I am, but how did you know?"

Marie Dumont laughed and her long earrings swayed. "I make it my business to know who everyone in New Orleans is and what they look like. You are a trader who imports and exports various goods. You were pointed out to me, and I was told you are most successful."

"Moderately successful," he said, still wondering about her knowledge of him.

"You're too modest. I am Marie Dumont, and it was one of my employees who tended you when you came down with the fever."

Michael's eyes widened. Was his angel one of Madame Dumont's ladies of the evening? He remembered now that he had heard of Marie Dumont. René had mentioned her several times. She owned this hotel, which was also a place where men could meet women for secret assignations. "Don't call it prostitution," René warned. "We think of it quite differently. Besides, many of New Orleans' most powerful men are married to women they met at Madame Dumont's hotel."

"I've only come for dinner," Michael said awkwardly. "However, I would like to thank the woman who tended me."

Marie smiled slyly. "I'm sure that both can be arranged. Would you like to sample a simple local dish, or do you have a special request?"

"I'll let you choose," he said.

"Ah, a man of adventurous appetites. I shall see you are served something very special and then I shall send the woman who tended you."

"I only want to thank her." He wondered if his words sounded ingenuous. The truth was that if she was as beautiful as he remembered, he would hire her for this evening and perhaps other evenings as well. He smiled; the driver had been right. One-thirty might be too early after all, and dinner might be only one of the pleasures he would enjoy this evening.

"Please, come this way," Marie said as she led him down a narrow corridor. She opened the door to a small room. In its center was a little table with fresh flowers. In the center of the table a candle burned slowly. To one side was an amply cushioned chaise longue. The room was heavily scented, though he could not immediately identify the enticing aroma.

"We only have private dining areas," Marie explained. "Should I send someone to entertain you?"

Michael looked into her eyes. "When can I meet the woman who tended me?"

"After dinner. I'm afraid she is occupied till then."

He wondered if the disappointment showed on his face. In fact, it was more than disappointment. He felt for a second as if he had been hit. He did not like the idea of his angel with another man, but then, he reminded himself that she was for sale. What did he expect? "I'll eat alone," he replied a little sullenly.

"I shall bring some wine," Marie said, and her mind danced over assorted possibilities. Chantel had said she did not want to sell her body, but perhaps she would change her mind when she learned who the buyer would be. Then again, perhaps she would not. Marie decided to let nature and fate take their course. However it turned out would be the way it turned out. Some things were simply ordained, and she was a great believer in fate.

"A fine French wine is not best in our climate," Marie told him as she set a decanter of golden liquid down on the table.

It was Chantel's special recipe and she called it "the wine of love." It was made with white wine, sherry, brandy, sugar, water, and lemons. Michael poured a glass of the liquid and sipped it. It was strong, but soothing as well as thirst quenching.

Some time passed and Michael wished that at least Marie had remained to keep him company.

After what seemed an eternity, Marie returned with a tureen of soup. "Won't you join me?" he asked.

Marie smiled. "I knew you would grow lonely. But all right, I will join you. In any case I want to see how you like the soup."

Michael watched as Marie slowly lifted the lid on the tureen. He inhaled with enormous pleasure as the scent of almonds was released into the room. Again, his dream returned. His angel was always surrounded by the aroma of almonds.

Marie ladled out a bowl full of the rich golden liquid. It was sprinkled with fresh green parsley. The smell rekindled not just his dreams, but pleasant memories of childhood. The appearance of the soup was delightfully colorful, and when he lifted the first spoonful to his mouth, he realized it was a delicate brew of almonds, chicken broth with bits of white meat, dry wine, cream, and what he believed was mustard.

"Surely there is mustard in this," he ventured.

"You have a good palate for an Englishman," Marie joked.

The soup was intoxicating and the next course was equally so. The final course was a chocolate dessert that was divine beyond description.

Marie left him and he reclined, a little tipsy and totally satiated, on the chaise longue. Then, as in a dream, his angel entered the room.

She was lovelier in reality than in his imaginings. She wore a white dress that, although modest in the extreme, did not hide her fine figure. Her hair was gathered up and fell in ringlets down her back; her heavily lashed brown eyes were filled with curiosity and intelligence.

"Are you the woman who tended me?"

Chantel nodded. "I am glad to see you're better."

"I wish you had been able to join me for dinner."

"I am afraid I had other commitments." She had decided not to tell him just yet that she had prepared his meal.

Perhaps, she thought, he did not have a lover after all. Perhaps he was free and had honorable intentions. "Did you enjoy your meal?"

"It was a divine meal."

Chantel smiled.

Michael lurched to his feet and without preamble pulled the shocked Chantel into his arms and placed the kiss he had dreamed of so often on her full lips. She seemed surprised and tried to pull away from him, but he held her even tighter, and kissed her neck and then her lips again. He felt her go slightly limp in his arms and he held her against him. It was a sensuous moment, a moment of supreme pleasure as he felt her warmth against him. The swell of her full breasts pressed against his chest and he clumsily covered one with his hand.

"So delightful," he whispered. "I want to have you. Cost is no object, I just want you—"

He felt her go rigid as she pulled away from him. Then he felt, with great surprise, the sting of her slap across his face.

"I am a chef," she said angrily. "I prepared your 'divine' dinner." She lifted her head proudly. "And I am a lady who is most assuredly not for sale. You are no gentleman!"

Was there something he did not understand? This hotel was a place where women were available—she was here, she even worked here. "I'm sorry," he stuttered. "I don't understand."

"You have insulted me," she said coldly. He might be good-looking and strong, but that did not give him the right to make assumptions about her. She trembled with anger.

"You tended me when I was ill. I wanted to—"

"Seduce me in return!" Her hands on her hips, she glared at him.

Perhaps one was supposed to build up to these things slowly, he thought. Perhaps such sexual liaisons were different in New Orleans than they were in Boston.

"I wanted to thank you," he stumbled.

She continued to stare at him, her eyes blazing with anger, though inside she felt hurt.

He turned about. "I think I should go."

Chantel's expression did not change. He opened the door and strode from the room only vaguely aware that he was slightly drunk. He hurried down the corridor and out into the street. Musicians were playing at the end of the street, and a small group of people were dancing. There was laughter and merriment everywhere. Somehow it all served to make him feel more miserable.

Michael saw his carriage parked at the curb, just beyond the dancers. It was after one, the driver was waiting, and he walked rapidly, restraining himself not to break into a run. He felt angry and knew he had made a fool of himself. He didn't understand this culture, and certainly he did not understand this woman who haunted his thoughts and occupied his dreams. Worse yet, he had clearly insulted her. He climbed into the carriage and ordered his driver to take him home. Perhaps he could write her a letter of apology. Perhaps then she would allow him to return.

"Damn," he muttered. He had never had such an experience with a woman. He did not normally have to try very hard with women; they almost never said no to him. But this one had shown herself to be quite different. She had not just said no, she had slapped him. Abstractedly, he touched his cheek. She had, in fact, slapped him quite hard and he could still feel the sting. "Damn," he repeated. He still wanted her, and he admitted he wanted her more than ever now that he had finally tasted her sweet lips.

* * *

"Such a handsome and wealthy young man, Chantel. And you turned him away?"

Marie Dumont's pride and joy, the great clock that stood by the front door, struck eleven. Most of the women who lived in the house were still asleep, but Chantel was up and, surprisingly, so was Marie. They sat at the kitchen table sipping hot tea with honey.

"He only wanted me for my body. I will not sell myself."

"Would you give yourself in love?"

"I want to give myself in marriage."

Marie's golden cat-eyes looked at her sympathetically. "You're a good Cajun girl," she allowed, "even if you are the mistress of erotic cookery."

Chantel looked down. "I am sure there is a place for erotica in marriage—surely it is not just for those who are single."

Marie laughed. "I'm sure it is more important in marriage. Every good wife must also be her husband's mistress. If she is not, he will find another."

"I did like Michael Hamilton. But he had no right to assume I worked here in *that* capacity. He had no right to assume I was—"

"Perhaps it was more wishful thinking than assumption."

"I still do not find it flattering."

"I think you will hear from him again. I should take time to see him. Perhaps he will come to understand that you are a lady."

"I'll see," she said, running her fingers through her thick dark curls.

"If he frequents this establishment again, will you cook for him?"

"If he pays," Chantel replied. "Your establishment is a business and I work here."

Marie nodded. "I have a feeling this relationship will flourish," she said as she stared into her teacup.

Chantel simply looked down. Was Marie talking about their business relationship or her relationship with the brash young American? She decided not to ask. There was no way she wanted to admit to Marie that she had thought of little else since last night. His kiss had ignited a flame of passion within her; the feel of his arms around her had made her reel with desire. Yet he had angered her and, oddly, she remained angry in spite of remembering her every sensation in his arms. Yes, she wanted him to return. But he would have to return on her terms or not at all.

The new white plantation-style house on the edge of Faubourg Ste. Marie was the largest home in the wealthy American neighborhood. It was owned by Gordon Walker, a banker from New York, who was a newcomer to New Orleans. Having only just arrived, he was a mystery to his neighbors, though gossip about him was plentiful. All that was actually known was that he was a widower with a very beautiful daughter. It was, therefore, not unusual that considerable excitement was generated when invitations to his housewarming party were delivered to the other inhabitants of Faubourg Ste. Marie.

"I envy you," René said cheerfully. "People here are curious enough, but in the French Quarter everyone is buzzing with gossip about this Mr. Walker."

"Then you can come with me to this housewarming and return to the Vieux Carré with all the news."

"The invitation is for you. I hardly think it includes me."

"You're my assistant and interpreter. It's important for you to know anyone who is likely to become a business associate. I insist. I doubt this Walker is such a snob. He is a businessman; he can't afford snobbery."

René grinned. "I shall come with you then, if only to test your theory. But of course there is an added reason. I hear his daughter is quite lovely."

René was very much a ladies' man. Michael was tempted

to confide in him, to ask his advice about Chantel. But he did not. He had decided instead on a letter. He felt he had to handle this himself. He had to make her understand that the last thing in the world he had wanted was to insult her.

"When is this party? How is one to dress?" René asked.

René's question interrupted his musings about Chantel. "Oh, let me see. It's at ten P.M. on November twenty-sixth. It says 'formal attire.' Can you make it?"

"Of course. 'Formal attire.' How very British. At least it begins at a proper hour."

René was right. Britishness had not ended with the revolution twenty-six years ago. This seemed especially true here in New Orleans, where so many diverse cultures came together. Many Americans affected formal teas, afternoon garden parties, and evening dinner parties. In this way they differentiated themselves from the frontiersmen who crossed the Natchez Trace and built farms upriver. They also stood apart from the French, Spanish, and free blacks. Those cultures favored costume balls, which enabled the celebrants to dress casually while pretending to be someone they were not. Michael felt adrift. The truth was, he enjoyed the celebrations of the majority of the population more than the gatherings of his countrymen. Still, when he attended a public event such as a costume ball, he felt himself a stranger looking in.

He examined the invitation again, and half smiled. "You're right. The time of the event is not British. Perhaps there is hope for this Gordon Walker."

René nodded. "I hope there is hope for his daughter too. I hear she is a stunning blonde. I love blondes. I once met a girl from Norway. She was the daughter of a sea captain. She and her father spent some weeks here. Her eyes were like bluebells, her skin like milk. I think of our short affair as one of the highlights of my life."

Michael laughed. "And you are going to tell me about it in the most minute detail, aren't you?"

René grinned. "But of course."

* * *

Chantel sat among the plush cushions on the sofa. They were covered with bright, bold African material and they were the first thing everyone noticed when entering the room. The other pieces of furniture were all made of dark wood and were large and heavy in the Spanish fashion. Incense burned from many small pots and filled the room with the aroma of musk.

Chantel examined the envelope that had just been delivered. Then she carefully tore it open and unfolded the paper inside. It was from Michael Hamilton.

My Dear Miss Boudreau,
  I want to apologize for my shameful behavior night before last. I fear I consumed far too much of the special drink that was served. I was overcome by your exquisite cuisine and, I confess, deeply attracted by your rare beauty. I beg your forgiveness and ask that I might again come to the hotel and sample your exquisite dishes as well as come to know you better. Please, I beg you, let us begin anew."

                                    Sincerely,
                                    Michael Hamilton

Chantel let the letter drop into her lap. "I do want to see you again," she said to herself. For a moment she let her thoughts wander back to the moment he had pulled her into his arms and roughly kissed her. A little chill passed through her, and she knew there was no denying her attraction to this man. Still, if anything were to come of a relationship with him, he had to understand that she was her own person, that she had standards, and she had no intention of becoming anyone's mistress. "It all depends on what you want," she said to the letter's author. She frowned a little. Something told her he was a man who usually got what he wanted. Something also told her he was a good lover, a man who could fulfill her own dreams.

She decided to write him back. She would tell him that Marie Dumont's establishment was a hotel that served all who paid, that she was the chef, and that she would be happy to see him again as long as he minded his manners and understood that her affections were not for sale.

"Mon Dieu," René muttered as he stepped down from the carriage to join Michael in the driveway of the home that had been so recently built by Gordon Walker. "This is not a house, it is a palace."

Michael did not disagree with René's assessment. Walker's house was a palatial mansion built on a slight knoll. It glimmered white in the moonlight and had a wide portico supported by tall, white Doric columns. The steps led to the wide drive and the surrounding scythed green lawns, which were dotted by pruned shrubs. It was located some distance from the American business district, which was across the common from the Vieux Carré, and was where Walker lived in a large house that combined home with office.

The grand double doors were opened for them even before they knocked, and they were ushered into a wide center hall, off which was a large room. It was filled with well-dressed Americans—"The cream of the crop," Michael whispered to René, who nodded in agreement.

Silent servants bearing trays of refreshment and drinks circulated among the guests.

"The cream of several crops," René said, gesturing toward the Spanish and French officials who mingled easily, but stood apart from most of the Americans. This, they both knew, was less a matter of nationality than it was a matter of common interests. The officials and diplomats present were aristocrats; they were a different breed than the tradesmen, and most of the Americans present were tradesmen.

A heavy-set, tall American with steel-gray hair and a firm jaw walked toward them. Both instantly guessed that this was their host, Mr. Gordon Walker.

He held out his hand, and Michael shook it.

"Gordon Walker," he said, turning to shake René's hand as well.

"Michael Hamilton and my assistant, Monsieur René Gaston."

"Good to know you both. I'm glad you could come."

Walker had a ready smile, a firm handshake, and a somewhat thunderous voice.

He turned slightly away and called out, "Susanna! Over here."

A young woman turned and came toward them. She had flowing blond hair, blue eyes, and a fine, slim figure. All of her natural endowments were enhanced by the light blue gown she wore.

"Michael, I'd like to introduce you to my daughter, Susanna. Susanna, this is Michael Hamilton, one of New Orleans' up-and-coming young importers. And this is his assistant, Mr. René Gaston."

Susanna Walker smiled warmly. "I'm happy to meet you."

Michael immediately thought that she was an attractive woman, but not as attractive as Chantel Boudreau. Moreover, she only glanced at him. Her smile immediately settled on René. Michael almost laughed. René appeared quite ready to live up to his reputation as a ladies' man extraordinaire.

"We're serving a buffet. Please, let me show you to the food."

She took René's arm and Michael walked abreast of them as she led them both across the room.

"My soul for a good caterer," Susanna said lightly.

"I know of a wonderful chef," Michael said quickly. As soon as he said it, he realized how close Chantel was to his every thought.

"You must introduce me. We entertain a great deal. My

father always expects the best, but it is I who must do the planning.''

"You've done a wonderful job,'' René praised, squeezing her arm ever so slightly. "This array of food is most impressive.''

Susanna looked up into René's eyes. "Impressive, but not as varied as I should like it. You're Cajun, aren't you? I would like to serve Cajun food. I've heard so much about it.''

She was flirting with René, and René, who had already confessed his fondness for blondes, was obviously enchanted by her.

Michael could all but feel the attraction between them. It had the suddenness of an electrical storm in the afternoon. Clearly René was interested in Susanna just as Michael was interested in Chantel. This new liaison could provide a way for him to see Chantel again, to make up for his past behavior. "Perhaps we could all have dinner in the Vieux Carré next week. You must sample this chef's cuisine. I know you'll be impressed.''

René grinned. "Yes, what a good idea. Would your father allow you to dine with us?''

Susanna's eyes revealed her interest. "Of course he would! I should adore it!''

"Then let us come for you at nine next Friday.''

"I shall look forward to it.''

CHAPTER THREE

Gordon Walker leaned back in his chair and lit a cigar. It was not just any cigar, but a cigar from Santiago de Cuba. It had a splendid wrapper leaf, strong and elastic with a silky texture and a dark brown color. Its flavor was pleasing, but then, in his opinion, Santiago de Cuba produced the finest cigars in the world.

"One of the few pleasures of living in New Orleans," he said to himself. Cuban cigars were readily available because the Spanish aristocracy could not live without them. The story went that Columbus had discovered the Indians smoking a long, thick bundle of twisted tobacco wrapped in a palm leaf. Within fifty years, cigar smoking became a symbol of wealth in Spain. Gordon's father had smoked cigars and he smoked cigars. He considered his cigar to be almost a symbol of his banking profession. Who could trust a banker who did not smoke a good cigar?

"New Orleans is a strange city," he muttered. He often had conversations with himself. It clarified his thoughts. "Yes, a strange city but a place of opportunity, a place where there is much money to be made.''

It was only a matter of time before America owned Louisiana. Gordon knew from his contacts in Washington that agreements had been made, that the entire territory owned by the French would be sold to the U.S. He expected the final news at any moment. Of course, he was not the only one who expected it. Americans were flocking to New Orleans like bees to honey. He cursed the slowness of communications and the closemouthed habits of the politicians. It took weeks to find out anything.

He let out his breath slowly and turned his thoughts to his position in New Orleans. A banker needed respect. People of all kinds had to feel he was their friend. Most important, he needed the indulgence of powerful men. He thought of his recent housewarming. It had gone well; he had entertained the powerful and he had set Susanna off on the right foot.

Michael Hamilton was a young man of means, of ambition, and fortunately also quite handsome. He had been told that there was no woman in Michael's life, and he judged Susanna to be a perfect match for him. Not only did Michael have a good reputation and would doubtless make a good husband, but such a marriage could unite his bank with a growing import-export business.

The import-export business in New Orleans last year had grossed over two million, a large amount of money, and Gordon wanted an interest in it. He had considered buying Michael out, but he deemed the young man to be an excellent manager and wanted him around to run the business. Why bother to buy someone out if you could achieve virtually the same end through a peaceful marriage? In any case, it was long past time that Susanna married.

He looked up from his musings when he heard a knock on his door. "Come in," he called out.

Susanna opened the door a crack. "Are you busy?"

"No, not at the moment."

Susanna came into the room and sat down. "This is the night

I'm going to dinner with Michael and René. I just wanted to remind you.''

"I hadn't forgotten," Walker answered. "In fact, I've been thinking about what you should wear. You know, you dress far too modestly. I know it's odd for a father to say that, but what I mean is, your clothes are out of style. Lower necklines are the fashion.''

"I'm not sure I want to wear lower necklines.''

"Posh! I've taken the liberty of buying you a dress. It's being delivered this afternoon. Wear it tonight.''

Susanna tried not to frown at her father. As was so often the case, this was more of an order than a suggestion. His tone diminished the quality of his gift, turning it from something that ought to have been delightful to something that was necessary. It seemed patently obvious to her that he was trying to match her up with this Michael Hamilton. The trouble was, she liked his assistant, René Gaston, much better. But she would not mention that to her father. He would not approve of her becoming involved with René, who was Cajun, not powerful in his own right, and who worked for Michael.

In fact, not only would she not mention René, she would not argue with her father. It was a fruitless endeavor. "I'll wear it," she said somewhat wearily.

"And you'll have a good time too. When he comes for you, I shall ask Michael to accompany us to the masked ball in the *Cabildo* next week. You'll enjoy that too.''

Now he was practically ordering her to enjoy life. There was no end to it. Her father had ordered her about for years. It almost seemed worth getting married so she could be her own boss. She suspected, however, that with her luck she would probably marry a man who ruled her just as her father did.

"You don't look very happy. He's a very presentable young man, you know. And he's both rich and well connected.''

Susanna drew in her breath. "He's all of those things, but I don't think he's interested in me." She did not want to say that she was not interested in him either.

Gordon Walker smiled. "You let me worry about that, my dear. Anyway, I'm certain you're wrong."

Susanna turned away. Was her father intending to buy Michael Hamilton for her? All that gave her comfort was the conviction that she doubted he was for sale. Still, she knew her father. He was a stubborn man who almost always got what he wanted.

"Well, if I'm to be out late, I ought to rest," she said, using the coming evening as an excuse to leave.

"Yes, off you go. You must always get enough rest. It helps you remain beautiful."

Susanna turned and left her father's room, wondering why she had come in the first place. Why was he so single-minded? It seemed that when he made up his mind about something, he could think of nothing else. "I wish he'd find a woman," she said to herself. Yes, perhaps if her father had a woman he would think less about her and planning her life.

It was once again Marie Dumont herself who greeted Michael at the door. She smiled warmly, and if she was surprised to see Susanna Walker in the company of Michael and René, she did not show it.

"How delightful—you've brought friends."

Michael kissed her hand. "Madame Dumont, please let me present Miss Susanna Walker and my assistant, René Gaston. You did get my note, about tonight?"

"Of course I did. Miss Walker is even lovelier in person than people say. And of course I remember René. He comes here now and again, and he has visited my shop more than once."

"Is Chantel here?" Michael asked anxiously.

"She is here. I shall send her out so you can tell her yourself what you would like her to prepare for your meal."

"Thank you."

Without further conversation, Marie beckoned them to follow

her. She led them back to the same room in which he had eaten alone. This time, the table was set for three.

"I am sure you'll enjoy dining with others far more than dining alone. Friends do so enhance the food, especially if one of them is a beautiful woman." Marie smiled seductively. Was this a *ménage à trois?* No, she decided not. She was quite certain Michael wanted Chantel to make it a foursome.

"We're only friends," Susanna said quickly.

"But of course," Marie purred even as she took their measure with her golden cat eyes.

Michael felt his face turn red, and he wondered if he should have brought Susanna here. Still, her father had seemed pleased. When he and René had picked her up this evening, her father had asked him to accompany him and Susanna to the masked ball at the *Cabildo.* He had agreed because René, who was clearly taken with Susanna, had nudged him hard in the ribs. He was very much aware of the attraction between Susanna and René, although he had said nothing, and René, for once, had said little to him.

In a few moments the ravishing Chantel appeared. Michael smiled at her nervously and then introduced Susanna and René.

"Did you get my note?" Michael asked anxiously. He wanted to pull her into his arms and kiss her this instant. Each time he saw her, he realized how much more beautiful she was in reality than she was in his dreams.

"Yes. I accept your apology," she said a little curtly.

He smiled with relief, but could not help but notice that she seemed cool.

Move slowly, he cautioned himself. He had moved too quickly the first time and made a terrible mistake. This time he had to take as much time as necessary and avoid insulting his angel in any way.

"What do you suggest?" Susanna asked enthusiastically as she leaned toward Chantel. "I've been told your culinary creations are divine."

"I should like to prepare a drink I call Passion Delight."

"I hope it's not as potent as the last drink you served me," Michael said, trying to make light of his previous disastrous experience.

Chantel did not answer. "It's made from two glasses of port, eight drops of a liquor called curaçao, and two thin lemon slices studded with cloves."

"That sounds intriguing," René said, brushing a stray hair off his brow. He well knew that such aphrodisiac drinks should be lightly indulged in by men, but that they were known to set women aflame or, at the very least, free them of inhibitions.

"Next I would suggest some broth supreme, sweet potatoes for sweethearts, and then some vermicelli for lovers, followed by King Crab and for dessert, some delightful pudding."

"Do you share your recipes?" Susanna asked.

Chantel smiled. "If there is a special one you desire."

"They all sound wonderful. I shall choose one."

"May I suggest the vermicelli?" Chantel ventured.

"May I watch you prepare it?"

"Of course. I'll come for you when it is time. But first the drink and the appetizers."

Chantel hurried back to the kitchen, where she found Marie waiting.

"I see that he's returned," Marie said, watching Chantel's expression.

"With another woman," Chantel said flatly. "A beautiful blonde."

"I do not think that Miss Susanna Walker is really with Michael Hamilton. Indeed, I don't think she even wants him. I think it is René she longs for. I think her father would not approve of René. I daresay they are, for the present, a threesome of convenience."

"Do you really think so?"

Marie nodded. "Let nature take its course. You'll see that I'm right."

Chantel turned away to set about preparing the first course. Maybe Marie was right, or maybe it was just wishful thinking. *I will not indulge in fantasies,* she promised herself. At the same time, however, she decided to watch and listen.

Long after the first course had been delivered, Chantel summoned Susanna to her kitchen.

"First," she instructed, "you sauté two cloves of garlic in three tablespoons of olive oil until they are soft and ever so light brown—like this."

Susanna watched, inhaling the mouth-watering aroma.

"Next, you add six and one half ounces of cleaned clams, two cups of tomato sauce, two teaspoons of chopped parsley, and one cup of water. You add salt and pepper to suit the palates of your guests, and then it should all simmer for about forty-five minutes till the sauce is rich and thick. Then you cook the vermicelli and drain it well. It is then heaped on plates and covered with clam sauce."

"It smells wonderful."

"Clams are believed to make men amorous."

Susanna smiled slyly. "I have a man I wish to make amorous."

Chantel said nothing. She was far from certain Marie was right about just which man Susanna Walker was interested in. This cool-looking blond woman had arrived with both men. Was it really René she desired?

"I must prepare some food for the masked ball," Susanna confided. "As you know, everyone must bring something. May I bring this wonderful sauce?"

Chantel nodded. "I shall be attending as well. The costume balls at the *Cabildo* are the only occasion on which all the inhabitants of this city come together."

"I don't understand why the English—and I include my father—are so stand-offish."

Chantel smiled at Susanna's observation. Susanna might

mean something to Michael, or she might not. Considering her own attraction to Michael, she ought to dislike Susanna, but she did not. Perhaps Marie was right; perhaps she was interested in René. She hoped so, not just because she liked Susanna, but because Susanna was so attractive.

"I'll see you at the ball," Susanna said as she left the kitchen. Then she turned warmly toward Chantel. "This is an enchanted kitchen and you are quite wonderful."

Michael looked about him at the interior of the *Cabildo*. He had been told that once this building had been called the *Casa Capitular*. The *Casa* had been rebuilt in stone and was now the *Cabildo,* the seat of government.

On either side of the large double doors that had given them entry, a guard stood at attention. The foyer was a large area, and in its center a winding staircase led to the second floor.

There were paintings everywhere. The ceilings were beamed and the walls whitewashed and made of stucco. A large chandelier was suspended from the center beam. But it was not a crystal chandelier, such as might have been found in New York or Boston. Rather it was made of wrought iron, the same wrought iron that covered windows in New Orleans and was used to build staircases and little rounded balconies.

Tonight, the huge foyer of the *Cabildo* was gaily decorated with painted animals made from papier-mâché, multi-colored gourds, and long chains of blue, yellow, and red beads.

The chief decorations, however, were the guests themselves. They numbered one hundred and represented the elite of the various cultural groups in the city. Regardless of whether they were Spanish, French, Cajun, African, European, or a mixture such as Marie Dumont, they all dressed in wild costumes and wore or carried masks.

At René's urging, Michael reluctantly came dressed as Marc Antony while René chose to come as a nameless Roman gladiator.

Susanna came costumed as a lady of the English Court, while Chantel, wearing her long hair loose, dressed in a white Grecian gown trimmed with gold. It fell in flowing folds over her body. Around the top of her head, she wore a garland of green leaves. Her gown was designed by Marie Dumont herself, who proclaimed it to be a replica of those worn by the famed Aphrodite, goddess of love.

Gordon Walker, who muttered darkly about the excesses that took place in the Vieux Carré, declared such balls to be influenced by the "foreigners" who ran the city. Nonetheless, he finally gave in and agreed to wear a costume. Appropriately, he came dressed as Caesar, a cigar-smoking Caesar to be sure.

Almost as if she knew Gordon Walker's choice of costume in advance, Marie Dumont came as Cleopatra. Her embroidered costume was elegant, her dark hair magnificent; her high cheekbones and slightly slanted golden eyes gave everyone the impression that she might indeed be the reincarnation of the famed Queen of the Nile.

Marie surveyed the scene with an amused expression on her face. Marc Antony was not one whit interested in Cleopatra, he had eyes only for the beguiling Aphrodite. The Roman gladiator looked with considerable lust on the English lady in waiting, while Caesar looked somewhat stiff and uncomfortable. "I shall change that," Marie vowed under her breath.

"There is nothing more charming than an ill-at-ease man of power," Marie whispered to Aphrodite. "I adore men of power. I do believe I shall have to help Mr. Walker to relax."

Aphrodite laughed. "I fear you shall need to find someone to help you."

Marie arched one brow. "I will need no help from anyone else. But I trust you did bring some—well, shall I say encouraging food or drink?"

"I think the punch will embolden the gentleman."

"What are its ingredients?"

"Muscatel, brandy, milk, cream, sugar, and nutmeg."

"It sounds more than sufficient. I will, of course, accept help from the God of Wine."

Chantel watched as Cleopatra walked to Caesar's side. Yes, these two were matched, she thought.

"Madame, I should like to dance with you," René said, from beneath his helmet. He tried to disguise his voice, but was reasonably certain the lovely Susanna would know him.

Her blue dress was cut daringly low in the style of the court. Her hair fell over her bare white shoulders invitingly, and her pink lips seemed to beg to be kissed. At least that was how it seemed to René in his current amorous state.

"I should love to dance with you," Susanna answered.

"I will thank Michael for leaving you unattended."

Susanna looked into his eyes boldly. How tired she was of games! She had decided she wanted René and she saw no reason to disguise her desires. "I asked him to leave when I saw you coming our way," she confessed.

"I feel this is going to be quite an evening," René replied as he guided her onto the dance floor. "You're a most unusual woman."

"Sometimes it's necessary to do things differently, to take matters into one's own hands."

He looked into her sky-blue eyes. She was being forthright and not bothering to play the coquette. He liked that. It was most refreshing.

Michael walked across the room toward his vision of loveliness. She was the breathtaking woman of his dreams, the woman whose soft hands he remembered from his delirium. Her white, gold-trimmed gown fell over her curved and most alluring body. *How I want to hold you,* he thought. If only he had not insulted her. If only she felt about him the way he felt about her.

Chantel watched as Marc Antony came toward her. His costume was as revealing as her own. He wore a sleeveless leather vest and short leather skirt in the Roman fashion. His arms were brawny and his chest broad. His legs were as muscular as his arms and they were well shaped and covered with hair. She smiled to herself. His body was no mystery to her, but still, he looked very handsome in his costume. She remembered how he looked naked and how his skin felt to the touch. A little shiver ran through her as she wondered how it would feel to be held down by such a large, strong man, to be joined with him in a passionate embrace, to be touched by him in that certain intimate place—

"You look flushed, Aphrodite," Michael observed.

"It's warm in here," Chantel returned.

"I find it warm too. Come walk outside with me. I understand there is a small garden behind the building."

Chantel looked into his eyes. They were so unusual. They were sea green, and if she stared hard into them, she could almost feel cool ocean water caressing her.

"Would that be appropriate? You did come with someone else."

Michael looked into her eyes and felt his desire for her growing by the second.

"I came with Susanna Walker and her father. We're only friends."

Only friends. Chantel liked his answer but wondered if she should completely forgive him so soon. Was this the moment she should encourage him? Did he really understand that she was not a woman who was free with her favors?

"I shall walk with you," she said slowly, "but only for a short time. The governor is going to make an announcement, and we must not miss it."

Michael took her arm and led her across the room and toward the garden.

It was December and in New England it would be freezing cold. But here the air was still unseemly warm and filled with the heady aroma of magnolias and oleander. The garden path was illuminated by torches set into the ground. They burned slowly in the damp night air and gave off little clouds of white smoke. Statues of illustrious governors past filled the garden, just as the sound of millions of katydids filled the air while the crickets competed for attention.

"I'm still unused to this warmth," Michael said, trying to make casual conversation.

"Many who come here do not remain because of the heat," Chantel answered.

"And you—were you born here?"

"Yes, but my family came from upriver. Originally they came from Canada. My heritage is Acadian. That's why they call us Cajun."

"Why do you work for Madame Dumont?"

"I'm an orphan. I must support myself, monsieur. It is not so easy for a woman to be on her own."

He felt tongue-tied. He wanted to know everything there was to know about her, but he also wanted to hold her, to feel her against him, to taste her luscious lips.

"You're very beautiful," he said awkwardly. "The most beautiful woman I've ever seen."

Chantel stopped and turned slightly. Michael could not contain himself. He drew her into his arms suddenly and kissed her full lips. It was a divine kiss, a kiss given by Aphrodite.

"You are most appropriately costumed," he whispered, breathing into her perfectly shaped ear. Then he kissed her neck and was quite certain he felt her move against him just as her lips had moved beneath his. His hands slid down her suggestive gown, over its silky folds, down over her rounded buttocks. It was then he felt her pull away from him. He looked into her face, aware of the heat that filled him. She brushed her hair back and he could see she was struggling to regain her own composure.

"It is far too soon for that sort of thing," she managed.

"I'm sorry. When I'm near you, desire overcomes me."

She looked down, avoiding his eyes. "It is time we went back inside," she said quickly. "We'll miss the governor's announcement."

She began walking quickly back toward the *Cabildo*. Michael followed, watching her hips undulate with each step she took.

I will win her over, Michael promised himself. When he kissed her, he could feel the heat of her body, smell the tantalizing aroma of her perfume, hear the shortness in her breath. Surely she was attracted to him too. Surely he could overcome her resistance to him if he kept at it.

Chantel shivered with delight as she walked ahead of Michael. He was quite a man! And yet for all the physical attraction she felt, she was emotionally wary of him, afraid that he still thought of her as a loose woman, a woman for hire or, equally bad, only desired her for a short affair. How could he imagine how sheltered her upbringing had been? Especially as she was considered the mistress of erotic cookery.

But fanciful imaginings were one thing and reality was another. She sighed. Prolonging desire would most assuredly make fulfillment more exciting. Great love, she had always been taught, was the same as a fine appetite. The hungrier one was, the more delightful the feast. *So we will wait,* she said silently to Michael. *We will wait till I am sure of your intentions and until you are sure I am the only woman you will ever want.*

Such an odd evening! Such a peculiar feeling! Gordon Walker sipped some more of the punch Madame Dumont had given him. It was strangely refreshing, yet it seemed to fill him with thoughts he had not had for many years. This Marie Dumont was said to be a witch, but the word he would have chosen was enchantress. Her voice was lulling, her eyes hypnotic, her intelligence and business sense utterly surprising. And yet when she stood close to him and he could inhale the aroma of her perfume, it was not business that came to mind.

"The governor is taking the podium. I believe this will turn out to be a most surprising evening," Marie said.

"A surprising evening indeed," Gordon Walker muttered. "When it is over, may I escort you home?"

"I should be delighted," Marie purred.

The governor was dressed in red and white. His uniform dripped with gold braid and his chest was filled with colorful medals. He cleared his throat and spoke loudly and clearly. "I have chosen this occasion to make an important announcement," he proclaimed. He waited for a long moment until the room filled with silence and anticipation.

"An agreement has been reached. After long negotiations, the Louisiana Territory—including this great port—has been sold to the United States of America."

Hardly had he spoken the words when all the Americans and most of the Spanish burst into cheers.

"The territory will be officially turned over at the end of this month, and in February we will have a week-long celebration, not just for the wealthy but for all of New Orleans. We will have a grand costume ball, dancing in the streets, music and food, and important guests! Till then, things will continue as they are."

Again there was a great cheer and then the musicians began to play and the governor stepped down from the podium and, taking his wife's arm, led her onto the dance floor.

"I do believe I have been deserted," Susanna said as she looked about.

René took her in his arms and led her out onto the floor. "Michael knows when to disappear," he said, smiling. "And that is most certainly my gain."

"I meant my father. I don't see him anywhere."

"Ah, well, that too is my gain. Let me kidnap you."

Susanna blinked up at René and felt suddenly quite reckless.

"All right," she replied, touching his metal breastplate. "I cannot turn down the protection of a Roman warrior, even one who is hidden beneath a mask. That is you, is it not, René?"

He grinned beneath his mask and slipped his arm around her tiny waist. "You shall only be certain when we discard our masks at midnight."

"It is near midnight now," she said.

"Then let us go somewhere alone to shed our masks and reveal ourselves."

Susanna nodded. "I should like to reveal myself to you," she whispered. Michael had vanished with Chantel and her father was nowhere about.

"Your father will not approve," René warned.

"It does not matter. I approve. My father has been running my life for years. It must end."

"Are you certain you won't regret this action?"

Susanna looked into his eyes. "I shall not regret it." At that moment, she knew she had made the most daring decision of her life.

CHAPTER FOUR

At two in the afternoon, Susanna Walker ventured from her room and crept down the stairs. In her mind, she had prepared various versions of her evening to tell her father, and specifically of her return home. In reality, René had brought her home in the early hours of the morning, and she had entered the house through the servants' entrance, which led to the kitchen. She had then made her way stealthily up the back stairs and gone directly to her room. Once there, she climbed into her bed beneath her mosquito netting and, holding herself tightly, relived every moment of her stolen hours with René.

"I am no longer a virgin," she whispered happily under her breath. It had all been wonderful! René was the only man for her, and her father be damned! Still, he had the power to ruin everything, and she vowed not to allow that to happen.

If all went well with her father, she had decided she would go to see Michael immediately. He would help her, of that she was quite certain.

The house was unseemly quiet, Susanna thought as she walked through the rooms. But then, she reminded herself, it was Sunday and most of the servants were off. The dining room was empty, so was the living room, and mysteriously her father was neither in his study nor in the library.

Beyond the kitchen, working in the storeroom, Susanna found the cook. "Has my father had lunch yet?" she inquired.

The woman looked at her and shook her head. "He hasn't even had breakfast, missy. He's not home."

Not home? She wondered if she looked as perplexed as she felt. She shrugged and went back toward the front of the house. Was it possible that all of her subterfuge was unnecessary? It seemed that her father had not even been home to catch her returning in the wee hours of the morning. But where could he be?

Susanna had just reached the front door when she heard the carriage in the drive. She went into the parlor and in a moment, her father came into the house.

"Oh, you're here," he said, flushing slightly.

Susanna sensed her father's ill at ease at once, and she felt overcome by a devilish desire to make him squirm. Certainly if he knew of her activities last night, he would forbid her to see René again, and he would, to boot, watch her carefully. But now, by some quite delightful quirk of fate, the tables were turned.

"You didn't come home last night! My goodness, I've been worried to death!" she said with a tone of disapproval.

"I'm sorry," her father muttered. "I was overcome with a headache and the hour was late, so I went to a hotel."

A hotel indeed! He had probably gone to Marie Dumont's. He had no doubt availed himself of some woman. It wasn't at all like her father, but it seemed to Susanna as if nothing else could possibly account for his embarrassment. And it wasn't just embarrassment—he also looked different. He looked satisfied with himself, but not satisfied in the same way as he looked when he clinched a big business deal. This, she could clearly see, was quite a different kind of satisfaction.

"Would you signal the driver not leave just yet?" Susanna

asked. "I want to go for a short drive before the carriage is put away."

Still flushed, and more than a little confused, Gordon Walker opened the door and called out to the driver who had just turned the carriage about.

Susanna sailed past her father and slung her light cloak over her dress. "I'll be off now, but back in a short time."

Her father nodded dumbly, and she thought that he looked just like a little boy caught with his hand in the cookie jar.

In less than fifteen minutes, Susanna was on her way to Michael Hamilton's home. She couldn't remember when she had felt more gleeful or more devilish.

Michael showed Susanna into his study. It was a cluttered room, filled with shipping schedules. The desk was covered with plans for a new wharf that Michael wanted to build. It would move his business from his home to the waterfront, where, in his opinion, it belonged.

"I'm surprised to see you," he confessed. "Can I offer you some refreshment?"

Susanna shook her head. "Why are you surprised to see me?"

"I was something of a cad last night. I should have seen you home, but when I returned you were already gone."

Susanna smiled. "I saw you with Chantel. Please, I like you and I don't want to be insulting, but I really didn't want you to take me home. René took me home—more or less."

Michael furrowed his brow at her candor. Still, as he and René were obviously close, she no doubt realized there was no need for her to hide anything. He smiled. "More or less?"

Susanna blushed. "He took me to *his* home. But I did not come to detail my evening. I came to ask you to help me."

"How might I help you?"

Susanna drew in her breath. "I'm in love with René. I know

you will say we hardly know one another, but I know it is love. I have waited a long while to find such a man, now I must have time to get to know him, time for our love to grow.''

"Should you not tell this to René?"

"I'm sure he already knows my feelings. That is not my problem. You are my problem.''

"How am I a problem?" Michael asked, mystified.

"My father is a businessman. You are a businessman. You are both easterners, both successful. My father wants me to marry you. He will see to it that we are together again and again, Michael. But I know you want someone else, and now you know how I feel about René. My father will not approve of René so I must be very sure of René's feeling for me before my father finds out about us.''

"How can I help you?" Michael asked.

"Take me out, and I will leave immediately with René. Let my father think you are courting me so that I can be with René.''

"I'm sure your father only wants to protect you," Michael said, hoping to draw her out.

"No, he wants to run my life as he has for twenty-three years. He wants to marry me to the man of his choosing, not the man I choose. Not that I don't like you—please, as I said, I don't want to be insulting.''

Michael laughed. If only she knew how relieved he was! He had sensed Gordon Walker's plans for him and Susanna and admitted to himself that he might have been interested had his heart not already belonged to another. "I am not at all insulted. René is my good friend.''

"I promise you that when the time is right, I will confess to my father and not implicate you. But I must be free to know my own heart. Please help me . . . well, us.''

Michael smiled. "Can we dine often at Marie Dumont's?"

Susanna laughed. "It will be my pleasure.''

* * *

Gordon Walker hurried to his study. There, he poured himself a strong drink and sank into his favorite old blue chair.

What had happened to him? All his life he had only pursued business. He had been straight, moral, and upright, a credit to his community, a credit to the banking profession. But last night he had been overcome! Now, his whole world seemed to have turned topsy-turvy.

He thought about Marie Dumont. Some said she was a witch; others called her a Voodoo Queen. Now he had good cause to wonder if such allegations could be true. He shook his head. No, he did not believe in witches or Voodoo. He sighed. If she was a witch, she was a most desirable witch. Oh, she was quite a woman! She was a sensuous, exotic woman. She was a woman he had been unable to resist, and no matter how topsy-turvy his life, she was a temptation he had to give in to. And damn! He was glad he had. What an experience! In his whole life he had never dreamed of such lovemaking. Susanna's mother had always blown out the lamp and worn a wool nightdress. She was impatient with him, and though he had loved her deeply, he now realized that she was cold by comparison to this wild exotic beauty who had seduced him.

Ah, Marie Dumont! She had taken him to her perfumed boudoir, excited him beyond all endurance, then pleasured him in ways of which most men only dreamed.

He grinned boyishly and ran his fingers through his iron-gray hair. If he did say so himself, he had given pleasure as well. Yes, he had turned Marie Dumont into a writhing wanton creature as hungry for him as he was for her.

"I shall have to see her again," he said to himself as he entirely cast aside all his objections to life in the Vieux Carré while at the same time seriously reconsidering many of his other previously held plans.

Suddenly, an idea came to him. What better way to see more

of Marie than to hire her to help him with the celebrations in February! What a team they would make! They would bring all of New Orleans to one gigantic party—a party where everyone would be both satisfied and satiated.

His mind raced ahead. Everything was going perfectly. Michael Hamilton seemed quite taken with Susanna. The more often he took her out, the freer he would be to see Marie. He would know incredible personal satisfaction with Marie and no doubt he would have business success as well. Eventually, the two businesses, his and Michael's, would be joined in wedded bliss.

He rang the bell by his desk and his butler entered. "I want you to go into town and buy a box of the finest imported chocolates, a bottle of the best French wine, and a bouquet of fresh flowers. All these are to be delivered to Madame Marie Dumont."

The butler nodded, but Gordon Walker did not see the smirk that crossed the butler's face as soon as he turned away.

Chantel delicately rolled the spicy, rum-flavored dough between her hands until it formed a hard round ball. That done, she picked up more dough and began again. It was a lovely feeling. The warm dough was soft and pliable, and the aroma of cinnamon, cocoa, oranges, and rum filled her kitchen. Soon that smell would fade and be replaced by the odor of sweet potatoes and bits of spicy meat cooking.

As she rolled the third pinch of soft dough between her hands, her mind filled with thoughts of Michael. The rippling of his sinewy muscles and hard, strong arms and legs made her shiver with anticipation. The idea of making love with Michael Hamilton excited her, but never having made love before, she could not help but wonder if the expectation was greater than the reality. She felt certain he was a good lover. She concentrated on her memory of him. His eyes burned with desire for her, and when he kissed her in the dining room, and in the garden more recently, his lips had moved slowly on hers. She had felt the promise of a slow, tantalizing waltz of seduction. That was what she wanted. "Lovemaking," her brother had once told her, "is like eating a fine meal. In order to enjoy it completely, you must eat slowly, savoring each morsel, prolonging the experience as long as possible."

Chantel had always listened to her brother. She missed him because he had been her friend as well as her brother. He told her about the world, and of course, it was he who had taught her to cook. It was all such an irony, she thought as she began to lay the spicy rum balls out on a tray. In the intellectual sense she knew all there was to know about lovemaking, but she had never done it! Until now, she thought with a smile, she had not met a man to whom she wished to give herself. It seemed, judging from the way she felt when she was with him, that Michael was the man—although, she reminded herself, it was important to know him better, to make certain that he was the right one.

Chantel finished rolling the last ball and looked up as Marie came in.

"You look quite devastating in that gown. Aren't you rather dressed up for cooking?" Marie commented dryly.

"Do you like my dress? Michael is coming tonight."

"More important, I think he will like it," Marie replied. "Yes, it suits you. And it's most suggestive."

Chantel smiled slyly. "I haven't seen you much of late."

"I have discovered a new pastime."

"I suspect it is not a pastime but a man."

"And what a man! He's a mature man, a man who has waited far too long for love. I adore the love-starved! They're so anxious and so very grateful."

"Have you seen him every night?"

"Yes. Secretly of course. So, your Michael Hamilton is coming tonight?"

"For dinner. But he is not 'my' Michael. I have not yet decided whether he is the one for whom I have been waiting.

We did not get off to a good start, but I have decided to give him another opportunity.''

''I'm going out this evening,'' Marie imparted. ''I hope your evening is as eventful as I'm sure mine will be.''

Chantel only nodded. Marie would make her own evening memorable. She was afraid to tell Marie that she thought Michael was the one for her, afraid something would happen. It was simply too soon. It was bad luck to speak of a love not yet in full blossom. Still, in her heart, she felt confident. His kiss in the garden and their embrace was a sweet memory, a memory filled with mutual desire.

''I feel a bit devious,'' Michael admitted as he guided the buggy along toward the Vieux Carré. The moon was full, and it shimmered off the water. It was an exceptionally bright night, and as they passed the *Cabildo,* the ironwork on the balconies, railings, and gates caught the glint of the moon.

''I don't want you to feel guilty because of me,'' Susanna assured him, ''for you have no need. My father wants me to marry you. He doesn't really care about my happiness. All he wants is to unite his banking business with your trading business. He really wants a merger, not a marriage.''

''I'm sure you're exaggerating.''

''No. You just don't know him as I do. My mother died when I was quite young. My father didn't just rear me; he picked out my clothes as well as my friends. He sent me to private schools he chose, and he always took me with him when he traveled.''

''That sounds as if he really cares about you.''

''I'm sure in his own way he does. But to me it seemed that he always wanted me at his side to impress his business cronies. When I grew older, I was expected to see to his dinner parties, be the hostess, play the dutiful daughter. My father has made all my decisions all of my life, but I cannot let him decide whom I shall love. That is the one decision I have decided to make on my own.''

"Why don't you tell him that?''

"Because he will pack me off to my aunt in Philadelphia and I shall never see René again.''

"Are you certain René is the one?''

"I adore him," Susanna said wistfully. "I have given myself to him. I love him.''

Michael felt his face flush, and he was glad she had not seen him. He hadn't realized that their affair had gone so far in so short a time. It was sudden but not, he reasoned, necessarily bad. René appeared to feel the same way about Susanna as Susanna felt about him. It would work out, and if he felt a trifle devious about his own role, he also felt vindicated. Gordon Walker was a sly businessman, more than a little devious himself, and while Susanna was a bit harsh in her judgment of him, she did understand her father, about that there could be no question.

"You will help me, won't you?'' Susanna pleaded.

"I am helping you, and I will continue to help," he promised. His hesitation had made her feel insecure. He was quite certain she had good reason. Her father could be a fearful man. He was most certainly a man used to getting his own way in most, if not all, matters. It was also obvious that this was Susanna's first rebellion against her father. "What's the plan for tonight?''

"You drop me a block from Madame Dumont's hotel. René will be there and we'll go off together. Then at two in the morning, René will bring me back to you.''

Michael nodded his acknowledgment. He would ask Chantel to join him as soon as Susanna left. They would have a long supper together and then—perhaps—she would let him kiss her again. He felt his spirits rise. He felt certain Chantel really liked him in spite of her hesitation. Maybe he would get further than mere kisses.

As planned, Susanna disappeared with an anxious and somewhat flustered René. Michael watched as they left together. He wondered where they would go for their assignation. Maybe, he thought, grinning, they would go back to his house since he was out and René's own room was so small. Once again, he contemplated asking René to move into his house. After all, the entire third floor was empty, and he often felt as if he were rattling about. The house was far too large for one person, and even if he were to marry Chantel, there would still be a host of empty rooms. Now, as he thought about it, it seemed altogether convenient. He would invite Susanna for dinner and then leave. She and René could be alone together without her father growing in the least suspicious. Yes, it could all work out very well. He would be here courting Chantel, and Susanna and René would be alone together in his house.

He hurried off down the street to Madame Dumont's.

"Are you enjoying your meal?" Chantel asked as she floated into the room.

Michael looked up. She was a vision to behold. She wore a red dress that was cut low and revealed her deep cleavage. It fell off her shoulders, pinched her tiny waist, and fell in folds to the floor. Each of the folds was lace trimmed. Her wealth of dark curls tumbled over bare shoulders and framed her lovely face. Her full lips looked utterly inviting.

"You're ravishing," he whispered, aware that he was so taken with her that the words fairly caught in his throat. "But surely you're not cooking in that gown?"

"I supervised the preparation of dinner. There is no need for me to be in the kitchen every moment."

"I'm glad to hear that." He stood up and walked toward her, then took her hand and kissed it. It was soft and smelled sweet. "Join me for dinner," he said, looking into her dark eyes.

"I would like that," she whispered.

They dined on soup made with black beans, a main course

of *petits pois* with sausage and rice, a side dish of stuffed mushrooms, and a dessert of forbidden fruit.

Each dish was flavored to perfection, a treat for all the senses—as was, he thought, his dining partner.

Chantel finished her dollop of forbidden fruit and smiled. "You cannot still be hungry."

Michael looked into Chantel's dark eyes. He felt drawn into them. Again his mouth went dry. All his instincts told him to seize her and kiss her, to hold her close, but he did not want to offend her as he had once before.

He reached across the white tablecloth and took her hand in his. She stared back at him, her wonderful lips slightly parted. Was he mistaken? Or did she desire him as much as he desired her?

Slowly, almost as though he hoped she would not notice, he moved his forefinger across the inside of her wrist. It was a slow, tantalizing motion, tantalizing because he imagined it to be some other part of her quite perfect anatomy. She seemed to shiver, but he continued.

Chantel stared back into his green eyes. The movement of his finger on her wrist was causing her face to flush. It was a deliberate movement, but it was not improper and she did not wish to withdraw her hand. It was entirely too pleasant a sensation.

"I think of you all the time," Michael confessed. "You fill my dreams. I have memories of your caring for me when I was ill."

Chantel blushed and hoped his memories were, at least, unclear. "I was simply doing my job," she whispered.

"Your hands were cool and soft." He continued to rub her wrist seductively.

"You were fevered."

"I dreamt you were in my arms. I dream that dream often."

"Am I immoral in your dreams?" she asked mischievously. He moved his fingers from her wrist slowly up her arm.

Then he stood up and walked around the tiny table, pulling her up and into his arms.

"In my dreams, immorality does not enter into our relationship. I want you, I take you, and you are excited and we enjoy one another."

His words were strong and she felt weak as he held her. She felt past struggling; she felt as wanton as she knew him to be.

He bent down and kissed her. He kissed softly at first, then with more pressure. He moved his hand on her bare neck, descending now and again to her rounded shoulder. He circled her ear and was rewarded with her sigh, with the warmth of her body, with the way she pressed against him.

"Oh," she gasped as he bent and kissed her neck, then her ear. He held her fast round the waist with one hand and suddenly dipped his head and kissed her cleavage.

She shuddered against him, but she did not push him away.

"You are the most beautiful, most desirable woman I've ever known. Before I met you all I thought of was business and work. Now I dream of holding you like this, of taking you, of feeling you against me. Let me love you, Chantel. Let me make love to you till you desire me as much as I desire you. Let me kiss and caress you till you cry for fulfillment in my arms. My darling—I hunger for you."

Chantel felt utterly seduced by his voice, by the promise of his words. Oh, she did want him so! She felt damp and flustered, excited by his promise, by the feel of his manhood against her. Everything in her wanted to cry out, "Take me now," but a small voice warned her to protect her virtue, to wait till he made some commitment to her.

"I want you," she gasped, returning his kisses. "But I promised myself long ago to wait until I married. Please, do not try to weaken my resolve."

He kissed her again, slowly. She was all he could ever want in a woman—in a wife. He would gladly marry her, and though every part of him ached for her, he decided he would wait because that was her desire.

"It will be difficult for me," he whispered. "I will want you again and again, and I can't promise not to kiss you and hold you again like this. But if you want to wait, then we shall wait. I only hope the wait will not be too long. If you want marriage, then it is marriage you shall have."

Chantel leaned against him. "Thank you," she whispered.

He kissed her neck again. "My mother used the expression, 'you would try the patience of a saint.' I'm sure that is true of you, my darling, but I am no saint. So imagine how you try the patience of this rogue."

Chantel smiled up at him. "Are you such a rogue?"

"I'm used to getting my own way."

"You almost got it tonight."

"We'll wait," he said again. "I'll come here as often as I can. Chantel, I love you."

She looked into his eyes. "And I love you," she whispered.

The morning sun shone through the windows and filled the downstairs room of Michael's house.

"You look a very satisfied man," René said, eyeing Michael with a smile.

"Satisfied, but not very satisfied," Michael returned.

"I'm not certain what that means," René answered.

"It means I am well on the road to satisfaction."

"Well, let me say that I am completely satisfied."

"So I gathered from Susanna," Michael replied. "She's a most likeable woman. I hope your intentions are honorable."

"Honorable but guarded. I don't think her father would be enthralled to discover our relationship."

"He's bound to find out sometime."

"Susanna wants time to prepare him. I think she is wise. So, for the moment our affair shall remain a secret."

"I have an idea that might well make the secret easier to keep. Why not move in here? Susanna can come to dinner with me, and the two of you can be quite alone."

"While you are courting your Cajun beauty?"

Michael grinned. "Exactly. I want to open an office on the waterfront. It might be better if I moved into a hotel for a few weeks while I get things set up."

René all but laughed. Was this the same Michael Hamilton he had known before? The young man who was all work with no distractions and no enjoyment? Was this the man he had to drag to the Vieux Carré?

"I'm glad to hear you're learning to relax, my friend. Yes, I will come and live here. It will be a great improvement on my current living quarters. It is certainly a more romantic place to court Susanna."

"Do you intend marriage?"

René laughed. "I do. There is no need to continue the hunt when the prize has been found and captured. We must only prepare her father for the shock. He will not be happy."

"How do you propose to prepare him?"

"We'll wait till after the celebrations, till the territory is part of the United States. That way, at least, she will not be marrying a foreigner. She wants to win him over to her way of thinking. I'm not sure she can, but what can it hurt to try?"

"None at all," Michael said thoughtfully. "None at all."

"I suppose you will go to Madame Dumont's to stay," René ventured.

Michael quickly shook his head. "I fear the temptations would be far too great. No, I want to be near the waterfront and I want to be free in the evenings without riding back and forth every day. In any case, Chantel will be busy preparing for the celebrations just as I will be busy setting up the new office."

"This is, as you say, a perfect arrangement. I will be able to entertain Susanna without arousing the slightest suspicion."

"I expect you to."

"I shall not disappoint you," René replied.

* * *

"And where might you be off to?" Gordon Walker asked his daughter as he watched her adorn her riding habit.

"To Michael's. He asked me to come over and plan the decorations for his party—the one he is holding to celebrate the official turning over of the territory. I shall probably have to go there each day. There is just so much to do."

Gordon Walker smiled broadly. "I can't tell you how pleased I am that you two are getting on so well."

"He won't be home now, but I shall see him later in the day," Susanna imparted. She turned about toward the door. René was waiting and she wanted him so badly that she ached for him. Her mind was full of thoughts of the future, a future when they would live together, a future with home and children, with love and family, a future without subterfuge.

"I'm off to town," Gordon Walker said, as he waved good-bye to his daughter. Yes, Susanna was a good girl. She was a big help and most certainly Michael would soon ask for her hand in marriage. A man like Michael Hamilton needed a good, solid woman, a woman with social stature and breeding. Susanna was such a woman and she would make him a fine wife.

Gordon strode into Madame Dumont's Hotel. It was lunch hour. As he had already learned, lunch hour in New Orleans was always followed by a rest period, a siesta that lasted for some hours. People usually began to drift back to work around three or four in the afternoon when the heat of the day had passed. They then worked till after seven. At nine they had dinner, and on weekends most partied all night long. Up till now, he had thought this afternoon siesta frivolous in the extreme. But now he found merit in the break. It gave him time to spend with Marie, and in the middle of the day, he always found himself in top form.

He walked down the long corridor and stopped short when he got to the reception room. Michael Hamilton was there, standing by the window with his back to the door. The beautiful young cook, Chantel Boudreau, was in his arms. She seemed flustered, and considering where he himself was headed, the situation seemed obvious enough.

He hurried on before either of them saw him. But his forehead knit into a frown, and for more than a few moments he felt totally distracted. It was not that he expected perfection. Most young men had dalliances with women, especially women of easy virtue such as he imagined this Chantel Boudreau to be. But he did not want his daughter hurt, and she was a beautiful young woman who ought to be enough for any man—at least in the short term.

Not that he could entirely blame Michael. Chantel was an exquisite little creature, and she had a most delightful talent for food preparation. He vowed to speak with her rather than confront Michael with his indiscretions. He felt certain that a small financial remuneration and the knowledge that Michael was practically engaged to Susanna would be quite enough to make Chantel break off the relationship. He shook his head; the difficulty was that Susanna was just not demanding enough.

He reached Marie's door and knocked lightly.

She called out to him and he opened the door. He was once again greeted by the heady aroma of her perfume and by the raging colors of her interior decoration. He grinned like a schoolboy when he saw her. Her statuesque golden body was draped only in red beads which, as he drew closer, he realized were not beads at all but berries. At first taste, he discovered them to be lightly dipped in some liquor. He drew in his breath in anticipation.

"I do hope you're hungry," she said throatily.

His face turned red. He would not have dreamed of his own

response a few weeks ago. He felt he had entered a strange new world, a world much to his liking.

"I'm starved," he said, bending toward her awkwardly.

"I love a man with a healthy appetite," Marie replied with a broad smile and a twinkle in her golden cat eyes.

Susanna dismounted and hurried toward the house. René opened the door and walked toward her. He opened his arms and embraced her, holding her tightly.

"I want to carry you directly to the bedroom," he whispered, as he gently bit her ear.

"Then do so," she whispered back.

He did not wait, but swept her up into his arms and laughed. "The garden house is closer."

She snuggled next to him and in moments he had deposited her on a lounge in the garden house. All around them tropical plants gave off a heady aroma.

"I feel drunk," she said, reaching up to undo the buttons of his jacket.

He buried his face in her cleavage even as his hand fumbled beneath her skirt. She groaned and wiggled as he touched her.

"Not there," she whispered.

"Yes, my darling, there."

"René," she breathed as she fumbled with his trousers. "Oh, René, I love you so."

"Mademoiselle Boudreau," Gordon called out.

Chantel emerged from the pantry to face Mr. Gordon Walker.

"Good day," she said cheerfully.

"Good day. I've come to speak with you."

"Would you like a meal catered?"

"I would indeed. During the week of the celebrations I should like to have you oversee the preparation of the food for a party to be given at my home."

"I am doing several other parties and of course some of the food for the main celebrations at the *Cabildo*."

"You are both talented and famous."

"Thank you," Chantel replied. "Tell me more about what you have in mind."

"I have in mind offering you this much money." He handed her a bit of paper with a large amount written on it.

For a moment she stared at it uncomprehendingly. Then she looked up. "This is much too much. I charge much less than that."

He smiled and cocked his head. "This is not entirely all for the preparation of the food. I should like you to promise not to see Michael Hamilton again. He is, after all, virtually betrothed to my daughter."

Chantel stepped backward and her mouth opened slightly in surprise. She trembled slightly. "Is this true? Is Michael going to marry Susanna?"

"Yes," Walker replied confidently.

How could Michael have tried to make love to her when he planned to wed another? And he had even told her he would wait till they were married. Or was that really what he had said? She fought to recall his exact words. No, he had not actually said, "will you marry me?"

Chantel fought back tears. Had Michael said the things he had only so that he might buy time to wear her down? Michael had first approached her thinking she was for sale, and it seemed that in spite of her explanation, in spite of all she had told him, he continued to think of her as a loose woman. Apparently, he assumed she was a woman with whom he could have an affair if he played his cards right, if he pretended to respect her.

"I did not know about his relationship with your daughter," Chantel said, struggling not to reveal her emotional state.

Walker nodded. "You must try to understand. Susanna is the kind of woman a man like Michael Hamilton must marry. You're very attractive, and I'm sure many men desire you."

Yes, Michael had only wanted to seduce her. Well, he had nearly succeeded.

Chantel bit her lip. Could she be certain that what this man said was true? *I don't want to believe you,* she thought. She pursed her lips together. She was as angry with this Gordon Walker as she was with Michael. The difference was that if Walker was telling the truth, Michael had not just angered her, but hurt her, lied to her, and led her on. She decided to prod further. "If what you say is true, there is no need to pay me to stay away from Monsieur Hamilton."

Gordon Walker grinned. "I certainly did not mean to insult you, little lady. But if you doubt me, you will find Susanna at Michael's house now, waiting for him to come home to her."

Chantel turned away. Clearly he thought her a woman of doubtful virtue, worthy of no more than a dalliance on Michael's part.

"Will you prepare the food for my party?" Gordon pressed.

"Yes, and I'll send you a bill for considerably less than you offer. I am not for sale, Mr. Walker. I work for a living, but it is honest work. I do not sell myself." She turned away and went back to her pantry.

"I'll be speaking with you," he called after her.

Chantel stared into the pantry, waiting for him to leave. When she heard the front door close, she hurried away and out the back door. She would ride out to Michael's house, and if Susanna was there, she would know that Gordon Walker had told her the truth.

Chantel climbed down from the buggy and walked up to the front door. "I will not hide in the bushes and spy on you," Chantel said under her breath as she stood for a moment before the front door.

She took a deep breath and then knocked. It was Anton who answered.

"Good day, Missy Chantel," he said, bowing ever so slightly.

"Good afternoon, Anton." Chantel stepped into the house. In a rush all her memories of Michael returned. She thought of caring for him, of massaging his back, of putting cool cloths on his fevered body.

She was about to ask for Susanna when she saw the cloak hanging on the hook near the door. It was the same cloak Susanna had worn the night she had come to the restaurant.

"Mr. Hamilton isn't here," Anton said.

Chantel nodded. "Is Miss Susanna Walker here?" she asked.

Anton looked down; in fact, he looked embarrassed.

"She be upstairs in the bedroom," he replied in a near whisper.

Chantel felt herself go stiff. Everything Gordon Walker had told her was obviously true. She was filled with warring emotions. When Gordon had told her about Michael and Susanna, her first reaction had been anger. But on her ride to Michael's house, her anger had turned to a feeling of betrayal. She was hurt and she had a deep emptiness within her.

"Should I go see if she can come down?" Anton asked. Obviously he was uncomfortable at the thought of having to carry out his own suggestion.

Chantel quickly shook her head. "No, I'll come again another time."

"But it's so far—"

"It's all right. I have another errand in the neighborhood." She felt absurd and Anton looked confused. She turned about and practically ran from the house. Tears had already formed in her eyes and all she could think of was that she wanted to get away, as far away as she possibly could. *How could I have been so wrong about a man—about Michael?* The question haunted her. She felt completely betrayed not only by Michael but also by her own judgment. Sadly, she thought, it would be a long while before she trusted another man, or even herself.

CHAPTER FIVE

Michael wiped his brow. It had been a long, difficult day. He had worked through lunch and even during the siesta. But he felt rewarded. He had hired men to begin building his new warehouse on the waterfront and had begun the process of moving his office from his house in Faubourg Ste. Marie to the foot of Canal Street.

In addition, he had rented a room in a small hotel some blocks from Madame Dumont's more lavish establishment. Now, having cleaned up and changed his clothes, he headed toward Madame Dumont's to eat his dinner and to be with his beloved Chantel.

"Good evening," Marie said as she showed him to his room.

Michael kissed her hand warmly, but he immediately sensed a coolness about her, and her expression seemed one of distress.

"Is something the matter?" he asked.

"It's Chantel. She's disappeared. Not that I don't have another cook—"

"Disappeared? I don't understand." Michael felt confused and distressed. He was aware of a sudden panic, a fear that something had happened to her. "I was to see her tonight. Could something have happened to her?"

"I think not. You will forgive my prodding, but has something happened between the two of you?"

"No, I—we had a wonderful evening night before last. I don't understand."

Marie seemed to look beyond him, her expression one of deep thought. Then she looked into his eyes. "Some strange misunderstanding has occurred, I feel it. I don't sense danger for Chantel, but I do feel sadness. I must make inquiries. One does not disappear so easily in such a small place. I'll find her and get to the bottom of all this."

"I wish I felt as confident as you. I'm worried about her. I can't think why she would run off."

"She'll come back," Marie said. "She has obligations to fulfill, and if I know one thing about Chantel, it is that she takes her obligations seriously."

"I must find her," Michael muttered. "I love her and I must find her."

Marie nodded. "Since you're here, you may as well eat."

Michael shook his head. "I'm not hungry now," he replied. And it was true. He felt empty; he felt a yearning, a desire to know that Chantel was all right and that all was well between them. But at this moment he felt no hunger, save his hunger to hold her close and tell her he loved her. "I'm going to look for her now," he said, although he had not the foggiest idea where to begin to look.

Marie Dumont sat at her dressing table and, looking in the mirror, wound her elaborate African headdress about her head.

Behind her, Gordon Walker watched from the bed. She was utterly naked except for her headdress, and he deeply enjoyed watching her as she began her ritual of dressing. In fact, however perverse it might be, he enjoyed watching her dress almost as much as he enjoyed watching her undress. She moved with a snake-like grace, and her body was golden, like her most unusual eyes.

"You're a damn admirable woman," he commented. "I mean, you're one hell of a businesswoman too."

Marie did not turn around. "You're my banker. You know exactly how good a businesswoman I am." She did not bother to mention that less than half of her considerable assets were in his bank. Marie did not deem it prudent to keep all of her money in one place. She had many businesses and many employees. There were powerful people all over the territory who were beholden to her, if not for one thing, then for another. Someday, she thought with satisfaction, Gordon Walker would be beholden to her too.

Marie still did not turn, but she could see him in her mirror and she spoke to his image. "Have you thought about politics?" she said casually.

He swung his long legs over the side of the bed and sat looking at the curve of her back, at the way her rounded buttocks were flattened by her sitting position.

"Of course I've thought about it."

"You would be the perfect man to run for governor of the territory once it's been ceded to the United States. When it becomes a state—well, you could become a senator. Think about it, Gordon. You have friends in Washington, powerful friends. You're a man of influence in New Orleans—and naturally, you're American. We'll need an American governor to negotiate for us in Washington. I sense you are just the right person."

He rubbed his chin thoughtfully. "The trouble is, I haven't been in New Orleans long. Then too, I want to continue to see you."

Marie laughed. "Darling, for a man of your experience, you are being quite naïve. I know everyone who is anyone and I can deliver many votes to you. I know others who can also deliver votes.''

"Have you that many friends?'' he asked.

"Friends? An intelligent person does not always count on friendship. Believe me, I know many secrets about the powerful people in this territory. I possess information they would not like to have made public. They will do as I ask them.''

She really was phenomenal! "That sounds a trifle like blackmail,'' he said with a grin.

"I like to think of it as a favor returned.''

"Do you really think I would stand a chance of winning?'' He hoped he did not show how truly interested he was in the idea. Politics was his passion—next to making money, of course. In truth, he saw one as an adjunct to the other.

"I would not even suggest it unless I thought you were the perfect candidate.''

"And what about us?''

"We will continue to pursue our pleasure together, and we will continue to be discreet. After all, you would not be the first or the last politician to have a mistress. I have heard that even Mr. Jefferson has a mistress. In fact, I believe she is like me, a woman of color.''

Gordon pulled himself up off the bed and walked over to Marie. He ran his hand over her shoulder and down to her breast. "You're as smart as you are stunning,'' he said.

She covered his hand with hers. "I think we'll make a good pair. We understand each other.''

"By the way, will that young woman who works here— you know, the cook—return in time to prepare the food for the celebrations?''

Marie nodded. "She's very conscious of her obligations.''

It was early evening when Gordon returned home. He bathed and then decided to try on the new suit he had purchased to wear to the official ceremonies.

He stood in front of the mirror and admired his new suit. He congratulated himself on the fact that he was still in fine form at the age of fifty-five. He was slim, in shape, and though his hair was gray, it was thick. He also felt secure in his virility. Marie was a test for any man, but he had proved himself by satisfying her again and again.

"The prime of life," he said aloud. Yes, he was in the prime of life and all his hard work was coming to fruition. When Susanna and Michael were married, the two businesses would bring him more power. And he was already well known among the powerful in the territory. With Marie's help, he was even going to enter politics. She urged him to do so, and it seemed an excellent idea.

Yes, he thought happily, he would announce his intentions during the celebrations. It was the perfect time to let it be known that he intended to run for governor.

"Father?"

Gordon turned toward the door. "Come in, Susanna. See what you think of my new suit."

Susanna opened the door and entered her father's room. She looked at him and nodded. "It's very nice."

"I'm glad you're here, Susanna. I haven't seen much of you lately."

"I've been busy," she answered.

"I haven't seen anything of Michael either."

"He's building a warehouse at the foot of Canal Street." She did not say that she had not seen Michael either, or that he was distressed by Chantel's disappearance and spent all of his time looking for her.

"Well, I think it's time he did something formal about your relationship. I'd like to announce your coming marriage at the celebrations."

"Marriage?" Susanna felt stunned.

"Well, you've been together a lot. I want him to come and see me, so you can become formally engaged."

"I'm not sure we're ready," she said nervously.

''Ready or not,'' her father laughed, ''send him round.''

Susanna felt like a statue. What was she going to do? ''All right,'' she stuttered. Then she whirled about and hurried away. She had to talk to René immediately. And to Michael as well. Whatever were they going to do?

Overhead the pale moon was partially obscured by ghostly low clouds. Chantel let the dugout drift toward the side of the bayou, and then she used the oar to pull the little boat still closer to the bank. She grasped the rope in one hand and slung it round the post of the old dock. Then she secured it and, watching where she stepped, gingerly climbed out and stretched.

This area was deserted now. Once it had been a thriving settlement, but the fever had come and the river had risen as storm after storm battered the area. It was deemed unsafe, and most families had moved on. Hers remained, and in time the fever that followed the floods took her father and brother, just as it had taken her mother long ago. No one lived here now. The nearest community was on the main bayou; this one held only the ghost houses of the past.

Chantel walked through the tall grass toward the now deserted cabin in which she and her family had once lived.

She pushed open the door and went inside, glad to be out of the wind, which was rising. The weather had changed suddenly, as it often did in January. It was a cold wind that had blown in from the north and, judging from the darkening skies, it would no doubt bring considerable cold rain.

''A big blow,'' she said to herself. The cabin creaked, the wind whistled through the trees, and the oft-peaceful bayou, which she had just come down, rippled wildly, as if calling out a warning into the night.

She reached into her pack and withdrew a lantern and her flint. She lit the lantern and looked about, marveling at how little had actually changed. She sank into one of the chairs and was met with a puff of dust. It was an uncared-for house, a house without a family.

After her brother and father died, she had closed the door of this house with all of its memories and gone to New Orleans.

Some people might have found it surprising that others had not come and inhabited this house. But she understood why it was deserted, and indeed why it would remain so. It was because this little bayou was famous for its storms, for the way the water swirled, for the winds that seemed to be circular, for the rapidly rising water. This bayou was a death bayou, a place of storms and fever. It was a place where people died. Her people were superstitious; they would not try to resettle here.

Most of the Acadians in this area lived on the main bayou. They lived in small villages, which they generally built in a square around their church. Her family had been a little different; they were fiercely independent and had tried to make a go of it alone. They had paid the price.

Chantel leaned back and closed her eyes. She wasn't at all certain why she had come here, but when she left New Orleans she knew she only wanted to get away for a short time, to consider what had happened, to be alone. She did not want others to see her crying, to know about Michael, to know how much she loved him and how hurt she was by his duplicity. She felt the tears again coming into her eyes and she let them flow, unabated.

In a few days, she knew she would return to New Orleans and fulfill her obligations. Then, she thought, perhaps she would take the money she'd earned and go elsewhere. She shook her head sadly. She still loved Michael, and she loved him so very much that she knew she could no longer live in the same city as he. Especially after he married Susanna.

"I'll go west," she decided. Yes, it was a big country and surely she could escape the memory of Michael Hamilton. She continued to cry softly, thinking only that it did not matter if the ghosts saw her cry.

* * *

René folded Susanna in his arms and rocked her back and forth comfortingly.

"Whatever will we do?" she sobbed. "My father will send me away. He'll send me back home and we'll never see each other again."

"I would follow you to the ends of the earth. Besides, I have no intention of allowing your father to send you away from me, cherie."

"He'll not allow you to marry me."

"We'll go to him together. I'm not afraid of your father."

"That is only because you don't know him as I do. Why are all these terrible things happening at once? Chantel is gone and Michael is miserable, my father wants me married right away—"

"I wonder if your father has something in mind, if there is a reason he wants you married right away?"

"My father is always planning something."

René said nothing, but he well knew that Susanna's father was a bit of a schemer. Surely he did not want her to marry Michael simply because he believed them to be in love. In fact, a halfway observant person would have known that they were not in love. When together, they stood apart; they never touched; there were no stolen looks. Clearly there were no secrets between them. That was not the case when he and Susanna were together; they could not keep their hands off one another. They stood close; they laughed at the same things. In a thousand ways he knew their love for one another and the intimacy of their relationship was entirely obvious. "We must talk with Michael before we talk to your father," René suggested.

Susanna nodded. As confident as René seemed, she felt as if her world were coming to an end.

* * *

Michael got up from the settee and walked anxiously to the window. The sky was black and the trees shuddered in the growing wind. Some of the smaller trees bent with the gale, their tops nearly touching the ground. Sheets of water fell from the skies, and now and again lightning broke the sky in two just before thunder rocked the house.

"You got home just in time," René said, looking over his shoulder. "This is certainly no time to be down on the docks. This is a hurricane, a big blow."

"I can't go home now," Susanna said. "Father will be concerned."

"He knows where you are. And what a pity." René smiled at her. "I guess you'll have to spend the night."

Susanna half smiled back at him. At least, she thought, he retained his humor.

"If only I knew where Chantel was," Michael said abstractedly.

"I'm sure she's quite safe. Michael, I know you're preoccupied, and I hate to trouble you, but Susanna and I have a bit of a problem."

Michael turned about. "It's all right. It is I who should apologize for being so preoccupied. You've practically been running the business the last few days. Please, tell me your problem."

"My father wants you to visit him and set a date for our wedding. I didn't know what to say or do, so I just came here right away."

Michael was not surprised. "What do you propose?"

Susanna hung her head. It was René who answered. "I intend to go to him and tell him the truth. I love Susanna and she loves me. We want to get married."

"My father will never allow it. He'll send me away," she said, repeating herself once again.

Michael smiled. "You're of age, he doesn't own you—or at least he won't once the territory is part of the United States."

"I'm afraid he will challenge René to a duel or—or I don't

know. I only know the law is not the problem. My father is the problem. He is used to getting his own way. He'll find a way to get it this time too.''

Michael looked at her sympathetically. Tears were beginning to run down her face, and her skin seemed even paler than usual.

"Tell me why your father wants me to marry you now."

"I don't know. I really don't know why he is in such a hurry."

"Perhaps that is what we should explore first. I should like to know more of your father's motives. I think I will talk with him. After that, we'll decide what to do," Michael said.

"How can we thank you?" Susanna asked, wiping the tears from her eyes.

Michael laughed. "Name your first son after me."

René grinned. "Will the French version do, *mon ami?*"

"But of course. I'll go to see your father tomorrow."

The walls of Gordon Walker's study were lined with bookshelves and each shelf contained a row of books. They were odd books, Michael thought, completely uniform in color and size. One shelf had all red books, another green, yet another orange. They were all nine inches high and no more than two inches thick. Michael picked out first one volume and then another and another. All of them were unopened! They were brand new, with uncut pages. It was puzzling. Why would anyone have a library of richly bound leather volumes that they clearly did not read?

He looked up when Gordon Walker came in. Walker was dressed in a velvet smoking jacket and he looked rested.

"Glad to see you, my boy. What did you think of the storm? It was quite a wind. I was forced to remain in the Vieux Carré all night. I thought all those flimsy buildings would blow right down. I suspect they were all held in place by those absurd little balconies."

"I rather like the architecture," Michael said dryly.

Gordon waved his hand in the air. "Utility is all I care about. Can I offer you a drink? Cognac? Oh, I see you've looked at my books."

"Yes, they look interesting."

Gordon laughed. "I wouldn't know. I buy them by the yard. Now how about that drink?"

Michael nodded. He presumed he might well need a drink.

Gordon went to a small cupboard and opened it up. On its shelves were many decanters and he took out two goblets. He poured two shots of cognac into each glass.

"This is an unhealthy climate. I drink to ward off mysterious maladies," Gordon announced.

"I've come to speak with you about Susanna."

"Good. You've been seeing a great deal of each other, and I thought perhaps it was time we made some solid plans."

"She's a lovely woman. I want to get to know her better," Michael hedged.

"She's more than lovely! She's clever and well educated. She would be an asset to any man in business. She knows how to entertain and she plays the piano very well indeed."

"I know what an asset she would be. Tell me, why do you think I would make her a good husband?"

Gordon frowned. This was not quite the conversation he had imagined he would be having. But as long as Hamilton had asked, he decided to lay his cards on the table. "Frankly, I'm not sure you would make her a good husband. I know about your dalliance with that little French girl who cooks for Madame Dumont. In fact, I had a little talk with her. I told her you were going to marry Susanna and I let it be known that I didn't approve of your outside interest. I offered her some money, but she would not take it." Gordon laughed. "Naturally, I'm a man of the world. I understand that an unmarried man has his needs, and I'm quite willing to overlook your—shall I say, 'distractions'."

Michael stared at Gordon Walker. He felt his anger rise to

a hitherto unparalleled level. How dare he speak to Chantel! Of course she had run away! The terrible misunderstanding Gordon had caused was suddenly clear to him.

"You meddling son-of-a-bitch!" he said, advancing on Gordon, whom he seized by the collar. "If you were not an older man, I would throttle you right here and now."

Walker looked truly shaken. His eyes were bulging and his face was flushed. "Unhand me!" he shouted.

Michael let him go but at the same time forcefully pushed him into a chair. "I am not marrying Susanna. I'm not in love with Susanna, though she is a fine young woman—a characteristic I presume she inherited from her mother. Susanna wants to marry my business partner, René Gaston. I intend to marry Chantel Boudreau, when and if I can find her."

Gordon's face paled. "Business partner?" he said lamely. "I thought he was your assistant."

"I am making him my full partner."

Gordon appeared to be fighting for self-control. At length he said, "I want my daughter to come home."

"I am not your errand boy," Michael snapped. "Ask her yourself. She's at my house with René."

Gordon's face was getting redder by the minute.

"Get out of here," he muttered. "Get out before I have you thrown out."

"I really wouldn't want to stay another minute!" Michael turned on his heel and quickly left. All he could think of was finding Chantel and telling her the truth. He rode home in a fury, still angry with Gordon, feeling as if he had failed Susanna and René, and more worried than ever about Chantel's whereabouts.

René and Susanna were waiting when Michael returned. He hardly said a word before he poured himself a cognac and then, after gulping it down, he turned around and blurted out the whole story without preamble.

Susanna was ashen-faced. "My father told Chantel we were to be married? He offered money? How could he have done such a thing? This is all my fault! I should never have asked you to pretend to be seeing me so René and I could be alone."

"It is I who agreed to do it. It's certainly not your fault. I should have told Chantel about the two of you."

"I should have gone with you to see Susanna's father," René said. "It is I who have to face up to him and tell him that I intend to marry his daughter."

"He's furious now. He'll never allow it—I know he won't," Susanna cried.

"You must defy him," Michael said, looking at her steadily.

"Yes," Susanna agreed. "I hope I have the will."

"I will be with you," René said, putting his arm protectively around her. "Susanna, I won't let him take you away."

Michael poured himself another drink. "I told Susanna's father something I have not had a chance to tell you, René."

"And what might that be?"

"I told him I intended making you my full partner. I intended to discuss this with you before, but then Chantel disappeared and I was distracted. I hope you will accept."

"Accept? How could I not? What a wonderful opportunity."

Michael nodded. "We'll talk about this later. I have to see Marie Dumont again."

"Of course," Susanna said. "We'll stay here."

Michael waved them good-bye and hurriedly left. He hoped that Marie was not occupied with customers. She needed to know everything if she was to help him find Chantel.

The small Acadian community on Bayou Teche was no different than other such villages. The cluster of simple houses surrounded a small church, which was visited by a traveling priest once a month.

Almost every such village was self-sufficient. The land around and behind the houses had been cleared for farming.

Cows and chickens were kept to produce milk and eggs, and the skins of any game caught were prepared in a tannery on the edge of the village and used to make clothing. Each community also had a headman or leader. The headman of this particular village was one Monsieur Tremblay. Chantel spoke with him now, having explained who she was, and how she had come to this village on Bayou Teche.

"Of course I remember your family. They lived about twenty miles from here on the Bayou of Ghosts. The years of the flood and the fever were a great tragedy."

"I've been away for a long time. I came back to think, but the storm came up and the water began to rise."

"You're fortunate you made it here. At least we're on higher ground. You can't continue your journey for at least three days," Monsieur Tremblay told her. "It's very dangerous, but then, I should not have to tell you that."

"But I must go back to New Orleans."

"It is quite impossible. There's a small room in the back of the church where the priest stays when he comes. You may stay there, and of course you can eat with any one of the families."

"You're very kind." He was, in fact, a very nice man even though such hospitality was to be expected. All that was asked in return was that the guest did a share of the work. "I'm very grateful," Chantel added.

"No need. We must all look after each other. Come along. I'll show you the room and introduce you around."

As Chantel followed him toward the church, she shook her head in dismay. When she got back to New Orleans, she would be busy indeed. Time was running out; the celebrations were to begin next week. But being busy was good, she decided. She would have no time to think about Michael.

She could tell herself she would have no time to think of him, but it was not true and she knew she was only fooling herself. Busy or not, her thoughts would fly to him. It was like a terrible curse, this hunger she felt for Michael Hamilton. For days now she had tried to hate him, tried to retain her anger, tried to cast him from her thoughts. She told herself again and again that she never wanted to see him again. But the truth was, she did want to see him. And even though he was going to marry another, she yearned for his arms around her, his lips on hers, and the sweet promise of his love. Perhaps it was for the best that she could not return to New Orleans immediately. Her delay only postponed her rendezvous with temptation.

CHAPTER SIX

Marie sat on the edge of her chaise longue and slowly massaged Gordon Walker's back. The cream she used had a pungent odor, and he felt both relaxed and excited by the combination of the aroma that filled the room and her slow, tantalizing movements. It was as if her long fingers were dancing on his flesh, commanding him to forget the troubling thoughts that crowded his mind.

"You're very tense," she observed.

"Perhaps it's just desire."

Marie laughed throatily. "That, my darling, is a different kind of tension. One which Marie recognizes instantly."

"I'm angry," he said, and she could hear him trying to restrain the emotion in his voice.

"Tell me about it. That is the trouble with you American businessmen—you think your emotions should be kept in a little compartment. In fact, you have many little compartments. You have a compartment for love, for lust, for family, for friends, and for pleasure. You have one very large compartment for making money. Don't you see? You cannot separate all the parts of your being. You must carry all your emotions with you all the time. Open up your little compartments to me. Tell me what troubles you.''

''It's my daughter, Susanna.''

Marie continued her massage. In truth, she knew quite well what was troubling Gordon Walker, but she deemed it necessary to get him to talk about it, to confide in her, and in the end to ask for the advice she intended giving him. But with a man like Walker it was important for him to think that such a thing was his idea. He had to be made to believe that his new understanding, was, in fact, a result of his own insight.

''Susanna is a very attractive woman.''

''I still think of her as a girl.''

''Perhaps that is part of the problem. She is a woman now and no doubt has a mind of her own.''

He grumbled something inaudible. Then, after a moment of silence, he admitted, ''She doesn't understand at all.''

''What is it she doesn't understand?''

''I wanted her to marry Michael Hamilton. I wanted her to have security, to marry a man who came from the same sort of family she comes from.''

''And?''

''And she has gone and fallen in love with this René Gaston. I'm sure he's a fine fellow, but he's—he's French.''

Marie ran her finger about his ear slowly. ''I'm part French. You do not seem to be attracted to women who come from the same sort of family you do.''

''Men are different.''

''No, they aren't. I know René. He is a fine man. Besides, Michael is making him a full partner in his business. Susanna will have the same security with René that she would have with Michael. Indeed, she will have more because René loves her and Michael does not.''

Gordon was silent and Marie knew he was thinking about what she had said.

"Personally, I thought you must have planned to have Susanna marry René. I mean, it is terribly clever, you know."

Gordon frowned and half turned to look into her face. "Clever? How is it clever?"

"If I am not mistaken, you once told me you wanted Susanna to marry Michael so the two businesses would be united. If René is a full partner, the two businesses will still be united, yes?"

"Yes, but—"

"It is even more clever! You want to run for governor of the territory. Many of the people here are Cajun! With your daughter married to a Cajun, they would all say, 'he is one of us!' Darling, having Susanna marry René is perfect! It is, as I have said, so clever of you!"

Gordon made a guttural sound of semi-agreement, then turned his head away. It really was clever. He hadn't really thought of it that way at all, but now that he did, he entirely saw the merits of the matter. Yes, he would send a message to Susanna giving her his permission to marry René. He was learning a few words of French from Marie, so he supposed one day he might come to understand René, who at the very least had exhibited abnormally good taste by falling in love with Susanna.

"What about that little French girl?" he asked after a few minutes. "Will she be back in time to prepare the food for my party? I want her to fix that erotic food she's famous for."

"I'm sure Chantel will be back in time," Marie assured him. She knew about Gordon's role in Chantel's disappearance too, but she did not say anything. When Chantel got back, she would tell her everything. She had assured Michael all would be well, and in her heart, she knew it would be.

"I have been worried about you," Marie said, ushering Chantel into the parlor. "I knew you would come back in time to fulfill your obligations, but I was concerned when the weather got so bad."

"I could not get back till the water went down," Chantel said. "I went back to the cabin where I once lived. You're right, I did come back to fulfill my obligations, but when the festivities are over, I am leaving New Orleans forever."

"You might change your mind."

"I think not. I went home to mull matters over. I think I have to start anew."

"Really. And why is that?"

"I gave my heart to someone and I was betrayed."

"You gave your heart to Michael Hamilton and thought you were betrayed. Nothing could be further from the truth."

Chantel stared at Marie. "I don't understand."

"Gordon Walker told you that Michael was going to marry Susanna. He is not. He was only pretending to see Susanna so that René and she could secretly meet. Now the truth is known. Susanna will marry René and you will no doubt marry Michael. He has come here every day looking for you. He has turned New Orleans upside down searching for you. He loves you, of that there can be no doubt."

Chantel's face flushed with excitement. "Are you certain?"

"Of course I am certain."

"I must see him right away," Chantel said, almost breathlessly.

"No, no, no. You will ruin everything. I will see to it that he knows you are back safely and tell him that you will see him the night of the celebrations at Gordon Walker's mansion. You have much too much work to do to prepare for the festivities. In any case, his enthusiasm will grow with the waiting. I want you to prepare the most succulent meal you can so that all of us will experience its effects. I have arranged everything. It is to be a night of the heart, an evening of romance. I shall see to it that Father Bourget is invited and is prepared to marry those who feel so inclined."

Chantel smiled. "You are putting my cookery to the test."

"Not at all. You already love and desire Michael, and he you. René and Susanna are also in love."

"And you?"

"I am the mistress of the serpent, Mr. Gordon Walker. I will play a song of seduction and charm him. He will dance to my tune."

Chantel smiled. "It's only a few days away. I suppose I can wait a few days."

"Yes, you can and will wait, and so will Michael. Now come. As we prepare this meal, you will tell me your secrets. After all, when you and Michael are married, you will be cooking only for him. I cannot have my business suffering as it has suffered in your absence. I have the need to train others to cook as you do."

"I think you will learn very quickly," Chantel predicted.

The morning sun streamed into the kitchen as Marie sat across the table from Chantel, listening as Chantel read from what she called, her "Formulas for Sensual Delights."

"It is a book written by my ancestor and passed on from generation to generation. My brother made each and every recipe with me; it was he who showed me how to turn these instructions into succulent meals. Its pages are delicate now."

"It must be copied over," Marie said. "As soon as possible."

"I have not read the books that are spoken of in this volume, but it says that there are many ancient books on erotic cookery. Many of these books my ancestor seems to have read while cooking for the King of France."

"And what might these precious books be?"

"There is a Roman cookery book, a book of potions from material on witches, an ancient book of herbs, a book of magic and alchemy, and some books from the Far East such as the one called *The Perfumed Garden.*"

"And what knowledge do these books pass on to us?" Marie asked.

"As I told you many months ago, the cuisine of love is divided into those foods that suggest love and those which make one feel amorous. But let me start with the obvious.

"For as long as we all remember, the apple has been called the forbidden fruit. Fruits and nuts are the very seeds of life, and they are said to make a man fertile. They are also colorful and please the eye. Remember the Bible?"

Marie smiled knowingly. "And the woman saw that the fruit of the tree was good to eat, and fair to the eyes, and delightful to behold."

"It was sinfully delicious," Chantel said with a smile.

"Tell me more," Marie said.

"Breads are used mainly because of the shapes into which loaves may be fashioned. A loaf of French bread can be so much more than a loaf of French bread, madame."

"Ah, yes. I know that breads in phallic shapes are often carried in the procession during the feast of Corpus Christi."

Chantel smiled. "The priest would rather we make buns marked with a cross."

"Old customs die hard," Marie acknowledged. "They still carry phallic loaves."

"Next in importance are eggs, madame. They are the everlasting symbol of fertility. It is said that raw eggs sucked from their shells are the most powerful of all love potions."

Marie fingered one of the eggs that lay in a basket on the table and smiled knowingly.

"Here, so close to the sea, shellfish are important to our cookery and it is said that shellfish make men virile."

"And hot, spicy peppers combined with other spices made women burn, and thus yearn for lovemaking."

"That appears to be a physical fact," Chantel allowed. "Just as Spanish Fly makes men strong for love."

"You prepare many vegetables."

"Yes, and many, like asparagus, are suggestive as well as tempting."

"Ah, yes," Marie nodded, "asparagus is suggestive of the

male at readiness and the artichoke is like the rose. It flowers in a female way."

"Spirits are useful too, but only to make a woman pliant. Too much spirit makes men snore."

"And usually before rather than after!" Marie laughed.

"Of course herbs and spices are at the heart of it all. They reawaken memories and create dreams. It was the search for rare spices that brought Columbus to America."

"Have you a specific menu planned for our night of love?" Marie asked.

Chantel smiled slyly. "Oh, yes, madame. We will begin with wine as red as rubies, to stimulate the lips and warm the chest. Then we shall have Hot Onion Soup, made only as the Cajuns can make it. That will be followed by Brazen Bean Salad, Throbbing Shrimp on a Bed of White Rice, and finally a dessert of Lover's Chocolate Mousse."

"It is a menu that sounds positively inspired," Marie said as she kissed her fingers and made an appreciative smacking sound.

"Now that I am to be one of those benefiting from the results of this feast, it is much easier to plan."

"I know it will be a success."

"I shall prepare it all, but someone else will serve it. I hope to be quite busy with other activities."

"All of New Orleans is dancing in the streets," René said as he combed his thick, dark hair.

"And will continue to do so for many days," Michael added cheerfully.

"I'm mystified by Walker's invitation. He seems to have accepted the fact that it is I who will marry Susanna and not you." René grinned and added, "Unless he plans to poison me at this intimate dinner party."

René wondered if he sounded convincing. He thought himself

a good actor, and if this evening were to be a true surprise for Michael, it was necessary for him to be just that.

"If he intended to poison you, I hardly think Walker would invite so many witnesses."

"It does seem odd that Madame Dumont will be attending," René observed. "You don't suppose Walker has some relationship with her we don't know about, do you?"

"Now that I think about it, I have seen them together more than once," Michael replied. He smiled, knowing full well that Marie Dumont was behind Walker's change of heart, Walker's deep apology concerning Chantel, and his acceptance of René. He himself would not have considered going to Walker's house had Madame Dumont not asked him personally and assured him Chantel would be there and that all would be well.

"Well, well." René nodded his head. "If they're having an affair, I think I might forgive him."

"All's well that ends well," Michael said. "I'm relieved by Madame Dumont's letter, even if I don't understand why I couldn't see Chantel immediately."

"What exactly did she write?" René asked. "You never did tell me." It was always good to ask questions, even if you knew the answers.

"I'll read it to you," Michael offered. He walked to his desk and from the side drawer withdrew an envelope. He opened it carefully and took out the parchment on which madame's most welcome letter was written.

My dear Mr. Hamilton,

I have sent this message by the fastest means possible and would indeed have delivered it in person had time permitted. Chantel has returned and has been told that you have no intention of marrying Miss Walker, and indeed, never did. She understands now that Miss Walker's father made an assumption based on the fact that he believed you two to be seeing one another regularly. She also understands that it is Monsieur Gaston who is

*to marry Miss Walker. As a result of these revelations,
Chantel is most eager to see you. She asks, however, that
you wait and rendezvous with her on Friday night when
the six of us—René and Susanna, Monsieur Walker and
myself, and you and Chantel—will dine privately at his
home. As you know, this intimate dinner is to follow the
public reception to celebrate the transfer of the territory
to the United States. Look forward, my friend, to the
expected and to the unexpected.*

> *Sincerely,*
> *Marie Dumont*

"Fascinating," René said, lifting both brows. "And almost
as mystifying as Susanna's letter from her father."

"It does seem strange that he decided to accept you so
suddenly."

"Perhaps I owe that to the fact that you generously made
me your partner."

"A position you earned with hard work, my friend."

René leaned forward and craned his neck so he could see
the big grandfather clock in the hall. "It's time we were leaving," he said. "I'll call Susanna."

Susanna called back, "I'll be right down."

"She's still nervous," René said softly. "She can't believe
her father changed his mind so suddenly. She was quite certain
he would try to prevent us being together."

"This is a night of mysteries," Michael said.

René shrugged, then again grinned. "Romantic mysteries,
mysteries of love, my friend."

In a few minutes, Susanna appeared at the top of the staircase.
Her long golden hair was curled and caught up on each side
so that her curls caressed her white shoulders. She wore a
stunning off the shoulder black dress trimmed in red lace. Its
bodice was low cut and her tiny waist was corseted tightly.

"You're a vision," René said, unable to hide his admiration.

"You look beautiful," Michael added.

"That's high praise from a man who only has eyes for one woman."

"I'm truly anxious to see her," Michael said, feeling no need to hide his desires.

"I'm so glad it's all turning out well. I was so worried."

René reached for her velvet cloak and held it out. He put it round her shoulders and then turned her about slowly and looked into her face. "We're off to find out what changed your father's mind," he said, "although Michael has a theory that Madame Dumont has played a large role in the resolution of our dilemma."

"Perhaps she has," Susanna said, sounding almost relaxed. In moments they were on their way.

The grand reception room of Gordon Walker's mansion was festooned with American flags. On a podium, a small orchestra played lively music while many guests danced and others sampled culinary delights from a long table.

Gordon Walker circulated among his guests, shaking hands and chatting with each person.

"I must see Chantel," Michael said anxiously. He left Susanna and René and went to ask after her. In a few moments he returned. "She's not here," he told them. "She's not coming till later."

"She must be exhausted. Look at this array of food! It's most impressive," Susanna said, waving her hand over the long table.

"Of all the parties given in New Orleans this week, including the one at the *Cabildo*, your father's will no doubt be the best," René said.

"It certainly looks as if he went all out," Michael agreed.

"We're not to eat any of this food," Susanna said, taking a roll from René's hand. "We're all eating later, privately."

"I'll have quite an appetite by then." René laughed.

"Why don't you two dance? I really don't mind. I'll just circulate," Michael suggested.

René took Susanna's hand and led her onto the dance floor. They were, Michael thought, a very handsome couple.

At eleven sharp, Madame Marie Dumont made her entrance. And a grand entrance it was! She wore a tightly fitting dress, the fabric of which shimmered in the subdued lighting. Her hair was hidden beneath a gold headdress and she wore long, dangling amber earrings that seemed to match her eyes. On a long golden chain, she led a large South American cat, an ocelot or the like. It followed her tamely but a path of frightened guests parted nonetheless, giving the animal a wide berth. Madame Dumont, Michael thought, was quite a showman.

Shortly after Marie's arrival, Gordon mounted the podium and raised his hand to silence both the orchestra and the guests.

"I want to welcome you all to my home," he announced in a loud, clear voice. "Not only are we here to celebrate the joining of this great territory to the United States of America, but we are here to celebrate several personal events!"

Michael glanced at Susanna and René. They were standing together and Susanna looked a trifle apprehensive. He turned back to the podium. Gordon Walker, he had to admit, was a fine orator.

"First, I should like to announce the pending marriage of my daughter Susanna to Monsieur René Gaston. They will be wed this very night at a private supper!"

"My goodness," Susanna whispered. "Did you know about this, René?"

René bent and kissed her neck as she blushed deeply. Everyone clapped and turned toward them.

"I knew about it," René said. "I met with your father two days ago and he told me then." He reached into his pocket and withdrew a lovely ring. "It was my mother's, Susanna. I want you to wear it."

She looked up into his eyes, and as everyone who was watching could plainly see, it was as if they were quite alone.

Gordon Walker raised his hands again. "And that's not all."

Clearly, Michael thought, he was enjoying his role as the magnanimous benefactor.

"It will be a double wedding. Mr. Michael Hamilton will be wedding Mademoiselle Chantel Boudreau, the finest chef in all of New Orleans."

Michael drew in his breath. Had Chantel really consented to marry him? He felt stunned, but dizzy with anticipation. If only he could see her, embrace her, be with her alone for a few minutes. But it seemed this was not what was planned, and thus far he could not argue with a single thing that Gordon Walker had planned.

"Next," Walker announced, "I should like to announce my partnership with the most unusual woman I have ever met, Madame Marie Dumont."

"My father and Marie Dumont!" Susanna whispered. "I don't believe it!"

René squeezed her arm. "Believe it. He is a changed man. Bewitched, I believe."

"Finally, I should like to announce my candidacy for governor of this great territory! I would lead us to statehood!"

The entire gathering clapped and shouted. Michael smiled to himself. Gordon Walker was a natural politician, but his enchanting mentor had helped him to understand changing opinion. Walker had a golden tongue and was ambitious. He seemed certain to get elected and would no doubt do so with Marie's help. Like her ocelot, Gordon Walker would follow her on a gold chain, invisible though it might be.

Gordon left the podium and began again to circulate among the guests. Then, within the hour, they were all signaled to adjourn to the private dining room upstairs.

There, beyond the double doors, Michael's bride Chantel was waiting.

"A fantastic sight!" Michael whispered. Chantel wore a beautiful ivory gown with tiny seed pearls sewn onto the bodice, which was cut daringly low. Her lovely face and dark curls were hidden beneath a veil. When he saw her, Michael felt as if the breath had been sucked out of him. She was a divine goddess, the vision in his dreams.

"Chantel," he whispered as he went to her side. "I adore you, I want to marry you, but it is only right that I ask you myself, now in front of everyone." He dropped to his knees and took her hand. "Will you be my wife?"

"Yes, my love, for we are destined to be together."

"I have no ring," Michael stammered. On the one hand, he was ecstatic that Marie had planned this wonderful surprise; on the other, he felt ill-prepared.

"Ah, but I brought one. I confess I've been in on this," René said, handing him a small box.

"Come along," Gordon urged. "Stand over here next to the good priest."

The four of them stood together and the priest took out a small book. "This is most unusual," he muttered, glancing at Marie. "But I do expect to see all four of you in church this Sunday."

They all nodded and the priest, who came from the Cathedral of Saint Louis, began the wedding ceremony, delivering it to both couples simultaneously.

When he was finished, René kissed Susanna and Michael nervously lifted Chantel's veil and kissed her.

"This is a most enchanting gown, and you are the most incredible woman I have ever seen," he said breathlessly.

She blushed as he bent to kiss her, and she returned his kiss.

"And now to the most divine of meals," Marie announced. "Please be seated."

They sat at three small, separate tables, each decorated with flowers and candles.

"Are you looking forward to dinner?" Chantel asked, as she leaned close.

"I am looking forward to dinner and beyond," Michael said, lifting the goblet of ruby-red port to her lips.

Chantel sipped it slowly, her eyes fastened on Michael. It was as if each of the three couples were alone with each other.

First the waiters brought the soup. The aroma of the onions and the succulent melted Gruyère cheese filled the room.

"A soup to take the chill off," Chantel said as she wrapped the cheese around her fork delicately.

"It's chilly outside, but not in here," Michael said. The flavor of the soup and port mingled inside him. He felt warm, and he could see that Chantel's lovely face was slightly pink.

Next came the cool sweet-and-sour flavor of the Brazen Bean Salad. Its bright greens and reds were a sight to behold.

After that, the Throbbing Shrimp on their bed of snow-white rice were served. This time, Chantel fed Michael the shrimp, one by one. Their flavor was truly succulent, and he licked the sauce from her fingertips, half closing his eyes.

"Dessert later," he said.

Chantel looked around. "We are quite alone, Michael. The others have all gone to their rooms."

As much as he had hungered for this fantastic meal, he now hungered for his bride. He stood up and carried the covered dish with the dessert with him; Chantel took the wine as they retired to a room just down the long corridor.

Michael closed the door and they both set down what they carried. Michael took her into his arms. "I feel a new kind of hunger, a different desire," he whispered in her ear.

She looked up into his face as he wrapped his strong arms about her. "I have saved myself for this night. You must be gentle with me."

"I shall be as gentle as I can, my wife."

He drew in his breath. She was a tiny woman, yet he knew her to be strong of spirit and will.

"And slow," she whispered. "As you once promised me, you must be slow."

"You are to be savored, like your cuisine," he breathed into her ear.

His large fingers fumbled on the tiny buttons of her elaborate gown, but at last he was able to push the material aside and slip the dress down as far as her rounded hips. She wore beneath her dress a snow-white corset that drew her small waist in even further and caused her lovely full breasts to swell over the top as if they were trying to escape its confines.

Never had he felt so dizzy with desire, a desire so great that it was palpable. His blood seemed to be boiling as he slowly pushed away her pantaloons and left her naked save for her seductive white corset.

He held her rounded buttocks and kissed her neck as she fairly swooned in his arms. "Loosen me," she begged. "Please."

He ignored her plea for the moment and carried her to the bed. "I want to ravish you, my angel," he said as he kissed her neck, her deep cleavage, and her rounded white shoulders.

He felt her undoing his clothes, and he quickly assisted her until he was naked and spread out next to her. He kissed her again and again, then touched her intimately and felt her sigh beneath him as she lifted her hips to meet his prodding movements.

"I am so afraid of hurting you," he said as he once again touched her. But she said nothing, only kissing him in return, running her hands over his chest and through the hair that covered it.

He ran his hand between her legs and found her warm and moist. She quivered as he kissed her as intimately as he had touched her.

"Oh!" she cried out. She panted and wriggled about. Her body flushed. He turned her over and kissed her buttocks, then he again turned her over and intimately caressed her till she was writhing and crying out in his arms. He continued, and in a moment she arched her back and shuddered.

"Now you are ready," he whispered as he slipped his fingers inside her secret place. She squirmed delightfully in his arms and moaned again.

Next, he slowly undid the laces of her corset and set her

free. He kissed her breasts and suckled them till again she was squirming in his arms.

"Oh," she cried out. "Please, pleasure me again."

He entered her slowly, and she let out a little cry, but she was so moist that she almost immediately responded by lifting herself to him.

He fastened his mouth on her lovely, nut-colored nipple and nibbled. Then he moved within her, knowing he could hold back no longer. They moved together as one, two lovers satiated on fine cuisine, wine, and their own lovemaking.

When they had finished, they cuddled in one another's arms.

"You are my beloved," he whispered.

Chantel nuzzled against him. Then she whispered, "The chocolate mousse awaits. Is it not time we had dessert?"

Chantel's Sensuous Delights

Recipes marked with an asterisk are often better the next day, when the flavors have had a chance to blend thoroughly.

DESIROUS ASPARAGUS

10 to 14 asparagus tips
4 medium tomatoes
salt and pepper to taste
¼ cup melted butter
¼ cup grated cheese (Romano or Parmesan)

Boil asparagus in salted water until nearly tender. Drain and set aside. Scald, peel, and core tomatoes. Arrange tomatoes in an oven-proof baking dish. Roll asparagus in melted butter and sprinkle with grated cheese. Stand the asparagus tips in the tomatoes. Bake at 350 degrees for 25 minutes.

PEPPER POT SOUP*

1 small onion, chopped
1 small green pepper
2 celery stalks, diced
2 T olive oil
3 T flour
4 cups chicken broth
1 cup tomato sauce
2 tomatoes, peeled and chopped
½ lb fish (Boston Blue, Cod, or White Fish)
½ cup rice
1 t celery salt
1 bay leaf
½ t white pepper

Note: Chicken broth can be made by boiling a chicken or chicken parts and adding one bouillon cube for flavor, or a commercial broth may be used.

Sauté the onion and green pepper in the olive oil until soft. Stir in the flour until smooth. Add the chicken broth, tomato sauce, tomatoes, celery, fish, rice, celery salt, bay leaf, and white pepper. Cook until all ingredients are done, about one hour. All soups benefit from slow simmering and often their flavor is better when they are rewarmed after being refrigerated for 24 hours.

A TASTE OF FIRE: CREOLE FILÉ GUMBO*

This is a dish that each cook can make her own way by varying the ingredients. This basic recipe leaves room for creativity.

1 large chicken breast
1½ cups water
1 small onion, chopped
1 clove garlic, minced
1 small green pepper, chopped
3-4 tomatoes, chopped
½ lb fresh okra, sliced
¾ lb cooked shrimp
¾ lb crabmeat
1 t filé powder
Salt and black pepper to taste
2 T olive oil
¼ t Creole Seasoning (More if you
    dare! Most commercial Creole or
    Cajun seasonings are made with a
    variety of red peppers. They vary
    in strength and should be added
    sparingly, tasting as you go.)

Simmer chicken in water until tender. Bone chicken and set aside, retaining the water and adding one chicken bouillon cube for flavor. Sauté the onion, garlic, and pepper in 2 T olive oil until soft. Stir in the tomatoes and simmer for 5 minutes.

Mix all of the above into the chicken broth and add the okra. Cook over low heat for one hour or until the okra is tender. Add the chicken, shrimp, crab, salt, Creole seasonings, and pepper to the broth and simmer for 15 minutes. Remove from the heat and stir in the filé powder. Serves four.

RUM FLUFF

3 T butter
3 T flour
1 cup warm milk
4 egg yolks
½ cup sugar
1 pinch salt
3 T rum
4 egg whites
3 oz rum

Melt the butter and blend in the flour. Add the warm milk and 3 T rum and stir until the sauce thickens. Beat in the egg yolks with the sugar and salt. Beat the egg whites until stiff and fold into the first mixture. Pour into a buttered casserole dish. Place the casserole dish in a pan of warm water and bake at 300 degrees for 35 minutes. Before serving, pour 3 oz rum over the top.

LOVE WINE

4 cups dry white wine
1 cup sherry
½ cup brandy
2 cups water
1 cup sugar
3 lemons, sliced

Combine sugar and water. Stir until sugar is dissolved and add the other ingredients. Serve in tall glasses over ice with lemon wedges. Drink sparingly and have someone else drive your carriage.

TANTALIZING BROTH*

2 cups chicken broth (use water from boiled chicken
   plus 1 bouillon cube or commercial product)
1½ cups water
1¾ cups clam broth (use water from cooking clams and
   1 T fish stock powder or a commercial product)
2 T sherry
1 small avocado, sliced and peeled
whipped cream (optional)
parsley
paprika

Combine broths and water. Heat until they boil. Remove from heat and add sherry. Place pieces of avocado in each soup dish and pour broth over them. Top with a dollop of whipped cream and sprinkle with parsley and paprika. If you prefer, eliminate the whipped cream and just sprinkle with paprika and parsley.

SWEETHEART POTATOES

4 medium sweet potatoes
½ cup brown sugar
1 T softened butter
1 egg yolk, beaten
1 egg white, beaten
⅛ cup sherry
1 dash nutmeg
1 dash cinnamon

Boil potatoes until tender, peel, and mash. Cream sugar and butter. Add egg yolks, sherry, potatoes, and spices. Fold in egg whites. Place in buttered oven-proof dish and place dish in warm water. Bake at 350 degrees for 40 minutes.

KING CRAB SALAD FOR LOVERS TO SHARE

> 1 cup light salad dressing or mayonnaise
> ½ cup chili sauce
> 1 t horseradish
> ½ t chopped chives
> 1 t lemon juice
> ½ t capers
> 1 lb king crabmeat
> 2 hard-boiled eggs, sliced
> 1 cup julienne beets
> salad greens

Combine first seven ingredients and place on salad greens. Garnish with eggs and beets.

EVE'S GIFT: FORBIDDEN FRUIT

> 8 large cooking apples
> 1 t cinnamon
> 1 T butter (or margarine)
> 4 eggs, beaten
> sugar to suit your taste

Peel, core, and slice apples. Cook until tender, drain, and mash. Add cinnamon and butter. Set aside to cool. When the apple mixture has cooled, stir in the beaten eggs. Heat some butter or margarine in the skillet and drop spoonfuls of the mixture into the hot butter. Brown slightly on both sides and sprinkle with sugar.

CAJUN HOT FRENCH ONION SOUP

*The main preparation can be made a day ahead, but the bread and cheese must be added just before serving.

    3 large onions (yellow or red)
    ¼ cup butter or margarine
    1 quart water
    6 T beef bouillon
    1 T Worcestershire sauce
    1 dash pepper
    6 slices French bread (toasted) or 2 cups croutons
    Gruyère cheese

Slice the onions thin. In a large saucepan sauté the onions in the butter until tender. Add water, bouillon, Worcestershire sauce, and pepper. Simmer for 20 minutes. Pour into heat-resistant soup bowls and float the bread or croutons on top. Cover the bread or croutons with slices of Gruyère and place under broiler or in microwave till the cheese is melted and bubbling.

If you prefer, follow the above directions and put all the ingredients except the bread and cheese into a crock pot and cook for 6-8 hours. Serves four.

Note: Some French onion soup requires only a round of bread with melted cheese (often Parmesan). Real Cajun Onion Soup comes from Quebec and calls for the entire top surface of the soup to be covered with bread and topped with melted cheese (always Gruyère).

BRAZEN BEAN SALAD

8 oz cooked green beans
8 oz cooked garbanzo beans
8 oz kidney beans
8 oz black beans
1 cup chopped green pepper
1 cup chopped sweet red pepper
1¼ cups sugar
1½ t salt
1½ cup cider vinegar

Combine all ingredients and marinate for a minimum of four hours before serving.

THROBBING SHRIMP ON A BED OF WHITE RICE

2 lbs raw shrimp
lemon juice
1 onion, chopped
1 clove garlic
3 T butter or margarine
2 large tomatoes, peeled and chopped
1 bay leaf
1 cup palm hearts, sliced
¼ t Creole or Cajun seasoning or to taste. (Test
    as you go when adding hot ingredients!)
Salt and pepper to taste

Marinate shrimp in lemon juice for one hour. Drain. Discard lemon juice. Brown onion and garlic in butter. Add tomatoes, shrimp, bay leaf, Creole seasonings, salt, and pepper. Simmer slowly for 15 minutes or until shrimp are cooked. Add palm hearts and heat thoroughly. Remove bay leaf. Serve over hot white rice. Serves six.

LOVER'S CHOCOLATE MOUSSE

2 cups milk
3 oz unsweetened chocolate
4 T cornstarch
¾ cup sugar
¼ t salt
1 t vanilla
Sweetened whipped cream, chopped toasted almonds,
   and cherries

Heat milk; add chocolate and vanilla. Stir over low heat until chocolate dissolves. Mix cornstarch, sugar, and salt with a little cold milk and stir into chocolate mixture. Cook over low heat until sauce is smooth and thick. Pour sauce into top of double boiler and cook over hot water for 20 minutes (do not allow water to boil). Remove from heat and add vanilla. Pour into a lightly buttered mold. Chill and serve with whipped cream, toasted almonds, and cherries.

A TASTE OF MAGIC

Julia Hanlon

CHAPTER ONE

Jesse Calvin figured the rifle stock would numb his shoulder if he kept it jammed against himself for much longer. He'd been squinting down the sights at the approaching stranger for so long that it would be a wonder if his eyelid ever unsquinched. His trigger finger felt about ready to freeze in the shape of a cup hook.

One of the dogs whined as if commiserating with his discomfort. The other two growled low in their throats, quivering and ready to attack. Jesse quieted them with a whispered command.

He considered shooting the intruder just to ease his own misery, but there was something about the way the man's torso listed to the left just before each slow step, the way his leg swung out to the side before setting foot on the narrow, twisting trail, that tugged a familiar chord in Jesse's memory.

A man who walked with such difficulty had no business climbing this far up the mountain. A man who probably couldn't run had to be a fool to approach the lair of a recluse. Someone ought to have warned him that mountain men in general seldom welcomed visitors.

Jesse Calvin in particular *never* tolerated intruders.

"Stop right there!" he bellowed when less than a hundred yards separated him from the stranger.

The stranger froze in mid-stride. "Jesse Calvin—is that you?"

It had been a long time since Jesse heard someone else say his name. The rifle wavered.

"Who wants to know?"

"It's me—Hobe. Hobe Merckel. I got something real important to tell you."

Jesse lowered his weapon. Now he understood why the man's awkward gait had seemed so familiar. Six or seven years back, Hobe had stumbled half-drunk out of Keppel's Saloon and right into the path of a fast-moving wagon. He'd gotten clipped and sent sprawling face-first into the dirt. Hobe's legs had never worked quite right since then.

Jesse closed his eyes and willed the memory back into that gray, frozen place where he locked away such things. Hobe's accident wasn't a particularly important event in Jesse's life, but he couldn't afford to let even one memory escape—the next thing he knew, everything he wanted to forget would clamor for release, and he'd find himself sitting staring at nothing for hours while he replayed his mistakes over and over again in his head, even though nothing could change what had been done.

Lately it had grown harder and harder to keep those thoughts at bay, and this time it took even more effort.

By the time Jesse won the battle, Hobe stood no more than a dozen feet in front of him. Exhaustion lined Hobe's face, and his limbs shook a little, lending credence to his claim that he had important news to impart. A person as bad off as Hobe wouldn't risk climbing the mountain without good reason. He bent, bracing his hands above his knees, and drew a few deep breaths. He kept an eye on the dogs, which had taken a stance between the two men. Stiff-legged, fur raised along their hackles, they bared their teeth in silent threat.

Jesse murmured a command, and the dogs sat.

"What brings you up here, Hobe?"

Hobe kept his attention on the dogs. "Glad to hear you can still talk."

"No reason why I wouldn't be able to talk."

"I've known a few mountain men lost the use of their voices entirely. Just froze up on them from not being used. Or maybe they forgot how to use words, not talking to anyone for years on end."

"I'm about ready to not talk to you, if this conversation is the best you can manage after coming all this way." Truth to tell, Jesse had more interesting discourse with his dogs, which was probably why his voice still rang clear and true. Talking to dogs alleviated the quiet when silence grew unbearable— but he'd die before admitting such to Hobe.

And he'd shoot his own self with his own rifle before admitting to Hobe that he was so company-starved that he welcomed their witless conversation as eagerly as dry earth soaked up soft rain.

Hobe fished a flask from his hip pocket and took a hearty gulp. Then he pulled a grubby hunk of linen from his inner coat pocket and mopped his forehead. "Damn hot climbing," he said. "Seemed downright cold when I started out a couple days ago. Never expected it to heat up so much, this early in the spring."

"It's not hot yet," said Jesse. "That trail takes a lot out of a man. You shouldn't be climbing at all with those gimpy legs of yours."

"Yeah, well, someone had to come up here to tell you. You said you wanted to know."

"Know what?" Jesse asked, while the excitement within him slowed into a thumping dread.

"Ezra Lowell. He up and died last week."

The memories battered at Jesse's skull, shrieking to be let out. He kept them in abeyance by a force of will that betrayed itself with a shakiness in his voice. "He suffer much?"

"Nah. Went quick."

"I wouldn't call dying by inches over five or more years a quick death."

"Hell, he didn't die from that old gunshot wound, Jesse—he went to the fever. Raged through Dry Falls good and proper last month. Ezra was one of the last to take sick. He'd been bragging all over town that all the liquor he swilled pickled his blood too much to interest a fever, but down he went."

"Fever alone wouldn't kill a man stout as Ezra. I ought to know."

"You're set as ever on blaming yourself," Hobe observed. "Well, maybe the rest of my news will set your mind at ease. That fever took a toll on the Lowell clan, including someone you never shot. Ezra's mama. She died, too."

"You mean his sister," Jesse corrected automatically while guilt wrenched his innards. He hoped Hobe might be joking about the girl. He couldn't be sure. He didn't think folks joked about things like that. Going so long between conversations apparently blunted a man's ability to separate sarcasm from truth. "Ezra lived with his sister. Alice."

"Alice is just fine. I'm telling you, it's the mother who died. No surprise you didn't know about Mrs. Lowell. She kept to the house for years—one of them flighty females who stay inside all the time."

Jesse couldn't summon grief for someone he'd never met. Especially as relief washed through him at hearing the girl lived. If he was the type of man who still believed in prayers, he could give thanks for that.

"She's all right, then. Alice."

"Depends on what you mean by all right. Alice tended her mama. Took care of Ezra, too. Poor gal's spent most of her life looking after one person or another, and now she ain't got nobody or nothing to show for it. Mama and brother both dead. She's going to have to move out of their shack, too, now that Ezra's gone. That house goes with the job. I hear Keppel's already hired someone."

Jesse shuddered, remembering the pain and despair in the little girl's eyes when they'd carried her brother home after the gunfight that had torn a gaping hole through Ezra Lowell. Jesse, blinded by rage and whiskey, had aimed for the man's heart—but too much drinking had blunted his skill. His shot had skewed to the right, tearing out a slab of Ezra's chest muscle and a good hunk of his upper left arm. A miracle, the doctor had said, that Ezra hadn't died immediately, but he'd warned that Ezra's life could be drastically shortened.

Alice Lowell, a skinny, scrawny gal who couldn't have been more than ten or eleven years old, hadn't flinched when accepting the news that she'd have to nurse her brother back to health. "Maybe this will keep him out of the saloon for a while," she had said. "Maybe." Her quiet despair had haunted Jesse over all these years. Those wide, tormented, startling blue eyes, dull with defeat, had been the one memory he'd never managed to squelch, no matter how hard he'd tried.

"Ezra wouldn't have died if he'd been full-strength." Jesse reiterated his guilt. "And he probably brought that fever home to his mother." His hands tingled. A murderer's hands, responsible now for two deaths; responsible for turning a young girl into a homeless orphan. "Where will she go? Alice?"

Hobe shrugged, took another swig from his flask, and shook the final few drops into his open mouth. "Someone'll probably take her in. You got any 'shine up in your cabin, Jesse?"

"I don't have anything to do with alcohol these days, Hobe."

Hobe grunted his disappointment. "Well, I can understand that. Guess I'll settle for coffee."

"No coffee." *For you,* Jesse added silently. He didn't allow anyone, ever, into his cabin—not even the traders who kept him supplied with luxuries like coffee and herbs.

"Cold water, then." Hobe heaved a disgruntled sigh. "And a spot in front of your fire for the night. I'll head back to town in the morning."

"Plenty of cold water in the stream. And it's too early in

the day to start worrying about where you'll sleep tonight. There's lots of good camp cover along the trail.''

Jesse could almost see Hobe's mind working over his comments, and could just about tell the exact minute when Hobe realized he was being denied the basic courtesy of a night's lodging.

''Well, hell, Jesse. I ain't Ezra Lowell. I don't have a pack of cards in my pocket, and I ain't going to try to get you drunk or trick you into gambling this godforsaken place away. You got no call to take it out on me for what Ezra done to you, Jesse.''

Jesse tightened his jaw. ''I just don't like having anyone on my property, Hobe. Nothing personal.''

''Personal enough to me. I'm purely tired out.'' He turned to wheedling. ''You remarked my bad legs yourself. Why, I'm apt to fall. Or maybe doze off against a rock and get eaten alive by hungry wolves.''

''I guess I'll chase them off if they get too close,'' said Jesse.

Hobe's eyes widened and his lips parted, and Jesse knew the man was about to pepper him with questions. He tightened his grip around the rifle, and Hobe's mouth snapped shut.

Though Hobe's silent acceptance suited Jesse, he figured he'd better explain. Explaining was important to people. He would have some explaining to do to Alice Lowell, so it might be a good idea to get some practice.

''I'll see to it that little Alice finds herself a home. It's the least I can do.''

''You're coming down? You're going to Dry Falls?''

Jesse didn't see any need to reconfirm what he'd just said.

''I'm not so sure you'll be any better company than the wolves,'' Hobe grumbled when the silence had stretched out for a while. He studied Jesse's appearance for a moment. ''So you're really coming back to Dry Falls. You're clean enough, but you'd best let me trim that hair. Ought to hack at the beard a little, too. Otherwise, folks'll think a big ole brown bear followed me down from the mountain.''

* * *

Ezra Lowell's shack hadn't changed much in the five years Jesse had spent atop the mountain. Maybe the boards had turned slightly more silver-gray; maybe the sag in the porch step was more pronounced. Maybe he just didn't remember it right.

The place sat fifty feet or so behind Keppel's Saloon. Ezra had earned his keep by sweeping out the saloon each morning and spelling old man Keppel behind the bar when the saloon's owner tended to his other business interests. Ezra must have found the house a handy place to live.

It was hard to imagine how women could live there, though. The saloon blocked all air and sunlight from reaching the front. A decrepit stable stood a dozen or so feet off to one side, and a padlocked storage shed cozied up against the house on the other end. Women had delicate sensibilities, and Jesse couldn't imagine them being happy so close to the noise, the smells, the sight of staggering cowboys who left the place only long enough to relieve themselves against the saloon's rear wall. No wonder Ezra's mother had never ventured out of doors.

Jesse had never seen the front door or windows opened, no doubt because of the proximity of the saloon, and today was no different. His whole being, accustomed to the sweet air and fresh breezes of his mountain cabin, rebelled at calling that squalid, closed-in collection of wood and tar paper a home. But Alice Lowell had grown up in that place. The girl was bound to be despondent at the thought of losing the only shelter she'd ever known.

He stood in the shadows pooling out from the small stable. The wall at his back felt comforting, the gloom a welcome protection from the blatant stares that had followed him ever since he'd walked into town with Hobe. He hadn't expected the rush of anxiety that had struck him while navigating Dry Falls' only street. People were everywhere. Looking at him. Smiling. Calling his name.

Asking why he'd stayed away so long. Saying it was nice

to see him looking so fit. Acting like they didn't remember
what he'd done, or the shame he'd brought upon himself.

Bad as that walk had been, though, the few dozen feet now
separating him from the Lowell shack promised to be worse.
But he couldn't stand there cowering in the shadows all day.
He shrugged off his coat. The day had turned too hot for the
buffalo-hide garment, and by wrapping it over his arm he was
able to hide his rifle, so he wouldn't appear too threatening to
the young girl. Despite halfway undressing, he didn't feel one
bit cooler. He craved home with such an ache that it threatened
to paralyze him. His gaze flicked toward the small square of
sky visible between the two tumbledown buildings. He couldn't
see his mountain, but he knew it loomed out there, dark and
tall against the horizon, ready to welcome him back as soon
as he settled Ezra Lowell's little sister with some decent, kind
family.

He doubted that Alice would come to the front door if he
knocked—she'd probably worry it was someone from the
saloon bent upon mischief. He drew a deep breath and then
darted from the stable to the side of the shack. He crouched right
beneath an open window. Soft, small sounds floated through;
someone was moving about inside. A chair scraped against a
wood floor. A drawer slid open, and back shut again. He held
himself still and listened—and then let out a shaky laugh. He
was behaving as if he were tracking a deer bound for the stew
pot instead of calling on a girl he meant to help. If she caught
him sneaking around, spying on her, she'd never believe he'd
come only to see to her welfare.

"Alice?" He rose, but as tall as he was, the window ledge
stood higher. He couldn't see inside. "Alice Lowell?"

Nobody answered his hail, maybe because whoever was
inside had commenced working a hand pump with such vigor
that Jesse could hear the water splashing. He swallowed. His
throat had gone dry the minute he walked into town. Though
he didn't really believe mere thirst was responsible, thinking
so had allowed him to feel less apprehensive.

"Miss Lowell?" He called the name out loud and made plenty of noise with his feet as he walked around to the back of the house.

A flatiron propped open the door, admitting sunlight to the small room. A female stood at the sink, with her back to the door. Her thick, honey-brown hair brushed against her waist from one side to the other as she worked the water pump.

Jesse was just about to call out again when she began singing.

Singing. He couldn't really recall the last time he'd heard a woman's voice lifted in song. He hadn't sung at all, himself, since a long-ago day when a traveling piano man had worked a stint at Keppel's Saloon. This woman sang an exceptionally merry tune that kept rhythm with her pumping. Her voice was soft and low, but she sang with such joyousness, in such rich, womanly tones, that Jesse knew at once she could not be sad little Alice Lowell.

Jesse gripped the door jamb, paralyzed into immobility. He thought he could stand there for hours, listening to her sing.

But then he realized that this woman's presence meant he was too late. Alice Lowell must have already been evicted. The new man Keppel hired had already moved in with his family.

Maybe they would know how Alice fared. "Ma'am?" he called, quietly, as if his subconscious rebelled against interrupting her. He tried again, louder. "Ma'am!"

She spun around. Her trailing hand caught the cascading water so that it sprayed in front of her, glittering like diamonds before it soaked into the worn cotton of her dress. She stiffened when she caught sight of him. Her eyes, huge and blue and instantly wary, stole Jesse's breath right away. Those eyes were the same shape, the same shade of blue, as the eyes that had haunted him for years.

Alice Lowell's eyes.

It couldn't be. He shook his head. He hadn't been up on the mountain that long. This full-grown woman could not be the young girl he sought.

"I'm looking for Alice Lowell." He pulled off his hat and balanced it on top of the coat folded over his arm. The room still seemed to echo with the crystal purity of her singing, making his voice sound extra rough, as if he truly were one of those old-time mountain men who'd forgotten how to speak.

"What do you want?"

"I have business with Ezra Lowell's sister."

Her shoulders slumped a little. "If he owed you money, you're out of luck. He's dead and buried."

"I know that, ma'am."

"So, what business . . . oh." She clasped her hands together at her waist. Jesse felt pretty certain that she did not realize how the unconscious gesture called a man's attention to the way her body curved in, and then out. "You must be the new saloon keeper Mr. Keppel hired. He said you weren't expected until next week. It's all right that you're here early. I planned to be out of here by morning. My things—the things I want to keep—are all packed, and I assure you I am quite ready to go."

"*You're* Alice Lowell?"

"Of course."

There hadn't been many times that Jesse Calvin had found himself in need of physical support. Only once before that he could recall—when he'd looked down at Ezra Lowell's writhing body and the realization of what he'd done had penetrated his alcohol-induced stupor. And now. His weight fell against the door jamb, and he let the crooked portal hold him up while his brain raced.

He ought to be rejoicing. Alice Lowell was no sobbing orphan in need of a foster family. She was a woman grown, albeit a bit on the small side. A woman who sang and didn't appear the least bit devastated by her recent losses. He'd made the trip into town for nothing. He could just nod, turn, walk away, and go back to his mountain.

"Where will you go?" he found himself asking.

"That's none of your concern."

"It is." He lurched upright. He'd come to admit his guilt and apologize, and that's what he would do. "It's my fault you have to leave."

She laughed, a short, humorless sound. "You're welcome to this house. All I ask is that you let me come back once, after I find some asparagus. I'll need to gather a little spinach and a few spring onions from the garden so I can make my soup. You're welcome to the bulk of the harvest. I just need enough spinach and onions for one pot of soup."

Soup? He knew women liked to talk about cooking and such, but he couldn't indulge her domestic interests just then. He had to let her know who he was, so he could spit out his guilt and make his apologies—now.

"I'm not the new saloon keeper, Miss Lowell. I'm the man who killed your brother."

"Oh, well, if you're not here to take over the house, then it's no concern of yours if I come back for the spinach and onions for my soup."

He scowled at her. "I don't think you heard what I said. I killed your brother. I guess you don't recognize me."

She looked at him then, with a boldness unusual in a woman, letting her gaze probe every inch of him from head to toe. "I guess I don't," she said.

"I'm Jesse," he said. "Jesse—"

"Calvin?" she finished.

"You do know me, then."

"Oh, I recognize your name all right, Mr. Jesse Calvin. My brother cursed you out loud twice every day. Once each morning when I forced him to wake and cross the yard to his so-called work. And once each night when he fell through that door so drunk he couldn't manage to stay upright."

"Did you curse me twice a day, too, Miss Lowell?"

"More than twice, sometimes. For not properly finishing the job." She bit her lip, then bent her head toward the floor, but not quickly enough to hide the rosy flush that bloomed on her cheeks.

He couldn't have heard her right. "Well, you can go ahead and spew out a few curses right to my face." Jesse stiffened his shoulders, ready for her to unleash her invective. Or worse. An iron cooking pot sat on the stove. "You can even throw that cook pot at me, and I won't flinch."

To his astonishment, her lips curved into a smile. Those eyes, whose sadness and resignation had haunted him for so long, now sparkled with delight.

"Curse you? Throw pots at you? To tell the truth, Mr. Calvin, right now, I'm more inclined to walk on over there and give you a kiss."

CHAPTER TWO

Alice groaned inwardly as she pressed fingers to her lips. "Oh, goodness, just listen to me! I'm not usually so—forward, Mr. Calvin. My mother always fretted I'd acquire bad habits, living so close to a saloon, and it appears she was right."

"No offense taken, ma'am."

Jesse Calvin looked away from her. He pretended great interest in the shelf hanging above the kitchen table, even though its battered pine surface lay bare. She'd carefully packed away the two genuine bone-china figures and the Bible that once sat upon it. The small house, home for so many years, no longer bore any trace of her occupancy. She wondered, sometimes, if she would ever leave her mark on anything.

A woman who'd lived as Alice had these past years knew how to size up a person with just one quick glance. Her mama had often tried to keep her pain and suffering a secret, but Alice had learned to recognize the thin lines of strain, the extra watery sheen in the eyes, the almost imperceptible trembling of lips that told her when Mama was being too stout-hearted for her own good. The skill had been even more valuable when

Ezra dragged himself home. A drunken man's face was as good as a road map to a woman who knew how to read the signs that told her when to keep quiet, when to pour a cup of coffee, when to load a plate with food, when to stay in her room with the door locked.

Jesse Calvin wasn't so easy to decipher. His deep-set eyes, the same rich green as a mountain pine, betrayed the soul of a man who was not at ease with his spirit. And yet he exhibited a steadiness of purpose in the way he held himself, a firm determination in the jut of his jaw, that marked him as someone who would not rest until he'd accomplished what he set out to do.

Her brother had indeed cursed Mr. Calvin twice each day— along with a litany of other names, names of people Ezra believed had done him wrong. Folks in town often talked about Jesse, too, though they usually changed the subject when they thought she might overhear. Everyone seemed to think Dry Falls had lost a valuable citizen when Jesse Calvin took to the mountains, that everyone would have been better off if Ezra had vanished instead. Alice had never known how to tell them she agreed, without sounding like a traitor to her own blood kin. Young women, in particular, mentioned how they hoped he might come back some day.

And now he stood here in her kitchen, intent upon apologizing for an action performed in the grip of white-hot passion. She wondered what he would say if she told him she had often thought the Lowells owed an apology to *him*.

She ought to look away now, the way he was doing. That would be the polite thing to do. That's exactly what she would have done, had not her quick, practiced eye caught the flash of interest that lit him before he quelled it.

Interest. In her. She couldn't remember the last time a decent man had looked at her with interest. And so she stood there with her fingers pressed to her lips, staring at him.

"I didn't recognize you," she said.

"That makes us even. I didn't recognize you, either."

"It was a long time ago. And we've both changed."

Not only that, but Alice seldom looked back on the day they'd brought her wounded brother home. And when she did remember it, all that came back to her was the blood, and the dreadful despair that had gripped her when she realized she was bound even more closely now to the brother she despised.

Still, it surprised her that she hadn't recognized Jesse Calvin right off—considering how she couldn't seem to stop trying to memorize his looks now.

He didn't care to be studied. She could tell by the way he shifted his heavy buffalo coat from one arm to the other. She caught the glint of metal and realized he concealed a firearm under his coat. Well, she didn't think he meant to shoot her. He seemed self-conscious, clearing his throat as his attention skipped from the empty shelf to the wall she'd denuded of all decoration, to the window from which she'd stripped her gingham curtains.

He seemed determined to look at everything except her, the woman who'd just blurted out that she felt like kissing him.

Maybe it was a good thing he'd sealed himself away on that mountain for all these years, if it bothered him so to have a woman's attention fixed upon him. He was the kind of man that automatically drew female interest: tall, broad of shoulder, and lean in the way of a man who carried a lot of hard-working muscle on his bones. He probably spent most of his time outdoors, hatless, because his hair was the shade of golden molasses, a few shades lighter than his beard and the curls peeping above his shirt collar.

Someone had taken a knife to his hair recently, judging by the short tufts that poked free here and there from the carefully sleek way he'd combed it back and tied it with a leather thong. A shame, that the job had been so badly done. She'd tended Ezra's scraggly locks with better care. Trimming her brother's oily, thin, mud-colored hair had been a chore; tending hair like Jesse's—thick, soft, and clean—would be a pleasure.

Clean. His hair, his beard, his hands and face showed him

to be a man who valued cleanliness and was comfortable with it, not like some she knew who visited the baths no more than once every six months and who spent the next several days tugging at their clothes as if the feel of fresh-laundered cotton irritated their skin. Jesse's garments bore out her opinion. The cloth had faded from many washings and lay soft against his skin. His shirt collar drooped from not being ironed, but she imagined a mountain man didn't think much about ironing collars.

"I expected to find you more distraught," Jesse said.

He had a beautiful mouth. Maybe holding her fingers still pressed against her lips while he talked made her wonder what his mouth might feel like against hers—and her fingers on their own account increased pressure against her lips, reminding her that she still stood there staring. She twisted her fingers into her skirt, wrapping them tightly within the folds.

"Miss Lowell? Pardon me for saying so, but you seem a little out of sorts."

"Oh. I expect I am." His comment did not surprise her. Most folks, not knowing the hell her life had become, expected her to be prostrate with grief over losing her mama and her brother within a few days of each other.

She'd learned to adopt a sober demeanor over these past couple of weeks, when what she really wanted to do was stand out in the meadow with her arms spread wide, her face tilted to the sun, while she spun in circles, celebrating the sheer joy of being free.

"I've set my mourning aside, Mr. Calvin," she said. "I do thank you for your sympathy."

"More than sympathy, Miss Lowell. I can't help but believe much of your grief has been brought on by what I did in the past to your brother. I've come to apologize, and to see if I can somehow lighten your burden."

She sagged back against the sink in surprise. "You've done nothing to me, Mr. Calvin."

"I shot your brother."

"If you hadn't shot him, someone else would have. I felt like shooting him myself on any number of occasions. My brother was a mean-spirited drunkard before you shot him, and he was a mean-spirited drunkard until the day he died."

"Suffering can turn a man cruel."

"Believe me when I tell you that Ezra recovered quite well from that wound. His failure to live up to his responsibilities as a man stemmed from his own moral weaknesses, and not from anything that you—or anybody—did to him."

"He provided a home for you and your mother, and now you're being forced to find a new place to call home."

The notion that Ezra had cared about where they lived almost made her laugh aloud.

"Ezra hung onto his job at Keppel's Saloon because a good part of his salary was paid to him in whiskey. The fact that this house came along with the job was of incidental interest to him. I had to haul him to his feet every morning and point him out the door, or Mr. Keppel would have fired him long ago. If not for my mama being so ill and not up to moving along, I would have gladly turned my back on my brother's so-called providing."

"It's not always easy for a woman to understand what goes on in a man's head. Could be you don't give your brother enough credit."

"Could be you've been wallowing in guilt over a no-account drunk," she said. "Please don't insult me by telling me I should have held my brother in higher esteem. I don't know what's going on in your head, but if you've turned your back on this town because of what happened with my brother, you've made an unnecessary sacrifice."

His jaw tightened. "I have often regretted shooting your brother, but that's not why I chose to live as I do." She waited for him to explain himself, but he changed the subject. "I didn't know about your mother, and I am sorry you lost her."

"Mama's passing was a blessing." Alice swallowed hard against the pain. "She'd been gone from her mind for a long,

long time. I found myself nursing a shell for these past couple of years.''

He frowned at her. ''Regardless, now that Ezra's gone, you're without a home.''

''I am not some helpless female, Mr. Calvin. I have a job awaiting me, one that provides room and board as well as a small salary. Mr. Palmer's wife plans to join him now that he's built a house to suit her special needs. She's something of an invalid and requires constant companionship. I begin in three weeks' time.''

She wondered if he noticed the distinct lack of enthusiasm in her voice as she mentioned her new job. He seemed, however, to be entirely focused on his own stubborn concerns.

''You said you're planning to move out of this house tomorrow. Where will you live until you take up residence with the Palmers?''

''I don't need a place to live.'' Excitement shivered through her. ''I shall be roaming the territory, hunting asparagus.''

''Roaming the territory?''

She nodded. ''Hunting asparagus.''

''It does not ease my mind, Miss Lowell, to hear that you mean to wander out all alone, looking for a vegetable. Coupled with what you said to me earlier—well, I can't help wondering if you're so affected by grief that your recent losses have left you touched in the head.''

''For someone who spends his time wandering free as you please up in those mountains, I can't understand why you are so against my doing the same.''

''I'm a man, Miss Lowell. You're . . . not.''

With that, he focused his full attention upon her once more, and she swore she could *feel* the strength of his regard. Never before had she been so conscious of the way her breasts pushed against the fabric of her dress, or the light slide of her cotton petticoats against her bare legs. ''I mean to find asparagus,'' she said in a faint whisper.

He blinked and shook his head. "I swear I've never heard of anyone so fond of it."

"I don't know if I'll actually like it at all," she admitted. "I've never tasted asparagus."

"Some folks relish the taste. Others don't."

"And you? Have you ever tasted it?"

He cleared his throat, and she wondered what it was about asparagus that made him so uncomfortable. "I'm fond of it. I can't say it's worth three weeks of camping out in the cold to find it, though."

"Oh, but it is!" She didn't know exactly how to put her mission into words. "Whenever our situation grew . . . onerous, Mama and I would lock ourselves in the bedroom, and she would tell me about a magical soup that would help a woman find her heart's desire. We would giggle together like school-girls and make up the most outrageous dreams, and assure one another that the magic soup would make everything come true."

Speculating over the magical properties of the special soup had helped the two of them turn many moments of terror into togetherness. She missed her mother suddenly with an almost physical pain. She laughed to cover the momentary weakness. "Just before Mama died, her head cleared for a few hours. All she wanted was to hear my *real* hopes and dreams. She swore they could come true. Mr. Calvin, she made me promise I would make that soup for myself, and I will keep my word."

If he mocked her promise, she would order him right out of the house. But he appeared thoughtful, as if he well understood the gravity of a deathbed vow.

"Surely someone here in town grows asparagus and would offer you a few spears."

"No one does." She had searched, as well as she could considering she'd never dared to spend more than an hour away from her mother. Uppermost had been the fear of fire striking their tinderbox of a shack. Ezra, always drunk, had taken to smoking cigarettes, and he took no care with the ashes or the burning cigarette itself. "Mama told me asparagus grows in the wild, sometimes."

"Can't you make the soup without the asparagus?"

"Asparagus is the most vital ingredient. Without it, there could be no magic."

Besides, hunting asparagus gave her a purpose for her wandering, which she did not care to explain to Jesse. He was right: grown women didn't take to the woods and the fields. Hunting asparagus gave her a shaky, but plausible, excuse for doing so. She wasn't sure she could explain—or that he would be interested in hearing—that when her three weeks of freedom ended, she would once again be confined within a sickroom, waiting hand and foot upon an invalid, on the inside looking out while fresh breezes teased the tall grass, while the sun warmed the earth, while children's laughter created a music she would be paid to silence. She felt an old, familiar despair stir within her, but he jolted her right out of it.

"I'm going with you."

"You don't have to say that."

"I'm not just saying it."

"Sure you are. You're trying to apologize, and you feel guilty, and it makes you feel better to offer to accompany me. Don't worry. I don't expect you to come with me."

"But I do mean it."

His voice had notched a little higher with each declaration, as if he meant to convince her through volume alone. How alike all men were, she thought. Determined, always, to show themselves in a good light, if only for a moment. "I'm sure you're very sincere right now. I do believe men *mean* to keep their promises. They somehow never manage it, though."

"You don't believe me."

"I've had too much practice with men and their promises to ever believe in them again, Mr. Calvin. Besides, the last thing I need is to spend nights in the woods alone with a man."

He blushed. Blushed! And his jaw clenched even tighter

with determination and responsibility. "If you're worried about losing your good reputation—"

"A woman who lives in a shack behind a saloon and who claims the town's worst drunkard as her brother doesn't have a good reputation to worry about. No, what worries me is the demands a man makes upon a woman."

Once again his eyes flared with interest, and he straightened, calling attention to his full size. A man like him would certainly make some bold demands upon a woman. Oh, she'd chosen her words poorly! She felt a slow heat begin low in her belly.

"You wrong me." His voice vibrated, low and husky. "I am not the kind of man who demands a woman do anything against her will."

"What I meant," she stammered, "was that you'd no doubt expect me to do all the cooking and keep the campsite clean. I'll be caught up in that kind of work soon enough. I have no desire . . ." Her voice caught. "I mean, the only cooking I intend to do over the next three weeks involves that magic vegetable soup."

He sent her a slow, brooding stare, as hot as a campfire flame licking dry oak, and she couldn't help thinking that maybe it wouldn't be such a chore to do a bit of cooking and cleaning for Jesse Calvin.

"Women don't know the first thing about camping in the wild."

"And men can be useless, annoying creatures who expect the comforts of home without the amenities."

"There's a lot more to survival than making stew over an open fire."

He didn't need to know that she'd spent years imagining running off into the woods, all alone. Those daydreams had helped her through days that seemed unbearable. When her mama died and she knew she'd have a chance to make this one very minor dream come true, Alice had meticulously planned her three-week interlude, down to the tiny hoard of wood shavings that would help her start a fire in a downpour.

"I have prepared well for my search, Mr. Calvin."

"Show me."

He stood there, stubborn and responsible to the core, with his chin thrust out, ordering her to prove the adequacy of her preparations. Well, she wouldn't. Women like her knew how to get things done. The weak-willed of the world depended on them. She'd soon have enough trouble training the Palmers, who no doubt expected her to conform to their ways. She'd bring them around. But for these three weeks, she had to answer to no one but herself.

She tipped her chin and glared right back at him, though she doubted she appeared half as imposing as he.

"I have no intentions of unpacking my saddlebags for you."

"Saddlebags?" His interest sharpened. "So you have a pack animal. I know a thing or two about them."

He was either exceptionally modest, or reluctant to acknowledge the past. Cowboys treasured their Calvins—the horses Jesse had raised and trained before losing his ranch to her brother. Some said that Jesse would have made Dry Falls famous for turning out prime horseflesh if he'd stayed in the business. "I have a mule," she said. "He is grain-fed and well rested."

"A good woodsman carries a small pack of personals and emergency items."

Her glance skipped involuntarily toward the door of her bedroom, where the very sort of pack he'd just described sat awaiting the last-minute items she would stow in it in the morning, after using them here for the last time. He noticed where she was looking and moved as if he meant to unpack her bag there and then.

"I don't believe I care to have you pawing through my intimate belongings."

He paused, but sent her a disdainful look. "You no doubt fear I will be proved right. You've probably packed all the wrong things."

"I did not."

He leaned back against the wall and crossed his arms, the very image of a man who would not be budged. "I'm not leaving until you show me."

She recognized a strength of will equal to her own. They could stand there all day bickering. She didn't want to waste another minute of her precious free time on such an unproductive exercise.

"You'll leave me alone if I show you my pack, right?"

"Yes, ma'am."

She heaved a huge, annoyed sigh and stomped across the kitchen to her bedroom. She snatched up the bag from her bed, stormed back toward him, and flung the bag at Jesse's feet.

"Thank you, ma'am." He sent her a crooked half-smile and crouched down and drew the bag toward him. She thought she would die of embarrassment as he reached in and drew out her sole indulgence—silk underdrawers. She could not bring herself to say out loud that they were as durable as they were pretty, not with his long, strong fingers rubbing the silk and judging their texture.

He cleared his throat and then folded the dainty silk back into a neat bundle. He reached back into the bag. His look of bemusement shifted into one of surprise, and then grudging respect.

She knew what he'd found: the small packet of matches that she'd carefully sealed in paraffin; a waterproof pouch holding a goodly supply of beef jerky that she'd made herself; a two-edged hatchet for chopping kindling. She'd purchased a coffee-pot that could double as a cookpot suitable for single-sized portions, and into it she'd packed a small ball of strong twine, needle and thread folded carefully inside clean cotton suitable for tearing into bandages, and a long-bladed penknife.

Though she shied away from consuming alcohol, she understood its medicinal properties and had packed a small flask of strong whiskey. A second, larger flask remained empty, awaiting fresh water.

"I will fill that just before I begin my journey," she said when he held it aloft.

"And what is this?" He held up a canvas-wrapped packet.

"A map."

He lifted his brows but made no comment as he delved again into the leather pack.

Nestled in the bottom of the pack were her spare clothes. She prayed he would not take them out, but he seemed to be a thorough man. He pulled free the plaid flannel shirt that had been Ezra's. She'd cut it down substantially to fit her, but even so it looked rather large when he unfolded it. But the shirt was nothing compared to the gathered-in and hemmed britches that Jesse shook open. He stared down at them with consternation.

"I don't mean to traipse through the woods wearing a skirt and petticoats," she said, defending her outrageous choice of garb. "Are you satisfied now, Mr. Calvin?"

"You chose well," he admitted, surprising her. She'd never known a man to admit a mistake. "I'll just put these things back now."

She didn't think she could bear watching him handle her silk drawers again. "I can repack my own bag. Now, if you don't mind, I have much to attend to."

He rose slowly to his feet. "I don't like the idea of you going off on your own."

"What I do and where I go are no concern of yours."

"But—"

"Mr. Calvin—whatever your purpose was in coming here, I assure you it was not necessary. I do not hold you responsible for my brother's death. I do not expect or want you to escort me through the woods while I hunt asparagus. I don't need your approval of my pack contents, and I certainly don't need your permission to do as I please for the next few weeks."

He glowered unhappily at her.

"Go on with you now. Get." She made shooing motions at him.

She didn't really know what she would do if he flat-out

refused to leave, and then realized how odd this whole interlude had been. A large, strange man had simply walked into her kitchen, and she'd never felt a moment's fear or apprehension— even when she'd realized he hid a rifle beneath his coat, even when he'd touched her underwear. She remembered all those nights when she and Mama had closed themselves in their room to stay out of sight and out of mind of Ezra's drunken cohorts. She'd never felt a minute's fear with Jesse Calvin, not a single minute.

She imagined that if she had been the sissy type of woman who required a man's presence, Jesse Calvin just might be a pleasant, safe companion to rely upon during an asparagus-hunting trip.

Rely upon? There was a farfetched notion. Men could not be relied upon for anything.

"Good-bye," she said.

He stepped outside, onto the small stoop. The kitchen at once felt too large, too empty. If such a familiar space seemed suddenly overwhelming with loneliness, how would she feel with only herself surrounded by the great outdoors?

She shook off the sensation and hurried quickly to the door. "Good-bye," she said again, and closed the door in Jesse's face.

CHAPTER THREE

Lantern light flickered on from inside the house well before dawn. Jesse moved away from the stable door and back into the darkest corner of the stable, where stacked bales of hay provided convenient places to hide. He didn't expect Alice to bound out of the house, ready to leave just then—but he also didn't feel quite right about standing there and watching her when she couldn't know she was being observed through the uncurtained window.

He allowed himself a moment to study the dozing mule and the packs hanging from nails in the wall, where mice couldn't easily help themselves to the contents. He'd been very careful when examining the packs and replacing everything. He didn't think she'd notice they'd been inspected.

She'd done a fine job with both the animal and her provisions. The mule's legs were sound, its back straight and strong, and judging by its placid acceptance of Jesse's examination, docile enough for a woman to handle. Her saddlebags held a good supply of coffee, salt, canned beans, and canned corn. She'd laid in bacon, salt beef and flour, and the makings of a snare to keep her supplied with fresh rabbit if she was so inclined. She'd stuffed one side of the saddlebags with oats for the mule. A pouch held a dozen shotgun shells. A couple of heavy blankets, even a pillow—she would fare well on her little adventure.

It should ease his mind to know she wasn't setting off ill-prepared. Hell, she was better equipped than he was. There was no earthly reason for him to be hiding there in the stable. No reason to continue to feel responsible for a woman who was obviously quite capable of taking care of herself.

He told himself it was just curiosity, nothing more, that kept him there to watch over her. If he was really all that concerned, he knew exactly where she could go to find her precious asparagus. He'd almost blurted it out when she'd asked him if he'd ever tasted the stuff. Alice could find all the asparagus she needed right in his own garden.

He'd noted the first shoots breaking ground a day or two before Hobe came up and gave him the news about Ezra. Some of the spears might be ready to pick by now. Planting that patch had been one of the first chores Jesse had tackled when claiming his remote hunk of mountain. He'd snuck back to his old horse ranch late one night and dug a bucketful of asparagus roots out of the plot he'd established there. Later, when he'd heard Keppel had turned hogs loose in the garden, Jesse had been glad he'd salvaged some of the roots. A thriving asparagus patch made a place feel like home. Almost.

Funny, that the only tie between his old life and the new was the very asparagus that Alice swore held magical properties.

But just the idea of granting anyone—especially a Lowell—access to his property made his belly clench. Never. If it turned out she pursued her asparagus hunt stupidly, he could always tell her to sit tight for a few days while he raced home, picked what she needed, and came back with the makings of her soup. He had everything she'd mentioned—the spinach, the onions, the carrots, even some dried celery.

He heard the creak of the kitchen door. He eased down onto the floor, concealing himself behind the tallest stack of bales.

A pool of golden lantern light illuminated the rickety old stable. The mule wheezed a rusty-sounding greeting. "I know just how you feel, Lightning." Alice's voice trilled with happiness as she patted the mule. "I can scarcely believe it myself— we're really leaving."

She started to sing again. A bright, lilting melody, but as she'd done the day before, she kept her words soft and low, like someone who was afraid to be overheard. Not because she was a bad singer, either. Jesse found himself unconsciously straining toward the sound, as if something sore inside him yearned to get close enough to bathe from head to toe in the sweet huskiness of Alice's voice. He edged forward so he could peek around the edge of a bale. His shirt caught against a few protruding strands of hay and caused it to rustle some. He froze in place, holding his breath, hoping Alice hadn't heard, and relaxed when her soft singing continued amid the splash of water and the swish of grain against a bucket as she tended to her mule.

She wore clothes that he remembered seeing Ezra Lowell wear. Men's clothes, just like those he'd found in her pack the night before. She'd altered them, but the shirt and pants were still far too large. She also had on a pair of men's boots. Judging by the clumping, sliding way she moved her feet, she wasn't accustomed to the weight or size of them yet. To keep them from slipping off, she'd wound short lengths of rope around each boot, under the sole, over the top, and around the ankle. Those boots were bound to cause her some trouble, later.

"Three weeks, Lightning," she said while the mule's strong teeth ground corn. "Three weeks of fresh air and sunshine. Well, it's spring so it might rain, but I won't even mind. I will hold my face up to the sky and let raindrops roll right down my cheeks. Three weeks."

Most women in Jesse's experience would make that "three weeks" sound as if they'd been sentenced to bread and water in a work house. Alice Lowell whispered "three weeks" with the reverence of a pilgrim predicting how long a miraculous vision might last.

He remembered her saying she had a job awaiting her in three weeks' time. You would think, then, that these three weeks were days for her to live through with uncertainty, without the stability and security of a roof over her head and a salary to pay her expenses. It seemed to Jesse that a woman accustomed to living indoors, accustomed to an indoor water pump and activities no more strenuous than tending to sick folk, ought to be less than exhilarated at the thought of letting cold spring rain wash over her face.

Not Alice. She sang as she tied the bundles to her mule with an excited fervor that told him she couldn't wait to set out from that stable and begin her asparagus hunt.

"Three weeks, three weeks, three weeks," she sang in a nonsense way, no particular melody, and softly, as if afraid to say the words too loudly. It struck Jesse then that she might have been forced to dampen her singing voice for quite a long time, to avoid disturbing a sickly mother, to avoid annoying a headache-plagued drunken brother. Maybe she couldn't risk singing too loudly now, either, for fear of getting into the habit. She meant to work in a sick room, after all. Mrs. Palmer might want it quiet all the time.

Jesse had heard a story about a fellow who'd captured a meadowlark and kept it in a cage. The bird would chirp once in a while, as if to remind itself that it was a bird. But the meadowlark never sang. The bird had lived, but its feathers grew dull and unkempt. The trapper decided to set it free, but by then the bird had lost its spirit and simply clung to its perch, never venturing out of the cage.

Alice Lowell was no bird, but Jesse couldn't help thinking that locking herself away in a sickroom wasn't much different than confining a meadowlark to a cage.

"Three weeks," she sang in the soft, fervent tones of a

prayer, as if these next twenty-one days were to be her limit of heaven on earth.

He knew then that he couldn't stop her. That it wouldn't be right to even try.

Nor could he just let her go out there all alone. She might know how to tend sick folk. She knew nothing about surviving in the wilderness.

She extinguished the lantern. "Let's go, Lightning," she said, a little breathless in the way of a child anticipating her Christmas stocking. The ridiculously named mule made no objection as she tugged on its headgear and led it from the stable.

The smart thing to do, Alice knew, would be to aim for one of the abandoned homesteads that lay beyond the perimeter of Dry Falls. Out there, she might come across the remnants of a kitchen garden. She might find asparagus growing alongside a caved-in log cabin, or amid the rubble of a collapsed wall. Asparagus was said to be a hardy perennial. Some might have survived even if the homesteaders had given up.

Or she could head straight for one of the places where more determined settlers still clung to their claims, and chances were good she'd find her asparagus, poking its green spears up toward the sun well before the winter-deadened weeds quickened with their own life. Her searching time had been so limited while her mama lived that she'd never been able to risk the day-long trek to the closest of the outlying homesteads. Now she had all the time in the world—three weeks!—to visit them.

She didn't think it too likely that she'd be seen leaving town at this early hour. But if someone spotted her, it would no doubt lead to questions and explanations that would delay her departure. So she left town the back way, leading Lightning along the narrow alley that ran perpendicular to Dry Falls' main street. The alley and street merged just beyond the edge of town, and within a few hundred yards the wide, well-packed surface narrowed into little better than a rutted trail. If she stuck to the trail, she'd eventually come to faint paths branching off, leading to the sorts of places she ought to go.

Yes, heading for a well-established homestead was definitely her best choice, with her surest chance of finding what she sought. Within a few days, a week at most, she'd have what she wanted, and she could return to town and take a room in the hotel, waiting for her job to begin.

She veered from the trail and made for the hills.

"Asparagus can spring up most anywhere," she informed Lightning. "Birds can pick up the seeds from a garden and carry them out into the wild places. In fact, if I was an asparagus plant, that's exactly where I'd like to grow—out there where I have to fight for every inch of space, but wild and free and never, ever fenced in."

The nice thing about talking to a mule was that as long as you phrased your comments the right way, the animal's head-bobbing motion made it seem as if he were agreeing with everything you said.

She concentrated on her walking. These boots of Ezra's were almost like new. He'd never stinted on his own clothes and footwear. He hadn't been an exceptionally large man—nothing at all like Jesse Calvin—but he'd still been a good deal bigger than she, even in the feet. At least an inch and a half separated her toes from the tips of Ezra's boots. She'd pulled on six pairs of knitted socks to try to make up some of the difference, and packed another sock in the tip of each boot. She'd even tied ropes around each boot to hold it in place. The ropes felt tight around her ankles, but at least the boots didn't slip.

She'd practiced wearing the footgear for a good week, but even so, walking across open ground put a strain on her legs that she hadn't anticipated. What looked like a flat, smooth walking surface from a distance was instead rocky and uneven. Weed stalks that had been flattened to earth during winter's snows wrapped themselves around her ankles. Tough clumps of grass, half dead stuff from last year and half new green shoots, caught at her toes. The extra inch and a half of boot length made it hard to judge where to place her feet. She hadn't counted on making such slow progress. She had hoped to reach the hills by noon. She had relished the notion of striking camp and eating the first meal of her adventure out there beneath the trees.

Besides, she'd wanted to be well out of sight of the town before people were up and about. She doubted anyone would come racing across the open ground to demand an explanation for her behavior, but even so, she'd feel better once the woods enfolded her.

She glanced over her shoulder at the thought, and saw a solitary figure following her, a few hundred yards back.

She gripped Lightning's bridle a little tighter and quickened her pace. Almost at once she stumbled over a big rock lying half-buried in the dirt and hidden by the newly emerging spring grasses. She caught her balance before falling, but tugged so hard on Lightning's leather that the mule brayed an objection. The familiar sound steadied her. She swallowed, and laughed a little shakily. Plenty of folks traveled the area. There was no reason to suspect the man coming behind of following her. Even though a normal person would stick to the trail. Or follow one of the paths leading to a homestead.

She peered over her shoulder again. The man was making no effort to conceal his presence, though he probably couldn't hide himself even if he wanted to on this wide-open, sunswept valley meadow. He looked big, but then he wore a buffalo coat that would make most anyone look on the huge side. She couldn't tell the color of his hair on account of his hat. He moved with a solid, rolling stride that spoke of familiarity with negotiating the grassy, treacherous footing.

There were a hundred different ways to approach the hills. No reason to follow in her wake . . . unless it was Jesse Calvin following her, still stubbornly intent upon watching over her.

She paused, waiting for her agitation to kindle into anger. Instead, a silly little thrill tingled through her, to think that

Jesse Calvin had meant it when he'd said he was interested in her welfare. But she shook that silliness away. Jesse's interest was spurred by guilt—misguided guilt, but guilt nonetheless. He'd made no secret of it.

"C'mon, Lightning." She pulled at the mule, who'd dropped his head to lip at the new grass peeking through the dried, winter-burned blades.

She refused to look his way again, even though she could think of little besides the man following her. Well, of him and things related to him, such as, if Jesse had spent the night in the town's only hotel, then how had he spotted her leaving, since she'd left by the back alley, which wasn't visible from the hotel? Such as, did he intend to catch up to her, and if so, why hadn't he done so by now?

His long-legged stride had seemed unaffected by the uneven turf. She recalled the way Jesse's boot leather hugged those long, muscled legs of his. He wouldn't have as much trouble walking as she, and without a mule to tug along, he ought to be making better time.

But he stayed well back. Almost as if he respected her need to take these first steps on her own.

With his presence quickening her pace, she made the edge of the valley by noon after all. The sun had been directly overhead for only a quarter-hour or so when she and Lightning splashed through a wide, shallow creek curving along the base of the mountain. She stopped and let the mule take a few sips of the cool running water, and then tied him to a tree so he wouldn't overdo and bring on a gut cramp.

She peeled off her coat and hat, then knelt at the edge of the creek and caught some of the crystal-clear water in her hands. She splashed it against her face, surprised to find that her hat hadn't shielded her skin as well as she'd thought it would. Her cheeks were a little hot from her long walk beneath the springtime sun. She dipped her hand again, with her palm cupped, and lifted it dripping to her lips. As she tilted her head back to drink, she felt his shadow block the hot sun.

"Mr. Calvin," she acknowledged without looking at him.

"Miss Lowell," he answered, and if he was surprised that she'd guessed his identity, he didn't betray it. He carefully balanced his rifle against a tree trunk and then shrugged off his big buffalo coat. He fashioned it into a clumsy bundle which he set on a grass tuft and placed his hat on top. Alice admired neatness in a man, but decided against admitting it aloud, and was glad she'd held her tongue when he rolled his shoulders and then twisted his torso from one side to the other. He sure looked like a man who meant to settle in one spot for a while.

"I seem to recall telling you I wasn't interested in your company."

"I'm not interested in your company either, Miss Lowell. It's pure coincidence that you've followed my favorite route home."

"*Favorite* implies you travel this route with some frequency. And yet from what folks in town say about you, you haven't left the mountain in five years."

She regretted the shrewish outburst the minute it left her lips, but it was too late to call back the words. She knew, somehow, that Jesse would be embarrassed at hearing that folks in town still talked about him. What she didn't understand was why she should be so concerned about hurting his feelings, when he obviously had no qualms about trampling all over hers.

"I like it more than I expected, living up on the mountain," he said. He squatted down next to her and caught water in his huge, cupped hand, and did just as she'd done in splashing it all over his face.

"What's to like about living all alone?" Until her mother died, Alice had seldom spent a moment on her own. These past days, by herself in the shack, had stretched long with a heady mixture of freedom and panic. Part of her enjoyed the solitude. Part of her stirred with restless anxiety, telling her that something was missing from her life.

Well, she'd soon put those disturbing feelings to rest. She'd never be alone again, once she took up her job with the Palmers.

"I don't suppose most people can understand the appeal of pitting your strength against the elements. One puny human being up against everything nature can toss at you. The funny thing is, Miss Lowell—nature plays fair. You know what to expect from a bear, a wolf, a bobcat. You can never be sure about people."

Alice had always suspected there was more to Jesse Calvin's retreat to the hills than guilt over a long-ago street fight. He spoke with the sad resignation of someone who'd learned all about human frailty, the hard way. But she didn't think he knew how much he'd revealed, because he was concentrating so hard on a bunch of lines he was drawing with a stick in the soft mud lining the creek bed.

"Up on the mountain, you grow your food or learn to forage for what you need—or you starve. The occasional trader passes through. But there aren't any neighbors handy to help out with a pound of flour or beans."

"Some neighbors would just as soon steal your beans as lend them to you," she said, letting a handful of water trickle through her fingers. "Apt to criticize your every move, to boot."

He shot her a surprised glance.

She drank again, mostly to keep her mouth occupied so she wouldn't blurt out more inane remarks. She couldn't imagine what Jesse Calvin must think of her—wandering all over while wearing men's clothes, complaining about concerned neighbors. His opinion of her didn't matter, anyway. It was no business of his what she thought, or how she looked. Still, she caught herself smoothing her hair back from her face, even though she knew her cheeks were still flushed from the sun and her quick splashing hadn't done much to clear the dust from her skin.

The water trickling through the rocky creek bed sounded

wonderfully cool and refreshing. She curled her toes in the too-large boots, thinking how nice a good soak would feel.

She stood. "Lightning and I will be making camp here," she said. "I don't want to overdo on my first day. So I guess I'll be saying good-bye to you now."

"What do you know. Another coincidence." Jesse stood as well, towering over her. "I intend to camp here, too. As you pointed out, it's been a long time since I traveled this far, and I don't want to overdo, either."

She didn't believe for a single minute that his presence was purely coincidental. Nor did he look the least bit tired. She would point that out to him, if she could get him to admit they were close to his home. "How far up the mountain do you live?"

"No need for you to worry about that. You won't be visiting."

She caught a breath in surprise at his vehemence. He seemed to realize how abrupt he'd sounded. He cleared his throat and stared off into the pines. "It's nothing personal. I don't let anyone on my land."

"Nobody?" She bit her lip, and forced herself to sound nonchalant. "Not even a wife?"

"No wife."

"Sweetheart?" Alice could scarcely believe her daring, but Jesse Calvin's romantic status had always interested the girls in town, and curiosity had plagued her since meeting him. Not because she herself was attracted to Jesse. No, she wasn't attracted to him at all. Well, maybe a little, in a general way. Any woman would find herself a little breathless in the presence of such a handsome, well-put-together man.

He didn't seem to mind her prying into his romantic attachments, which surprised her, considering how he'd struck out when she'd asked about his home. "The gal I wanted to marry loved Jesse Calvin, horse rancher—not Jesse Calvin, mountain man."

Shame for the damage her brother had wrought flared high.

He'd cost Jesse a lot more than a horse ranch. "Ezra never kept any of his promises," she said. "Not to our mama. Not to me. Not to you."

"Looking back, I know I made a mistake in forcing Ezra to say he'd give me a chance to buy back my land. Forced promises aren't worth anything. The truest promises are the ones a man makes from deep in his soul."

"Are those the kinds of promises you make, Jesse?"

"I don't make promises to anyone anymore," he said. "Except to myself. I've promised myself that nobody will ever get close enough to take anything precious from me, ever again."

"That's why you won't allow anyone on your land."

"That's part of it."

She felt annoyed with him suddenly. Annoyed that he felt so guilty about shooting Ezra all those years ago, when Ezra had done something so much worse to Jesse. Annoyed that Jesse seemed so sure and confident about taking care of himself, and so utterly certain that she wasn't capable of the same.

"Then you're no doubt anxious to get back to your precious land. Someone might trespass."

"My dogs will take care of them."

"Dogs? Well, you'd better hurry back and feed them."

He laughed. "Those hounds can out-hunt me any day. They're fine on their own."

He was sounding more and more as if he meant to follow her for a long time. "You probably have a cow to milk. She'll be in distress since you won't allow a neighbor to come by and take care of her."

"My cow's nursing a new calf. I can help myself to some milk if I have a craving for butter or cream, but the calf does the milking just fine on its own."

"And I suppose the dogs will take care of anyone who tries rustling off your cow."

"Yes, they will. Why, I'd guess I could camp out here for weeks on end without anything going wrong at my place."

She dropped her last lingering hope that his following her had been purely accidental. "Go on, say it—you mean to keep watch over me," she accused him.

He shrugged. But he had not lied to her when he said he no longer made promises. He didn't come right out and say that he would watch over her, even though it was obvious that was exactly what he intended to do.

CHAPTER FOUR

Jesse had just about forgotten how well a woman could make her mood known without saying a word. Alice stormed over to her mule and loosened the saddlebags with angry tugs. With quick, economical movements that nonetheless conveyed her annoyance, she picketed the mule where it could reach water and grass, and then turned her back very definitely on Jesse Calvin while she fashioned a quick meal from her provisions.

She didn't ask him to join her.

He minded more than he knew he ought. He hunkered down near the creek and reached into his pocket for a pouch of pemmican. The greasy crumbled meat reminded him that he carried a jar of his homemade salve in his coat.

"Here," he said, handing the salve to her when she'd finished her meal. "Be careful of the jar. They're hard to come by."

She stared suspiciously at the small container. "What is it?"

"Something for your face." He swallowed hard. "And your neck. You ought to rub it into the part that shows where your shirt isn't buttoned."

She glanced down at the small vee of skin that had reddened

from the sun. The sunburnt state of her skin made it hard to tell if she blushed. Her fingers slid, smooth and silky, against his hand as she accepted the jar from him.

His hand felt emptier, when her touch left him, than the mere absence of the jar's weight could account for.

She grimaced as she sniffed the jar's contents, and Jesse didn't know whether it was from the odor, or from the pain of wrinkling her sunburnt nose.

"Mostly bear grease," he admitted. "And a few other things."

"Guess I don't really want to know what the other things might be."

"Guess not."

She dabbed the salve onto her cheeks and forehead. "A little higher," Jesse instructed. "To the left a little. Now to the right. No, not that far—"

She scowled at him.

"Here, let me." He dipped his fingers into the jar and caught a goodly portion of salve. Standing up close to her like this, she seemed so delicate. He found himself touching her skin with the gentleness one might accord a china doll, and then realized that she was ever so much finer than fired porcelain. The purely medicinal intent of his touch gave way to the sheer pleasure of stroking a woman's skin. He traced the tender places beneath her eyes, and then his hand stroked down, along the curve of her face to the exquisitely soft skin beneath her chin. His hand trembled, and it was one of the hardest things he'd ever had to do in his life to stop his fingers from sliding down, down, to where the sun-blushed vee disappeared inside her shirt.

"I reckon you can handle the rest yourself," he said, his voice hoarse.

"I can," she said, sounding as unsteady as he felt.

Jesse had never considered himself an exceptionally imaginative man, but watching Alice smooth bear grease into her flesh roused all manner of troubling fantasies. He knew he ought to look away, but when he tried, he found himself contemplating the way her breasts pushed against the soft flannel of Ezra's old shirt, and the tight-cinched waist of Ezra's old pants.

"Well?" she said eventually.

He jolted, embarrassed at being caught staring at her.

"Did I get it all, or do you intend to order me around some more?"

"You did just fine," he said. "But now that you mention it, there is something else you ought to do. Strip off those boots and socks and dunk your feet in that there creek."

"I planned on doing that anyway," she said.

Watching her remove her footware was an exercise in torture, and Jesse had to bite his lip to keep from shouting "keep on going" when she finished. She rolled the hems of her pants to her knees and waded out into the shallow creek. The water improved her mood; he heard a muffled giggle when a bird, diving for bugs, sent a fine spray of droplets over her.

"Are you all right?" he called.

"Feels good," she answered. And then, a little grudgingly, she added, "You ought to come wading yourself."

"My boots fit fine."

"Do it just for the fun of it," she said. "You don't always need a reason to do something that feels good."

Jesse could think of a number of things they might do together that would feel downright wonderful. Come to think of it, soaking his feet in ice-cold water might help redirect his mind away from the path it had decided to follow.

And so he found himself standing out in the middle of the creek with his hairy legs bared to the knees, staring fixedly at the top of a tall pine to avoid noticing how water spatters had pasted Alice's clothes against her skin.

Alice laughed. "A little fish just nibbled my ankle."

It didn't seem fair that a stupid fish got to enjoy one of the very diversions that had been uppermost in Jesse's mind. Wading with Alice wasn't cooling his inappropriate thoughts at all.

He sloshed back toward the creek bank. To his dismay, she followed right behind.

"What will we do next?" she asked while her hands busied themselves with pulling her clinging clothing away from her body.

"Do? We?" His mouth had gone dry.

"Well, if we're going to camp here for the night, together, we ought to find some way to pass the time. Nothing too strenuous, since you're so tired and all."

"There's nothing to do in a camp." Jesse had seldom uttered such a bald-faced lie. He could think of a dozen things he'd like to do with Alice Lowell, none of them in the least bit appropriate for a man who'd taken on the responsibility of acting as her guardian.

"I guess we'll just have to talk, then."

"Talk?" God, this could lead to trouble, too. Jesse began mightily regretting his pure-hearted impulses. "Talking is women's sport."

"Talking's not a sport. Talking's important."

She reached up and did something to her hair that made it cascade down around her shoulders with a luxurious bounce. It looked cooler and more slippery than the creek water. Jesse jammed his hands in his pockets, when he really wanted to plunge his fingers into the wealth of her hair.

"Talking isn't necessary." Jesse proved his point by meaning two things at once, though he fervently hoped she didn't grasp the full meaning. Alice Lowell shouldn't understand that a man and woman didn't have to talk, all the time, to thoroughly enjoy one another's company. "Chattering doesn't accomplish much of anything."

She made a disbelieving sniff and lifted her hair at the back of her neck and let it bounce back down again. She shook her head and her hair billowed out like a silken cloud, and then she tucked it behind her ears.

Jesse decided he better get her talking quick, so she would stop fooling with herself. Watching her graceful movements made him wish he could fool with her instead. His mind raced, seeking an acceptable topic for conversation.

"Take your asparagus hunt, for example. You've told me at least three times that you have to find asparagus to make some kind of magic soup. Well, that doesn't make any sense. There's nothing magical about soup. I don't mean any disrespect toward your mama, but I can't help thinking you mistook fever ravings for the truth."

She grew still. She gripped her hands together, which accomplished Jesse's goal of turning her immobile. But instead of bringing him relief, her frozen stillness made him want to gather her close in his arms and warm her back into motion.

"This one special soup is magical," Alice whispered after a moment's silence. "It's made up of all the things that come to life in an early spring garden—tiny onions, spinach, asparagus—and a few things left over from the year before, like flour and carrots and dried dill. That way, the wealth of the past is tied to the promise of the future."

Her words shook him; not so long ago, he'd been thinking how his asparagus patch was the one link he'd maintained between his old life and the new. And now with Alice talking about tying the wealth of the past to the promise of the future, he wanted to blurt out that he understood the concept all too well. But he couldn't tell her about his asparagus patch. He couldn't.

"Nothing magical about gardening. Digging and weeding are hard, dirty work." He'd always considered the time spent toiling in the dirt to be a necessary evil. Now that he thought about it, though, he realized that for some people a garden might be more than yanking weeds and swatting mosquitoes. People who had wives and kids to feed, maybe, could look on the endless gardening tasks as a link between the past and future.

He'd never understood the pleasure some folks took in gardening. But then he'd never looked on the chore through Alice's eyes.

"Seems to me that soup has enough vegetables that you could do without the asparagus," said Jesse.

"Oh, no—the asparagus is the most important ingredient. Asparagus implies commitment, you see. It can grow in the wild, but a really good patch of asparagus requires care. The plants come back year after year. You have to dig a deep, wide trench and enrich the soil with leaves and such. And you have to wait for the pleasure of enjoying your asparagus. You can't pick too many spears the first few years or you'll stunt their production forever."

Jesse let her tell him all these things he already knew, for the sheer pleasure of watching her speak . . . and to avoid admitting that he'd done exactly as she described when planting his own patch. He ought to tell her, here and now, that they could dispense with the hunt and go straight to his cabin, where he could help her harvest what she needed from the first shoots poking from the ground.

The wealth of the past, tied to the promise of the future.

But that would mean willingly bringing someone onto his property. Impossible. His land was the one place in the world where he didn't ever have to look another person in the eye and admit the truth about himself: That Jesse Calvin valued *things* more than he valued human life.

He'd been so crazed to hear that Ezra had sold his horse ranch that he'd shot him. And he'd aimed to kill. If he hadn't been as blind drunk as Ezra, the bullet would've hit Ezra's heart instead of tearing out a chunk of his arm.

He guarded his new home with zeal. But that wild mountain land protected him in return.

There was no way on God's earth that he would ever allow Alice Lowell, of all people, onto his property.

He'd never considered himself a particularly imaginative man, so it was a shock to him when his mind started flashing images to him. Images of Alice, with her hair hanging loose and moving softly in the wind, singing while she gathered the wealth from the past and the promise of the future from his garden. Alice sitting across the table from him, laughing and talking while they ate home-grown produce for dinner. Alice, stepping half-dressed from the bedroom, with a sweet-smelling rose tucked behind one ear. . . .

Good Lord, if he was thinking thoughts like this now, after spending only a few hours in her company, what would happen if she actually visited his place? The unaccusing quiet of his cabin, the safe emptiness of his private retreat, would be haunted with the memory of her presence.

No, he couldn't tell her about his asparagus.

He couldn't take the chance that his only refuge might become a place of loneliness and misery.

"Now you see, that's exactly what I mean about talking not accomplishing anything," he said. "You tell me this soup is magical, and then you give me a list of everyday, ordinary ingredients. None of that stuff sounds magical at all to me."

"You have to prepare the soup with your heart's desire uppermost in your mind, and while you're eating it you have to wish for your dreams to come true." Alice's expression took on a dreamy cast; her lips curved in a secret smile. And then she started, and shook her head, as if to chase her pleasant thoughts away. "I guess it does sound a little crazy."

"A sane person wouldn't expect that this soup will grant you your heart's desire."

"It . . . it doesn't seem likely."

"Then why are you so set on making it?"

Her chin tipped. "I told you—I made a deathbed promise. Unlike some people, I always keep my promises."

But there was more in her eyes, more in the set of her shoulders, than determination to honor a vow. Alice had the look of a woman quivering with expectancy, almost as if, deep down inside, she believed that making and eating this magical soup would truly bring about her heart's desire.

A desire that, for all her blathering about meaningful conversation, she didn't see fit to share with him.

He wondered what desires a woman like Alice held close in

her heart, what dreams she cherished, what hopes she treasured. It seemed wrong to be plagued by such curiosity when she obviously didn't care to let him in on her secrets. It seemed even more troubling that he should wonder such things about a woman he barely knew, a woman he meant to exclude from his life the minute he felt his obligation to her had been fulfilled.

Coming down off his mountain had been a big mistake. Indulging his curiosity about Alice Lowell would be an even bigger one.

He heaved a huge, grizzly bear of a sigh, one designed to discourage further discussion. "So we're back to where we started. This whole conversation didn't accomplish a thing."

But as he walked away from her, he knew he'd spoken a lie right out loud. That brief conversation had challenged him to look inside himself. He'd had to admit to himself that it was shame over betraying a flaw in his character, not shame over shooting Ezra Lowell, that had sent him into hiding for five long years. He didn't think he'd ever had a more meaningful conversation in his life.

Alice knew she ought to just let him walk away. She ought to pray he kept on walking right out of the camp, leaving her to blessed solitude, the way she'd wanted from the first.

Instead, she found herself tagging along after him like a puppy eager for another stroke of its master's hand. That touch of his, slippery with bear grease and meant only to soothe and heal, had roused a confusion within her unlike anything she'd ever known. She wanted him to touch her again . . . she was afraid to let him touch her again. Her usually sensible mind urged her to let him take his surly self off into the pines, while her newly awakened woman's cravings demanded that she stay close enough to breathe in his scent, to bask in his warmth, to lean into his strength.

Jesse's strength was something new to her—not his sheer physical strength, for she'd always been aware that men possessed more physical power than women. She'd never before realized, though, that one could find peace and comfort just from being in the presence of someone who wasn't drunk. Someone who had his mind made up about what he wanted to do, and who took his responsibilities seriously. Someone like Jesse.

How strange, that she should believe so implicitly that he was dependable. He'd never made her an actual promise. He just . . . did things.

"Ouch!" Something sharp pierced the sole of her bare foot, and she instinctively caught the foot in her hand while she hopped to a stop on the other. Jesse's big feet probably had the horned consistency of a callous, judging by the way he strode unflinchingly along the same rock-strewn path. At her outcry, he paused and glanced back over his shoulder.

"Did something bite you?" True concern marked his suddenly rigid stance.

"No. Just stepped on a sharp-edged stone."

With a few ground-eating strides, he came back to her. He crouched down and stared at her foot.

"You're sure it wasn't a thorn, or a sliver of wood? A clean cut, and not a puncture?"

He seemed unduly concerned, Alice thought. Not like herself. For some reason, she'd relaxed completely, now that he was close enough to touch.

"Let me see." He reached for her injured foot, and she hopped back. Much as she'd wanted him to touch her again, she feared that letting him get his hands on her would only intensify those inappropriate cravings she'd developed.

"It's nothing. Just a little cut."

"You're out in the wilderness, Miss Lowell. There is no such thing as 'just a little cut.' Any injury can fester, and out here there aren't any doctors to tend to you. You'd think a grown woman would know better than to get her feet all nicked up."

His criticism stung, especially since she knew he was right.

She had only her inexplicable craving to be near him to blame for traipsing over the mountainside in her bare feet.

"I don't exactly walk around without shoes all the time, you know."

"I can see that." And before she could protest, he scooped her up into his arms. She had to wrap her arms around his neck and hold on tight. He headed back to the camp.

"Put me down! What do you think you're doing?"

"I'm taking you to water."

"I can walk. I'm not hurt bad at all."

"You need to clean that wound, not track it through the dirt. I knew your feet would cause me trouble sooner or later."

That was the sort of comment Alice figured she ought to take exception to, except it felt so good to be slammed up against Jesse's chest while his strong arms supported her at the back and knees. She could feel the steady thump of his heartbeat against her breast where it lay mashed up against his ribs. He felt incredibly firm, and yet soft, like a layer of rough velvet covering steel. Ezra's soft, doughy skin hadn't felt the least bit like Jesse's when she'd had to prod and poke her drunken brother into action. A few stray golden-brown curls poked from the neck of his shirt. She wanted to touch them, to twine her fingers through them, but doing so would mean loosening her hold around Jesse's neck, and she didn't want to do that.

What she'd like to do, Alice realized with dismay, was stay cuddled in his arms, exactly like this, for a long, long time.

She had to do something, anything, to drive that notion from her mind. "So, that's what you think about," she said, resolving to retreat into mindless chatter.

"Huh?"

"My feet. You spend all your time worrying about the trouble my feet will cause."

He paused at the edge of the creek. "No, ma'am, I only spent about a minute noticing your boots and figuring out your feet were going to be a problem. You have other . . . parts that cause me considerable more worry."

Take **4 FREE** Books!

Zebra created its convenient Home Subscription Service s
you'll be sure to get the hottest new romances delivered
each month right to your doorstep — usually before they
are available in book stores. Just to show you how
convenient Zebra Home Subscription Service is, we woul
like to send you 4 Zebra Historical Romances as a FREE
gift. You receive a gift worth up to $24.96 — absolutely
FREE. There's no extra charge for shipping and handling
There's no obligation to buy anything - ever!

Save Even More with Free Home Delivery!

Accept your FREE gift and each month we'll deliver 4 bran
new titles as soon as they are published. They'll be yours
to examine FREE for 10 days. Then if you decide to keep
the books, you'll pay the preferred subscriber's price of jus
$4.20 per title. That's $16.80 for all 4 books for a savings
of up to 32% off the publisher's price! What's more...$16.8
is your total price...there is no additional charge for the
convenience of home delivery. Remember, you are under r
obligation to buy any of these books at any time! If you ar
not delighted with them, simply return them and owe
nothing. But if you enjoy Zebra Historical Romances as
much as we think you will, pay the special preferred
subscriber rate of only $16.80 each month and save over
$8.00 off the bookstore price!

She wondered if it were her imagination, or if his arms really tightened around her, holding her infinitesimally closer for the space of a few heartbeats before he let her legs slowly slide down the length of his body. And even when her troublesome feet were safely planted in the cold water, he kept one arm tight around her shoulder for just a little longer. Of its own accord, her body pressed back, enjoying the feel of having him so close against her. He drew a deep, shuddering breath, and she could feel his pulse quicken just before he stepped away.

She didn't know why she felt like smiling. Or why it suddenly seemed like a very fine thing, to be a woman possessing a number of worrisome . . . parts.

CHAPTER FIVE

Alice pretended to be resting while Jesse yanked on his boots and then shouldered his rifle. "Eat when you're hungry," he said.

"You bet I'll eat when I'm hungry," Alice retorted toward his back as he left the camp. She thought she'd made it clear that she wanted no part of being the designated cook and cleanup person.

She meant to stick to her resolve, too, even though Jesse didn't seem to have much in the way of supplies besides that boring old pemmican. Considering how concerned he was over her health, it seemed just a tad small of her to refuse to share her provisions. He had, after all, examined her foot and carried her to the creek, then tended her wound with a concern she found oddly touching. Cooking him one meal, strictly prompted by gratitude, wouldn't be all that much of a bother.

She pushed those thoughts away as Jesse disappeared into the woods. Their small campsite immediately felt empty and echoing. The pines appeared almost black, the quiet so profound that she wouldn't be surprised to learn that everything on the mountain had been buried in a layer of golden pine needles. A strange heaviness filled her. Despite her sassy assertions about eating when she pleased, she doubted she'd feel hungry any time soon.

Maybe, by the time he returned, she'd have worked up an appetite.

Jesse knew she wasn't accustomed to camp cooking. He might poke fun at her, but he wouldn't be surprised if she accidentally prepared just a little more than any woman could possibly eat. He might not think she'd gone to any extra effort if she casually offered him a few bites of her food, and told him she meant to throw it away if he didn't eat it. That way it wouldn't look as though she'd gone to any extra trouble, or that she'd backed down from her no-cook, no-clean stance.

"I swear, Lightning, I'm acting just like a smitten miss planning on preparing a box lunch for her beau," she grumbled to the mule as she donned her socks and boots. "I ought to be hoping Jesse Calvin starves to death out in those woods and never comes back to this campsite again."

But she found herself hoping the very opposite thing. She wandered along the creek, alternately studying the ground for asparagus shoots and gazing about at the beauty of the wilderness. Hawks circled far above, graceful shapes soaring against an azure sky. Wind ruffled the tall pines, creating a whimsical impression that the feathery branches were waving to her, welcoming her into their midst. She had imagined herself spending hours drinking in such beauty. Instead, she found herself glancing back over her shoulder at the barren campsite, again and again, wondering where Jesse had gone.

He hadn't promised to come back.

Eat when you're hungry, he'd said. That curt command might have been his last conversation with her.

Returning to the empty site held no appeal. Nor could she summon any enthusiasm for following a bend in the creek that would take her out of sight of the camp.

She heard the far-off crack of a rifle shot. "Jesse!" She

turned to run to him, to see if he was all right. A second bullet crashed, and the echoes of both shots mingled and bounced against her ears. She realized she had no idea where to look. "Silly," she called herself out loud. "He took his rifle. He went hunting. He probably shot a deer or something."

He hadn't promised to come back.

"Oh, this is ridiculous," she muttered. She had to find that asparagus and rid herself of Jesse Calvin's presence. She was the type of woman who took care of people. She was probably mistaking her naturally caring nature for something different, something that made her afraid Jesse might be worming his way into her heart. She took one last look back at the campsite, and, after sucking in a long, deep breath, left it behind her.

She had some hunting of her own to do.

It would help, she thought, if she knew exactly what new-grown asparagus looked like, but all she had to go on was the verbal descriptions her mother had painted for her. Mama had said a person could find asparagus in a sunny spot, poking right up through the ground with no leaves to announce its presence. She might think at first that those tender young shoots were nothing more than extra-thick, fast-growing blades of grass, but upon closer look she'd realize that the asparagus burst forth from its wintry hibernation with an unequalled, delicate, first-green-of-spring beauty.

Unequalled beauty, the first sign of life in a desolate landscape . . . a magical ingredient for a magical soup that would help a woman realize her heart's desire . . .

If she found asparagus alongside this creek, she could no doubt hunt down some wild onions and some leafy edible weed to take the place of spinach. After all, asparagus was the only essential ingredient—she could find substitutes for everything else. She could whip up a pot of that special soup before Jesse came back to camp.

Good Lord—what was happening to her? She'd sent him on his way with the clear impression that she didn't intend sharing anything to eat with him. Now she was scheming up ways to spoon-feed him the soup that was so special to her that she'd vowed to devote three weeks of her life to finding the necessary ingredients!

All this inner turmoil, and she didn't know if he'd even come back to her.

He will. Something inside her spoke up for him, something deep and secret that held utter confidence in Jesse Calvin.

It must be the pure mountain air, she decided, that was turning her a little rattle-brained. Fresh air, and the almost giddy sense of freedom that came from not having anyone to take care of, at least for the moment, could give any woman an excuse for acting a little silly. Soon enough she'd be mired back into sober respectability. No more men's britches, no more mules, no more mountain man lifting her in his arms and stroking her foot with tender care. Utter desolation swept through her, so quick and so powerful that she almost cried aloud from the force of it slamming against her heart.

And then she saw it. A tree, its branches tipped green and red with budding leaves, sheltered a few delicate curls of green poking from the dark, rich earth.

Asparagus. Had to be. Her search was over. She could pick a few stems and break camp. Go back home, wait out the time in Dry Falls until her new job started.

Her heart thudded, heavy and hard, the way it did after intense disappointment.

She stooped down to study the emerging plants and her spirit lightened a little. Her mama had been quite adamant about the asparagus standing straight and tall—these little fellers curled like snail shells at the tips and were sort of hairy, to boot. They might not be asparagus shoots at all.

Jesse would know. He'd said he enjoyed asparagus. That meant he knew what it looked like.

She carefully noted landmarks to make sure she'd find the spot again and hurried back to the camp. Yes, Jesse might know whether or not she'd found the right thing. His knowledge was the reason she felt so anxious to find him back in camp with the mule and the supplies. Yes, his knowledge of plant lore was what she craved, was what set her running, sore foot and all. Hope, that Jesse could confirm that she'd found asparagus. Nothing more.

Jesse shifted in his tree, wincing at both the discomfort of his perch and the knowledge that he'd turned out to be no better than a goldarned cat, slinking around and spying on a helpless critter. The critter, in this case, being one Alice Lowell, and he crouching like a tomcat with his head swinging back and forth following every move she made. Watching her for hours, watching her rush back into camp with such speed that he'd almost abandoned his lookout to make sure nothing was wrong. Watching her simmering excitement gradually fade into disappointment, and then eventually into a firm-lipped determination as she built a fire and began preparing her dinner.

A fanciful-minded fellow could study those shifting expressions and begin to believe she'd been disappointed at not finding him there.

Well, he'd had to watch her, he rationalized, without her being aware of it to make sure her foot wasn't bothering her. She was just stubborn enough to pretend everything was fine if she thought it would ward off his concern. He'd never known a soul who resented attention more, despite needing it so bad that the need all but oozed from her.

Of course, she no doubt thought she hid that need. Could be most people didn't notice it. Could be he recognized it because he'd spent a fair amount of time hiding a similar need within himself.

He snorted aloud, annoyed at the direction his thoughts had been taking of late. He hadn't done this much thinking about his own self in years. Odd, how a person who chose to live all alone found it easiest to survive by not thinking much about himself. He wondered how long it would take him to recapture that comfortable state of oblivion after he'd left Alice behind and returned, all by himself, to his home in the mountains. He waited for the usual wave of homesickness to sweep through him, the way it had done when he'd started down the mountain trail.

The wave didn't come.

She'd taunted him about his dogs and his cow. Odd, how he didn't miss his critters at all, either. They could get along just fine without him.

Alice needed him. She didn't think so, but she did.

He hadn't felt needed for a long time. Not since Mary Grace had informed him that the cabin he'd built on his mountain didn't suit her as well as the ranch house he'd lost to Ezra Lowell. He realized then that it was what he'd owned, not himself, that she needed. He'd heard Mary Grace found herself another horse rancher, with a fine big house.

Jesse wondered what Alice would think of his house.

Mary Grace's desertion had hurt less than Jesse expected. He halfway understood how she might value a ranch and house over a man. He'd shot a man, after all, over a ranch and a house.

He hadn't thought about Mary Grace, or all that he'd lost, for a long time. His regrets, and his secrets, had started escaping about the time he'd first heard Alice Lowell singing.

Chores would pass easier, back home, if he had some singing to listen to, to set up a rhythm for his work. . . .

No. Alice wasn't welcome there—nobody was. His mountain home was his retreat. But home, which he'd expected to tug at his heart every minute of every day, seemed to have lost a good bit of its pull over these past couple of days.

He didn't want to even begin exploring the reasons for that. He slid from his branch and caught up the two rabbits that he'd shot, and went to join Alice near the campfire.

She glanced up when his foot crunched a brittle twig, and a look of sheer, radiant welcome blasted him with so much heat that it made him ache inside. He couldn't remember any ever greeting him with such joy. It stopped him dea tracks, and God alone knew what sort of sappy grin it pasted on his face, because something in the way he looked seemed to make her realize what she'd done. She flushed, and looked down at the ground, and when she looked up again that happiness at seeing him had smoothed into a blank indifference that smote his heart with the force of a hammer.

He yearned to see her eyes light with welcome, for him, again. Yearned with a power and craving that made all his former homesickness seem less troublesome than a gnat buzzing around his face.

"If I'd known rabbits came that way out here in the mountains, I'd have come hunting out here myself," she said, nodding toward the game hanging from his hand.

"Uh." He didn't know what she meant. "Rabbits are rabbits, no matter where you shoot them, I would say."

"Mmmm . . . but back in Dry Falls, they don't come skinned and gutted like those two." She cocked a brow. "Don't tell me you cleaned them out in the woods to spare my delicate sensibilities?"

That's exactly what Jesse had done, but he shrugged and pretended otherwise. "I like to get the messy parts over with, that's all."

"Uh-huh. And did you get both of those rabbits with one shot?"

"No. Took two shots."

"I've heard tell that a really good shot can bring down two at once."

"Never happen," Jesse said, although he'd heard some brag the same thing.

"Then you must be awful hungry, to hunt down two rabbits for your dinner."

"I don't mean to eat both of them," he said. "One's for me, and one's for—" He snapped his mouth shut before he could say *you,* because her chin had tipped up and anger snapped in her eyes. Women. Smiling at a man one minute, ready to crack him in the jaw the next, and all because he'd brought her some fresh meat. "Later," he finished.

She blushed, and then looked embarrassed. She fooled with the cans she'd set next to the fire and surreptitiously slid one back into the pack, as if she'd drawn it out for him despite her declaration that she wouldn't share with him, and now regretted that impulse.

"I'll fetch some wood for that fire," he said. "That is, if you don't mind my helping out."

"I don't mind," she said, her voice small, and with a little hitch in it as if she choked back a sob. "Could you . . . I mean, would you mind if I came with you while you got the wood? And if we went over that way to pick it up?" She pointed downstream, where the creek meandered into the forest.

"I reckon that's as good a place as any to find wood," he said, even though plenty of deadfall lay only a few paces away.

"Well, yes, but also—I think I might've found some asparagus. I'd like you to look at it and give me your opinion."

Jesse's heart plummeted straight to his feet. "That's good. That you found asparagus, I mean. You won't have to spend all your free time hunting it down, I guess."

"I guess not." She sounded dispirited.

He walked a step behind her as she led him to her find and found it hard to keep from reaching out to touch her when she lurched to the side at a rough spot, when she tripped over a rock at another. The walk was torture, not only from watching her from behind, but from wondering why she'd decided he was an asparagus expert. Could it be that she somehow knew he had a nice little patch of the stuff up at his house and was just waiting for him to invite her to gather some? "Over there," she said at last, pointing toward the base of a tree.

She knelt and plucked something from the ground, and then came back to him and rested it gently in his palm.

"Hell, that's not asparagus," he said, surprised at the lilt in his voice. "That's nothing but a fern frond."

"A fern frond?" She looked up at him, delight dancing in her beautiful eyes.

"Fern frond."

"You're sure?"

He figured she ought to be sounding a lot more disappointed than happy, but she sure had the look and the smile of a person who'd just been handed a gift. "Cross my heart," he said solemnly, and made the motion to go along with the words. Somehow, the fern frond tangled her hand with his as he placed it against his heart. She let it rest there, warm and soft, for the space of a few heartbeats.

"So I have to keep looking," she said, and it sounded as if it were hard for her to speak.

"Yeah."

He expected she might droop at the confirmation; instead, she made an excited little hop. She lost her footing yet again and grabbed onto his arms for support. "I'm sorry," she said. "I'm not usually so clumsy. It's these boots."

With her squeezing his muscles like that, his darned arms acted as if they were caught on pulleys and jerked forward until his hands gripped her around the waist. "I know."

She made another little movement, her waist bending lithe and firm within his grip. Without thinking much about what he was doing, Jesse lifted her in the air like some damned fool lovesick dope. He smiled up at her while her hair cascaded down over her shoulders and tickled his nose and chin.

She laughed, a joyous, ringing sound that filled those empty old woods with vibrant life. He laughed, too, a sound so rusty and disused that it might've been an old bear growling from a cave, but the sound seemed to delight her even more. He spun them in a circle.

"Stop it, Jesse!" she shrieked, not sounding as if she meant it at all. Hearing his name come from her lips did something odd to his heart. He didn't know what was wrong with him. He spun even faster, until she gripped onto him tighter and clamped her legs around his waist, hanging on for all she was worth. He felt her core hot against his belly, and desire shot through him so swift and so hard that it stopped him in his tracks.

"Thank you," she gasped, still giggling. "I was afraid you'd make me so dizzy I wouldn't be able to look for asparagus anymore."

He wanted to hear her say his name again. He wished she would burst into song again, but with full voice and unafraid of making too much noise. He wished she would call back what she'd said about hunting asparagus. Her declaration was a reminder that she wasn't out in these woods, ready to climb this mountain, because she wanted to be with him. She had a purpose in being there—a dumb purpose, but a purpose nonetheless, and he had no business holding her and breathing in her scent and reveling in her laughter.

"Sorry," he said.

He loosened his hold on her waist, but didn't completely let go of her—he couldn't lest she fall. She instinctively hung on, tightening her legs around his waist, pressing her breasts into his chest. Waves of bliss rocketed through him. She let out a small, wordless sound, breathy and filled with startled pleasure. Her lips were only inches from his, parted slightly, lush and full and so kissable that he had to grind his teeth together to keep from swooping down and plundering her sweetness.

His breath stirred a stray tendril of her sun-scented hair. He wished his fingers had the freedom to touch her, too, to stroke across her smooth skin and wind themselves into the silken strands of her hair, to tilt her head back and claim her lips.

She held on, wrapped all around him, and every male instinct within him recognized that she was confused, uncertain . . . and interested in the sensations that had to be sweeping through her body. He need only press her closer, kiss her the way he ached to kiss her. He could savor her taste and the feel of her while he carried her to that soft, ferny place beneath the tree and loved her until she screamed from the pleasure.

But initiating Alice Lowell to the joys of lovemaking had

not been his intent when he left his mountain sanctuary. He closed his eyes, forcing himself to remember. He owed her. He'd vowed to see she was protected and cared for. He'd harmed Alice Lowell enough without taking from her the one thing a woman had the right to hold precious and sacred. That gift was hers to bestow upon the man she would marry someday.

A man Jesse suddenly hated with every fiber of his being.

"I have to tend to those rabbits," he said.

"Oh!" She flushed, as if suddenly realizing for the first time that she clung to him like a kitten caught in a tall tree. She let her legs drop to the ground, and he wanted to bend them back around his waist and tell her to stay just as she was. Her arms still clung to his neck, and he had to bend a little, because he was so much taller than she, but all too soon she broke that hold, too, and he was left standing there, all alone.

Alone, solitary, the way he'd wanted to be. It had never before seemed so very lonely.

Funny, Alice thought, how touching a man, being held by a man, could act like strong drink in a person's body. Or at least the way her brother Ezra had claimed strong drink affected him—one sip, and he had to have more, more, more until he was a dizzied, babbling wreck.

Alice felt exactly that way now. She had reveled in Jesse's touch, wanting more, wanting harder, wanting . . . She didn't know what she wanted. Only that letting go of him had been the opposite of what she'd wanted to do, and that now she lay in her bedroll on her own side of the campfire, craving more of his touch. Aching to drown herself in the feel of him until her senses swum and her mind went blank and all was oblivion except for the reality of him.

Something was wrong with her, terribly wrong.

"Jesse?" she called softly.

He made a sound, not a word exactly, but enough to let her know he wasn't asleep.

Her heart hammered. She couldn't flat-out ask, "Why do I feel this way with you?" And so she said nothing.

"Is your foot bothering you?" he asked into her paralyzed silence.

"No, my foot's fine. I just wondered . . ." She swallowed, and tried to find the courage to ask him to come close, but she could not summon it. "I just wondered why you left Dry Falls. I know there's more to it than the shooting of my brother."

He was silent for so long that she feared he'd fallen asleep. But eventually she heard him stir in his bedroll. "Do you know why I shot your brother?"

"Because he cheated you at cards. He stole your ranch from you."

"Not exactly," Jesse said. "Ezra won that card game fair and square. He cheated on his word. He swore he'd give me a chance to buy back my ranch. But no more than two days later, he'd turned around and sold it for less than half its worth to old man Keppel."

"For drinking money," Alice whispered. Her brother had never told her that part of the story, but she had no trouble believing it. "You had every right to shoot him."

"No, I didn't. It's never right for a person to value possessions more highly than a human life, but that's what I did when I aimed my gun at your brother's heart."

"But Jesse—your land. Most men love their land with a passion."

"Yeah, I loved my land." He gave a short laugh. "Well, I learned a lesson that day. I learned never to let anything become so important to me that I'd do something crazy if I lost it."

"Anything?" she asked. "Or any*one*?" She held her breath, waiting for his reply.

"Both," he said. "You can't let passion overrule your common sense. I looked down on your brother's blood soaking into the dirt and knew that if I'd gone that crazy over losing some land, there was no telling what I'd do if I lost a person I loved. I vowed then and there to cut passion out of my life altogether."

"A person can't live that way."

"It's easier. And safer."

"That's not true."

"Then why are you going to cage yourself up in a sickroom like some captured meadowlark?"

He sounded angry, and she couldn't understand either his anger or his talk about meadowlarks.

"I'll always know where I stand," she said. "I'll have a place to live and food to fill my belly. I won't have to put my soul into earning those things—only my labor. My heart won't break from hoping and dreaming that things will get better. You don't know what it's like to believe in promises, only to have them broken again and again."

"So in other words, you're not taking any chances. You like blaming your brother for making your life miserable, and from now on you'll be able to blame your job for doing the same."

"That's not true! I like taking care of people. And I need that job."

Her protest rang out against the quiet, and the mountain threw her words back at her, daring her to acknowledge the truth.

"I guess there's all kinds of places for a person to hide," Jesse said. "Some of us pick mountains. Some of us hide in plain sight."

"Good night, Jesse," she whispered. She couldn't continue this conversation. Her belly clenched, and she shook from head to toe. For so many years she'd resented the demands her family had placed upon her. She'd dreamed of the life that could have been hers if she'd been born into different circumstances. But now that she had the freedom to do whatever she chose, she'd proven herself to be a coward. Instead of striking out in search of happiness, she'd settled for safety. Instead of searching for excitement, she'd settled for routine.

The rest of her life would be no more fulfilling than the first part had been. And she had only herself to blame.

"Good night, Alice."

Jesse lay within reach, a man who had vowed to cut passion out of his life. And he was right about her—she had done the same, but without the clear-headed understanding of what she was doing. She'd arranged a life for herself that meant always burying her hopes and dreams. He alone, of all the people she'd ever known, had recognized it at once.

She felt utterly alone. And filled with the sinking sensation that for the rest of her life, no matter how many people she might coax and bully and tend, she would always feel frigid and empty inside. She was like a pile of kindling heaped in a stove, capable of burning, but doomed to stay forever cold without a spark to ignite her into flame.

CHAPTER SIX

Jesse spent a sleepless night, tossing and turning with a restlessness that could not be relieved. It seemed that every rock in the territory lay under his bedroll, gouging into flesh that had become extraordinarily sensitive since hoisting a certain young woman in his arms. The physical discomforts were even more difficult to endure because of the devilish voice inside him that whispered throughout the night, reminding him that right across the other side of the campfire lay the softest pleasure known to man.

Alice. Just as determined as he to shield her heart from caring too much about anything.

He'd never told a soul how humiliated he'd been when he'd bared his weakness for all the world to see. Jesse Calvin, a man so consumed by love for his land that he'd been willing to shoot another man to death.

But he'd told Alice all about it as easily as if she'd asked him to merely snap his fingers.

And instead of making him want to avoid her, this ease of talking with her made him want to hold her close.

Talking's important, she had said. He'd spent five *years* without engaging in conversation more meaningful than establishing how many wolf pelts ought to be bartered for a pound of coffee. He couldn't spend more than five *minutes* talking to Alice without baring his innermost secrets.

Except for the truth about his garden. He still hadn't mentioned that asparagus patch of his. No reason on earth why keeping that particular secret ought to make him fight with his conscience throughout the interminable hours of darkness. Alice Lowell had no right to walk on his land, no right to pick his asparagus. He had no obligation to provide her with the ingredients for her magic soup. He lay as rigid as a fence post, with his hands clenched into fists at his side, listening to Alice's soft breathing and the occasional low, womanly murmurs she made as she moved in her sleep.

One night like this, he could survive. He'd survived worse. But he didn't know if he could endure two, and the mere thought of prolonging this ache for three nights . . . well, impossible. For the sake of his own sanity, not to mention Alice's reputation, he had to get some asparagus into her hands and send her back home to make her damn-fool magic soup. But what if there was no asparagus to be found? Was maintaining the sanctity of his home more important than helping Alice fulfill that deathbed promise she'd made?

He could, in his mind's eye, see those tender young asparagus shoots growing in his garden. More than one man required. And all of it destined for plain, ordinary eating when she wanted to make magic from it. Maybe it wouldn't be so bad to take Alice there, to the garden. He wouldn't have to allow her in his house, of course. Just the garden.

He'd once caught Hank Barlow, a fellow recluse, snooping near his garden. A load of rock salt had sent the old man scampering, never to return, especially since Jesse had called out loud and clear that the next time he caught Hank on his land he wouldn't bother changing ammunition. He'd been so enraged by Hank's intrusion that he'd gritted his teeth for hours.

But maybe he could give Alice a few minutes to pick what she needed.

He waited for rage to build in him at the notion. Instead of rage, he felt a tender yearning to hear singing echo through the air. Somehow, a singing woman, all starry-eyed with the ridiculous notion that eating soup would help her find her heart's desire, didn't rouse his territorial instincts at all. If anything, thinking of Alice on his land made him wonder if he'd ever be able to let her go.

Wouldn't it be something, if her soup really could help a person achieve his or her heart's desire?

He broke out in a sweat despite the coolness of the night.

The first bands of pink lightening the sky had never felt so welcome.

Jesse sprang from his bedroll well before actual sunup and busied himself with coffee making. He hoped Alice would continue sleeping, but she bolted upright as if she, too, had been waiting for an excuse to leave her bed. He glanced over at her and almost dropped the coffee pot. He'd very studiously avoided looking at her the night before, so he hadn't realized that she'd changed clothes.

"What are you wearing?"

"My nightgown, of course."

"I never heard of anybody deliberately wearing anything so ridiculous on a campout."

She glanced down at the garment he found so offensive. A ribbon threaded through the lace at her neck, but only for decoration, for the gown's neckline dipped a lot lower than the clothes she usually wore, down past the sun-reddened vee, baring the merest hint of creamy white swells to dawn's pink glow. She'd pinned up her hair in a loose knot, and as he watched she stretched, gave a ladylike yawn, and shook her hair free of its restraint. She sent him a sleepy smile.

"I understand. You're grouchy in the morning. Mama said most men are."

He couldn't form words. He grunted something that he hoped

sounded like a greeting and pretended great concentration upon the coffeepot.

He had to end this trip. Had to get her off his mountain before every tree, every blade of grass, every rising of the sun taunted him with the memory of how much more beautiful and precious it all seemed with Alice Lowell in its midst.

He couldn't take her to his place. He couldn't.

But he also knew every inch of the surrounding area, and he knew there wasn't a sprout of asparagus to be found in the wild places. He wasn't so sure about the territories staked out by his fellow mountain recluses. Maybe Fate had had a good reason for reminding him of Hank Barlow. Hank's shack was maybe half a day's journey from their camp. And even if Hank had no asparagus, he'd be a welcome presence, providing he didn't kill them both on sight. Another person might help dilute the tension that sizzled into life every time Jesse realized how utterly alone he and Alice were, together.

"I have an idea," he said. "I know a place where we might find your asparagus."

"Oh." She blinked, her smile dissolving. "That's . . . that's nice."

"Stop here," Jesse ordered, after they'd been traveling through the woods, uphill, for more than three hours.

Alice nodded, too tired to speak. Her ankles felt wobbly and her legs shook, worn out from the unaccustomed climbing. Her shoulders cramped from the effort of dragging Lightning along behind them, but she'd refused Jesse's repeated offers to take over control of the mule. Her calf muscles ached from the effort of walking in the overly large boots. Jesse had several times inquired about her feet, seeming to worry about that stupid little rock puncture that she'd had, but she'd stoutly declared herself fine to deflect his concern.

A girl could get used to having a man like Jesse worried about her welfare. She couldn't afford to let that happen. She took care of other people; nobody took care of her. She'd learned that lesson long ago, and it hurt too much to hope it would ever change.

She started to untie the packs, figuring they would make camp now that Jesse had ordered a halt to their travels, but his arm shot out and pushed her against a tree trunk. He held her immobile. "Don't move," he said. "It's not safe yet."

"A bear?" she whispered, her heart slamming. "A wolf?"

He gave a short laugh. "Worse. A fellow by the name of Hank Barlow. He's not expecting company. He's apt to blow off our heads first and ask questions later."

"Doesn't seem very neighborly."

"That's the way things are, up here."

"Is that the way you are? Ready to shoot anyone who walks onto your land?"

He swallowed; she could see the motion of his Adam's apple, and the slight flinch of his jaw, as if she'd struck him. "A man can turn a little over-cautious when he's not used to being around other people."

"Or maybe a man can forget to act like a human being," she shot back. "People aren't meant to live alone ..." Her voice trailed away as she realized she was lecturing a man who'd chosen a hermit's lifestyle, a man who had come down from his own high-mountain lair only from some misguided sense of responsibility.

A man who'd sworn off passion rather than ever allow himself to care deeply about anything—or anyone—ever again.

It hit her suddenly, with a force that was almost physical, that once she and Jesse parted, he would once again return to his self-imposed isolation. He never allowed anybody on his land. There would be no one to delight in the sight of his rare smile. She wondered if he smiled at all, when he was alone. There would be no one to thrill to his touch, to ache for his kiss, to take pleasure in simply being with him.

She, on the other hand ... She ...

As he had unerringly pointed out, matters might not turn out much different for her, once she returned to Dry Falls and took up the life she'd arranged for herself. She wouldn't be alone, in the literal sense of the word. She'd be mired in the midst of the Palmer family. Someone else's family. She'd be no better than bought-and-paid-for labor, and nobody but herself would give a hoot about her smiles or care one little bit that her life was expiring by slow degrees without her ever experiencing the joys and accomplishments that were a woman's due.

How strange. Until now, when she'd been slammed against a tree and might at that very moment be framed within a crazy old man's rifle sights, she hadn't realized that she had a right to expect more than life had handed her.

She'd endured the hell her life had been, and had deliberately sought a refuge that would grant her safety and anonymity. She'd seen to her basic needs. She would be fed and clothed and safe from drunken rages and days of hunger when the food money had been confiscated and used for whiskey.

But Jesse roused other needs within her, needs that were not so easily slaked.

Her mind snapped out of its reverie when Jesse bellowed a greeting to the still-unseen Hank Barlow. She jumped, and cried out in alarm at the unexpected sound.

"I told you to stay still," he scolded in a harsh whisper. And then he drew a great lungful of air and hollered out again. "Don't shoot, Hank! It's me, Jesse."

His greeting was still echoing in the wind when a quavery, old-man's voice shouted back, sounding unexpectedly close. "I see two varmints and a nice mule skulking in my woods. Jesse Calvin's only one varmint, far as I know."

"Have a gal with me, Hank."

"Don't say!"

A loud crashing commenced off to the side, and within a few seconds an apparition burst from the brushy cover. A wild-eyed, wild-haired, sour-smelling old man gazed at Alice with such open-mouthed hunger that she instinctively leaned into Jesse.

His arm circled her with light possession, and she felt him tense. Something in his stance communicated itself to Hank, and he shook his head, then sent them a wry, gap-toothed smile.

"What you doing, traipsing around with a gal, Jesse?"

"Hunting asparagus."

"Well, why on earth don't you just—"

Jesse tensed again, and Alice wondered what sort of warning Hank sensed that time, because he snapped his mouth shut and scowled down at the rifle that he'd jammed butt-first into the dirt.

"Thought we might explore the area around your shack, Hank. See if we might find some."

"Ain't no use disturbing my peace to hunt something that ain't there."

The recluse's not-so-blunt refusal of their company reminded Alice of the way Jesse had lashed out when telling her she would never be welcome on his property. She tried to put herself in Hank's place—living alone, with no human companionship for days, weeks, maybe months. You would think the old man would beg for them to come to his house for a visit.

Alice, safe and warm in Jesse's arms, studied Hank and felt like bursting into tears. The hair, long and stringy and unkempt . . . she couldn't help remembering her first sight of Jesse and thinking that someone had recently attempted to bring his hair into order. Hank had shown an almost paranoic fear of approaching strangers. There had been something in Jesse's reaction to her comments on the subject that told her that he, too, tended to shoot first and ask questions later. She rested in his arms, feeling the firm, reassuring thud of his heart against her shoulder, reveling in his clean scent and the thrill of his touch, and felt the horrible certainty that Jesse meant to return to his home and turn into a younger version of Hank Barlow.

It didn't seem right. She'd spent such a little amount of time in his company, and yet she knew in her soul that Jesse Calvin possessed a loving, caring nature. He'd make some woman a fine husband. He'd be a proud, protective father for a brood of children. A man like Jesse had no business hiding away. Not when there were women like her who needed men like him.

She did need him, she realized. She needed Jesse Calvin. Because until he'd come along, she'd been content to bury herself away in her own version of a mountain sanctuary.

"No asparagus at all in these immediate parts," Hank said, idly scratching his stomach through rag-tag layers of torn clothing and moth-eaten wool. He sent Jesse a devilish smirk. "I hear tell there might be some higher up."

"Jesse?" Alice said tentatively, anxious to get the both of them away from this foul old man and all the emotions he conjured within her. "Maybe we ought to go—um, higher up like Hank says, and look."

"Yeah, l'il gal, you help him look somewheres else," said Hank. Without another word, he hoisted his rifle to his shoulder and melted back into the forest. Silence reigned for a few moments, and then a bird let out a call, soon joined by others. A small woods critter darted between the trees with a soft rustling sound. Jesse's heart thudded strong and sure into Alice's pulse, and she realized that there was no good reason why they should be standing there, so close, now that Hank had departed.

And yet . . . she could not bear the notion of stepping away from him. Of placing even a handful of inches between them. She could not shake the ridiculous notion that if she allowed Jesse to even temporarily retreat into his self-imposed isolation, she would lose him forever. Jesse Calvin was no asparagus plant, sending out shoots visible to the discerning eye. No matter how carefully a woman hunted, she might never again find the tiny crack that had temporarily developed in his shield. If she lost it now, he'd only seal it up, hide it, recontain himself in his carefully constructed isolation.

She turned, careful to do so slowly, making sure she didn't break the light hold he had on her. She pressed her forehead into his shoulder, scarcely daring to breathe. She fashioned a secret kiss against his shirt, wishing she were brave enough to let him feel the pressure of her lips. He tensed, and for one glorious moment his hands tightened, possessing her, claiming her as his.

And then he stepped away.

She made a small, embarrassed sound and whirled away from him. She wrapped her arms around her mule's neck and buried her face against the animal's glossy fur.

He wanted to apologize. Wanted to tell her he'd gloried in her yielding in his arms, wanted to tell her that his blood roared with need for her. He couldn't do it.

"Hank is out there, watching us," he said by way of explanation.

"Why? He obviously doesn't want our company."

"He'll want to make sure we leave. He's probably sitting up in a tree, cackling his fool head off, trying not to blink until we're out of his sight."

"To make sure we really get off his land."

"Not just that." He swallowed. He suddenly felt embarrassed that he knew exactly what Hank was doing, because he'd do the same things himself. Now that he'd opened his big mouth, he'd have to explain. Alice peered at him over the mule's neck with so much curiosity that he knew she'd just keep poking and prying away at him until he told her everything. "He hates having someone breach his privacy. But he'll keep watching to store up the sight of us. He'll go over every word we said, every move we made, times he gets to feeling lonely."

"You understand him so well," she whispered.

"Let's go." Jesse took the mule's reins without giving her the chance to refuse his help, and struck out in the opposite direction from where Hank had disappeared—as if physical distance could separate Jesse from the old recluse and all he represented. As if walking away could prove he were completely different and unlike the cackling old fool.

Walking away from Hank, but heading in the direction of

his own place, where he was indeed all too familiar with what it felt like to want to chase someone away when you were dying inside for a little companionship.

Yes, he understood that well—the basic craving for ordinary human contact. But now he realized that his isolation would be even more difficult to bear. His restless, sleepless nights would now be haunted with the remembered feel of Alice yielding in his arms, with Alice's warmth thawing the frozen shell of his heart, Alice's body a perfect fit to his . . . and him pushing it all away.

"How's that old fellow's eyesight?" Alice hollered.

He frowned over his shoulder at her, and realized she'd fallen a good thirty paces behind. "Your foot bothering you?"

"Will you forget about the foot? You're just moving so fast, Jesse, that I don't have a chance to look for asparagus."

"There isn't any around here."

"How can you be sure?"

"I'm sure."

"Then maybe I ought to take my mule and get myself off this cursed mountain." She'd come to a dead stop, and stood there with her hands planted on her hips, glaring at him. "I'm wasting precious time."

He took a quick look around to gather his bearings and realized that he must have set a brutal pace—they'd probably covered two miles or more since turning away from Hank. Miles closer to the one place on this mountain where she would find what she sought, the one place where he dared not take her, not if he meant to hold on to any shred of sanity. He couldn't take her to his place, just couldn't, and yet he seemed to keep aiming them there as though he was some big old goofy homing pigeon.

He ought to pounce on her suggestion that she take herself off his mountain. Hell, he ought to escort her himself, so she'd make better time, and stand there waving good-bye as she headed back toward town. The last thing they should do was camp out for another night.

"We'll stop here," he said. Before she could protest, he tugged free the ropes holding the mule's burden and tossed their bedrolls down on the ground. "Rest your foot."

She sighed, but it seemed to lack conviction. If anything, she looked a little pleased as she came forward to join him and the mule. She pulled the saddlebags from the mule and let them drop near the bedrolls.

"We're out of Hank's range, too." He felt uncomfortable with the easy way they worked together. A man like him and a woman like her shouldn't find it so natural to work side by side. "Don't have to worry about him watching us anymore."

"Well, that's a relief. Now we can do . . . well, private things."

His blood surged at her words. "Private things?"

She blushed. "Say, like one of us has to make a trip into the brush. Or maybe, if you really insist on looking at my foot, I don't have to worry that Hank's watching me shuck off my boots."

"I'll go on ahead a ways, if you have to use the brush."

"No, I'm fine. I'll just take off my boot, because I know you're going to make me do it anyway."

She bent. He fiddled with the ropes that held the remaining packs on the mule's back, but the diversion didn't help. His mind could imagine plain as anything the sweet, graceful curve Alice's body made as she bent over the rope wound around her boot. Even a decidedly unladylike curse did nothing to dispel his daydreaming.

She swore again. "Damn this knot!" Her hand darted out toward the mule's leg for balance. The mule chose to shy from her touch, which meant Alice's questing hand landed on Jesse instead, at almost the worst possible place for a woman's hand to come to light, right at the sensitive junction of his thigh and groin.

"Sorry." She snatched her hand away, as if she'd been scalded by the heat flaring through him.

He bit back a moan and dropped to one knee to conceal the

effect her touch had on him. "Let me," he said, hoarse. He propped her foot on his thigh and directed his trembling fingers to work on her knot.

"No, I can—" Her fingers accidentally tangled with his. He caught, and held on.

CHAPTER SEVEN

Something wild and sweet within Alice unfurled, as if it had been waiting for that certain touch—firm and sure and vibrant with longing—before bursting into life.

She let her foot slide off Jesse's leg, but she didn't let go of his hand. He said nothing, and Alice wondered if he were struck as speechless as she by the sensations surging through her. A pleasurable ache curled around her heart. An unfamiliar hunger set up its craving far below her belly.

His position had sent his shirtsleeve traveling up his arm by an extra inch or two, revealing his wrist, and a fresh-looking scrape that ran along the edge of his palm. He must have hurt himself somewhere during this trip, while he'd been taking care of her, and he'd never flinched, never made a sound, to let her know. She doubted that anyone, ever again, would be as concerned for her well-being as Jesse had shown himself to be. Nor would anyone care what happened to him, all alone on his mountain.

"Once I'm gone," she said, "there won't be anybody to fret about you."

"I don't need anyone to worry about me."

"I never thought I did, either." She wasn't sure she'd said it aloud, until he chuckled.

"Maybe we ought to stay together for a little while longer, then, so we can worry about each other."

He had tried, she could tell, to inject humor into his offer, but the unsteadiness of his voice, the tremor she felt in his grip, told her that he wasn't feeling at all lighthearted at the moment. Nor was she. She didn't know what it was that she was feeling, except that she was utterly certain that the answer to the mystery lay somewhere in Jesse's arms.

She had spent a good many years turning aside the attentions of men. Trail-weary cowboys who'd presented her with wilted buttercups they'd plucked from the roadside and promised to give her blood-red roses someday. Failed silver miners who'd spent their days in Keppel's Saloon alongside her brother and swore they'd find work and quit drinking if she'd walk out with them. She'd declined the gifts. She'd ignored the promises she knew they never meant to keep.

She wished now that she'd allowed herself a little practice. She didn't know any women's tricks. She didn't know how to tell when a man told her the truth.

"You never once promised to take care of me, but nobody's ever looked after me the way you do."

"I thought you didn't put much stock in the promises a man makes."

"I haven't had cause to believe in anyone." *Until now,* she realized with stunned surprise. Jesse had proven to her that it wasn't what a man said, but rather what he did, that proved his worth.

The knowledge was too new, too tentative, to overcome a lifetime of disappointments. She sensed the call of his body, and the answering cry of hers, but her soul demanded a verbal assurance that there was more in this heat flaming between them than a lonely man amusing himself with an equally lonely woman amid the anonymity of an isolated wilderness.

She waited for words. He gave her himself. And while her mind whispered that she hadn't heard the one promise she needed to hear, her woman's heart gloried in his need for her.

With a low groan that rumbled straight through him into her, he pulled her into his arms. His lips, firm and warm and demanding, closed over hers. Pure pleasure jolted through her, stealing her breath, sending her heart skittering like a wild thing. She turned all but boneless, startled by the desire that weakened her, while he seemed strengthened with purpose.

He swiveled so that she was supported by his bent knee, and this left his hands free to travel her body. She felt his touch at her hips, her waist, and she shivered with the pleasure of it. One huge hand cupped her breast, and she wished that no cloth separated her sensitive flesh from his questing fingers. As if he'd read her mind, he thumbed open the buttons lining the front of her shirt.

"You're not wearing any underwear, Miss Lowell." Her skin lay bare, awaiting his touch. But he didn't use his hands. His head swooped low, and she quivered with startled delight when she felt the scratch of his cheek, the wetness of his tongue, starting down below her navel. His mouth traveled up. His breath fanned hot against her flesh as he tasted the contours of her breast. When she thought she would faint from the sensation, his lips closed over her nipple, his tongue teased her, and she couldn't help it—she cried aloud at the pleasure that throbbed through her.

"Oh, Jesse," she gasped. "I want . . . I want . . ."

"I know, sweetheart," he murmured into her flesh, adding yet another pleasurable sizzle. He rose, lifting her easily and, never once taking his lips away from her, walked them over to where they'd unloaded the mule. He kicked at one of the bedrolls until it rolled open, and then set her down until she stood unsteadily, holding on to him, never wanting to let him go.

He tipped up her chin until she looked him straight in the eye. She'd thrilled, before, when he'd fixed his gaze upon her, but he'd never before seemed . . . hungry for her. He'd never shown such a proprietary gleam, a pure masculine intent, coupled with the resolve that warned no other man would ever have the right to look at her in that way, once he'd done with her what he would.

"Unless you tell me to stop right now, Alice, I'm going to take off your clothes," he said. "And then I'm going to take off mine. After that, the two of us are going to spend a good long while in that bedroll. Things will never be the same for you if we do this."

It was a promise of sorts. And a demand, which nonetheless offered her a choice.

In answer, she lifted her trembling hand and undid the first button on his shirt.

He wasn't wearing any underwear, either.

The crisp curls adorning his chest were a darker golden brown than his hair. She pressed her cheek against him, loving the mixed textures of him, the tickling hair, the firm muscle, the heated skin. She loved the way his hands moved over her, tugging free her clothes. She moaned a protest when he moved away from her, but it was only for the space of a few heartbeats, and only for the purpose of shucking his own garments. And then he was back, holding her close, creating the dilemma within her of wanting to look at him, drink in the male beauty of him, but never wanting to allow an inch to separate them, ever again.

He lowered her to the bedroll. He moved over her, accustoming her to his weight, amazing her with the myriad ways a man's body could make a woman's come to life. With each stroke of his hand, each sweep of his tongue, he wakened new sensation within her, in places she'd never suspected of possessing sensation.

It all seemed so right. So perfect. "Yes," she murmured, as his fingers left a trail of fire along her inner thigh. "Oh, yes," she gasped when he touched her where she'd never imagined anyone would touch her. He found her small, sensitive nub and with gentle pressure made her writhe and cry out his name. He covered her fully, and she gloried in his weight, and most especially in the hard, demanding part of him that pressed into the wetness he'd coaxed from her. He moved with exquisite slowness as he entered her. She could feel the tension in him, the trembling in his muscles as he restrained himself.

"It won't hurt the next time." His mouth closed over hers, as if he wished he could swallow her pain into himself when he thrust, hard, and made her his. He moved within her, slowly at first, and then faster, filling her with his power and strength. He took from her, and yet he gave her so much more.

The next time. The implication that he meant to do this again, coupled with his full possession of her, sent waves rippling through her, a plunging sensation that made her hold him tight, wanting to take him with her while she fell into the glorious, giddy world that held only the two of them.

Falling, falling ... she'd fallen, all right. She'd fallen into love.

She loved Jesse Calvin.

She loved a man who had vowed to cut passion out of his life.

Alice had spent hours, sometimes, standing by the small kitchen window while her mama slept. If she leaned exactly the right way, she was able to see beyond the stable and outbuildings. For as long as she managed to maintain the uncomfortable position, she could treat herself to the sight of the valley, long and verdant and dotted with wildflowers, sweeping toward the mountains.

She'd always been fascinated by the wildflowers. They started out so insignificant, fighting for sun and water against the tougher and stronger weeds. The flowers often prevailed. They budded, and bloomed, delighting the eye, perfuming the air, intoxicating bees and humans alike with the heady proof of their triumph. But only for a little while, as if such exquisite beauty could not be permitted to live for very long.

Maybe we ought to stay together . . . for a little while, Jesse had said. He'd placed a term on their togetherness. There was no reason for her to feel hurt or betrayed. He'd been honest with her from the first.

"Are you all right?" Jesse murmured into her hair.

She wondered if he'd noticed the tremor that had shook her when she'd realized she'd fallen in love with a man who could not love her in return. "I'm fine."

"Tomorrow . . . well, tomorrow could be a little uncomfortable for you. Or so I've heard."

She wanted to cry. No wonder she'd fallen in love with him. She loved *this* Jesse, the warm and tender and caring man who held her in his arms. The man who worried that she might be a little sore in the morning.

What if . . . what if the Jesse she held in her arms was the real Jesse? Maybe the other one—the man who'd foresworn passion, who'd said she would never be allowed onto his land—maybe his reluctance to reach out for what he needed stemmed from the same fears and uncertainties as her own.

She had spent all her life accommodating herself to whatever happened. She'd been afraid to reach out and grab onto what she wanted, because disappointment hurt so bad. It was so much easier to let herself get swept up in circumstances and let circumstances determine what happened. A person who never tried never had to take the blame for failing.

If she wanted Jesse, she would have to take a chance.

"Tomorrow? There are a lot of tomorrows, Jesse. How many are you talking about?"

He tensed. "It's best to take them one at a time."

His words were like fingers of frost blackening the frail bud of hope she'd dared nurture within herself.

She shivered, remembering the wild-eyed, ill-kempt Hank Barlow. Jesse's perfect comprehension of the old man's ways, the way he'd interpreted Hank's behavior, betrayed his familiarity with such moments. Jesse would melt back into that life, and all trace of the man she loved would vanish forever. She understood, because she knew how to lose herself, too. But where he disappeared into isolation, she submerged herself in the lives of others. She knew how to hide her hopes and dreams so well that even she could pretend she didn't have any.

She was so afraid of having her hopes raised and ruined again that she'd been willing to spend the rest of her days hidden away, with no hope of making her own life blossom with fullness. With Jesse, she stood a chance. If she dared to help him, she would help herself. She had to try again.

"Well, you're the kind of gal that thinks she can save folks from themselves. Maybe you wouldn't mind trying to save me, Alice." He loomed over her and trailed kisses from her chin to her navel. "I swear I'd feel redeemed after a few minutes of this."

"That's what you want from me?"

"Part of what I want. After we do that for a while, we'd build up our strength with your fine cooking, and do some of this." He captured the tip of one breast with his lips and did something with his tongue that sent pleasure jolting through her. She couldn't lie still; she surged against him, a moan betraying the sensation coursing through her. He laughed, a low, masculine sound of triumph, and with a quick shift of his hips claimed her once again. He thrust hard and deep. "We'll do this all the time, Alice. All the time."

She held him as tightly as she could, matching him thrust for thrust, while she felt herself splintering apart. One fragment of her soul went soaring with the pure physical delight he gave her, while another thudded to earth like an angel stripped of its wings. *Save me, Alice . . . your fine cooking . . . we'll do this all the time . . .* He'd made no mention of love. No mention of marriage.

Save me, Alice.

She'd never been able to save anyone. Her mother's poor health and lack of will to live had been beyond anyone's ability to cure. No amount of cajoling, bullying, begging, or pleading had coaxed her brother into changing his life for the better. Jesse was just like everyone else, expecting her to take care of things.

He was just like everyone else. . . .

No. Not exactly. Jesse had never promised her anything. She was the one who'd read meanings into his words that he'd obviously never intended. He'd told her exactly what he meant to do with her, and he did it now—he touched her secret places and taught her an ecstasy she would never feel again. She heard herself crying his name while waves of pleasure coursed through her.

She could have him for a little while. But not too long. If she stayed, she wouldn't be able to save herself.

Jesse wanted to make her a hundred promises, a thousand promises, and hold her in his arms while he made every one of them come true. But she was a woman who'd been lied to so often that she no longer believed a man when he said what he meant to do.

All he could do was show her.

Especially now. Jesse knew he ought to be hating himself with every ounce of his being. He had done it again—allowed passion to overcome his common sense. He'd given up his mind and his heart to passion, and taken something precious and irreplaceable from another person.

And he didn't feel the least bit remorseful.

The last time, he'd been willing to kill because of the land he'd lost. This time, he'd cast aside all honor and responsibility and taken what he wanted from Alice without caring that he was claiming from her a woman's most precious possession. Glorying, in fact, in knowing that he was the first, that he had made her his own before any other man had so much as touched the glorious silken texture of her skin.

Worst of all, he'd done this with a woman from whom he'd

already taken so much. Set her brother on the path to death. Brought about the loss of her home. He'd made an oath to himself to watch over her and protect her while she went on her wild-goose chase for asparagus, and vowed to see her settled safe into her new job before returning to an isolation that no longer beckoned with any allure.

Even enumerating all the wrongs he'd inflicted upon her, he couldn't summon one speck of disgust for himself. In fact, he felt downright pleased with what he'd done. He'd never felt so complete. He'd never felt the joy of his masculinity so powerfully before, never experienced this sense that all was right within his world.

What he wanted to do, more than anything, was lift Alice into his arms and race up the mountain to his cabin, where the two of them would live out the rest of their days reveling in each other's company. Take her to his home.

He wanted Alice Lowell in his home, on his land, in his heart, forever.

She lay quietly, her eyes closed, but not asleep. Her skin bore the soft flush of a woman who'd enjoyed the ultimate pleasure. She was a woman who burst into song at the thought of hunting down asparagus to make a magical soup that would make her dreams come true. He was a man who'd forgotten how to sing, a man who knew dreams died with the rising sun.

With her, though, he felt like singing. He wanted to believe in dreams coming true.

"We'll head back to town tomorrow," he said. "We'll tell the Palmers you won't be taking the job."

She opened her eyes. Instead of the contentment, the faith in him that he longed to read in her eyes, he read that old despairing expression that had haunted him for so many years. An awful feeling churned within him.

"No, Jesse. I have to keep my promises. I must find my asparagus. And then I'm going back to town by myself to take that job."

CHAPTER EIGHT

Ribbons of gold, orange, and pink streamed through the sky, heralding a glorious dawn. Everything seemed so much more beautiful here in the mountains, Alice thought. The air seemed fresher and more invigorating. The air touched her skin with gentle coolness. The soft sounds of nature—rustling leaves, scampering woods critters, water splashing over stones—rivaled any man-made music she'd ever heard.

She tried very hard to memorize all of it. Once she returned to town, she'd be buried in dust and heat and staleness again.

Once she returned to town, she'd never again kneel side by side with a man who had loved her the whole night long. She ought to feel exhausted. His shoulder rubbed up against hers, and she wished no cloth separated their skin. She ought to feel bone-deep embarrassment.

No. What she ought to do was get away, before she found herself settling for whatever he offered.

"I've decided to leave the mountain today." Alice dunked her tin plate into the creek and hoped that the splash covered the quavering in her voice.

Jesse dropped his cup into the water, and seemed to have a little trouble fishing it back out again. "You haven't found your asparagus yet."

"I know." Her heart quietly broke. If only he'd said, *Don't go, Alice. Stay with me. Love me forever.* But all he was worried about was that stupid old asparagus.

Her mama had been so very, very wrong. Alice knew now what her heart's desire was, and finding asparagus and turning it into a magical soup wasn't going to do a thing to make her dreams come true. Her dreams were all wrapped up in one half-tamed man who didn't need any passion in his life.

"I give up," she whispered. She'd given up on finding asparagus, given up on honoring her deathbed promise. Given up on dreaming.

"You can't give up," said Jesse, and now it was her turn to drop her metal cup into the stream.

Well, they would certainly have clean cups the next time they drank coffee. That might turn out to be a blessing. When a person all alone drank coffee, at least they could look into the shiny tin surface and try to squint out a reflection for company.

And it was all so ridiculous. She knew in her broken heart that Jesse Calvin was as lonely as she, that he had found something magical in her arms, just as she had in his. She'd found a joy so profound that she was willing to change her life, to risk everything she'd tried to protect to hold onto it. But Jesse was content to savor it day by day, with no commitment to nurturing it until it was strong enough to last forever.

He crouched at the edge of the creek, scrubbing his tinware as if this washing had to last him the rest of his life, with such a grim set to his lips that she knew he meant to keep silent for the rest of the day.

"You're a fine one to talk about giving up," she said, her anger spilling out. "You can't wait to get rid of me so you can slink back to your cabin and hide for the rest of your life."

"I didn't say that."

"Not today, you haven't."

"There are a lot of things I haven't said today."

"Such as . . . such as what?" Her pulse hammered so hard that she wondered if she'd be able to hear him if he spoke the words she longed to hear. Hope stirred, not dead at all, even though she'd tried her best to flog it into submission.

He was silent for a time, a very long time.

"You can't give up," he said. "You gave your word that you'd make that soup."

"I gave my word to a dead woman. She won't care if I keep it or not."

"But you'll care," Jesse said. "Honoring a promise means a lot to you. You'll always regret it if you abandon your search now."

His words struck her like blows. He understood so well what was important to her, which only made his continued silence on the subject more meaningful. Jesse knew what it would take to keep her with him; he apparently didn't care enough to try.

"Maybe I put too much stock in keeping promises."

"Don't give up on your heart's desire, Alice."

Her mama had said those very words before she died, when Alice admitted that her dreams weren't so very special, that they might not be worth pursuing. A man to love, who would love her in return. A real home, and children.

She had found a man to love in Jesse. And she'd found that love because she'd followed through on her promise to find the makings of the magical soup. So a little bit of magic had trickled her way. Her hunting had given her a taste of life that she might never have dared savor.

"You're right. I do have to finish what I started out to do." Excitement, tempered by heartbreak, simmered inside her. She would have to find the strength to start all over again. "But everything I ever learned about asparagus tells me that I won't find any up here, away from civilization. Expecting to find asparagus up here is as ridiculous as . . . as . . ."

"As believing making some magical soup from it will make your dreams come true?" Jesse asked.

"Dreams do come true." Just saying the words strengthened her. "Maybe not here and now."

"You don't always find what you need in the place you think it ought to be."

"I thought you considered me a crazy fool for believing that dreams could come true," she said. "Well, I do mean to find my heart's desire. And I'm going to start with asparagus. My best chance of finding it is down below, no matter what you say."

Strangely, it seemed a blush crept up his neck. "Hank said there might be some up above."

She knew him well enough by now to realize that this was a half-hearted offer to continue to aid her in her search. She was about to refuse when he glanced at her, and she saw naked hope in his eyes. He wanted her to stay, even if only for a little while.

"Up above," she said.

"I'll take you," he said.

He led her toward his home.

With each step, equal measures of anticipation and dread pounded through him. He couldn't wait to see if Alice would appreciate the simple beauty that brought him so much pleasure. And yet he couldn't help remembering the pity she'd shown for old Hank. Maybe he'd show off his cabin, his land, his dogs, and Alice would express nothing but scorn for what meant so much to him. She might not understand that taking her to his home was the most significant thing he could think to do for her.

After all these days spent trying to convince himself she didn't belong on his land, he was sick at heart to think she might not like his place. Maybe he ought to change his mind about taking her there.

No. He was only lying to himself, something he'd done for years, and something he knew he could never do again. What he dreaded was the betrayal that would lance through Alice when he showed her his place and she realized he'd had asparagus all along and hadn't told her about it. It would be so easy for her to think that he'd deliberately sabotaged her efforts to find her heart's desire.

She couldn't be more wrong.

But what was he supposed to do—tell her? Say it flat out, *Alice, I love you, I want you to be happy, I want to spend the rest of my days seeing to it that life is a joy for you?*

She was a woman who doubted the spoken word, and for good reason. He had nothing but his word to give to her. His word, and the irrational hope that when she made her magic soup from ingredients grown by his own hand, she might find her heart's desire with him.

He broke into a sweat that had nothing to do with the effort of climbing the mountain.

He could say that, and more. But she'd spent a lifetime hearing promises made, living through promises broken. The only thing that would prove his love to her was for him to somehow show her how much she meant to him.

He had nothing. Except for the small patch of asparagus in his garden, about which he'd been less than forthcoming. If he took her there, to the mountain retreat where no other person had ever been welcomed, if he helped her gather the slim green spears, if he stood beside her and helped her make her magical soup . . . would she understand?

He prayed she would.

Three dogs came racing through the trees, their jaws agape, their tongues hanging. "Jesse!" she called, fright turning her voice a little shrill.

"Don't worry. They're my dogs. They won't hurt you."

His dogs? Then . . . they must be near his cabin. The cabin he swore nobody was permitted to visit.

The dogs aimed straight for Jesse and flung themselves against him in a frenzy of canine delight. Dogs possessed good instincts. Dogs wouldn't love a man who didn't know how to love in return. Dogs were kind of like asparagus—keeping them implied a commitment to caring for them.

Jesse issued some gentle commands and his dogs settled into a dancing prance at his side, gazing adoringly up at him while he pressed on, leading her . . . where?

In a moment, she knew. They came to a clearing in the woods, an acre or two that had been laboriously hacked free of trees and brush. A small, snug cabin had been built right in the center of the sunny open space. Jesse's home. The place he held so dear that he'd allowed no one to see it. She waited for him to say something, waited for him to welcome her to where he lived.

"This is hard for me, Alice," he said.

"I'll stay here while you fetch what you need."

"I don't need anything from *there*," he said.

He cupped his hand beneath her elbow. He took a deep breath, as if to fortify himself for a terrible ordeal.

"Jesse, it's obvious you don't want me on your land."

He shook his head. "No. I'm glad you're here. What bothers me lies out behind the cabin."

Oh, she was pathetic—thrilling to hear him say he was glad to have her there. She tamped down her excitement, and puzzled, she let him guide her to the rear of his house. She stole quick little peeks at the dwelling. It looked surprisingly welcoming for such a primitive structure stuck way out in the middle of nowhere. A lot of effort had gone into making it a snug shelter.

A string, with a number of brightly colored feathers tied to it, hung in one of the windows, a make-shift curtain that shimmered with glorious iridescence in the sunlight. Alice's throat tightened. A man who ruled out passion shouldn't be so aware of beauty.

"Alice."

She glanced up at him, and barely had time to wonder at the pale tension that marked his expression when he pulled her into his arms. It was the first time he'd embraced her since they'd made love, and her body reacted with traitorous delight. He held her tight, his heart hammering against her breast so fast that you would think he'd spent the past minutes cavorting the perimeter of the clearing with his dogs instead of just walking slowly with her.

"Don't hate me," he murmured. He swooped low to kiss her. She melted into him, saving the taste of him, the feel of him, wondering at his agitation, and wondering how she would manage to live without this for the rest of her life.

"What's wrong, Jesse?"

"Over there." He jutted his chin toward the edge of the clearing.

He seemed to be distressed by his garden.

She recognized the tubular stalks of spring onions. The rich velvety leaves of early spinach. And she began to understand his agitation when she spotted something else, something which she'd heard so much about but never actually seen—golden-green stems, poking from the bare earth and reaching for the sun.

"Asparagus," she whispered. "You knew it was here all the time."

"From the first minute you told me you meant to find some."

"Why didn't you tell me?"

"At first, the thought of bringing anyone here was impossible."

"And now you just want to relieve yourself of the responsibility of watching over me while I hunt."

"No, Alice. Now, it's impossible for me to think of living with myself if I don't help you make that soup."

Her throat tightened. He so easily said words that touched her heart. But never the promise she most longed to hear.

"Do you think the asparagus will remain edible if I wrap it in damp cloth?" she asked. "It will take a couple of days to get back to my old place."

"You're not going anywhere."

"I have to make the soup, Jesse."

"Make it here. In my kitchen."

"Here?" She didn't know how she managed to choke out the word. How could she go into his house and cook on his stove? She had a fanciful mind. In no time flat she'd conjure up the fantasy that there was more between them than a temporary passion inspired by loneliness. She'd stand there pretending she was Mrs. Jesse Calvin, preparing a special meal for her beloved. "I don't . . . I don't know the recipe off by heart," she lied.

"Well, I do," he said. "You told me often enough. I'll help you. You pick the asparagus. I'll get the spinach. We'll both pull a few onions."

"I need carrots," she protested. "And celery."

He sent her a half smile, but didn't point out that she'd just betrayed how well she remembered the recipe. "Plenty of carrots in the root cellar. Dried celery in the house. The makings for dumplings, too."

"Jesse, I don't know. Whenever I thought about that soup, I always imagined making it on my own."

"You can do it alone if you want to," he said quietly. "Or we could do it together."

"Together?"

"You and me, Alice. Together."

She felt her defenses crumbling. She'd been determined to hear a promise from him—and now she had to wonder why. Hearing promises meant nothing. A simple word from a man like Jesse—a simple word like *together*—held more promise than a torrent of solemn oaths made by a lesser man.

She nodded. No words were necessary.

* * *

He gave her a knife and showed her how to cut each asparagus stalk near the root. He moved to the far end of the garden where the spinach grew. He was usually careful, this early in the spring, to pluck only the outermost leaves, but he couldn't be bothered to concentrate on prolonging his spinach harvest just then, not while Alice Lowell knelt on his land, her hands buried in soil he'd turned with his own hands. He grabbed whole plants and yanked them out by the roots. The greenstuff wasn't being destroyed, but transformed into something capable of making Alice's dreams come true. Kind of like him. He'd ripped out all his battle-scarred defenses, and instead of getting wounded, his heart was being reborn with hope and joy.

The meanest of his dogs sat right in front of Alice, a goofy canine grin on its face as it watched Alice cut stalks of asparagus and tuck them into the pot Jesse had fetched from the house. Alice laughed and patted the dog, who swiped at her hand with an affectionate tongue. Jesse couldn't believe that old hound had taken to her so fast.

Well, why not? He'd done the same thing.

He waited for his instincts to rear up and point out the danger he was opening himself up to. Instead, he stood there stuffing spinach into a bucket, grinning like his dog.

He heard a beautiful noise.

It was Alice. She was singing. Singing soft, singing low, but she was singing.

"I can't hear you," he called. He ached to hear her voice echoing through the trees, joyous and unrestrained. "You need to sing louder when you're up on a mountain, on account of the air being so thin."

"I'm singing as loud as I can," she protested.

"No you're not. I can barely hear you."

"Well, you're a fine one to talk. You're not singing at all."

"I . . ." He didn't know how to tell her that he'd forgotten how to sing. "I've never heard that song. I don't know the words."

"I could hear the men singing it in the saloon. It's easy." She hummed a few bars, and then launched into a chorus. "Oh, my darling, oh, my darling, oh, my darling Clementine . . . come on, Jesse, sing with me!"

He'd picked enough spinach. He stood and walked over to her, dangling the bucket in one hand. "You want me to sing."

"Loud."

"You'll be sorry. I can't carry a tune."

"How would I know? I haven't heard you so much as hum." She cut another asparagus stalk. She sang the full verse of a song about a mining gal and her pa. She arched a coy glance upward at him. "Come on, now, sing the rest with me. Oh, my darling . . ."

"Oh, my darling . . ." His throat threatened to clamp up on him, because the words to the silly song suddenly took on new meaning. He reached for Alice's hand and pulled her to her feet. "Oh, my darling, oh, my darling, oh, my darling . . . Alice mine."

"Jesse?" she whispered, swaying.

He caught her against him, felt her heart pounding, and knew he had to say the right thing. Couldn't think of what would be the right thing. He dropped his bucket of spinach. It felt good to sing, damned good.

"I can't remember the rest of the words."

"Make them up. I . . . I like the way you sing it better than the real words."

"You might as well know that you can't expect much from me in the way of poetry," he said. "I'm not good with words at all."

"I don't think I'm especially good with them either." Tears glimmered in her wondrous eyes. But her expression was not the old despair that had haunted him. She glowed with joy, and he knew that he would never tire of seeing Alice glow for him.

He started over again. "Oh, my darling, oh, my darling, oh, my darling Alice mine." He paused, and swallowed, praying she wouldn't laugh, wouldn't run screaming from the garden. "You are mine, I'm yours forever, we'll do fine, my Alice mine."

She didn't laugh. She didn't run. He pulled her close until her face was pressed against his shirt. And then her shoulders started to heave a little—and by that time he didn't care if it was from laughter or tears. Especially since he seemed to be producing a combination of both things himself.

"Let's go home, Alice," he said, and he lifted her into his arms.

The spinach and asparagus hadn't wilted too badly, Alice noted as she rinsed them in the water Jesse had fetched from his stream, considering how long they'd lain out there in the garden. The crisp mountain air must have kept them so fresh, while she and Jesse . . .

A blush coursed warm and tingling from the top of her head to the tips of her toes, which were as scandalously bare as the rest of her legs. She wore nothing but one of Jesse's shirts, the hem of which barely grazed the tops of her thighs, affording her scarcely any modesty at all.

He'd told her there wasn't much sense in dressing just then. He had plans, he said, for passing the time they had to wait before adding dumplings to the simmering soup. He was kneading the dumpling dough himself with smooth, sensual motions that called to mind the things he'd done to her with those very fingers, things she felt sure he planned to do again, too, from the slow, anticipatory smile he gave her. There was an unspoken promise in that smile. A promise she knew in her bones that he meant to keep.

She thought she might have to spend the rest of her life learning all the ways Jesse Calvin kept his promises.

She slid a cast-iron lid in place on the soup pot.

Jesse wiped his hands with a damp towel and slouched back in the chair.

"Come sit with me, Alice."

"There's only one chair," she pointed out.

"It'll hold two."

She didn't see how, with him occupying every bit of it with a lazy sprawl that revealed so much of him to her hungry eyes. He'd pulled on his blue jeans when they'd left his bed, but he'd left the top button undone. His muscled torso rose in a firm vee out to broad shoulders. His arms, flexed against the chair, bulged with strength even though relaxed. His hair had come undone from its leather thong, probably because she'd buried her fingers in those soft, thick curls while holding his head close against her. He looked every bit as wild and untamed as this wonderful land he lived upon. As primal and anticipatory as she felt inside. She walked slowly toward him, wishing they were headed back to the bed instead.

Until he pulled her onto his lap, and arranged her so that her knees straddled his hips. The shirt rode up, well beyond modesty, and she couldn't pull it down. He gripped her tight around the waist, supporting her so that she hovered inches above him. He lowered her just a little. He must have undone the rest of his buttons while she'd been staring at him. She gasped at the intimate contact when her soft flesh met his heat.

"You're not wearing any underclothes, Alice," he said as he found a gap in the shirt that allowed him to stroke his tongue against her breast.

"Neither are you." She trembled, shivering with delight when a deft movement of his hips brought him hard against her. He let her down as he entered her by slow, infinitesimal degrees until he filled her more fully than she ever imagined possible.

"How long does that soup have to simmer?"

"Ten, maybe fif . . . fifteen minutes."

He thrust, sending exquisite tremors coursing through her. She would never feel empty, ever again. "How long?"

"Twenty! Twenty minutes."

"That might be long enough. This time."

Jesse had never in his life considered soup to be a thing of beauty, until he saw Alice's magical asparagus soup.

The broth, golden and rich, reminded him of the way the sunlight glinted against Alice's hair. Tiny flecks of dried celery and the deep orange cubes of carrots that he'd stored by himself in the cold of the last year mingled with the asparagus and spinach and onions that they'd picked together that very day. The dumplings he'd helped make floated on top like small sturdy islands offering safe harbor. The soup was just what she said it would be—the wealth of the past tied to the promise of the future.

"You taste it first, Jesse." Her hand shook as she spooned a portion into a bowl.

"No, sweetheart. You have the right to taste it first."

She gripped the edges of the bowl so hard that he worried her fingers might break. "I . . . I can't," she said. "I'm afraid."

"Afraid of what?"

"That the magic won't work."

He put an arm around her shoulders and guided her to the chair. With gentle pressure he got her to sit, and then he knelt in front of her. She held that bowl in such a rigid grip that the soup's surface shimmered like molten gold.

He took the spoon and dipped a portion of soup. "Your mama told you that the woman who made this soup and ate it would realize her heart's desire."

Alice nodded.

"Did she happen to say what would happen if a man ate it?"

"We didn't talk much about men."

"Hmmm." He ran the edge of the spoon against her lip, moistening the lush curve with rich, buttery broth. "Seems to me, the only fair thing would be if the soup worked the same for a man as for a woman.''

"Do you have a heart's desire, Jesse?"

"I sure do." He made another pass with the spoon against her lips, and smiled when her tongue darted out to capture a droplet of broth. "There's nothing I want more in this world than to hear you say yes when I ask you to marry me."

"You . . . you want to marry me?"

"Not if you refuse to eat. It's a hard life up here on this mountain. I can't have a wife who's too persnickety to eat magic soup."

Her lips parted. He tilted the spoon, sending the magic soup into her mouth while sheer radiance lit her from within.

"Will you marry me, Alice?"

She nodded. Her throat worked while she swallowed her magic soup, and he thought she breathed a quiet word. He couldn't actually hear what she said, because he caught the sound within himself as he kissed her. He tasted her; he tasted her magic soup.

"Did you say something, Alice?" he teased.

"No," she said, her lips still clinging to his, so that when she smiled he smiled with her. "Sometimes words aren't necessary."

Mama Lowell's Magical Asparagus Soup

7 cups vegetable broth
3 T butter
1 cup diced carrots
5 green onions, sliced (include green parts)
1½ cups celery, diced (or ½ cup dried celery)
12 asparagus spears
2 cups spinach leaves
salt and pepper to taste

Dumplings*

1 cup flour
2 t baking powder
1 t dried dillweed
¼ t salt
2 t butter
⅜ cup milk

Trim asparagus stalks. Remove tips and reserve. Cut stalks into ½-inch sections.

In soup pot, melt butter. Add celery, carrots, and green onions and cook over low heat, stirring occasionally, until vegetables are softened (about 15 minutes). Add broth and asparagus stalks. Raise temperature to medium and continue cooking until mixture comes to a full boil. Cover and cook about 15 minutes until vegetables are tender.

While soup is cooking, measure dumpling ingredients into a separate bowl. Work in butter with tips of fingers. Add milk gradually. Mix with knife until dough forms; set aside.

Return to soup and add spinach, asparagus tips, salt, and pepper. Cook for 5 more minutes. Drop dumpling mixture by tablespoons on top of soup. Cover and continue cooking until dumplings are cooked through, about 10 minutes.

*Modern-day cooks can make a simpler dumpling by using 1 cup plus 2 tbs. biscuit baking mix. Stir in ⅓ cup milk and 1 t dried dillweed. Add to soup as instructed above.

KISSES SWEETER THAN . . .

Jean Wilson

CHAPTER ONE

Laura Leigh Westbrook fumed all the way from her office in San Antonio to the train station in Horsefly, Texas. From the first correspondence she'd received from Mrs. Lawrence, she'd been appalled at the ridiculous name of the town. Later, she'd learned that the stop on the railroad had been named by German immigrants. The Americans had changed the name to something easier to say and spell. Hence the small town became stuck with the silly name of Horsefly.

Now she found herself on a dusty road struggling with a team of high-strung horses who kept trying to turn back to their stable. The man at the livery had directed her to the Lawrence place, a mere four miles east of town. After the exasperating day she'd had, the trip seemed more like twenty miles. A grove of trees in the distance caught her attention, and she hoped she'd reached her destination. Her arms ached from trying to control the team.

Because of a delayed train, this assignment had taken much longer than she'd anticipated. When she'd left the office that morning, she'd planned to meet with Mary Lawrence and return home on the evening train. According to the watch pinned to her lapel, it was after three o'clock. That left only three hour to complete her chore and return to Horsefly to meet the six o'clock train.

Dark clouds gathered in the south, making the horses ever more skittish than before. She turned the team down the narrow lane between the row of sturdy oaks. The Lawrence homestead appeared a neat, orderly farm. The fence posts stood in a straight line, and the outbuildings looked well cared for. Waist-high corn waved in the wind and a small herd of cattle grazed in the meadow. The doors and windows of the white house were thrown open, welcoming the summer breeze that had suddenly sprung up from the south.

She pulled the team to a halt and tamped down her temper. No use taking out her annoyance on the innocent Mrs. Lawrence; her anger was fueled by her father, who refused to recognize her talents as a serious journalist. She'd been assigned to what he called "lady's stuff." Although she'd worked with him for eight years, he still couldn't accept her desire to someday become publisher and editor of the *Advantage*. Since she was his only child, it was either leave it to her, sell it, or turn it over to her incompetent cousin, Arnold. Laura Leigh cringed every time she thought about the paper going to rack and ruin under other leadership. Herbert Westbrook, like many men in the enlightened year of 1895, believed that a woman's place was in the home. Like his own wife and this Mrs. Lawrence. He couldn't accept his daughter's desire for a career, or her involvement with the suffrage movement. Both remained a constant thorn in the side of the veteran newsman.

Hurriedly, she climbed down and smoothed the wrinkles from the skirt of her navy suit. Picking up her portfolio, she paused for a moment to study her surroundings. Instead of flowers, neat beds of herbs surrounded the porch. A sumptuous aroma wafted from the windows and a pie cooled on the sill. Mrs. Lawrence deserved the praises she'd already garnered for her recipes. Laura Leigh's stomach rumbled. In her eagerness to reach the homestead, she hadn't taken time for dinner.

As she started up the steps, a figure appeared from around the side of the house. A boy of about twelve skidded to a halt and stared in amazement.

"Afternoon, ma'am." Under a tumble of red hair, his green eyes sparkled with interest.

"Hello. Is this the Lawrence homestead?" she asked. Eye level with the young man, she flashed her brightest smile.

"Yes, ma'am."

When he didn't make a move or offer further information, she glanced into the screen door. "Is your mother home?"

A cloud passed over his face. "No, ma'am."

She was getting nowhere fast. "When are you expecting her back?" After the long trip, had she just missed the woman she'd traveled miles to see?

He shuffled from one scuffed boot to the other. "Don't rightly know."

"Billy," a gruff voice called from the direction of the barn. "Where are you?"

The boy glanced from Laura Leigh to the barn. "On the porch, Paw, talking to a lady." He turned back to her. "Paw didn't tell me we was expecting company."

Almost immediately, a figure appeared from the dark interior of the barn. A tall, powerfully built man stalked toward the house. He wiped his brow with a red kerchief and shoved it into the rear pocket of his denim trousers. A battered black hat hid his hair and eyes.

He approached the porch, and in a show of courtesy, he removed the hat and nodded. "Can I help you?"

Afternoon sunshine glittered off his perspiration-dampened dark auburn hair. Eyes the same green as the boy's met hers in a questioning glance. A heavy growth of dark whiskers shadowed his square jaw. Except for the scowl that narrowed his lips, he was quite nice looking. She stilled the pounding in her chest. She hadn't expected to deal with the woman's husband, especially one as large and intimidating as this man.

"Ma'am?" He narrowed his eyes and studied her under thick lashes.

Heat colored her face. She hadn't meant to stare and lose track of the conversation. "Sorry. I'm looking for Mary Lawrence."

His face paled. "Billy, it's fixing to storm. Stable the horses before it hits."

The boy glanced at the wide blue sky with its smattering of puffy white clouds. "Paw, you sure? Looks nice to me."

"Go," the man ordered in a voice that would brook no argument.

His hands shoved into the pockets of his coveralls, the boy shuffled toward the barn. He glanced over his shoulder and shrugged, clearly unhappy at being dismissed.

The man's gaze followed the boy, but he made no attempt to introduce himself.

His rudeness stuck another thorn in her side. "Sir, I repeat, I'm looking for Mrs. Lawrence. Is she expected back shortly?"

His glanced at the sky, then back at her. "No."

On a sigh, she shook her head. "Are you her husband?" Getting information from this stoic man was worse than pulling teeth.

"There is no Mrs. Lawrence."

Confused, she studied the closed expression on his face. "Do I have the wrong house? Is there another Lawrence homestead nearby?"

"We're the only ones." He slammed his hat onto his head. "You'd best head back to town before the storm hits."

Like the boy, she doubted the probability of an impending storm. Bright sunshine filtered through the trees, and only a few clouds drifted across the sky. "Sir, I have correspondence from a Mary Lawrence at Horsefly. The livery owner directed me to this homestead. Now you tell me there is no Mrs. Lawrence. Do you have a housekeeper? A mother? A sister?"

"No, there's just me and my son."

She shot a glance at the pie and inhaled the luscious aroma that came from the kitchen. Something just didn't add up. "Do you mind if I sit down for a moment?" She sank to the porch steps for a chance to think. "Could you fetch me a drink of water, please?"

Immediately, he retreated to the well to the side of the house. Her gaze followed his every movement. Muscles in his forearms bulged as he worked the pump handle up and down. He was quite a well-built man, so unlike the dandies her mother paraded in and out of the house as possible suitors for her only daughter. Mother couldn't understand that Laura Leigh was content to remain unmarried at the spinsterish age of twenty-seven.

Her wandering thoughts returned to the purpose of this trip. Could it be that Mr. Lawrence was hiding something? Somebody had sent in the prize-winning recipes that the *Advantage* had printed over the past months. Laura Leigh's instincts as a reporter kicked into gear. The man returned seconds later with a ladle of icy water.

"Thank you, Mr. Lawrence." She sipped the water slowly, studying the man while he studied her. This assignment could be much more interesting than expected.

He nodded and propped a wide shoulder against a porch post. "Mind telling me why you're looking for this Mrs. Lawrence?"

After a moment's thought, she decided to tell the truth and let him suffer the consequences. "I'm Laura Leigh Westbrook from the San Antonio *Advantage*. A Mary Lawrence—at least I think her name was Mary; the way the signature was scribbled, it was difficult to tell—submitted a recipe that took first place in our contest." She studied his expression. His eyes narrowed so slightly, only a trained observer would notice. "Since then, she's submitted other dishes, and our readers are quite taken with her concoctions." She sniffed the succulent smells wafting from the window. "They're clamoring for more. It seems she has employed a method of exact measurements and complete directions very similar to that taught at the Boston Cooking School. Even a new bride can follow her instructions."

Taking another sip from the dipper, she continued to ponder the man's reactions. So far, he'd shown little response. Now a slight blush crept up his thick throat. He folded his arms across his chest. An intriguing tuft of burnished hair peeked from the open buttons of his shirt.

When he remained silent, she plunged ahead. "We would like to publish a collection of her recipes with detailed instructions and advice for both the novice and the experienced cook. So you see, I'm desperate to locate the woman."

"Sorry. I don't know a Mary Lawrence."

He was lying through those straight white teeth. "Too bad we can't locate her." She stood and set the empty dipper on the porch. "The book could earn a tidy sum for her. Many women would jump at the chance to share their expertise with others, and help their families in the process."

The last brought a tightening to his lips. "I'm sure they would."

She glanced at her watch. "I'd best be on my way if I'm to make the last train back to San Antonio." A rumble of thunder sounded in the distance. "You may be right about a storm. If you hear from the elusive Mary Lawrence, please have her contact me." Digging into her handbag, she pulled out a business card with her name and the address of the paper.

Work-roughened hands brushed hers as he took the card. For a brief instant their fingers touched, and Laura Leigh wished she wasn't wearing her gloves. She wondered how his hands would feel holding hers. As quickly as the thought surfaced, she shoved it away. She was on an assignment, and she had no time for fanciful notions. But if she didn't think fast, she was sure to fail—and she'd never failed on a project in her life.

He studied the card and shoved it into his pocket. At least he hadn't thrown it away.

"You'd best hurry, ma'am. You don't want to be caught on the road in a storm."

The wind had picked up and dry leaves swirled around the

yard. Her wide hat fluttered. Before she could grab the brim, a gust of wind tore it away and flung it toward the trees. "My hat!" she shouted.

Laura Leigh lifted the hem of her fashionable gored skirt and raced after what was her very best hat. Mr. Lawrence also dashed after the fleeing object. The ivory hat lifted and soared like a kite caught by the breeze. A big sheepdog joined the chase, nearly tripping her in his enthusiasm. She snagged her hem on a thorny bush and paused long enough to tug it free. With his longer stride and added height, Mr. Lawrence snatched the hat from a low-hanging limb. She smiled her thanks, breathless from unaccustomed running. Holding it tightly to her head, she turned back to the hired wagon.

A crack of lightning lit the sky, and the team hitched to the wagon reared on their hind legs. "The horses," she shouted. Again she hastened her step. The dog scampered ahead, barking and dancing around the team. Frightened by the commotion, the horses broke loose and galloped away, dragging the wagon behind them.

Mouth agape, Laura Leigh watched her transportation dash helter-skelter toward town. "Go after them," she ordered. The man skidded to a halt at her side.

"No use," he said, his breath coming in short gasps. "They won't stop until they're safely back at the livery."

Another flash of lightning, followed by a loud blast of thunder, sent the dog darting under the porch. At the same moment, the sky broke open, and large raindrops splattered on the dusty ground. Mr. Lawrence grabbed her arm and propelled her toward the shelter of the porch.

"Get inside," he ordered. "I have to see to the animals."

"But . . . but . . ." she sputtered. He was already gone, sprinting toward the barn. Within seconds, sheets of rain pounded on the tin roof of the overhang. She retrieved her portfolio and cowered against the wall in a furtive attempt to escape being drenched by the wind-whipped cloudburst. To protect her new linen suit, she slipped inside the door.

In the parlor darkened by the cloudy afternoon, she located a lamp on a round table and struck a match to the wick. Feeling like an intruder, she glanced at her surroundings. A faded brown davenport fronted a stone fireplace. Beside it were a tattered easy chair and a wooden rocker. Books and newspapers lay on the floor beside the chair. She could imagine Mr. Lawrence's large body resting in the chair after a hard day's work.

She bit her lip, wondering who prepared his meals. Did he cook all the food, or was there a woman somewhere whom he refused to acknowledge?

The man was a mystery, and mysteries intrigued Laura Leigh. As a great fan of *The Adventures of Sherlock Holmes,* she often solved the mystery before the famous detective created by Arthur Conan Doyle. A good reporter was also a good detective.

The patter of rain on the roof brought her out of her reverie. After dropping her hat on the davenport, she carefully removed her jacket and shook off the raindrops. Rushing around the room, she closed the windows, and remembered the pie cooling on the sill. Fortunately, the porch had sheltered the pie, and she retrieved it before it became wet and inedible. It smelled wonderful. Unable to stop herself, she tugged off her gloves and dipped a finger into the filling and stuck it into her mouth.

She closed her eyes and sighed. It was heavenly. The fruit was a combination of strawberry and probably rhubarb, perfectly seasoned with a touch of sugar and cinnamon. She was tempted to take a slice and try the flaky crust, but she didn't dare be so presumptuous. Glancing around the kitchen, she spotted loaves of fresh, golden bread on a sideboard. She sliced a tiny bit off the cut loaf. It was finely textured and good enough to eat without butter. Somebody in this house was a talented cook and baker.

That was just the person Laura Leigh needed to contact. In spite of the indifferent man of the house, she intended to complete her assignment.

Laura Leigh stepped to the window and looked toward the barn. The rain beat angrily on a large vegetable garden filled with tomatoes, beans, and other plants. From the barn two figures appeared, their heads bent, running for the house. Mr. Lawrence and his son jumped onto the porch and shook their heads like wet dogs. They slipped into the kitchen and dripped water onto the clean floor. Laura Leigh stepped back and snatched two towels from the back of the door. She tossed one to each male.

Mr. Lawrence buried his face in the towel and dried his face and hair. His son pulled off his boots and headed into the parlor. "Paw, I'm going to my room to change."

Left alone with the man, she wasn't sure how to handle the situation. Every day Laura Leigh worked with male reporters, copyboys, and printers. None of them or the men she knew socially made her feel so small and intimidated as this big, gruff farmer. She shifted her gaze to the window and the rain that showed no signs of letting up. From the corner of her eye, she watched the man. His wet chambray shirt clung to his broad shoulders. He tugged the shirt from his denims and slipped it over his head. Rarely had she seen a man's bare chest and never one so masculinely interesting.

Unable to help herself, she stared at him. He rubbed the towel across his chest. Under a mat of dark russet curls, his muscles were as sharply defined as those on a bronze statue. Her gaze lowered to soaked denims that clung to his powerful legs the way her silk stockings clung to hers. Tingles skidded up her spine. What she was doing was indecent. A respectable woman would never lust openly at a man—a stranger she'd met only minutes before.

Mortified by her behavior, she lifted her gaze to his face and met his stare. Her breath hitched in her throat at being caught in such improper behavior. She froze in place. Seldom was Laura Leigh at a loss for words or ill at ease. Watching this man seemed to rob her of her sensibilities.

He found his voice first—a deep, husky rasp. "I'll change into dry duds and when the rain stops I'll drive you into town." His long strides left wet bootprints from the kitchen, through the parlor, and into the narrow hallway.

Only when she heard a door slam shut did she realize she'd been holding her breath. She swallowed hard, her throat dry. Needing a drink, she filled a cup from the pitcher beside the pump on a sideboard.

The rain continued to fall, and the gray clouds made the afternoon as dark as night. Thankfully, she was safely indoors and not on the road with a spirited team. Shivers raced over her at the thought of being caught outdoors, yet being stranded on the homestead with a handsome, enigmatic man was nearly as daunting.

As soon as the rain let up, he would drive her to town. There was still time to meet the train to return home. Only she would return empty-handed.

She sipped the water, and again took inventory of the kitchen. A modern Acme cookstove, as new and shiny as the one in the Westbrook home, stood against one wall. A large pot simmered on the burner, and a pot of coffee warmed on the reservoir. She turned to the counter. Behind the freshly baked bread, she noticed a tablet of writing paper. With a glance over her shoulder, she made sure neither father nor son had returned. Although it was rude, and terribly nosy, she picked up the pad and turned the top page.

Printed in a neat hand was a recipe for a pie. Scanning down the ingredients, she figured it was for the pie she'd already tasted. The precise instructions were printed with exact measurements. It was signed "Mary Lawrence." No, she was wrong. It wasn't *Mary;* the name was *Marcus.*

"That's private property." The rough voice came from over her shoulder and a large hand snatched the pad from her fingers.

She spun on her heel and stared at him. His plaid shirt was

open over dry denim trousers. She dropped her gaze from that intriguing wide chest to his large bare feet. When her eyes again met his, she nodded. "You're right. There is no Mary Lawrence. It's Marcus. You're Marcus Lawrence. You're the woman I'm looking for, and you're a man."

CHAPTER TWO

"I'm glad you noticed, ma'am." Marc shoved the writing pad on the highest shelf. He should have known better than to leave a reporter alone in his kitchen. The woman was determined to learn his secrets or die trying.

She studied him with a scrutiny that heated his skin like the warmth from the cookstove. She'd removed her jacket, and the damp shirtwaist clung to her full bosom. A row of tiny buttons and lace ran from her neck to the band of her skirt. He returned her stare with equal ferocity.

She set her hands on her shapely hips. "Well, are you ready to tell me the truth?" Her tone was that of a schoolmarm chiding a mischievous student. Only she was much prettier than any teacher he'd ever met. Her eyes turned a turbulent gray, much like the storm clouds that were now wreaking havoc with his crops.

"I've already told you there's no Mary Lawrence." He lifted the lid on the stew pot and stirred the contents.

"Are you Marcus Lawrence?"

With a nod, he dipped a spoon into the pot and tasted his

stew. His specialty was desserts, but man could not live on sweets alone. "That's my name." He added a dash of the spice mixture he'd created to make seasoning easier.

"You sent in the recipes, didn't you?"

"I don't know what you're talking about."

"Please, Mr. Lawrence. I'm no fool. You tell me that there's nobody here but you and your son. Yet you have a delectable pie cooling and a fragrant stew simmering on the stove." She gestured to the notepad he'd snatched from her. "And the recipe for said pie in detailed description. Do you expect me to believe that some gremlin or fairy entered the house and prepared these delicacies?"

"Do you believe in fairies?"

"Not on your life." A hint of humor curved the corners of her full lips as pink as ripe strawberries.

There was no use lying. The woman was like a bulldog. She would just hang on until she wore him to a frazzle. "They're mine."

She flashed a self-satisfied grin. Almost immediately, the smile turned into a frown. "Oh, my. That does present a problem." She tapped her chin with one finger.

"Problem? How so? You said my recipes were well received." He filled two mugs with coffee from the pot on the stove. "Cream, sugar?"

"Both, thank you." She stirred a large dollop of cream and two spoonfuls of sugar into the cup. "I had a proposition for 'Mary Lawrence,' but I'm not so sure it will work since she doesn't exist."

"If it's about wanting to publish the recipes, I don't see why you can't. Simply use my initial instead of my name." The idea of his creations being published excited him as much as the first five dollars he'd won in the contest months ago. Yet, it wouldn't do to let the woman know how much he wanted it.

"It isn't only publishing the book. There's something else."

She drummed her nails on the table. "We had another offer for her—you."

He narrowed his eyes and studied her. Strands of hair the color of coffee with rich cream had escaped an elaborate twist at the back of her head. Shapely brows lifted over expressive eyes that showed every thought and emotion. She wasn't wearing a wedding band, and she was past the age when most women took a husband. "Get on with it. What kind of offer?"

"My uncle owns Homestead Flour Mills. Since many of your recipes are for pastries and cakes, he would like to sponsor a tour to promote his product. He wanted to pay Mary, who I now know doesn't exist, to travel to various county fairs and give cooking lectures and demonstrations to the ladies. We could take orders for the flour, and sell the cookbooks."

His heart nearly stopped beating. Just the money from the sale of the books would be a welcome addition to his nearly non-existent bank account. "Since I'm a man, you're withdrawing the offer." He'd come a hairsbreadth from having his dream come true only to have it blow up in his face.

"I'm afraid so. Most of the participants in the domestic events at the fairs are women, and they might resent a man who can best them in what they consider their domain."

"Then it looks as if you've made this trip for nothing." Marc couldn't hide the disappointment in his voice.

"Not entirely." She stood and moved toward the parlor. Seconds later she returned with a paper in her hand. "We can still publish the cookbook, although it won't sell as well without proper promotion."

"Can't be helped. I can't change my sex."

She laughed softly, a throaty chuckle that was incredibly womanly. The sound settled in his chest and heated his blood. "No, even if you tried, you're much too large to pass for a woman." Her eyes sparkled with humor.

For just a moment he envied her husband, or lover, or any other man in her life. He'd been alone for too long if just being near this woman had him thinking about Miss Westbrook in such an unseemly manner.

He laughed to hide his growing discomfort. "I'd never fit into those shoes." He wiggled his toes, and garnered a full-blown laugh from her.

"We could hide your boots under a long skirt." Her eyes glittered with amusement. "But I doubt we could get a gown to span those incredibly wide shoulders." Her cheeks pinked prettily and his heart thumped at the admission that she'd noticed his body. He'd certainly noticed her womanly figure under the damp cotton blouse.

"I'm not interested in a corset, either."

"I don't blame you. These things were designed by the Spanish Inquisition torturer who hated women."

His gaze shifted to the line of her body shaped by the undergarment. Full, firm breasts pressed against the soft white fabric of her blouse, and her waist was nipped in above round, womanly hips. Fire streaked through his veins. Needs that normally only tormented him at night burst full bloom in his body.

"I suppose the tour is off."

"My father assigned me to escort Mrs. Lawrence and write about the reception of her, the cookbook, and her creations. Now it looks as if we won't be going."

"Hope you're not too disappointed."

She sipped the coffee. "No. Now I'll get back to some serious journalism."

Marc rarely had guests, and never a pretty woman, yet he found himself enjoying her company. "You're a reporter on the *Advantage*? I didn't think they usually hired women."

Her eyes shot fire. "That's the attitude I've been fighting for years. My father is the publisher and editor, and he allows me to cover the stuff the men don't like—women's issues, as long as they aren't serious or important. Once in a while I get in a story about the suffrage movement. Usually it's recipes and covering tea parties. Someday he'll accept me as a serious journalist."

"So I was your assignment."

"Mrs. Lawrence was. Of course, now that's a moot issue." She stood and moved to the doorway at the rear porch.

He followed her and glanced over her shoulder. She was taller than most women, hitting him in the middle of his chin. The fragrance of lavender surrounded her like a gentle mist. It was a welcome change from the barnyard smells and lye soap that were a normal part of his life.

She shivered and hugged her arms. "Is this rain ever going to let up? If we don't leave soon, I'll miss my train."

"Could settle in for the night."

"It can't." She spun and collided with his chest.

He clasped her arms to steady her. Her breasts touched his bare chest like hot coals. She gasped and gazed up into his face. Her skin was as white and smooth as thick, rich cream. He couldn't remember the last time he'd held such a lovely woman in his arms. Their eyes met and locked. Marc felt as if the lightning that had been striking all around them had hit him square in the chest. He lowered his gaze to her parted lips, as moist as a rain-kissed rose. Like a bee spying that succulent flower, he bent his head to sip at the nectar.

"Paw! When are we gonna eat? I'm starved."

Marc jumped back so quickly that Miss Westbrook staggered and stumbled into his arms. Her hands braced against his bare skin, warming his flesh like a hot bread fresh out of the oven. He squelched the hunger in his gut and steadied her on her feet. She dropped her hands, but the question remained in her gaze. Would he have kissed her? Even Marc didn't know the answer. But he'd sure as heck wanted to.

"In a minute, son," he called. Billy stood in the kitchen doorway staring wide-eyed at Marc and the woman in his embrace. This time she backed away and returned to stare into the stormy afternoon. He bit his lip to calm the storm thundering in his heart. Rebuking his own foolishness, he stalked back to the stove and the simmering stew.

"Is the lady staying for supper?" Billy asked.

"I suppose so. Until the rain lets up, she's kind of stuck with us."

Miss Westbrook turned and rubbed her hands up and down her arms as if to warm her skin. Sweat broke out on Marc's forehead. He wished those were his fingers stroking her soft flesh. Again he cursed the needs that tortured his mind and body with improper thoughts.

"Billy?" She stepped closer. "We were never properly introduced. My name is Laura Leigh Westbrook."

"Howdy, ma'am. I'm William Thomas Lawrence. Pleased to meet you."

His back to the pair, Marc grunted under his breath. The boy had shown much better manners than his father. "Set the table and we'll eat. Looks like the rain is letting up. After dinner, you can drive Miss Westbrook back to town." The sooner he got rid of the woman, the sooner his heart would slow to normal and his brain would stop being ruled by his libido.

Laura Leigh's knees trembled in spite of her determination to retain her composure around Marcus Lawrence. Her own behavior had shocked and appalled her. Usually when her suitors tried to take liberties, she quickly put them off with her wit or a sharp retort. With this man, she'd been ready and eager for the kiss that never came. Thankfully, his son had stopped them before she made a complete fool of herself.

He spoke little as he served up the stew. From the first dip of her spoon into the bowl, Laura Leigh was amazed at the taste of the meal. "Mr. Lawrence, this stew is wonderful," she said, unwilling to hold back her praise. "This recipe would make a fine addition to the cookbook."

The cloud that had darkened his features lifted at the sincere praise. "If there is a cookbook."

"Paw has been working on a cookbook for ages," Billy remarked. "He's probably the best cook in the county, Miss Westbrook. And he's always trying new dishes. I'll bet I eat better than anybody else I know."

"I wouldn't doubt that one bit." She took another dip into

the rich, thick gravy. "This is much more flavorful than most stews."

Marcus merely shrugged, but his son took up the cause. "I watch Paw sometimes." The young man stood and retrieved a pint glass Mason jar from beside the stove. "He uses this stuff a lot."

"Billy," Marc admonished. "Put that back."

She took the jar full of a substance with the consistency of salt, but sprinkled with a variety of colors. "What is this? Your secret ingredient?"

"Just some spices and herbs I mixed together to make cooking faster and easier when I'm in a hurry."

"Faster and easier." She shook out a few grains into her palm and touched her tongue to the mixture. It was salty, tangy, with a hint of what tasted like Mexican peppers. "Very interesting. Can you put this in other foods?"

"Paw has a couple of other mixtures. He uses them all the time."

An idea crept across her mind. "In addition to the cookbook, you could mix this up and sell it. Women are always looking for ways to make their meals easier and tastier. Why, I'm certain your concoction would be as well received as your recipes."

"Miss Westbrook," he said, taking the jar from her fingers. "We've already discussed the impossibility of the cookbook."

She glanced at the pie. As if reading her mind, he cut three large slices. The crust was flaky and tender, and the filling sweet and as tasty as something the angels would serve. He deserved all the accolades his recipes received. The big, muscular farmer was as much at home in his kitchen as in his barn. For some reason, she found this incredibly appealing. "We can still publish the book, and I'm certain I can get my uncle to help us market the spices."

"No." He set the dish in front of her.

"Oh, don't worry. We won't steal your secret formula. You

can make it here in your kitchen, and advertise it in the *Advantage*."

"Paw, that sounds great. Think of all the money we can make." Billy's face lit up like a child's on Christmas morning.

"I have a farm to run. I don't have time for some pie in the sky scheme." He moved to the window. "The rain is coming down even harder. Looks like you'll either have to battle the storm, or spend the night."

The idea of spending the night both excited and alarmed Laura Leigh. She shoved her empty dish away. "I don't care much for a soaking, but I really can't spend the night."

Marc shrugged his wide shoulders as if it didn't matter to him. "Your choice, ma'am." Even as he spoke, another flash of lightning lit the sky, and thunder rattled the window panes. "You have a husband or fiancé waiting for you?"

"No. I'm unmarried, and I live with my parents." She hugged her arms to ward off a chill. If she spent the night, her parents would worry. Yet, she often stayed at the office all night when working on a story. On a long sigh, she turned to face him. "Looks as if I'll be staying."

CHAPTER THREE

"Miss Westbrook can have my bed, Paw." Billy grinned at the pretty woman who had spent the past minutes staring out the window at the storm.

She turned and smiled. The woman had the warmest smile, as sweet as his grape jam. Her eyes lit up like stars on a clear night. "Thank you, Billy. But I don't mind sleeping on the davenport."

"Oh, no, ma'am, that wouldn't be right. You're welcome to have my room."

"Don't argue with my son, Miss Westbrook. He's trying to be a gentleman." Something Marc was having problems remembering to be. The woman had brought out needs he'd tried to deny and yearnings he'd struggled to control. Every time he looked at her, his brain turned to mush and his gut knotted.

"Thank you, Billy. That's very kind of you." She stood and gathered the dishes. "Since you did the cooking, I suppose I'm in charge of cleaning."

"No need, ma'am." His son took the dishes from her hands.

"We don't often get company, especially pretty ladies. I'll do the cleaning."

Marcus stared at his son. It usually took threats and bribery to get the boy to do the dishes. Tonight, he'd actually volunteered for the chore. "Is that my boy talking? Or did somebody steal him and leave this polite young man behind?"

"Go on, Paw. Don't make Miss Westbrook think bad about me."

Her eyes flashed with humor. "I hear that gypsies often steal children. Did they happen to come by here?"

Marc's blood turned to ice. The woman had no idea how close to the truth her jest had come. She'd inadvertently voiced the fear that he'd lived with for twelve years. Only Marc knew that his son was half gypsy.

She rolled up the sleeves of her blouse. "You wash, I'll dry."

With a shake of his head, Marc shoved aside the disturbing thought. He hadn't seen a Romany caravan in years, and he intended to steer clear of them at any cost. Needing fresh air to clear his thoughts, Marc retreated to the porch to watch the rain batter his land. True, the crops needed the rain, but too much would ruin his potatoes and tomatoes. A cup of coffee in his hand, he propped a wide shoulder against a post and ignored the splatter of rain that splashed on his feet. His attention turned to the problem at hand. The storm showed no sign of letting up. That meant that he would be forced to share his home with the woman who filled his mind with indecent ideas and made him feel more alive than he had in years.

Behind him, the sounds of laughter and voices poured from the kitchen. The pair seemed to be getting along well. His stomach knotted. Over the years, he'd rarely spent more than a few minutes alone with a decent woman. He'd forgotten how good a woman's laughter sounded, and how sweet they smelled. Miss Westbrook reminded him of everything he'd missed in his years of self-imposed celibacy.

A loud squeal brought him around. It was a woman's scream.

He turned pale. Had she burned herself on a pot of hot water? In a few long strides, he slammed into the kitchen. Miss Westbrook had soap bubbles on the tip of her nose, and Billy's hair was damp.

The laughing lady ducked under the table, and Billy trailed after her, his hands full of rapidly melting bubbles. "I'll get you," he yelled, his voice breaking with laughter.

Miss Westbrook popped her head up from under the table and let loose with a large wad of soap. Billy ducked and the soap plopped in the middle of Marc's forehead.

"What the hell is going on in here?" At the loud sound of his voice, the pair stopped and their laughter died in the noise of the rain beating on the roof.

Billy's eyes grew wide, and he looked properly chastised. As for the woman, she grinned like a contented cat. Hair stuck out from her once neat bun, and the front of her blouse was spotted with water. "We were just having a little fun. You know, to make the work easier."

He wiped the soap from his face before it dripped into his eyes. Marc wondered how long it had been since he'd heard his son laugh with so much abandon. Or when Marc had last felt like having fun. Watching the sparkle in the woman's eyes, he couldn't be angry with her or Billy. Turning toward the dishpan, he scooped up two wads of soap and in one quick movement that caught both of them offguard sent a glob at each of the combatants. Billy sputtered and backed away. Miss Westbrook darted for the dishpan, only to encounter Marc's body as he guarded the wet ammunition.

"Not fair," she said, reaching around his waist.

Her damp blouse pressed against his chest. As she moved from side to side, her bosom brushed his bare flesh under his unbuttoned shirt. Her touch shot rivers of awareness through him. Hands circling his waist, she stopped abruptly. As she lifted her gaze to his, the smile died on her face. Her hazel eyes changed to a deep, sparkling gray, like the hot ashes of a fire. The same heat sizzled through him, scorching his flesh where she touched. His pulse beat in his ears, drowning out the sound of the wind and rain.

For long moments, their gazes held. Marc felt as if he was floating on a river and headed toward the rapids. Any second, he would tumble over the rocks and be lost forever. Thankfully, his common sense took over. "Sorry, Miss Westbrook, game's over."

She jerked away from him and wiped her face on her sleeve. "I suppose it's best. You're bigger and we're at a disadvantage."

His gaze drifted over her. The damp shirtwaist clung to her body, and if anybody was at a disadvantage it was he. Abruptly, he turned away and grabbed his slicker from a peg. He had to get away before he made a fool out of himself. "I'm going to check on the animals." Within seconds he'd pulled on his boots and rain gear and stepped onto the porch. The rain hit his face, but did little to cool the fire in his blood. How he was going to spend the night under the same roof with her was beyond him. Marc suspected he was in for a long and sleepless night.

Laura Leigh tossed and turned all night. Billy had kindly given up his bed and moved to share his father's room. Without her nightclothes, she tried to make the best of the situation. Marcus had given her a clean chambray shirt that reached to the tops of her knees. She managed to comb out her hair and left it hanging loose down her back. Wearing only a shirt that smelled of lye soap, sunshine, and man, she felt slightly decadent. Especially since a handsome, eligible man slept on the other side of a thin wall.

Wouldn't her mother be shocked if she knew that her daughter had spent the night with a man and his son? That was one thing she'd never tell her father. Why, he would come after Mr. Lawrence with a shotgun. The thought made Laura Leigh laugh.

Sometime during the night, the rain had stopped. She awoke

to the silence of the night. For a long moment, she listened to
the sounds from the house. Faint snores came from the adjoining
room. The two males were sound asleep. She punched the
pillow and tried to return to sleep. Instead of growing drowsy,
her mind was racing in a hundred different directions. Mostly
she wondered about Marcus Lawrence.

The man was an enigma. A farmer who was a gourmet cook.
What a contrast. His green eyes had a troubled look every time
she'd mentioned his wife. Was he still in love with the woman
who was no longer a part of his life? And those recipes. She
remembered the note pad that he'd so rudely snatched from
her fingers. What other secrets were hidden in those notes?

Curiosity overcame good manners. Tossing off the blanket,
she sat up and swung her legs to the floor. She bit her lip and
reconsidered her actions. The Lawrences had been generous
hosts and had offered her shelter in a storm. Did she intend to
repay their hospitality by snooping into their private business?
Then her journalistic instincts kicked in. Before she could consider the propriety of her actions, she padded on bare feet to
the door. Carefully she opened the door and noted that the next
door was tightly closed. As silent as a thief, she crept to the
kitchen. A pale glow from the embers in the stove guided her
way.

On tiptoes, she stretched to reach the upper shelf. "Darn,"
she muttered. Her fingers barely touched the shelf, but she
couldn't reach the pad. Not to be hindered, she tugged a chair
from the table over to the shelves. She climbed onto the chair
and stretched an arm onto the upper shelf. Her fingers searched,
and came up empty. Leaning closer, she stretched her full
length, reaching into the corners. The shirt pulled up to the
middle of her bare thighs.

"Looking for something?"

Startled by the unexpected husky voice, she jumped and
staggered. Off balance on the chair, she swayed from the right
and to the left. She flailed her arms to regain her balance. With
nothing to grab, she felt herself flying through the air. Instead

of landing on the hard floor, strong arms snatched her as easily as catching a baby.

Eyes wide, she stared into the shadowed face of her savior. Even the darkened room couldn't hide the angry scowl on Marc's face. Common sense told her the man had every reason to be angry with a guest who was searching his house like a burglar.

Her back rested on one muscular arm, while her bare legs rode on an equally bare arm. She clutched his strong shoulders for balance. He was shirtless, and her chest pressed against his. Wearing nothing but his wash-worn shirt, she might as well be naked in his arms.

"Uh . . ." Her words stuck in her throat. Never had she been this close to such a virile man. "You can put me down now."

Slowly, he lowered her, sliding her body down his until her toes touched the floor. For what seemed like an eternity, she remained pressed to him—full, firm breasts to solid muscular chest, soft female belly to a hard male stomach, and smooth, bare silky limbs to sturdy legs under rough canvas trousers.

"You didn't answer my question," he said in a voice raspy with sleep.

"Question?" For the life of her, she didn't remember anything except the pleasure of the feel of the man who held her in his arms.

He slid his hands to her waist. "What were you doing in my kitchen?"

"What?" Her hands rested on the brushing of hair on his chest. It tickled her palms and sent erotic sensations up her arms. "What are you doing up in the middle of the night?"

His fiery green eyes locked with hers. "I heard something scraping across the floor."

"Maybe it was a rat." She tangled her fingers in those intriguing curls on his chest. His heart pounded like a bass drum. He pressed closer, his maleness hard against her stomach. Tingles settled in her most female part, something that she'd never experienced with any of her suitors. Marc sent yearnings sizzling through her unlike any she'd known before.

"We don't have rats." His mouth quirked in a bit of a smile. Heat glittered behind his lowered lashes. "At least not four legged ones."

"My mother warned me my curiosity would get me in trouble one day."

"Haven't you ever heard that curiosity killed the cat?" His hands were warm and his thumbs stroked the flesh under her breasts.

She nodded. "And the old proverb says 'Curiosity is ill manners in another's house.' I suppose I should heed warnings."

He lowered his face, his mouth inches from hers. The night's growth of whiskers made him look ominous and dangerous, like a dark figure out of her dreams. "If you wanted anything I have, all you had to do was ask."

At that moment, Laura Leigh couldn't even remember why she'd left the bed and entered the kitchen. All she knew was how safe and protected she felt in his house and in his arms. Desire streaked through her like a bolt of lightning. She'd never felt this way about a man. And she had no business feeling so attracted to a man she'd met only hours earlier. A man who was so devoted to his dead wife, he couldn't even talk about the woman.

Ignoring the tightness in her chest, she shoved out of his arms. No good could come of getting involved with a man she could never have. "I'm sorry I woke you. Please forgive my ill manners." Turning on her heels, she darted to the hallway and the safety of Billy's room. She shoved her fist in her mouth to control her emotions. She'd been wrong to leave the room and snoop around the man's home. She hugged her waist, her flesh still warm and tingly from his touch. No man had ever seen her so indecently clad, yet at the time she was neither embarrassed nor ashamed. Now she was only sorry that after tomorrow there was little chance she would see him again. A tinge of sadness settled in her chest. On a long sigh, she padded back to the bed and immersed herself in dreams of what could never be.

Marc's knees turned to tapioca. He sank into the chair Laura Leigh had used for a ladder. If he'd had any sense at all, he'd have left her alone to snoop into his belongings. A lonely man had no business holding an attractive woman in his arms. He breathed deeply to calm his racing heart.

Thank goodness for the darkness that had dimmed his view of her shapely form as she stretched to reach to the top shelf. In the pale light he'd gotten enough of a look at those long legs to torment his body nearly beyond endurance. Worse was holding her in his arms. When he'd startled her, and she'd begun to fall, he had automatically reached to prevent her from being injured.

Instead of releasing her immediately, he'd held her close to his body. He shivered at the loss of the heat that had sizzled through his blood like a drop of batter in grease. She'd been so soft, so appealing, so feminine. And he was so needy. He closed his eyes and pictured her lying on the narrow bed clad only in his shirt, her beautiful hair spread over the pillow like a halo. He'd felt those full breasts pressed to his chest, enjoyed the feel of her rounded stomach against his flat belly, and rejoiced when her long, silky legs touched his. Letting her go was one of the hardest things he'd ever had to do. Alone in the kitchen, his own private domain, he was as aroused as when she'd brushed her hand over his chest and he'd pressed his arousal against her.

Knowing he would never get back to sleep, he snatched up a towel from behind the door and stalked from the house. After the rain, the stream behind the house would chill him to the bone. And cool the ardor that now threatened his peace of mind.

* * *

By dawn, Marc had come to terms with his libido and his needs were under control. He'd returned to the house and proceeded to test a new recipe. In his cooking, he could lose himself and forget the loneliness in his life. He'd started experimenting with recipes after his parents died and he'd been left alone with a young son to raise. Cooking became both a passion and a necessity.

As he mixed the cake batter, Marc doubted he would ever create a recipe without thinking about Laura Leigh Westbrook and her offer to publish his cookbook. Or of the way she'd felt in his arms.

Shoving aside his desires, he put the cake into the oven and started on breakfast. As soon as she arose, he would send her into town to catch the next train back to San Antonio. And get her out of his life, forever. She was a reporter, the kind of woman who would snoop and delve into his private life and uncover secrets best left alone.

Marc sensed more than heard the woman enter the kitchen. His nerves jumped as he felt her presence behind him. Even after drenching himself in freezing water for half the night, his blood heated at her approach.

"Something smells good," she said, peeking over his shoulder.

He turned a piece of crisp bacon in the skillet. Grease popped and splattered on his hand. The hot grease didn't faze his toughened skin; the woman at his side scorched him with just a touch. "You'd better move back," he said. "You don't want to burn that pretty skirt and blouse."

She gave a soft chuckle, the sound that made him think of soft blankets and cold nights. And a passionate woman under the covers. Marcus growled under his breath.

"I'm wrinkled and mussed. I hope Billy doesn't mind that I borrowed his hairbrush."

His son was so smitten with the woman, the boy would give

his blood if she needed it. Marcus set the bacon on a platter and turned to the table. She jumped out of his path, and brushed against his arm. For a woman who'd been up late into the night, she looked refreshed and alert, while Marc felt like a bear cheated out of his hibernation.

"He won't mind," he said.

She settled at the table. "Is he still sleeping?"

"No. I sent him into town to send a telegram to your father to tell him that you were delayed, and to check on the train schedule." He filled two cups with coffee. "He'll drive you back to town in time to make your train."

"Thank you. Those biscuits smell heavenly."

"Help yourself."

She smeared butter on a biscuit and dabbed on a spoon of jelly. "Tell me, Mr. Lawrence, do you make your own butter and jelly?"

He slanted a glance over his shoulder. "Butter, no. I buy it from a neighbor lady. Jelly, yes."

"Delicious. You're amazing. Have you ever thought about opening your own restaurant?"

"It's crossed my mind, but I have a farm to run and a son to rear." His voice hardened. He rarely spoke about his dream, knowing it could never come true.

"A shame. Everything is wonderful."

Her praise brought an unbidden smile. "Thank you."

"Have you decided to sign the contracts for the cookbook?"

"No." After their encounter in the night, he hadn't thought about a thing but her. She licked the butter from her fingers in an action that was slow and unbelievably sensuous.

"I'll leave them with you. If you change your mind, let me know. Even without the tour, I'm sure your cookbook will be well received by our readers."

"I'll think about it."

"While you're thinking, consider what the additional funds will mean to your son. For his education. Or for your own eatery."

He shot her a hard glance. "Miss Westbrook, I think of little else."

"Good. Then I'll expect to hear from you."

"Maybe." Surely a business arrangement with her father couldn't hurt. And there was no reason he would have to deal with her.

She'd stirred his interest as easily as he stirred his stew pot. The idea had been simmering in his mind since she'd first mentioned the possibility. Marc had a decision to make and until she left, he wouldn't be able to think clearly about anything. Except her.

CHAPTER FOUR

Laura Leigh sorted her mail into piles on her desk. For the past two weeks she'd looked for a letter from Marcus Lawrence. So far, he hadn't so much as sent a note. And she'd received no new recipes.

If she didn't hear from him soon, she would be forced to confess her failure. That was one thing she'd never admitted to in her life. She wasn't about to let Marcus Lawrence be her first. Too bad he wasn't a woman. The very idea brought a smile. Never had she met a more virile, robust man. He'd been constantly on her mind and in her heart.

She touched a finger to her lips. Their almost-kiss had been a source of turmoil. The man who'd escorted her to the theater a few evenings ago had tried to steal a kiss in the carriage. At the first touch of his lips to hers, she felt her stomach recoil. Before she became sick, she shoved him away and demanded an apology. Immediately, he'd begged her pardon with profuse expressions of regret. She couldn't imagine Mr. Lawrence regretting kissing a woman. If she read him right, he would just take what he wanted and damn the consequences. He'd have kissed her that day if his son hadn't interrupted.

Tossing aside a note inviting her to the next suffrage meeting, she considered Billy. The young man had grown pale when she'd asked for his mother. Had she only recently passed away, leaving a grieving son and husband? That could account for Marc's hard look when she'd questioned him about his wife.

Just what she needed—to be attracted to a farmer who still loved his dead wife. She double-checked the date of the meeting. Since she wouldn't be touring the county fairs, she could attend. No matter that her father thought it all foolishness, Laura Leigh enjoyed working for her causes.

A note on her calendar reminded her of today's assignment—another tea party. On a long sigh, she pinned her small feather-covered hat to her upswept hair and grabbed her note pad. She suppressed a smile. She almost wished a cat fight would break out among the women—anything to liven up what promised to be a boring, run-of-the-mill story.

Checking the watch pinned to her lapel, she hurried down the hallway to the staircase. As she turned at the first landing, she ran headlong into a large, solid object. She staggered for a moment, and would have tumbled down the stairs had strong hands not gripped her arms.

"Sorry," she muttered.

"I beg your pardon," a man said in the same breath.

Her gaze lifted and met dark green eyes under a black hat. "Marcus!" His name burst from her lips.

He steadied her on the narrow landing, his hands strong and firm on her upper arms. "Miss Westbrook. Are you in a hurry?"

"Yes." Her heart thumped like a nine-pound hammer. "No. I mean, I was." She braced her palms against his chest.

A copyboy bounded up the stairs. "Ma'am, you okay?" he asked, staring at her practically swooning in a man's arms.

"I'm fine, Joey." She moved back and allowed the boy to race past on his errand. Once he was out of earshot, she turned to Marcus. Her breath hitched. He wore a black suit and a white shirt. His wide shoulders filled the narrow staircase. Tingles settled in the middle of her chest. "What are you doing here?"

His mouth quirked into a crooked smile. "You invited me."

Aware that she had twisted her fingers into his lapels, she released her hold. "I did?"

"Can we go somewhere and talk?"

The tea party would have to get along without her. "My office." She turned and retraced her footsteps. It had to be important to bring him from his home to San Antonio. She bypassed her father's open door and hustled Marcus into her own tiny office. Heedless of the impropriety of the situation, she closed the door behind him. She dropped her note pad on her cluttered desk and settled on the chair. "Please have a seat, Mr. Lawrence."

He removed his hat and brushed his hand through his hair. It was a few inches shorter than when she'd seen him earlier, and he'd shaved that morning. For a man who looked so much at home in a kitchen, he was vastly out of place in her tiny office.

For a long moment she stared at him, ignoring the good manners her mother had drilled into her. Her throat went dry, and her mind went blank. He was even better looking than the image she'd carried into her dreams every night for the past two weeks.

He cleared his throat. "Miss Westbrook, I would like to know if the offer is still open?"

"Offer?"

"Don't you remember presenting me with a contract for a cookbook?"

Laura Leigh felt like a complete idiot. Looking at him had chased any semblance of intelligence from her brain. "Of course. We want to publish your recipes. Did you decide to sign the contract?"

He nodded and reached into his coat. "I have it here, and

enough recipes to complete the book.'' He set the packet on the desk.

At least something was working out. ''That's wonderful. My father was a little disappointed that I came back empty-handed.'' She opened the packet and quickly perused the signed contract and the neatly printed recipes.

''What about your uncle? Was he disappointed, too?''

''Well, I must confess, I haven't spoken to him yet. I was hoping you could work something out.''

''That's why I'm here. I have a proposition for you.''

Laura Leigh leaned forward and propped her elbows on her desk. Excitement bubbled up in her chest. ''Have you come up with an idea?''

''I have. But I need your help.'' He rested his right ankle over his left knee. His boots were highly polished and his suit neatly pressed. He'd clearly worked to make a decent appearance.

''My help? How?''

''I've been considering our conversation. I don't think I would be very convincing as a woman, but if a real woman could take my place, things could work out for both of us.''

She set her chin on her fists and studied him. He'd said he didn't have a wife or sister. Was there another woman in his life? A fiancée? The prickle of disappointment annoyed her. His private life meant nothing to her except where it concerned his cookbook and tour. ''Have you found this lady?''

''Yes.'' He hesitated a moment before he continued. ''You.''

Her jaw dropped and her hands fell to the desk. ''Me?''

A pleased smile curved his lips. A scar at the corner made it slightly off center. ''You. It was your idea to conduct the tour to promote the cookbook, not to mention your uncle's flour company. Think of all the interesting stories you could write.''

''I still don't understand what you mean.''

''You can be 'Mrs. Lawrence' and give the speeches and demonstrations.''

Her voice came out in a squeal. "Me? That's impossible."

"Why?"

She took a deep breath to calm her pounding heart. The very idea was ludicrous, yet interesting. "First of all, I can't cook. I don't know the difference between a skillet and a stew pot." It was a bit of an exaggeration, but she truly knew nothing about the culinary arts.

"You don't have to know a thing except how to talk. And I've noticed you're very good at that. I'll be right there to tell you what to say."

"You and me? Together?" Tingles of excitement crawled up her spine. The idea of being with him both thrilled and frightened her. But wouldn't her mother be shocked at her traveling with a man?

"Certainly. You're pretty and well-spoken. The ladies would be more receptive to you than to a big, ugly farmer. We can give a few little hints and talk about the recipe book. You can tell them that I eat all these dishes, and that I love them. Which is the absolute truth. We'll be able to promote Homestead Flour and my seasoning mix."

Of all the things he'd said, the fact that he thought her pretty made her pulse race. She opened her mouth to tell him that he was far from ugly, but thought better of it. She settled back against her chair to consider the proposition. "Let me get this straight. You want me to be your wife—"

He cut her off with a resounding, "No. I want you to pretend to be 'Mrs. Lawrence,' the cookbook writer. I have no wife."

She stiffened her spine and glared at him. Was his grief for his wife so severe that he refused to acknowledge her? "I'm sorry I offended you. I merely wanted to clarify the situation."

"No offense taken. I apologize for my lack of manners. It was your suggestion to escort the tour. We'll simply switch places. You do the talking and I'll tell you what to say. We might have to judge a few contests, but I'll help you with that."

"Mr. Lawrence, I may not cook, but I can still taste." She stood and hugged her arms. The idea of spending time with him had her mind in a dither and goose pimples on her arms. Propriety demanded that she refuse. But if she ever wanted to be taken seriously as a journalist and go on other assignments, she needed to take a chance now and then. She reached into her desk to pull out the schedule she'd planned weeks before.

Loud male voices came from the hallway. Her spirits sagged. Her father and Uncle Fritz were right outside her door.

"Laura Leigh!" her uncle called, flinging open the door. He entered the office with the exuberance with which he did everything. "Where's my favorite niece?"

She shot a glance at Marcus, who had jumped to his feet at the sudden interruption. "Uncle Fritz, I'm your only niece." Offering her cheek, she accepted his quick kiss.

Her father followed at Fritz's heels. "I told this old goat that you're busy." Herbert stared at Marcus.

"You aren't interrupting, sir," Marcus said.

Laura Leigh stepped forward and quickly made the introductions. Her uncle's eyes widened as he gripped Marcus's hand. "Are you related to the lady who's going to promote my flour in her recipes?"

Hurriedly, Laura Leigh interrupted. "Mr. Lawrence brought the contract for the cookbook and new recipes."

Herbert grinned. "Excellent. I'm ready to publish the cookbook. My cook tried some of your creations, so I can testify that they're very good."

A flush crept up Marcus's thick throat. "Thank you, sir."

Fritz slapped the younger man on the shoulder. "So, are you and the missus ready to make the tour that Laura Leigh outlined? She promised me lots of orders and she should get a story or two out of the county fairs."

Her father laughed, and Laura Leigh cringed. "She'll send back lists of the winners of the pie and preserve contests," he said.

She set her resolve to show them that she could do a lot more than that. "You never know but that I might get something really interesting to report."

"There's a fair this weekend in Kendall County. Will you be able to make it, Lawrence?" Uncle Fritz's question was more of a command. He was a man accustomed to giving orders and having them obeyed.

"I think so, sir. If Miss Westbrook isn't busy."

"She'll go." This time it was her father who was ordering her life. He picked up the contract and recipes. "Let me get this to production. I have an artist who'll add some sketches, and it should be ready in a few days."

Everything was happening so fast, Laura Leigh's head was spinning. "I'm not sure I can leave on such short notice."

"Of course you can, Laurie. This was your idea from the start and you talked me into the project. A good reporter follows through to the end." His orders issued, he turned on his heel and started for the door.

"But Papa, it isn't proper." She didn't add that she didn't quite trust herself to be alone with the handsome farmer.

Her father stared at her over the rims of his eyeglasses. "Why in the world not? You'll be traveling with Mr. and Mrs. Lawrence. What could be more appropriate?"

Only there was no *Mrs.* Lawrence. She opened her mouth to report that truth, when Marcus interrupted. "Miss Westbrook will be quite safe and everything will be above board. I give you my word, sir."

"Then it's settled. Let me get this to production. I want the books ready in time. I'll even print up one recipe to give away free. That should draw interest."

Her uncle pulled a cigar out of his pocket and offered it to Marcus. "Bad habit. My wife thinks I smoke them just to annoy her." He laughed. "Sometimes I do."

Marcus accepted the cigar her uncle had imported from Cuba. "Thank you. I rarely get one of these."

"Enjoy it." Uncle Fritz followed her father to the door. "Herb, how about printing up some flyers to go with the books. My Homestead Flour is a fitting match for those desserts. Besides, I'm footing the bill for the tour."

"I've already thought about that. We'll print an advertisement on the back cover, to remind the ladies of your product." The brothers stalked down the hallway.

"Damn good idea," Fritz said. "Smart girl your daughter. A man couldn't have done a better job."

Coming from her uncle, that was quite a compliment. Their voices faded away in the hustle and bustle of the newspaper offices. She turned to Marcus. "Looks as if we'll be in Kendall County on Saturday."

He shoved the cigar into his pocket. "I'll meet you at the Kendall Inn in Boerne on Saturday morning."

She sank to her chair. There was no getting out of it. If she wanted to be treated like the male reporters, she would have to buck up and complete the assignment. "If we're going to pull this off, you had better write a script for me. I told you I can't cook."

"I'll select a simple recipe, and all you have to do is read the ingredients and pretend to follow the directions. Since we won't have to actually prepare a meal, we should be able to pull it off."

Her heart slowed to normal. "I hope you're right." But some gremlin in the back of her mind warned that it might not be as easy as they thought.

CHAPTER FIVE

Marcus picked up the valise containing a change of clothes and his recipes. He'd come on the early-morning train and already the crowds were gathering on the main street. He surely hoped he and Miss Westbrook could pull this off. He needed the money from the cookbook and he refused to pass up the golden opportunity that Fate—and Miss Westbrook—had dropped into his lap.

A box containing the jars of seasonings he'd spent the past days mixing waited at the railroad station to be picked up after he met Laura Leigh. His sleepy son had driven him into Horsefly, where he had caught the early train to Boerne. Billy had begged to go with him, but Marc reminded him that somebody had to stay behind and care for the animals.

His son had grumbled and complained. Marc had finally given in and promised to take him as soon as they could hire a neighbor to tend the stock.

As he made his way to the hotel, his heartbeat picked up. All week he'd tried to convince himself that his excitement was due to the tour, not to being alone with a pretty woman.

He frowned. It had been years—thirteen to be exact—since he'd been this attracted to a woman. Marc warned himself to control his emotions. The last time he'd lost control, his life had turned into disaster. Serafina had stolen his heart along with his money. However, she'd left him something much more precious—his son.

In spite of his gypsy blood, Billy was a good, hard-working boy. Marc's chest swelled with pride. His son would grow into a fine man, and he would make some girl a good husband. He prayed every day that his son wouldn't let passion override his good sense and marry the wrong woman, as Marc had done.

He'd fallen in love with the beautiful gypsy girl and ignored his own father's warnings. Serafina had captivated him with her exuberance and gaiety. Her dancing had brought fire and excitement into a farmer's dull life—a life that didn't suit her. As soon as Billy was born, Serafina had run away with another gypsy band. He didn't know if she was dead or alive.

Marc shook off the memories that had haunted him for the past weeks. Since he'd met Laura Leigh Westbrook, he'd considered his lonely existence. Until her, he hadn't realized how much he missed having a woman in his life and in his bed. Marc picked his way through the crowds and marched toward the hotel. Thinking about her was futile. As much as he hated the thought, he was married and not free to court a woman or fall in love. He was smart enough not to fall for a woman like Laura Leigh. The Westbrook family was one of the most prominent in San Antonio. Her father owned a newspaper and printing company, and they lived on King William Street amid the other prosperous merchants in the city. She deserved a man from her own social circle, not a dirt farmer without a dime to his name.

Once inside the hotel, he registered at the desk. Laura Leigh's train was due to arrive in about an hour. After placing his bag in his room, he hired a wagon and team from the livery and returned to the depot to wait for her. He propped a shoulder against a post and considered smoking the cigar her uncle had given him earlier that week. Instead, he shoved it back into his pocket. He decided to save it for a special occasion.

The train arrived later than scheduled, and more and more people were heading toward the fairgrounds at the end of town. They were running late, and their first lecture was scheduled just before the pie-judging event. He came to attention when the loud whistle and clatter of wheels announced the arrival of the train. He watched the passengers disembark, checking each woman as she stepped foot on the wooden platform.

He'd begun to think that he was being stood up, when a woman in a wide hat lifted her skirt and showed a bit of a slender ankle and lace-trimmed petticoat. His gaze followed the line of her dark pink skirt to a jacket with puffy sleeves. Laura Leigh smiled when she spotted him and nodded her thanks to the conductor who helped her down the steps. He let out the breath he'd been holding. Not for the first time since he'd accepted this project, he wondered how he was going to survive being in the company of such a lovely woman. His only salvation lay in never being alone with her.

"Mr. Lawrence, I'm so sorry to be late. You simply can't rely on the trains to be on time. Next week, I'll arrive the night before in order not to keep you waiting." She stopped her breathless ramblings and glanced over her shoulder at the porter, who tugged a cart piled with boxes.

"Are these all yours?" he asked.

She nodded. "I have the cookbooks, advertisements for the flour, and order blanks." She signaled for the black uniformed porter to follow her. "And of course my bags."

He groaned. It was clear that the two large valises held her personal belongings. "It's a good thing I hired a wagon. We'd never manage to carry all this to the fairgrounds." Marc picked up a box and heaved it into the back of the wagon. He hadn't seen the cookbook and couldn't wait to see his creations in print. More important, he wanted to get the reactions of women who tried the recipes and pleased their husbands.

"Good thinking. Since we're running late, I'll have to register at the hotel this evening. Did you get a room?"

"Yes." He helped the porter load the other boxes and valises, then handed the man a coin. Thanks to the advance payment that Mr. Westbrook had sent the day before, he had the extra money for such necessities, as well as for a fine room and meals.

Offering a hand to Laura Leigh, he helped her to the wooden seat and climbed in beside her. They used the few minutes' drive to the fairgrounds to go over their strategy. He hoped it went as smoothly as they'd planned.

"Ready, Miss Westbrook?" He pulled the team to a halt.

She set a hand on his arm. Her touch was gentle, but it did funny things to his insides. "Mr. Lawrence, we had best resort to using our Christian names. We don't want anybody to get suspicious, especially since I'm supposed to be M. Lawrence, the author of the cookbook."

"You're right, Miss—I mean, Laura Leigh. I'll try to remember." As if he could forget her name. He'd been saying it over and over in his mind for weeks. "It's a beautiful name."

"I can thank my parents for that. If I had my way, I'd call myself something more exotic, like Alexis or Anastasia. But I suppose I'm stuck with plain Laura Leigh."

He offered his arm. "You don't look like either of those. And there's nothing plain about you."

"Thank you, Marcus. That does make me feel more confident about this project. Let's cross our fingers that we can pull this off."

As they entered the tent where the contestants had lined up their pies and cakes, he spoke briefly to the judges. Women began to gather for the judging, and he and Laura Leigh made their presentation. She read the recipe for his apple cake along with the precise directions. Laura Leigh made it clear that for best results, one should always use Homestead Flour. When someone asked a question, Marc stepped in, and replied that it was so simple, even a man could explain. She passed out a sample recipe, and several women purchased the cookbook and ordered flour. For their first venture, it had gone rather well.

For the remainder of the day, they toured the exhibits. Marc checked out the latest in farm equipment while Laura Leigh made notes on the names of the winners of the various competitions. Later, they returned to the pie judging and awarded the ribbons. More ladies approached and purchased the cookbook. Marc had taken time to look it over, and he was pleased at what the publisher had done. He enjoyed sharing his creations with others. His seasoning mixes also sold better than he'd expected.

Although they hadn't introduced themselves as Mr. and Mrs., the fair organizers assumed they were a married couple and addressed them as such. It didn't matter to Marc. He rather enjoyed having men stare at him with an attractive woman on his arm.

As the sun was setting, Marc guided Laura Leigh toward their hired wagon. He hated to see the day end, but he feared he'd enjoyed her company too much.

"Where are we headed?" she stopped and asked.

"Back to the hotel. Where else?" He loosed the lines of the horse and offered her a hand up.

"So soon? Don't you hear the music? I understand we can have dinner here and then there's dancing under the stars." She glanced toward the crowd gathering in a clearing behind the tents.

"We can eat at the hotel." Gripping her elbow, he all but lifted her off her feet. He'd already spent too much time with this woman for his peace of mind. To touch her, to dance with her, would test his will power beyond endurance. "And I don't dance."

She pulled away and glared at him. "Well, I do. You go back to the hotel. I'm going to stay a while."

"It isn't proper to stay alone." When he reached for her again, she slapped his hand away.

Lowering her voice, she said, "Is it proper for us to be on

this tour without a chaperone? I'm a journalist always looking for an interesting story. I might find one tonight.''

Short of tossing her over his shoulder and bodily carting her away, he had no choice but to let her go. "I give in. We'll both go. But we have to get to bed early. It's been a long day." In a normal day, Marc rose at dawn and worked until dark. Often, he stayed up until midnight baking and creating new recipes. Those activities rarely tired him as much as fighting his emotions where Laura Leigh was concerned. He prayed the night would soon end.

"Thank you." With a smile that would melt ice in winter, she removed her hat and tossed it into the wagon. She looped her arm in his. "Mr. Lawrence, let's join the festivities."

For the next hours, Marc stood on the sidelines while Laura Leigh charmed the farmers and ranchers at the fair. She spoke to the wives about the recipes as if she actually knew what she was talking about. When he stepped away from her to fetch punch, a young cowboy swung her onto the dance floor. She went gracefully into the young man's arms. Marc's big feet felt like railroad ties. If he even tried to dance, he would surely smash her toes like pancakes. When one dance ended, she sipped a glass of punch and was promptly swept back onto the dance floor by yet another man.

Frustrated, he pulled the Cuban cigar out of his pocket and struck a match to the end. He puffed, and choked on the smoke. Only then did he remember that he'd meant to save the extravagant cigar for a special occasion. With a shrug, he reasoned that being with Laura Leigh was as special as his life would get. Forcing himself to remain calm, he continued to puff, while keeping his gaze on her. She sure seemed to be enjoying being with those other men.

As she spun past him, she smiled and winked. He downed both cups of punch to quench a thirst caused more by a woman than the warm night. The music stopped, and Marc stepped forward to claim his escort. He dropped the cigar stub to the ground and smashed it under his heel.

He cringed when Laura Leigh threw back her head and laughed at something the cowboy said. Her throaty laughter irritated him more than it should. That she was having a good time without him shouldn't bother him at all. But it did. He didn't like his reaction one bit. She had every right to dance with anybody she chose. They weren't married—heck, they weren't even courting.

"You naughty boy," she whispered too loudly for confidentiality. "Here's Mr. Lawrence."

He'd almost forgotten their charade. "It's time to return to the hotel," he said. "You understand, don't you?" he asked the man who continued to clutch her elbow.

The younger man nodded and grinned. "Yes, sir, Mr. Lawrence. If this pretty lady was my wife, I'd never let her out of my sight."

Laura Leigh's cheeks pinked. "Thankfully, Mr. Lawrence isn't the jealous type. Are you, *dear?*" She traced his jaw with her fingertip. Desire clutched at his gut. "Where's that punch you promised me?"

He studied the empty cups in his hands. "We'll have to get more." Holding both small cups in one hand, he removed her from the cowboy's grip on her elbow and led her toward the punch table.

"Not that one." She tugged him to another table. "This one is much better."

Marc hadn't noticed the other bowl surrounded by the younger men. They stepped aside when he and Laura Leigh approached. He dipped out two small cups and handed one to her. She drank it down in one long gulp, and he refilled her empty cup. Marc took a sip of the punch and rolled it around in his mouth. It tasted different from the drink he'd had minutes before. When she dipped her third cup, he realized the difference. The punch had been spiked with whiskey. And Laura Leigh was on her way to getting smashed.

"I think you've had enough," he said, taking the cup from her fingers.

She glared at him through glassy eyes. "I'm still thirsty."

"How many cups have you had?"

"Two just now, but earlier I had two, or three." She tapped her lips with a finger. "I don't remember. But it sure was good."

"It's spiked," he grounded between his teeth.

"Spiked? With liquor?" She grinned up at him. "That's rather funny, don't you think?"

"I don't see anything humorous about getting drunk." He clutched her elbow. "Let's go."

"Oh, Marcus. You're an old stick-in-the-mud." She pulled back and glanced at the cowboys watching them. "I'm having fun."

He lowered his voice for her ears only. "Do you want me to toss you over my shoulder and haul you off to the hotel?"

Again she laughed. "Mr. Lawrence, a gentleman would never propose something so outrageous," she challenged in slurred words. "You wouldn't dare."

"I'm no gentleman." Without further ado, he neatly flipped her over his shoulder. She yelped in surprise, her head hanging down to his waist.

"Marcus," she squealed. "Put me down this instant."

He gripped her legs to keep her from kicking him. "Madam, you'll learn never to challenge a man."

As if he was putting on a show for their benefit, the men laughed and applauded. Women giggled behind their hands.

"Help!" Laura Leigh yelled.

"Quiet." He smacked her on her well-padded bottom.

"You're a barbarian."

By then they'd reached the wagon. He stood her on her feet. "Yes, ma'am, I surely am."

She swayed and clutched his coat for support. "You made me dizzy."

"That punch made you tipsy."

"I am not drunk. I only had a little, bitty cup of . . ." She hiccuped. "Oh, my. How unladylike."

Marcus laughed and plucked her into the high seat. "Try not to fall off. We'll be at the hotel shortly."

"I'll try to hold on."

He climbed up beside her and untied the reins. She tilted toward him, and he slipped an arm around her to prevent her from falling off. Her head rested on his shoulder. It was a mistake; he knew it the instant he touched her arm. He'd already let himself become captivated by this woman. Getting closer to her both physically and emotionally could be disaster. He'd been down that road once, and he didn't need a repeat of that kind of heartbreak.

Marc steeled his resolve. They'd been thrown together temporarily, but when they'd toured their last county fair, he would return to the farm and she would regain her position in society. He guided the team to the livery behind the hotel. She jerked awake when the movement stopped. The livery owner stepped out and took charge of the team. Marc flipped him a coin and turned to the woman resting against his shoulder.

"Oh, my," she said, her voice heavy. "Was I sleeping?"

"It's been a long day. Let's see if we can get you a bed to sleep in."

"I wired ahead. So they should have a room for me." She yawned and reached out a hand to him.

Once her feet were planted firmly on the ground, she plucked her hat and jacket from the wagon. Holding both her bags in one hand, he caught her elbow to steady her stride. The hotel lobby was much more crowded than he'd expected. Laura Leigh's head dropped against his shoulder as they waited in line for the clerk's attention. "Name's Lawrence, may I have my key?"

The man scanned the register. "Room 201." He turned away and plucked a key from a hook. "Here you are. Do you need help with your bags?"

Marc shook his head. "No. Do you have a room for Miss Westbrook?"

Again he scanned the ledger. "Miss Westbrook? No, I don't

see her name.'' He studied them over eyeglasses propped on the end of his nose.

''She wired for a room. Surely you have her reservation.''

The clerk shook his head. ''When she didn't show up, I gave her room to somebody else. Sorry.''

At that, Laura Leigh woke. ''What do you mean? I need a room.''

The man straightened his narrow shoulders. ''We're completely full. I have three men in a room for two.'' He eyed them suspiciously. ''Aren't you Mrs. Lawrence? Your husband has a room. If Miss Westbrook comes, I'll put her in with some of the women who're sharing a room.''

Several people had stopped to stare. Not wanting to make a scene, he took Laura Leigh's arm. ''My wife is sleepy and she's confused. We'll go up to our room.''

''What do you mean? I'm not confused and I'm wide awake.''

''Sweetheart, we can settle our disagreement when we're alone,'' he said. Rushing her from the lobby, he all but dragged her up the stairs. ''We'll work something out.''

''It's your fault, you know. You should have let me register before we went to the fairgrounds.'' She propped a shoulder against the wall while he inserted the key into the door.

''If you'd been on time, this wouldn't have happened.''

A couple entering the next room stopped and glared at them. Marc shoved open the door and followed Laura Leigh into the room. She stumbled slightly and flopped down on the bed. ''Go find someplace to sleep. I'm staying here.''

''This is my room.'' He anchored his feet and refused to move. ''I'm not going anywhere.''

''You can't stay here.'' Her voice grew slow, her words slurred.

Marc agreed. For his own sake, he shouldn't stay in the same room. ''It's late. We'll just have to make the best of the situation.''

"Best," she said, as her eyes closed and her breathing became deep and even.

For a long while Marc stared at the fully clothed woman asleep on the only bed in the room. Her skirt was twisted around her legs, showing quite a bit of a well-turned ankle. The pink shirtwaist had pulled free of the tight waistband of her skirt. Her jacket and hat lay discarded at her side. In sleep, her disheveled appearance made her look sweet and youthful.

He removed his hat and dragged his fingers through his hair. How was he expected to make any best out of this debacle? He shrugged out of his jacket and draped it neatly on the back of a chair. The way he saw it, he had two choices: either stay, or leave. If he left, the clerk and other men would get suspicious and wonder why a man would leave the bed of such a pretty woman. Since they were posing as a married couple, it wouldn't do to arouse suspicion. If he stayed, there was no telling where things could lead. He wasn't made of stone, and being with her was more of a temptation than a normal man could bear.

Carefully, he plucked her jacket and hat from the bed and placed them on hooks behind the door. As much as he hated to disturb her, he had to wake her to at least take off her shoes. "Laura Leigh, wake up and take off your shoes."

One eye slipped open. "Shoes? What shoes?"

"The ones on your feet." He leaned over her and lifted one slender foot and cradled it in his big hand.

She lifted her head and looked down. "Oh, those." Her head dropped to the pillow. "If you want them off, do it yourself."

Marc gritted his teeth. He had half a mind to let her sleep in her shoes as well as her now wrinkled skirt. Instead, he quickly loosed the strings. He slid his hand along her silk-clad ankle and worked the shoe from her foot.

She wiggled her toes and sighed. "Other one." Lifting her skirt to her knees, she offered the other shapely leg.

Tempted almost beyond endurance, Marc took another steadying breath. How much torture was a man expected to endure before he threw all caution to the wind? Even a monk would be tempted by that soft, womanly body lying on his bed. As quickly as possible, he untied the laces and dropped the shoe to the floor with a plop. Unable to stop himself, he let his gaze drift over her silk-enclosed legs.

As he watched, her hands moved up her leg to above her knee to a lacy garter. "I can't sleep in my stockings," she whispered.

His gaze jerked to her eyes, now half closed and dreamy. Her mouth was parted in a pretty pout.

"Your stockings?" The words stuck in his throat like the pit from a peach.

"Help me."

It took several seconds before her soft plea penetrated his passion-dazed brain. He leaned closer and steeled his resolve. Hand trembling, he plucked the garter with two fingers and slid it down her leg. Her hands met his as she lifted her knee and began to roll the silk stockings down her leg. Fire sizzled up his arm, and he jerked away. With her skirt puddled near her waist, she was showing entirely too much of petticoats and underdrawers for a man to resist. He turned to the open window and took a cooling breath of air. If he had the sense of a doorpost, he would walk out and find a bed in the stables.

He turned to tell her he was leaving. It was too late. She had one silk stocking in her hand and was dangling it over the end of the bed. Lying on her side, her breathing was even and deep.

She might sleep, but Marc knew he wouldn't get a wink of sleep that night. Tugging the quilt from the other side of the bed, he wrapped her in a cocoon. Unsure how to handle the improper situation, he removed his boots, tugged down his suspenders and removed his stiff collar and necktie. With Laura Leigh installed on the bed, he looked around for a place to sleep. The chair was too small, and the floor hard and cold. She was curled on one side of the bed, leaving the rest too inviting to pass up. He slipped quietly onto the bed and lay flat on his back, his arms tucked under his head. Stiff as a board, he struggled to keep his distance from her.

Marc was in for a long, sleepless night.

CHAPTER SIX

Laura Leigh's head ached and her middle felt as if someone
had plunged a sword into her waist. She tugged on the blanket,
but found it caught under her body. In the dim light from the
window, she studied her surroundings. She was on a bed in a
strange room, and she was fully dressed except for her shoes
and one stocking.

Slowly, the truth drizzled into her fog-dazed brain. She dared
to glance to her side. A dark shadow reclined beside her—a
large figure as stiff and solid as a fallen log. Marc—lying on
the bed with her. She ran a hand along her body. Surely nothing
untoward had happened. She had on her blouse, skirt and
unmentionables, and Marc wore his trousers and shirt. The only
things missing were his stiff collar and black necktie.

She covered her mouth with her fingers to hold back a groan.
In her sleepy state, she'd asked him to remove her shoes and
stockings. Heat seeped over her. He'd held her foot and gently
brushed his fingers over her ankle. She'd fallen asleep with a
delicious sensation covering her like a warm quilt.

Now she'd awaken to find that she'd gone to bed with a

man—a virtual stranger. She didn't dare look any closer at him. She needed to do something about the tight waist of her skirt if she was ever to get back to sleep. Fortunately for her, she'd given up the torture of a tight corset. Slowly, she swung her feet to the floor and lifted her head. That proved to be a mistake. The room started to spin, and she flopped back to the pillow. Laura Leigh rarely drank more than a single glass of wine, but that night she'd had at least half a dozen cups of punch spiked with hard liquor.

In spite of her pain, a tiny smile curved her lips. Wouldn't her proper mother be shocked at her daughter's improper behavior? Not only had she gotten drunk, she'd gone to bed with a man. She bit her lip. Thankfully, Marcus had remained a perfect gentleman.

Again, she tried to rise. This time she made it to her feet, but she grabbed the iron headboard for balance.

"You okay?" the husky male voice asked.

She jumped at the unexpected sound. "I didn't mean to wake you."

"You didn't." He sat on the opposite side of the bed. "What are you doing up? I thought you would sleep right through the night."

"I have to loosen this skirt before I die." Her fingers trembled as she tried unsuccessfully to release the button. "Oh," she groaned.

"Need help?"

Lots, she thought. "No, thank you, Mr. Lawrence. You've done enough already." Twisting the garment, she tugged, and the button popped off and flew across the floor with a ping. "I'll look for it in the morning." Now that she could breathe, she again sat on the edge of the bed. Her stomach settled to a slow roll.

"Miss Westbrook, I'll close my eyes and turn my back if you wish to don your nightdress."

Changing out of the stiff and confining clothes sounded wonderful, if inappropriate. She rubbed her temples to ease the ache. Surely she wasn't thinking clearly if she even considered the offer. Standing, she let her skirt slip to the floor and stepped out of it. Too unsteady on her feet, she let the garment lie where it fell. The blouse proved more difficult. Each sleeve contained a row of six tiny buttons at the wrist, and a dozen down the front. Her maid would go into a hissy fit if she tore these loose. If she didn't feel so bad, it would be funny.

"I need help," she whispered.

He came to his feet immediately. In the darkness, he was nothing more than a large shadow. "What's wrong?"

She shoved out her arm. "Too many buttons."

"Is that all?" Laughter sounded in his voice.

Slowly, his large, blunt fingers loosed one button after another from their tiny loops. Her stomach trembled, and she wondered if it was from his nearness or from the liquor. How odd this was. Laura Leigh Westbrook, the daughter of the respected publisher of the *Advantage,* standing in her petticoats before a strange man while he unbuttoned her shirtwaist.

When the second sleeve was free, he paused as if unsure what to do next. Her head had cleared some, and she became aware of how vulnerable she was. "I can finish, thank you."

He turned away and moved to the window. "Miss Westbrook, I realize how difficult this is for you. If you wish, I'll go down to the lobby to give you privacy."

She stopped unbuttoning the blouse. He'd been nothing but kind, since she'd been the one to overindulge. "That won't be necessary, Mr. Lawrence. We're mature adults. I'm certain we can share a room without compromising ourselves. If you will remain where you are, I'll slip behind that screen and don my nightgown."

On unsteady feet, she snatched her smaller valise and moved behind the dressing screen. Removing only the blouse, she pulled the cotton nightgown over her chemise and petticoats. It wasn't entirely comfortable, but at least she felt more clothed.

He was still at the window when she returned to the bed. "If I lie down as before, you can have the other side." She curled into the quilt and closed her eyes.

The bed sank when he sat on the edge. He stretched out his long legs on the bed, never once touching her.

"Mr. Lawrence," she whispered.

"Yes?"

"Why don't you take off your trousers?"

He chuckled, a deep male sound that made her skin tingle. "Miss Westbrook, that sounds like a proposition."

Her skin heated. "I only meant that if you don't take off your trousers, they'll be so wrinkled, you'll look as if you slept in your clothes."

The bed again shook and she heard the sound of trousers slipping down his legs. She squeezed her eyes shut, but the image behind her eyelids made her heartbeat race. In her imagination, his shoulders were wide and his chest muscular. But it was when her thoughts lowered to below his waist, that her fingers curled into her palms. If she kept thinking about him, she would never get to sleep. Her hands itched to touch him, to learn the varied textures of the large, beautifully formed male body stretched out on the other side of the bed.

Shocked by the direction of her thoughts, she began to recite every Psalm she'd learned in Sunday School. When she ran out of Psalms, she started on the Beatitudes. His breathing was even and deep when she finally fell off to sleep.

Noise from the hallway woke Laura Leigh the next morning. Instantly, she remembered everything about the night before. Embarrassed at her behavior, her skin heated. At least the headache had eased, and she was once again herself.

Lifting an eyelid, she glanced from the corner of her eye. The other side of the bed was empty. She opened both eyes. Marc's jacket and trousers were gone. A relieved sigh escaped her lips. She hadn't been certain how she would have handled the situation if he'd remained in their room.

Taking advantage of the few minutes of privacy, she hurriedly dressed in a clean skirt and shirtwaist. Since she hadn't bothered to brush out her hair the night before, she took longer than usual to twist the long brown tresses into a topknot, allowing a few tendrils to dangle to her nape. Her stomach growled, and she wondered if Marcus had already eaten breakfast.

Notepad and handbag in hand, she entered the lobby. Several men were lounging on the davenports and easy chairs. A young cowboy tipped his hat and stepped aside to allow her to enter. She nodded and flashed a tentative smile.

"Finally awake?" Marcus stepped to her side and took her arm.

She jumped at the unexpected sound of his voice. "You must have gotten away early."

"I'm used to getting up at the break of dawn." He guided her toward a crowded dining room. "I have a table over here."

He held her chair and seated her. "I didn't think I would be able to eat a bite after the way I overindulged last evening, but I'm starved."

"No ill effects?"

She shook her head. "Not even a headache. Have you eaten?"

"Yes. But I'll have a cup of coffee and stay until you finish. We can go over our demonstration for today."

"What am I showing?"

"We're going to show a quicker way to make biscuits."

"Doesn't everybody know how to make biscuits?"

"Do you?"

She sipped the coffee the waiter had set in front of her. "No." Lowering her voice, she added, "But I have a cook and housekeeper."

"What if you decide to marry?"

"I'll steal my mother's cook." Her mouth curved in a sly smile. "Or I'll marry a man who can cook."

He laughed. "Good luck."

"I'm going to need it to get through this tour."

While she devoured her eggs and biscuits, he explained his method. All she had to do was remember what he told her and repeat it to the audience. "Are your biscuits any good?"

"You tell me. You're eating one now."

She studied the high, fluffy bread with the crisp brown top. "This? How?"

"You don't think I've been lollygagging around all morning, do you? I spoke to the cook and showed her the system 'Mrs. Lawrence' had developed. I must admit she was skeptical, especially that a man explained the method. But she was quite impressed with the results."

It was her turn to laugh. "Mr. Lawrence, you are a wonder. This is delicious."

He shoved back his chair. "While you finish, I'll fetch the wagon. Meet me at the rear entrance."

"I'll be with you shortly." She watched the big, rough-looking man swagger to the doorway. After this project was over, he would make a wonderful subject for a story. A farmer who developed recipes and wrote cookbooks. What an enigma he was. The past night, he'd been more of a gentleman than the so-called elite of her social circle. If he ever got over his grief for his wife, he would make some woman a wonderful husband.

She shoved back her chair. There was no use thinking about him in that way. She had her own agenda. Once she succeeded in this project, her father would be forced to give her meatier assignments and train her to take over as publisher of the newspaper. There was no place in her plans for marriage or a man. Someday everybody would know about Laura Leigh Westbrook and her success at the *Advantage*. Why she might even expand her sights to the *New York Times.* Anything was possible for women in the coming century, including winning the right to vote and hold office. Laura Leigh promised herself to be in the forefront of the battle.

That week, Laura Leigh filed her stories about the county fair. She faithfully listed the winners of the pie- and cake-baking contests, the preserve and jam blue-ribbon entries, and the names of the livestock contestants. Since nothing unusual had happened, her stories were run-of-the-mill and ordinary. She didn't write about the most exciting part of the fair—her spending the night in the same room as Marc Lawrence.

Every time she thought about that night, her stomach fluttered and her heart rate accelerated. None of the men who regularly called on her had made her feel so feminine or made her pulse race simply with a thin smile.

"What's making my girl smile like that?"

Her father's gruff voice from the doorway made her jump. She hadn't realized that she'd been lost in thoughts about Marcus. "I'm thinking about the tour. The cookbook is being well received, and Uncle Fritz should be pleased about the orders for his flour."

Herbert Westbrook stepped into the small office he'd given his daughter. As the only woman on the staff, he felt it best if she not share the larger room with the male reporters. In a way, Laura Leigh resented the distinction. At other times, she enjoyed her privacy.

"Your uncle is delighted. He's thinking about hiring Mr. and Mrs. Lawrence full-time as his representatives."

"Oh," she whispered. She'd forgotten that her father and uncle didn't know that there was no 'Mrs.' or that Laura Leigh was posing as the author of the cookbook. "I'm not sure they would be interested. They have a farm to run."

"Let Fritz worry about that." He glanced at her valises beside the door. "When are you leaving for Castroville?"

"I'm taking the afternoon train. I want to get there early and see that things are set up properly." Truth be told, she needed to make sure they had two rooms. Marcus had mentioned bringing his son with him.

Her father rolled his cigar between his fingers. "Did you speak to your mother about your project?" Not giving her a chance to reply, he continued, "She isn't at all happy about your going off alone. She thinks I should assign one of the men."

"No." She leaped to her feet. "This is my idea, and I expect to get some interesting stories."

"Calm down, honey. I'm not going to take this away from you. I explained to your mother that you're well chaperoned. Mrs. Lawrence is there, and Mr. Lawrence will see that no harm comes to you."

She sank back to her chair. Her mother would go into a swoon if she knew that she and Marcus had spent the night alone. No, she would have a stroke that they'd actually shared a bed. "You and Mother don't have a thing to worry about. I'm a mature woman, and I'm able to take care of myself."

"She would be much happier if she could escort you."

Having her mother looking over her shoulder was the last thing she needed. "Mother is much too busy with her charities and social obligations to waste time sitting around at county fairs."

He eyed her suspiciously. Herbert Westbrook had been a shrewd newspaperman for too many years to be fooled. "I'll calm her fears. Just be careful and stay out of trouble."

She stood and kissed her father's cheek. "Thanks, Papa. I promise to bring you some great stories."

"Let me know when you're ready to leave. I'll have Pedro drive you to the station."

"My train leaves at five o'clock. Since Ma—Mr. Lawrence took the books and order blanks with him, all I have is my own baggage."

Herbert shoved his unlit cigar between his teeth. "If you keep selling cookbooks, we'll go into the second printing."

She smiled. "That sounds wonderful." Marcus would be delighted. And so would Laura Leigh.

CHAPTER SEVEN

"Marcus, we're in big trouble." Laura Leigh pulled him from the entrance of the large tent away from the crowds. He'd met her as prearranged in the middle of the fairgrounds and found her pacing a rut in the dusty ground.

His heartbeat fluttered. Worry turned her hazel eyes a dark brown. Things had seemed to be going very well until now. "What do you mean? What happened?" He caught her icy hands in his large warm one.

She lowered her voice. "Him."

He followed her tilt of her head, ready to do battle with some villain or sinister brute in the shadows. The only people in the tent were several women and ordinary-looking men. "Who?"

"The fair manager."

If the man had accosted her or in any way frightened Laura Leigh, he would take his head off. Marc wasn't normally a violent man, but he wouldn't allow anybody to hurt a woman in his care. "What did he do?"

"He set up a stove."

His mouth agape, Marcus stared at her. "Laura Leigh, what are you talking about?"

A flush crept up her cheeks. "They set up a stove, and they want you—me—to prepare our recipe and give a real demonstration. We have to actually *cook.*"

"Is that all? You sound as if you've been asked to commit murder."

She pulled her mouth into a straight line. "I might as well. You know I can't cook. If I try, I might just kill a few people."

He laughed. "It isn't that bad. You've done well so far. I'll be with you."

Planting her hands on the hips of her pretty blue skirt, she glared at him as if he'd taken leave of his senses. "I can't do it. It was easy when all I had to do was talk. Doing is different."

Marc shook his head. It was almost comical. For a woman who was normally self-assured and confident, she was as nervous as a child on the first day of school. "I'll help you."

"It won't work."

The crowds were beginning to gather in the tent. They had thirty minutes before their demonstration began. "Let's go back to the hotel and think about this."

He helped her into the hired wagon. "Where's Billy?" she asked.

"I couldn't get anybody to tend the stock. But a neighbor promised for next week. He'll come with us then." Marc realized they would both be safer if his son had come along, but it couldn't be helped. Besides, he could control his impulses around Laura Leigh. He hoped.

Minutes later they reached the hotel. She'd arrived the night before and, as they'd planned, had reserved two connecting rooms. Once in her room, she sat on the bed, while he took the single chair.

"We'll do something very simple. Like a cobbler, or shortcake. I brought fresh blackberries and a sack of Homestead Flour. I'll write everything down for you, and you just have to read the instructions from the cookbook. It's easy, you'll see."

"Easy for you." She tapped her lips as if thinking. "We'll just let you give the lecture."

"We agreed that you would be me."

She held out her hands and pulled off her gloves. "No, listen. You can be me, or you. Whatever. I'll tell them that I have a rash on my hands, and I can't work with the food. You'll be my hands, while I read the directions."

It was his turn to look at her as if she'd lost her mind. "You don't have a rash."

Opening her valise, she pulled out a petticoat. "Do you have a knife?"

He reached into his pocket for his jackknife and opened the blade. "What are you going to do? Slit your wrists?"

"Don't be foolish." She held up the lace-trimmed garment. "I hate to do this, but it can't be helped. Cut between my fingers."

"You're going to ruin that thing?"

"No matter. I need bandages to make the scheme work." She tore the petticoat into long strips. "Now, just wrap these around my hands, and nobody will be the wiser."

Carefully, he bound her fingers like a mitten. "This might work. It's the only chance we've got."

She waved her hands in front of his face. "I'll explain that I have a rash, but my instructions are so precise that even a man can follow the directions. When you pull the perfect pastry out of the oven, you'll be a hit."

"If they don't mind an ugly farmer showing them up, it might work."

With a smile, she touched his cheek with her bandaged hands. "Mr. Lawrence, will you quit calling yourself ugly? You're rather fetching when you quit frowning."

Even with the cloth wrapped around her hands, her touch warmed his heart. "If we can pull this off, I'll buy you a bottle of champagne."

"We'll do it. But, remember, I can only have one glass."

He laughed. "I can't forget what happens when you overindulge." All week he'd thought of the way she'd looked lying on the bed, her face flushed, and struggling to remove her stockings. The picture of those long, shapely legs had haunted him night and day for the past week.

"Then I'm trusting you to watch out for me."

Offering his arm, Marc wondered who was going to watch out for him. His skin tingled from her touch, and his body heated whenever he looked at her. Since she'd invaded his life with her outrageous proposition, his world had centered around her and this project. The woman was constantly on his mind, and if truth be told, he would have followed her if he wasn't making a penny on the cookbook and his spices.

Marc chided himself for a fool. Only an idiot would risk his heart on a woman who wouldn't fit into his world any more than Serafina had. He set his resolve to keep his emotional distance—something easier said than done.

The women had gathered in the tent, eager for the judging of their homemade treats. From the expression on their faces, the contestants were slightly annoyed that the winners wouldn't be announced until after the baking demonstration.

Laura Leigh stepped up to the table on a small stage and smiled at the crowd. She was glad she'd worn her blue suit and perky hat, both of which drew the attention of the crowd. She'd heard the whispers and knew that the women admired her clothes. The outfit was new, and had cost nearly a week's wages.

"Good morning, ladies and gentlemen." She smiled at the men standing on the sidelines. "Welcome to our presentation of recipes from the new cookbook published by the *Advantage* and Homestead Flour." Removing her hands from her pockets, she held her wrapped fingers up for inspection. "Unfortunately,

I've developed a rather annoying rash, and I won't be able to prepare the dishes for you.''

Disappointed murmurs rumbled through the crowd. ''However, one of the best features of our recipes is the simplicity of preparation. Even a man can prepare a delicious meal simply by following directions and using my cookbook. Mr. Lawrence,'' she said, gesturing to Marc.

At the twitter of laughter, Marcus stood. The ladies stared at him, questions in their eyes. He'd removed his hat and coat, and rolled up the sleeves of his crisp white shirt. Muscles bulged under the sleeves. He looked more like a blacksmith than a chef. ''I'll do my best,'' he declared with a smile.

Under the bandages, Laura Leigh crossed her fingers. They'd decided to show the biscuit mix Marcus had created. As she read the ingredients and checked the skeptical expressions on the women's faces, Marcus dutifully mixed the dry ingredients, then worked in the lard.

A woman about her mother's age, wearing a calico dress, whispered loudly for all to hear. ''I've been making biscuits since I was a girl. What's so different about this?''

Marcus looked up, his hands coated with flour. ''The difference, ladies, is that at this point, you can store this mix in a tight container and when you're in a hurry, you need only add milk, and you have your biscuits ready within minutes.''

A younger woman, with a baby in her arms, stood. ''I'll be glad to save time when I have to get breakfast for my crew.''

''In addition to making biscuits, you can add other ingredients and make cobbler, shortcake, flapjacks, and even a nice yellow cake,'' Marcus said before Laura Leigh could respond. ''In fact, we have some fresh blackberries, and we want to show our Quick and Easy Cobbler.''

Laura Leigh backed off and let Marcus take over. Even the older woman who'd protested his method gave her full attention. By the time he shoved the finished product into the oven, he had the audience in the palm of his hand. While the dessert baked, he explained others of his recipes and talked about the spice mixture.

He answered questions that flew over Laura Leigh's head. When he pulled the finished cobbler out of the oven, the crowd gathered around for a taste. Laura Leigh tore pages from her notepad into small pieces, and Marcus spooned out the treat. Lips smacked, and even the men reached for samples.

By the time the pan was empty, they knew they'd been successful—at least, Marcus had. Women dug into their precious egg-and-butter money to buy the cookbook. Several merchants ordered quantities of the flour. The fair manager asked them to come back that afternoon and prepare another dish. Marcus agreed, his smile wide and charming. He looked like a child on Christmas morning.

He turned and winked at her. Her heart fluttered. She'd been wrong. The women accepted Marcus—a man—and respected his opinion. In fact, they looked at him with something akin to adoration in their eyes. A spark of jealousy seeped through her. He was clearly enjoying himself, as well he should. These were his creations, and he deserved the accolades.

When it was time to judge the pie-baking contest, Marcus and Laura Leigh were asked to sample the entries. The first was an apple pie that smelled wonderful. The lady cut a large slice, and smiled as she handed it to Marcus. He dipped a spoon into the apples, and savored the filling. With a nod, he passed the plate to Laura Leigh.

"I'm sorry, dear," he said, his eyes glinting with humor. "I forgot about your rash." Picking up the spoon, he scooped off a bit and held it to her lips.

Surprised, she opened her mouth and accepted the offered treat. She lifted her gaze and met Marc's stare. For a second, she forgot to swallow, but the intimate moment passed quickly. Somehow the pie slipped down her throat. A tiny bit stuck to the corner of her mouth. Before she could flick it off, Marcus reached out a finger and brushed her lips. His touch was gentle and warm. Sensations shivered to the pit of her stomach. She caught his wrist and carried his finger to her mouth. Slowly, she licked the crumb from his finger. His eyes heated.

"How is it?" he asked, his voice husky.

She released his finger. "Delicious." She wondered if his lips would be as sweet. If they'd been alone, she would have found out. As it was, the contestants were staring at them, waiting for their verdict. Embarrassed at her thoughts, she turned to will away the heat that warmed her cheeks. Thoughts like that could only get her into trouble. And man problems were something she didn't need. Laura Leigh had her sights set on being an important newspaperwoman and publisher. A man would only hinder her goals.

In spite of his resolve not to get too close to a woman, Marcus couldn't deny that he thoroughly enjoyed touring the fair with a pretty woman on his arm. Men often stopped to tip their hats at Laura Leigh, and the ladies stared at her stylish suit and hat. The second demonstration was better accepted than the first, as word of mouth had increased the crowd. He was delightfully surprised that the women enjoyed his presentation and bought his cookbook and spices.

As dusk fell, the crowds moved toward the area set up for food and dancing. When Laura Leigh began to meander that way, he pulled her toward their wagon.

"Marcus, I want to get something to eat."

"We will. I promised you champagne if we could pull off that act. Let's go back to the hotel for dinner. They might have champagne."

She smiled, and his blood heated. "How does a farmer know about champagne?"

Laughing, he helped her up to the wagon seat. "I've been around a bit, miss. I learned about champagne on a trip to New Orleans. That's also when I became interested in well-seasoned food. Of course that was . . ." He stopped before revealing that it was before he'd married Serafina. "Before my son was born."

Her eyes warmed with sympathy. He'd led her to believe he was a widower, and he didn't want to change the perception. "Did you and your wife honeymoon in New Orleans?"

"No." He didn't talk about his ill-fated marriage, and even his son knew nothing about his mother. "It was before then."

His harsh words silenced her questions. "I'm sorry, I didn't mean to pry."

"It's okay. I just don't like to talk about it."

The ride to the hotel was strained. His past was a wall between them, and a barrier to his future. After returning the wagon and team to the livery, they walked slowly to the hotel.

By the time they ordered dinner, his humor had returned. Laura Leigh deserved an explanation, but Marc hated to talk about his youthful folly. Only since meeting her had he begun to wonder if he should try to dissolve his marriage. If he had any idea where to find Serafina, it would be easy. However, if she'd rejoined the gypsy camp, they could be anywhere in the country. The Romany hated authority, and steered clear of the law. Even if he tried to find them, he probably wouldn't be able to. It was best for him and Billy to leave well enough alone.

To his delight, the proprietor had a few bottles of champagne. They shared the wine and a tasty meal. The conversation remained light, mostly about the day and their reception by the women. Laura Leigh was relieved that she would no longer have to give the demonstrations. They agreed that she would sell the cookbooks and take orders, while Marc did the cooking.

They toasted their successful partnership, and before they realized it, the bottle was empty. Laura Leigh giggled. "Looks as if I've done it again."

"Feeling tipsy?"

She tilted her glass to drain the last drop. "I feel wonderful." Her cheeks were flushed, and her eyes glittered.

He smiled. The woman was a beauty and a delightful companion. He hated to see the evening come to an end. He pulled back her chair and caught her elbow. "I think it's time for us to turn in."

Lifting her gaze to his, she grinned. "Already?" She took one step and stumbled. He caught her around her slender waist.

"And you said you weren't dizzy."

"Maybe just a little."

She pressed her hands to his chest. His heart raced like a wild rabbit with a hound on its tail. Holding her felt good and right. She tilted her head and swiped her tongue across her lips. His gut knotted. Needs surged through him like a tornado on the plains. He ignored the other diners and waiters. All that mattered was the warmth in his chest and the fire in his blood. He wanted her, and by the spark in her eyes, she wasn't immune to him.

"Do you need assistance, Mr. Lawrence?"

Marc jerked up his head to find the proprietor staring at them. "No. We're fine." He removed his arms from around her. When he took a step, she stumbled again.

"Oops."

In one quick movement, one he was certain he would live to regret, he scooped her up in his arms and exited the dining room. "If you can't walk a straight line, I suppose I'll have to carry you."

She circled his neck with her arms and rested her head against his shoulder. "You don't have to. I can walk."

"Sure, and I can fly." He climbed the stairs to their second floor rooms.

"I'm the one who's flying." She let out a long sigh. "I don't believe anybody has carried me since I was a child and Papa carried me to my room and put me to bed. Are you going to put me to bed?"

He swallowed hard. Holding her like this, feeling the touch of her fingers twisted in the hair at his nape, sent improper ideas into his mind. His body's reaction would surely shock her female sensibilities. He was sorely tempted to take her up on her invitation. But it was only the champagne talking. "No, you're going to put yourself to bed."

"What if I can't take my shoes and stockings off? Or unfasten all these tiny buttons. Will you help me?" Her lips nestled in his neck; her breath tickled his throat.

"I'll let you sleep with them on." His words were soft, without threat. He itched to remove not only her shoes, but everything up to that silly little hat perched on her shiny brown hair.

When they reached her room, he set her on her feet. "Stand still while I unlock the door." She kept her arms around his neck while he struggled with the key.

When the door swung open, he again picked her up and kicked the door shut with his foot. He looked around her room. Marc was treading on dangerous ground. As much as he wanted her, he knew better then to give in to his desires. Such folly could prove disastrous. In a few long strides, he reached the bed and set her down on the colorful quilt. When he tried to straighten, she tugged on his neck. Caught off balance, he tumbled to the bed on top of her.

"Are you tipsy, too, Mr. Lawrence?" Laughing, she tightened her grip on his neck.

His face was inches from hers. Her eyes sparkled with a challenge only a fool would accept, and only an idiot would reject. He caught her hands with his. "You're playing with fire, Laura Leigh."

"I'm already burning up."

Her body was warm and soft under his. Desire hit him in his gut like the kick of a mule. If he didn't move within a second, he wouldn't be able to. He held his breath. "Do you have any idea what you're doing?"

"Yes. I want you to kiss me."

He squeezed his eyes shut and prayed for strength. "If I kiss you, will you let me go?"

She smiled like a temptress out to steal his soul. She'd already taken his heart. "Kiss me and find out."

Her skirt had shifted, revealing the long length of her silk-clad legs. How much torment could a man endure before he went mad? He kissed her quickly on the lips and pulled back immediately.

"Is that the best you can do?" She tangled her fingers in his hair and pulled his face to hers.

He caught her wrists. "Laura Leigh, you've had too much to drink. That's only the champagne talking."

"Marcus, I'm feeling light as a feather, and I have complete control of my senses. I've wanted to kiss you since that first day at your farm when you were wet and incredibly manly. Don't you want to kiss me?"

On a long groan, he buried his face in her hair. She smelled as fresh as apple blossoms in spring. "You don't know what you're asking of me. I've been alone for a long time, and you're a very beautiful woman." Marc was hovering on the edge of a precipice with one foot over the edge.

"You think I'm pretty?"

"Woman, I've wanted you since the minute you set foot on my land. But I can't kiss you and then just get up and leave."

"I don't want you to leave. Make love to me."

Either he'd had too much champagne, or his imagination had him hearing what he wanted to hear. The needs he'd tried to quench burst forth like a flood from a broken dam. "Do you have any idea what you're saying?"

Her lips found the pulse at his throat. "Yes. I can feel that you want me. Will you deny both of us what we desire?"

He lifted his head and looked into her eyes, all dark and needy. "Lord knows I can't deny the truth. Have you ever . . ." He wasn't sure how to ask a woman the intimate details of her life. He was willing to bet his farm she was a virgin.

"Been with a man?" She lowered her eyelids. "No. But I've never felt like this before." Her eyes widened, and she smiled. "I'm old enough to know what I want, and I want you."

As much as it cost him, Marc rolled to the side and counted

to ten. He had to get his lust under control. Laura Leigh was too precious, too wonderful for him to use her only for his own pleasure. "You don't understand—"

In a quick movement that caught him off guard, she threw herself on top of him, trapping him on the bed, her legs straddling his. Her arms resting on his chest, she cradled his face in her hands. "I do understand, Marc. I care for you, a lot." She strung a row of kisses across his chin and mouth. "Will you quit arguing and kiss me? Really kiss me."

The fire in his veins burned out of control. Marc gave up fighting his needs and her desires. He stroked her spine and her side, his fingers stopping just short of her breasts. "Are you sure?" His arousal pressed against her stomach.

She shivered and covered his mouth with hers. She tasted of champagne and blackberries, passion and fire. He stroked her breasts, and the tips hardened under his touch. Struggling to remain calm, his hands trembled as he worked the tiny buttons of her clothing. His mouth followed his hands, tasting the sweetness of her flesh.

She tore the buttons from his shirt in her hurry to undress him. Her enthusiasm left him weak with needs. His body was on fire, and he prayed he could control his desires.

Their legs tangled; their bodies melted together as one. He gave with a passion he'd never before experienced; she responded with a joy that made him shiver with pleasure. He drank of her like a man dying of thirst. She offered the gift of her body with the generosity of a wanton and the purity of an angel.

When they reached the pinnacle of pleasure, he almost wept with the exuberance of her love. As they lay together, arms and legs entwined, Marc acknowledged what had been in the back of his mind for weeks. He was falling in love with the lovely and provocative woman.

She kissed his cheek and brushed her fingers along his beard-roughened jaw. "Is it always so wonderful?"

He pulled the quilt over their naked bodies. "Only when it's with somebody very special."

"You're special to me, Marcus. Very special."

His heart thumped and hammered against his chest. "I've never met a more special woman. Laura Leigh, you're one in a million." He stopped short of revealing how much he cared. Even in his half-drowsy state, his mind was alert enough to realize that he had no right to let her think there was a future for them. Aside from the fact that they were from different worlds, as far as he knew, he was still married to Serafina.

"Then why are you frowning? Have I done something wrong?"

Her voice hitched, and he realized he'd inadvertently disturbed her. "Of course not." He brushed a stray lock of brown hair from her eyes. "But it's time we got some sleep. We have another busy day tomorrow."

She snuggled into his arms. "We wasted money on that other room. Here we are sharing a bed again."

"Looks like it's getting to be a habit." He wrapped his arms around her and pressed a gentle kiss to her forehead.

"A good one. One I don't want to break."

Marc shoved his disturbing thoughts aside and enjoyed the pleasure of the moment. He couldn't remember a time when he'd felt such peace and contentment. If it only lasted a day, he would take what heaven had given him. Too soon he would return to a hell of his own making. He only prayed he wouldn't hurt Laura Leigh. She deserved better than anything he had to offer.

CHAPTER EIGHT

Marcus could hardly keep Billy still on the way to New Braunfels. The boy rarely left the farm, and he enjoyed the idea of an outing. Marc had hired a neighbor boy to tend the stock, in order to give his hard-working son the day off. On the first day of the tour, he'd promised his son he could come if he kept up with his chores.

He tamped down his own excitement. Marc didn't fool himself into thinking it arose only from seeing his dreams come true; he was realistic enough to acknowledge that he was eager to see Laura Leigh again. Over the past week, she'd been constantly on his mind. While plowing his fields, he'd thought about her bright eyes that had darkened with passion when they'd made love. When he washed his hands, he remembered the texture of her silk stockings when he'd removed her shoes and slid the stockings down her legs. Her skin was as smooth as the finest satin. It had taken all his will power not to leave the farm and spend the week with her. He could hardly wait to see her again.

With Billy along, they wouldn't be able to share a room,

but that didn't matter. He just wanted to be with her one more time—to hear her laughter, to see her eyes sparkle, to touch her hand, to smell her sweet perfume. Thinking about her had his libido on full alert.

Since the Comal County seat was close to his home, he chose to drive his own wagon to the town. He slowed the wagon near the central tent of the fair. The entire county must have turned out on the bright, sunny day for the festivities. Hundreds of farmers, ranchers, cowboys, and finely dressed women milled on the grounds. He spotted Laura Leigh by her wide-brimmed hat covered with large silk flowers. His heart thumped at the sight. Dressed in a pretty blue dress she stood out from the women who surrounded her like a rose among weeds.

"There's Miss Westbrook," Billy called out. "Oh, I'm sorry, Paw. I'll try to remember she's pretending to be my maw."

"It's only while we're on the grounds, son. We thought that it would be easier to sell the cookbooks if everybody thought a woman was the author." He tugged the team to a halt and jumped down.

Laura Leigh lifted a hand and waved. She separated from the other women and approached the wagon. "I see you made it," she said.

"We left home at dawn to make it on time. Is this where we'll give the demonstration?"

She lifted her face and whispered, "They think we're married. Kiss me." He glanced over her shoulder and saw the other women watching them. To avoid unnecessary suspicion, he kissed her briefly on the cheek.

Her skin was soft and inviting. He pulled back quickly before he let his needs overcome his good sense. "I have to unload the wagon," he said, turning away from her.

A frown tugged at the corners of her mouth. She glanced at his son and flashed a smile. "Hello, Billy. I'm glad your father brought you along."

The youngster's eyes lit up like a gas chandelier. "So am I. It's been a long time since I've been to a fair."

Marc grunted and lifted one of the heavy boxes. "Give me a hand, son. Then you can go check out the exhibits."

"Yes, sir."

It took only a few minutes to unload the wagon and set up a table in the tent. Billy ran off with the money he'd saved from working the farm. Marc hoped his son had enough self-control not to let a hustler swindle it from him.

As they had the week before, he and Laura Leigh judged several contests and Marc gave the demonstration. Again, the cookbook sold well, as did the flour. By day's end, both were stuffed from sampling too many sweets, pickles, and preserves. Yet they hadn't had a moment alone. As dusk fell, Marc pulled her into a darkened corner of the tent.

Immediately, she slid her arms around his neck. She smiled up at him, and he felt as if he were looking into the eyes of an angel. "You haven't given me one decent kiss all day," she whispered.

He didn't hesitate to correct his oversight. His mouth slanted over hers, and he parted her lips with his tongue. Her response was sharp and immediate. She met his searching tongue with a fervor that rocked him clear to his soul. When the kiss ended, they were both breathing heavily. "I'm going to miss you tonight," he said, raining tiny nips down her throat.

"I know. I've waited all week to be with you. More than once I was tempted to go out to the farm on one pretense or another."

He laughed. "I thought about going into San Antonio to check on you." Pulling back, he brushed a rough finger along her jaw. "I'm sorry about Billy being with us, but I promised him weeks ago he could come if he did all his chores."

"Don't apologize. I understand. We'll just have to be on our best behavior. You don't want to set a bad example for your son, do you? If you think you can slip out after he goes to sleep, I'll leave the adjoining door unlocked."

"I'll try to—"

His words were cut off by his son's shouts. "Paw, Miss— Maw!"

They jerked apart as Billy darted around the tent. "We're here, son," he said, as breathless as the boy who slid to a halt.

"Boy, this fair is great. You should see that prize-winning bull over in the livestock show. And did you know they even have a gypsy fortune teller? And dancers with gold bracelets that jingle, and men playing violins."

Marc's blood froze in his veins. He curled his fingers into his palms to keep them from trembling. "Gypsies? There's a gypsy band here?"

"Yeah, Paw. You've got to see them. The ladies have bright red and yellow skirts, and the men have shirts with wide sleeves. They have tents and wagons painted with flowers and stuff. And the men wear a gold earring in one ear."

His worse fear was coming true. Gypsies. A Romany caravan. He should have remembered the tribe followed the fairs. It was one of the reasons he and Billy seldom attended the festivities even in their own county.

Memories of Serafina flashed in his mind—pictures of her long black curls waving in the breeze as she danced, her arms flung over her head, her skirts flying around her long, shapely legs. The first time he'd seen her had been at a county fair much like this one. The farm boy had been swept right off his feet.

"Marcus, is something wrong?" Laura Leigh's soft voice snapped him out of his stupor.

He looked into her worried face. "No, I'm fine. Son, stay away from the gypsies, you hear me? They're nothing but tramps and thieves."

"Paw, I didn't do nothing wrong. The lady wanted to talk to me is all."

"What lady?" He gripped his son's shoulders and shook him.

"A pretty lady with black hair. She said her name was Sara something. She offered to tell my fortune. She even guessed my name. But she pronounced it funny, like the Germans—Wilhelm.''

His hands tightened. "Serafina?"

Billy nodded. "Paw, you're hurting me."

"Marcus, let your son go. You're frightening him." Laura Leigh pried his hands from the boy's arms.

"Stay out of this, Laura Leigh. This is between me and my son."

Her eyes grew wide and her mouth thinned into a straight line. "Excuse me for caring."

Afraid he was taking out his anger at his wife on the innocents around him, he dropped his hands. "I'm sorry. I didn't mean that. Son, be careful around those people. They'll rob you of your last dime if you're not careful."

Billy rubbed his arms. "Okay, Paw. I'll be careful."

Sorry for the way he'd treated his son and the woman he cared for, he forced a smile. "Let's load up the wagon, and I'll treat both of you to a fine dinner at the hotel."

"Yes, sir." Billy returned to the tent to retrieve the boxes of cookbooks.

Laura Leigh wasn't so easily put off. "What was that all about? He didn't deserve to be treated like that. He didn't misbehave. People are always fascinated by the gypsies."

He carried her small hands to his lips. "I know. I encountered gypsies a long time ago, and I don't trust them." An understatement at best. "I just want him to be careful."

By the look on her face, she didn't quite believe him. "Let's go eat. I'm starved."

"I'll help Billy. Meet you at the wagon." He glanced around, but saw no trace of the gypsies. If Serafina was there, he intended to stay as far from her as the moon from the earth. He didn't trust her, and she could only hurt his son. The only thing he wanted from her was a divorce. He promised himself he would see a lawyer as soon as he returned home.

Laura Leigh didn't protest. She left through the flap and headed toward where they'd tethered the team.

Marc hadn't taken two steps when a figure slipped from the shadows. Musky perfume wafted from the woman. Her wide skirts rustled, and she tossed long black curls over her shoulder. Bracelets dangled from her arms, and around her neck hung a chain with gold coins. His heart stopped beating.

"Serafina." Her name spewed from his lips like sour wine.

"Marcus. It has been a long time." The woman slithered toward him, like a serpent out to steal his soul. She'd tried it once and nearly succeeded. It wasn't going to happen again.

He ignored her attempt at cordiality. "What do you want?"

Her laughter twittered like the shrill cry of a bird. "Is that any way to talk to your wife? Your *first* wife?" She lifted a hand to his face. Quickly he sidestepped to avoid her touch.

"You deserted me twelve years ago. You aren't my wife."

She set her hands on her hips and thrust her breasts toward him. The top of her head barely brushed his shoulder. Her dingy white blouse sagged, showing an indecent amount of full breasts that overflowed her garment. With one false move, the dusky nipples would surely escape their loose covering. Long earrings skimmed her honey-colored shoulders.

"I am the mother of your son. Now I want Wilhelm to live with me." Her almond-shaped black eyes flashed like an angry cat's.

Fear knotted in his stomach. "You can't have him. You didn't want the baby, you can't have the young man."

"Why do you not ask him what he wants? My son may not want to be tied to that prison of a farm. I can show him the world. And he should take care of his mama." Her wide mouth thinned to an angry line.

"I'll never let him go." Unable to control his fury, he gripped her arms and glared into her face. "Leave him alone."

She stepped into him, brushing her voluptuous breasts against his chest. At one time that movement had sent him into a sexual frenzy; now her touch disgusted him. "I want you, Marcus. Do you not remember how it was for us? How you could not get enough of my body?"

He remembered everything—mostly the pain when she left, the anxiety of running a farm and tending an infant, of making up stories so his son wouldn't bear the pain of knowing his mother didn't want him. He shoved her away. "Don't touch me."

Her blouse sagged, and slid down her arm. "It is *Gorgio* woman, is it not? She is your wife. She does not know you already have a wife." With a swish of her skirts, she pranced around him with feline grace. "What would she say if she knew her husband is bigamist? That you are my husband?"

Marc tightened his hands into fists to keep from strangling the woman. The way she said *Gorgio,* their name for anybody not a gypsy, sounded like a curse from her lips. "Don't bring her into this. If you so much as speak to her or my son, I'll kill you." The threat came from anger and hostility built up for years.

His threat rolled off her like water off a duck. "You will do nothing."

Exasperated, he asked, "What do you want?"

"I saw you today. You have much money. You and the woman have fine clothes, and she wears gold around her neck and in her ears. I will not reveal that you have two wives, if you give me money. Since I do not have a son to work for me, I need gold, silver. You will give it to me."

He wanted to laugh. Laura Leigh was not his wife. But she would be hurt, and his son would be devastated if the truth came out. As much as he hated blackmail, he had little choice. Digging into his pocket, he pulled out the earnings from the cookbook plus the expense money Mr. Westbrook had sent. It would put them in a bind, but he would somehow manage to pay back the money.

"Take this. It's all I have."

Her eyes brightened as she snatched the money from his fingers. "It will do for now. I will be back tomorrow for more. Unless you want me to contact the woman."

"Leave her alone. She doesn't know anything."

"Does she please you, Marcus, as I did?" She gripped his wrist and carried his palm to her breast. "Do you not think of me when you take your pleasure in her body?"

Revulsion surged through him. His hand trembled. As if he'd been struck by a hot poker, he snatched back his hand. "I think of you like I think of a dreaded disease."

She glanced to the side. Over her head, he spotted Laura Leigh entering the tent. "Here is your woman. Will you not introduce me to her?"

"Get out of here." He shoved her toward the exit and dipped under the flap after her.

Laura Leigh covered her mouth with her fingers. When Marcus hadn't shown up at the wagon, she'd come looking for him. Billy had loaded all the goods, and he sat in the high seat waiting for his father. She'd opened her mouth to call his name when she saw Marcus with a beautiful gypsy woman. Dressed in a low-necked white blouse and flaring red-and-yellow skirt, she moved with the grace of a seductive cat.

She stopped in the shadows and watched, too shocked to move. He and the woman were deep in conversation as if discussing a business arrangement—or a personal assignation. From the distance, she couldn't hear their words, but their actions spoke volumes. He dug into his pocket and passed an amount of money to her. She could only imagine why he would pay the flamboyant woman. Men often lost all common sense when a woman whetted their sexual appetite. Laura Leigh's breath caught in her throat when he pressed his palm to the woman's breast. The gypsy's provocative laughter shot an arrow clear through Laura Leigh's chest. Her heart shattered like fine crystal thrown against a brick wall.

Marcus was no better than the worst of men. Whatever made her think that because he'd made love with her, that he cared for her or her feelings? No words of love were spoken, nor had he made any promises. If he wanted another woman, it was his right as an unattached male.

As if they sensed her staring at them, Marcus and the woman slipped out a flap in the tent. Alone, Laura Leigh sank to a bench to regain her composure. She hugged her arms to ward off the chill that seeped to her bones. Marcus didn't owe her an explanation—he didn't owe her anything. Only a fool would put her hopes and dreams in a man who kept secrets, as she knew he'd done.

Blinking back tears, she struggled with her temper. She had to face facts. Marcus didn't belong to her, and she had no say in whom he saw, or whom he bedded. Maybe he'd only told his son the people were tramps and thieves to keep the boy pure. What was good for the father was all wrong for the son.

With a composure she was far from feeling, she gathered her dignity around her like a shawl and returned to the wagon.

To her surprise, Marcus was waiting for her. In spite of her resolve, she couldn't hold back her tongue. "What took you so long?" she asked.

His eyes were troubled and he looked away. "I was talking to somebody."

"Who?"

"Nobody important." He offered a hand. "Are you ready for dinner?"

She twisted her fingers in her skirt. "You and Billy go ahead. I want to interview a few more people for the paper."

"Laura Leigh, it isn't safe for a woman alone out here."

"I'll be fine," she stated in a firm voice. Much better than with him. Until she was able to get her emotions under control, she didn't want to be near Marcus.

Clearly his mind was elsewhere, and his gaze drifted over her shoulders. "Just be careful. If you aren't back at the hotel in an hour, I'll come looking for you."

"Please don't bother, Mr. Lawrence. When I get my story, I'll return to my room. I hope you enjoy your evening." Her head held high, she stalked away from him. Demonstration or not, Laura Leigh planned to take the early morning train back to San Antonio the next day.

Let Mr. Marcus Lawrence keep his gypsy, his cookbook, and his demonstrations. Laura Leigh had plans of her own, and they didn't include having her heart broken by a faithless lover.

In spite of the warm evening, she was chilled to the bone. Hugging her shawl to her arms, she blinked back the tears that threatened to dampen her cheeks. She was a reporter, and if she ever wanted her father to accept her talents, she would just have to concentrate on her job.

She glanced over her shoulder and found Marcus's gaze locked on her. With a haughty toss of her head, she blended into the crowd and began to form a story in her mind.

CHAPTER NINE

Two hours later, Laura Leigh still hadn't shown up at the hotel. Marcus and his son had finished their meal and sat waiting in the lobby for her to return. He was certain she'd seen him with Serafina. If Billy hadn't been with them, he might have been willing to tell her the truth—to explain the strange situation. But how could he tell the woman who'd given so willingly of herself that he was married to a gypsy woman who'd deserted both her husband and her son? That there was no hope for anything lasting until Serafina was out of his life?

Worse, how could he tell her that the woman was blackmailing him? Or that, like a fool, he'd given in to her. For the last time. No matter what Serafina threatened, he would just have to stand up like a man and take his blows as they came. As soon as Laura Leigh returned, he would tell her the truth. Then he had to tell Billy about his mother. Marc had little choice. It would be disastrous for his son to hear her version of the truth from Serafina.

Tired of waiting for Laura Leigh, he stood and stretched.

"Son, I'm getting worried about Miss Westbrook. I'm going to look for her."

Billy rose and stood beside Marc. His son was a fine youngster with a good head on his shoulders. Someday, he would grow into a good man. "I want to go with you, Paw. I'll help you look for Miss Westbrook."

It was safer for Billy to be with Marc than where Serafina could get to him. "Okay, son. We'll go together. She's probably just talking to some women and lost track of the time." At least he hoped so. He prayed she'd had enough sense to stay away from the gypsies. There was no telling what they would do to a woman who wore nice jewelry and carried a bit of money in her handbag. It would be even worse if she had met Serafina and the gypsy filled Laura Leigh's head with her lies.

He settled his hat on his head. Without taking the time to retrieve the wagon from the livery, he and Billy walked to the fairgrounds. Once there, he led the way to the dance area, where couples were enjoying the music and socializing. More than likely she was enjoying a spin around the dance platform with a young cowboy or farmer. Determined not to be jealous, he scanned every woman wearing a wide hat and pink dress. Twice he started to tap a young man on the shoulder, only to find that the woman was not the one he was seeking.

They circled the clearing, but didn't see Laura Leigh among the revelers. Worried for her safety, he decided it best that they split up and cover the entire fairgrounds. He sent his son toward the exhibition area, while he headed toward the gypsy camp. Fear, anger, and apprehension bubbled up in him like a pot boiling over. If they had done anything to Laura Leigh, he would commit murder with his bare hands.

The brightly colored wagons were circled near the woods. Myriad campfires blazed in the distance. He remembered the time he'd sneaked into a similar camp to be with Serafina. Today, he regretted his youthful insanity with every bit of his being. Several tents stood open to catch the breeze. His gaze scanned the area. Gypsies mingled around the fires; men and women danced to the tune of a squeeze box and violin. Tambourines jingled, while others clapped their hands and cheered. Laura Leigh was nowhere among them. He stepped inside a tent and looked around. It was empty. He turned to leave and found his way blocked by four men.

The wind whipped their wide, flowing sleeves, and their pitch-colored hair hung below their shoulders. The tallest man wore a drooping black mustache. He slapped a stick against his palm. "*Gorgio,* you look for gypsy woman?"

Marc glanced from the right to the left and realized that the only way out was through their line. "No. I'm looking for a *Gorgio.*"

The shorter man, an ugly fellow with a scar-pocked face, wore a blue-and-white printed scarf knotted around his neck. "Gypsy woman not good enough?"

Another man separated from the others. "You *Gorgio* Serafina tell us about. She say you throw her out of your house and steal her son."

Marc anchored his feet and balled his hands into fists. "She deserted her home and family."

The tall gypsy shifted from foot to foot. "You lie. We teach *Gorgio* not to lie about Romany."

The quartet surged forward as one. Marc blocked the stick with his arm, but he wasn't fast enough to avoid the blows to his midsection. He struck out, catching one in the jaw, another in his stomach. When two men held his arms behind his back, the others pummeled him with the stick and their fists. He struggled to free himself, but the gypsies were hell-bent on killing him. The blows came one after another. Pain enveloped him until darkness overtook him and he slipped into unconsciousness.

Laura Leigh excused herself from the woman she'd been interviewing. She'd seen Marc circle the clearing where couples danced to the music. From a distance she'd watched his every movement. She'd started to call out his name, until she noticed that he'd separated from Billy and left in another direction. Her heart sank. Marcus headed directly for the gypsy camp— and the woman he'd been with earlier, of that she was certain. Although she knew it was wrong to follow him, Laura Leigh needed to be sure. Her pace slower than his, she watched as he entered a tent. Four men slipped into the same entrance. By their bright yellow and blue shirts, she recognized them as the Romany.

Her natural curiosity, as well as her concern for Marc, drove her closer. Grunts, groans, and the sound of blows came from the tent. Afraid of what she would find, she slipped under the flap. In the pale yellow light from a single kerosene lamp, she spotted them—four men bent over a prone body. Arms and legs flailed, feet kicked, and the man on the ground groaned.

She screamed. ''Marc!''

The four men spun toward her. One man bumped against the pole and knocked the lamp to the straw-strewn ground. The dry straw ignited immediately. Laura Leigh screamed again. The men darted past her, slamming her to the ground. She struggled to her feet and saw that the fire was rapidly spreading. By the time she reached Marc, flames licked at the tent's canvas walls.

She stumbled to his prone body. ''Marc,'' she cried. Shaking him, she tried to wake him. His face was bruised, and blood spurted from his lips and nose. His shirt and jacket were torn and dirty. Laura Leigh had to do something. Within minutes, the tent would turn into an inferno, and they both would be trapped.

Again she shook Marc. He moaned, and tried unsuccessfully to sit up. Determined to save him, she shoved him to a sitting position. She choked on the smoke and yelled at Marc, ''Get up! We have to get out of here.''

He stumbled to his knees. ''Laura Leigh, what—'' His words died in a series of coughs.

''I don't feel like being burned alive.'' She shoved him to

his feet and draped his arm over her shoulder. Using all the strength she could muster, she dragged him to the entrance of the tent. Men carrying buckets of water were racing toward them. One burly man grabbed Marc's other arm and dragged them to safety.

Laura Leigh sank to the grass and cradled Marc's head in her lap. Both of them were smudged with soot, but they were alive. He coughed and choked, gasping for breath. His face was bruised and battered, his eye blackened, and his lip split. Tears tumbled from her eyes to his forehead.

By then the tent was totally engulfed in flame, and the fire had spread to the others. Men with buckets of water tried to keep the inferno contained. The breeze fanned the fire, and they were fighting a losing battle.

Marc rolled to his side. "I've got to go." He clutched his middle with one arm and tried to sit.

She caught his arm. "No. You have broken ribs and your face is a mess. You might even have a concussion. I'll send for a doctor."

He shook his head and ran his fingers through hair dirty with twigs and straw. "The fire is spreading."

"The men are trying to put it out. There's nothing you can do."

"The tents, the wagons," he groaned. "Serafina."

"They're trying to stop the fire from spreading to them." Even as she watched, the gypsies were driving their horses away from the inferno. The breeze caught the fire, and lifted it toward the wood-and-canvas wagons. Flames licked and leaped from one to another, eating at the dry wood and cloth.

"I have to find Serafina." Marc shook off her arm and stumbled to his feet. Clutching his side, he bent double and staggered toward the middle of the camp.

Laura Leigh shuddered. After she'd risked her life to save his, he was risking his life for the gypsy woman. It was a courageous and foolish thing to do.

"Miss Westbrook." Billy's breathless voice drew her gaze. 'Where's my paw?"

She pointed to the silhouetted figure racing toward the wagons. "He's hurt, but he's going to rescue others."

The young man helped her to her feet, and they followed in Marc's footsteps. The gypsies were scattering, grabbing goods from wagons and racing for safety. Marc grabbed a young gypsy boy and asked him something. He pointed toward a wagon painted with flowers and banners of all the colors of the rainbow. Marc stumbled in that direction.

Marc's ribs ached and blood dripped down his face. Putting his own pain aside, he searched for Serafina. As much as he despised the woman, she was still his son's mother. Billy deserved to know his mother, and as much as he hated to admit to himself, she needed to know her son.

He spotted Serafina dragging a load of garments from the wagon. The bucket brigade now reached the wagons and fought a fruitless battle against the flames fanned by the wind. He grabbed her arm and pulled her into his chest.

"Serafina, you have to get away from here. The wagons will go up in a flash."

Her dark eyes gleamed with the wildness of a trapped animal. "No. I must save my belongings." She twisted out of his grip. "My money—it is in there."

"Let it go. You'll get more." He caught her wrist and spun her toward him.

She lashed out and caught Marc in the middle of his injured ribs. He doubled over in pain. Free of his grip, she scurried away like an angry cat and climbed into the rear of the wagon, the front of which was already in flames. He started to follow when a hand grabbed his arm.

"Paw, don't." Billy tugged him to a stop.

He glared at his son and the woman who'd only minutes ago saved his life. "I have to." His chest ached and he gasped for breath. "She's your mother."

If he'd slapped both of them with a club, they couldn't have been more shocked. "I'll explain later."

Smoke poured from under the door of the wagon and flames seared the dry wood. "Serafina!" he called as he struggled with the door that refused to open. He slammed a shoulder into the fragile wood. Thick black smoke blinded him. Inside the crowded, cluttered wagon, he searched for her. Flame and smoke hindered his progress. He coughed, and covered his face with his handkerchief. Water sizzled on the outside, but it did little good in the smoke-filled interior. He tore at the pieces of furniture, the bedding, and the goods piled in the corners. Gasping for breath, he touched flesh.

Voices yelled from the doorway for him to leave. He grabbed at Serafina and tugged. She'd wedged herself into a corner. His breath almost gone, he pulled with all his limited strength. Crawling backward, he managed to reach the door. Hands grabbed at him and at the woman. He stumbled to the ground and struggled for breath. In a loud whoosh, the wagon exploded in flames. Tears blinded his eyes.

"Serafina," he called, coming to his knees.

Laura Leigh knelt beside the woman who lay unmoving on the ground. The gypsy's skirts were scorched, and her hair was in wild disarray. In her hand, she clutched a cloth bag. "She's dead."

The simple words slashed through him like a knife. He stared at the body. His stomach clenched. He'd loved her and she'd given him a son. Although he'd cursed her a thousand times, he hadn't wanted her to die. His gaze shifted from the woman who'd stolen his youthful heart, to the pained face of the woman he loved with all the strength of a man.

Billy hunkered down and stared at his mother. "She's my maw?" His words were broken with disbelief and pain.

Marc nodded and crawled toward Serafina. Men surged around them in a futile effort to save the gypsy camp, yet he felt more alone than ever in his life. He owed explanations, but words failed him when he needed them most. He touched his fingers to the pulse at her throat to see for himself. It was true. She'd died of the smoke while trying to save a paltry bag of money. Marc buried his face in his hands. Guilt weighed on his shoulders like a heavy cloak.

"She was very beautiful," Laura Leigh said, her voice soft with sympathy. "And so young."

Billy touched his mother's face. "I don't understand, Paw. You said my mother was dead."

Eyes misty from the smoke, he lifted his gaze to his son. "She left us soon after you were born. I didn't know where she'd gone. I only saw her again today." His son sagged into his arms and buried his face in Marc's shoulder. Tears for the mother he'd never known flowed from him as from a riverbed in rainy season.

Laura Leigh slipped to her feet. "You are still married to her?"

"Yes."

Emotion washed across her face. "I see."

"No, Laura Leigh, you don't understand anything." How could he explain why he hadn't told her about his wife? How could he make his son understand the lie they'd lived with for twelve years? He hugged his son in a vain effort to comfort the boy.

"I'll leave the two of you to grieve. We'll talk later." Turning on her heel, Laura Leigh moved toward a group of gypsies watching their homes go up in smoke. So much loss, so much destruction. His own heart was in shambles. His life in turmoil.

A knot tightened around his chest. In one night he'd lost everything in losing Laura Leigh.

While trying to comfort his son and come to grips with his past, Marc watched his future walk away.

CHAPTER TEN

Her heart in shambles, Laura Leigh hurried away from Marc and his son before her tears blinded her path.

He was married. And he'd neglected to relay that singular detail of his life. He'd slept with her, made passionate love, and kept something so important from her. The reason was clear. If she'd known he was married, she wouldn't have given herself so completely to him. And maybe she wouldn't have fallen in love with him.

She watched the sweat-drenched men tossing water on the fire. Children gathered to watch the activity. Men shouted, and women cried. A small gypsy girl hugged her doll while her home burned to the wheels. An old woman sat on a pile of cloth and comforted the child. Women wept as they watched the destruction of their homes. Her instincts as a reporter kicked in and overran her own misery. Too many had lost more than she. She'd lost her lover, but she still had her position and home. In losing their tents and wagons, the Romany lost their houses and their livelihood—and some lost their lives.

Digging into her handbag, she pulled out a pad and pencil.

She wrote her feelings and impressions of the turmoil. All around her she saw both bravery and cowardice. The men who'd started the fire and left Marc to die were cowards of the worst kind. Injured, Marc had struggled to save the woman who'd deserted him years ago.

Stories formed in her mind as she interviewed the victims and the rescuers. She promised to engage her mother in the effort to help these people. If they would accept the help, Loretta Westbrook would plan any number of fund-raisers. She loved helping others and willingly shared her wealth and energy with those less fortunate.

Dawn was breaking over the horizon when Laura Leigh made her way back to the hotel. She'd long ago lost her shawl and hat. Her gown was torn and sooty. Her footsteps as heavy as her heart, she entered the hotel and asked for the key to her room.

"Miss Westbrook." She turned to see Billy enter the lobby. His shoulders sagged and his eyes were red-rimmed.

Heart aching for the boy, she opened her arms and welcomed him into her embrace. "How are you doing?" she asked for a lack of what to say. She kissed him on top of his red hair.

"Okay, I guess," he said, against her shoulder. "I didn't even know my mother was alive, and now she's gone."

Laura Leigh patted him gently on the back. "I'm sorry it had to happen like this. She was very beautiful." It sounded inane, and foolish, but it was all that came to mind.

Billy pulled away and squared his shoulders. Displaying a maturity beyond his years, he said, "We're taking her home to bury her beside my grandparents."

Her heart twisted. "How is your father?"

"Okay, I guess. He didn't care about her. I think he's glad she's dead."

"Billy, don't say such a thing. Your father is a good man. He risked his life to save her."

His eyes glinted with anger. "Then why didn't he tell me

about her? We could have looked for her. She didn't have to
live like that.''

She shrugged. ''I don't know. If she left him when you were
a baby, maybe she wanted to live with the gypsies. I understand
they prefer their nomadic life to settling down.''

''He probably drove her away.''

For some reason, she was compelled to come to Marc's
defense. ''Give your father a chance to explain. He's done his
best to be both a mother and father to you. He's the only one
who knows what really happened.'' She slipped her arm across
his shoulder. ''Go on upstairs and get some rest. You're about
to fall over.''

He nodded. ''I'm tired.''

She took the key to his room from the clerk and led the boy
up the stairs. He entered his room, and she went to hers. She
hated to leave Billy, but it was important to leave on the first
train out. Not only did she have to file her stories, she wasn't
ready to face Marcus. As she washed and changed into clean
clothes, she wondered if she would ever be ready to face the
man who'd deceived her and broken her heart.

His hand in the air, Marc hesitated before knocking. Laura
Leigh deserved an explanation, but so far words had failed him.
He'd given his son only a cursory account of his disastrous
relationship with Serafina. Gathering his waning courage, he
rapped lightly on the door.

To his surprise, the door slipped open. He stopped in his
tracks. Laura Leigh stood at the bureau mirror adjusting her
hat. Fully clothed in a pretty rose-colored suit, she looked like
the welcome first flower of spring after a frigid winter. Weeks
ago she'd come into his life and melted the ice that had too
long surrounded his heart. She'd given him back his life and
the chance for love. His heart constricted. Through his own
stupidity, he'd lost everything.

She spun to look at him. "Marc." Her eyes turned from warm gray to cold steel. "What are you doing here?"

He wrapped an arm around his middle against the pain in his chest. "I had to see you."

On a sigh, she picked up her handbag. "I'm in rather a hurry. I want to make the morning train back home."

"Can't you wait? We need to talk."

"Mr. Lawrence, we have nothing to discuss. I'm very sorry for your loss. It was a sad tragedy."

"Are we back to formality after all we've shared?" He stepped closer. Laura Leigh was the only real thing in his world turned into a nightmare.

She laughed, a sound shrill and without humor. "We shared a business arrangement that was profitable to both of us. Since you've made your mark, you don't need me anymore." Her voice cracked. "You never needed me."

More than anything, he ached to hold her, if he could only breach the wall that had sprung up between them. "You'll never know how much I need you, but I should have told you about Serafina. You deserved to know the truth."

"Yes, honesty would have been preferable to deceit."

"Do you mind if I sit down? I'm totally exhausted." In mind and spirit.

A frown pulled at her mouth. "Did you see a doctor?"

He nodded. "He cleaned the cuts and bandaged my ribs. You were right; a couple were broken."

"I'm very sorry."

Stretching out a hand, he reached for her. She jumped back out of his reach. "I don't blame you for not wanting me to touch you. I'm filthy. But I didn't want to take the time to clean up before I saw you. I didn't even thank you for saving my life."

She lifted one slender shoulder. "Anybody would have done the same."

"I don't think so. The thugs who beat me left us both to die in the fire."

"Do you know who they were?"

He shook his head. "They were Roms who blended into the crowd and probably ran away when their own people became the victims."

In the distance the shrill whistle of the train tore through the quiet Sunday morning. Laura Leigh jumped. "I have to go if I want to make my train."

It was too soon; the pain was too raw. He'd hurt her deeply. "I won't try to stop you. When will I see you again?"

"Mr. Lawrence, you're in mourning. Your son needs you. It wouldn't be proper for us to see each other. If you want to continue the tour, you can go on without me. I'm going back to my job and my home."

The finality of her words hurt worse than the pounding he'd received. "Laura Leigh, I love you." His confession shocked him. He hadn't meant to put that on her. Not until they resolved this conflict between them.

Moisture glittered behind her long, dark lashes. "Don't say that, Marc. It's only guilt talking. I didn't expect anything from you. I'm an adult woman. I knew what I was doing, and I don't want you full of remorse over what we shared." She lifted her valise from the bed. "I don't want to miss my train. I've already wired part of my report to my father. He's waiting for my story for tomorrow's paper. If I want him to take me seriously as a reporter, I must make my deadlines."

Heedless of his soot and grime, he surged from the chair and blocked her path. He grabbed her arms and pulled her into his chest. His mouth covered hers in a kiss hard and full of longing. Caught off guard, she gasped. He took advantage of her surprise and slid his tongue past her lips. Holding her, feeling her warmth against him, was sweet torture.

She melted against him, her mouth sweeter than strawberries. Desire swept through him with the swiftness of lightning. He wanted her, needed her to ease some of the pain in his heart. Her valise dropped to the floor with a thud and her hands clung to his shirt. His heart pounded against her fingertips. Memories of the past, thoughts about the future, drifted away on the delicious sensations that surged through him.

Her reaction was immediate and as strong as his. She returned his kiss with a fervor that left his heart pounding and his breath short. The kiss ended, and he slid his hands up her arms to her shoulders. "Don't leave me."

A tear rolled down her cheek. "I have to go." She twisted out of his grip, and this time he didn't try to stop her. "Goodbye, Marcus. Take care of Billy."

His hands dropped to his side. The finality in her words stabbed his chest like a Bowie knife cutting the life out of him. "I love you," he whispered to a room as empty as his heart.

Laura Leigh studied the front page of the *Advantage*. Her stories about the fire at the Comal County fair made the headlines for a week. "L. Westbrook," she read the byline. Her father had printed every word she'd written and asked her to write follow-up stories for each day's edition.

Pride swelled within her. The entire editorial staff had raved over the quality and professionalism of her work. Even the male reporters had admitted that her work rivaled theirs. The story about Marcus's daring attempt to rescue the gypsy woman brought a flurry of requests for the cookbook. She'd kept his relationship to the dead woman confidential. She doubted he would want that fact published abroad. Her stories focused on the brave men who'd fought the fire and the victims who'd lost their movable homes. Although the gypsies rarely were accepted by the community, funds began to arrive to assist them in getting new tents and wagons. Her own mother had already organized a ball as a fund-raiser to help the needy.

At the sight of Marc's name in the story, her heart contracted. She covered her mouth with her fingers. Since she'd walked out of the room after their soul-stirring kiss, she'd thought about him constantly. He'd lied and deceived her; he didn't deserve her consideration. Did he really love her, or was he simply trying to appease her after their indiscretion?

He needed time to get over the guilt about his wife's death. Billy, too, needed time. How sad to lose a mother before you even got to know her. Laura Leigh didn't know what she would do without her own dear parents.

The door to her office flung open, banging against the wall. She looked up, and for a brief second she expected to see Marcus marching into the room. However, it was her father and uncle who stood in the doorway. "Here's my star reporter," Herbert declared, pride in his voice.

Her uncle followed, a wide smile on his face. "Miss Laura Leigh, I think you owe me an explanation. I thought that a Mrs. Lawrence was our star. Now I learn that *Mr.* Lawrence is the cooking expert."

The story about Marc's success had spread back to the Homestead office. Her face heated. She'd neglected to tell her parents that she and Marc hadn't been escorted by his wife.

"We didn't mean to fool anybody. At first we thought that the ladies wouldn't accept a male cook. But when he gave the demonstrations, the women swarmed around him like bees to honey." Her heart sank at the reminder that she had done exactly the same.

Her father nodded. "Tell me the truth, Laurie, was the Mrs. with you?"

Caught, she was forced to tell the truth. "No. He doesn't have a wife."

Uncle Fritz chuckled around his unlit cigar, and her father snorted. "You wouldn't be laughing if it was your daughter who'd been traipsing all over the state of Texas with a man."

"Father, I'm a grown woman. And we weren't alone. His son was with us." She crossed her fingers at the partial lie.

"Don't tell Loretta," her uncle said. "You'll never hear the end of it."

Her father glared at his brother. "As long as nothing untoward happened, there's no use rocking the boat."

She turned away to hide her blush. Nothing untoward, hah! She'd fallen into bed with a man who already had a wife. Worse, she loved him with all her heart and soul. And willingly she'd given the gift of her body.

"Are you planning to attend the ball this Saturday?" she asked to change the subject. "Mother expects all of us to make her fund-raiser a success."

"Your Aunt Patricia and I will be there. Are you inviting Lawrence?"

"He's on the guest list." She'd added his name, but she doubted he would come.

"I want to thank him in person for the orders. They've been pouring in. That was quite a publicity stunt." Her uncle tossed the stub of his unlit cigar into the wastebasket.

"I'm going to do another printing of the cookbook. If we can get him back on the tour, we'll sell all of them in a few weeks." Herbert tapped the front page of his newspaper.

"He was hurt in the fire, and it will take time for him to heal. Maybe in the fall." By then, her heart might have mended and she could face him again. "Now if you'll excuse me, I have a deadline to make."

"Let's get out of here," Herbert told his brother. "I'm training my daughter to take over for me when I retire. Can you imagine? A woman as publisher and editor?"

Fritz laughed. "She's the best reporter in town. You should be proud."

"I am. And so is her mother." He flashed a secretive grin at Fritz. "Let's give her that gift."

She stared after the pair who were acting every bit like boys out to fool their mother. Minutes later, they returned, her father carrying a wooden box while her uncle toted a smaller package. He set the large object on her desk. Her heart beat faster when she spotted the name Remington stenciled on the box. She'd wanted this for so long, and she didn't dare hope her father had actually purchased it for her.

Laura Leigh felt as giddy as a child at her birthday party.

Her father lifted the wooden box and there it was—a shiny black Remington typing machine. She brushed a finger along the keys. She'd read about the machine, had attended a demonstration, and drooled over it in the Sears, Roebuck & Co. catalogue. The Universal keyboard was a wonder, as was the very idea that she could press the keys and have every letter uniform and perfectly legible.

Tears flooded her eyes. "For me?"

"Who else would want this thing? But if you're going to be editor one day, you'll need these modern contraptions. I even installed the Mergenthales linotype machine a couple of years ago."

"Thank you, Papa." She threw her arms around her father's neck. "And you, too, Uncle Fritz."

"Believe it or not, it was your mother's idea. She said if you're going to be a journalist, you need the finest, most up-to-date writing machine available."

"Mother? But I thought she didn't want me to work."

Herbert removed his handkerchief from his pocket. "She wants you to be happy, and if being a serious newspaperwoman makes you happy, then she'll support you." He dried her eyes as he'd done when she was a child and ran to him with her skinned knees. "But don't think she's giving up on finding you a husband."

Fritz opened the package of plain white paper. "Show us how it works."

She grabbed a sheet of paper between her fingers as she'd seen in the demonstration. Carefully, she rolled it into the machine. For a long moment she stared at the strange arrangement of keys. Hunting and pecking, she spelled out her name. It was the most amazing thing she'd ever seen. Not only would it make her work easier, but it showed her father's confidence in her ability. That meant the world to her.

If she concentrated on her new equipment, and worked hard to be a good journalist, she might get over Marcus. And of course, she also might fly to the moon on a butterfly's wings.

CHAPTER ELEVEN

The charity ball had been an overwhelming success. Loretta Westbrook had raised a tidy sum for the victims of the fire. Trying to hide her heartbreak, Laura Leigh had danced with every eligible bachelor and drank more than her share of champagne.

None of her efforts helped her forget Marcus. The champagne reminded her of the night she'd indulged and made love with him. Dancing made her think of when he'd stood on the sidelines choking on a cigar while she whirled past in another man's arms.

She wondered how he was doing. Was he coming to grips with his guilt? Had Billy come to terms with his mother's death? She'd half expected him to attend the ball. Every time she spotted a tall, muscular man in a black suit enter the room, her heart had skipped a beat. It was only foolish thinking. Surely it wouldn't be proper for a man in mourning to attend a gala. Of course, only she and his son knew about his marriage. To the world, he'd been a widower for years.

Back at the office, Laura Leigh used her new typing machine

to compose the story for the next morning's edition of the newspaper. Her fellow reporters mocked her use of the modern machine, stating that a real reporter composed his story on the run. Laura Leigh ignored their taunts. She loved the machine.

However, even hard work hadn't stopped her from thinking about Marcus.

She wasn't sure if she was disappointed or glad he hadn't come. Either way, she was spared having to face her feelings for him.

"Is that my favorite niece pecking away at that contraption?" Uncle Fritz stuck his head through the open doorway.

"Come in, Uncle. I'm working on my story about the ball."

He removed his bowler hat and took the chair at the side of her desk. He wasted no time getting to the point of his visit. "I rather was looking forward to seeing Lawrence at the party. Have you heard from him?"

"No." Her heart stumbled at the thought that he hadn't contacted her at all. "Why did you want to see him?"

Fritz pulled a cigar from his pocket. "I wanted to offer him another business proposition." She waited while he clipped off the end and shoved the cigar into his mouth. "I've been thinking about opening a restaurant, and I wanted to know if Lawrence would be interested in running it for me."

From the few things he'd told her, it was Marc's dream to own his own eatery. "You'll have to ask him."

He flashed a cajoling smile. "I wondered if I could talk you into presenting the proposal to him." When she opened her mouth to protest, he held up a hand to stop her words. "You convinced him to make the tour, and it was highly successful. If anybody can influence him, it's you."

If he only knew how much it hurt to even think about Marc, much less to try to sell an idea to him, her uncle would never have proposed such a thing. "I can't get away. I'm very busy at the paper. I have stories to write and people to interview."

"Your father will let you go for a day or two." He continued as if she'd agreed to his scheme. "I've selected a good location near the Alamo and the Menger Hotel. He'll be in complete charge of the restaurant. He can manage it any way he pleases, run the kitchen, do the cooking if he wants.''

''In other words, you want to hire him to run your business.''

''No, I want him as a partner. When you hire somebody, they can work or not and still make the same salary. But as a partner, he'll share the profits. I'll front the money; he'll do the work. We'll iron out the details later. It's up to you to convince him to accept the offer.''

Her stomach twisted. She doubted that anybody could convince Marc to do something he didn't want. On the other hand, Uncle Fritz was offering a chance of a lifetime. She'd gotten her wishes; now she had the chance to help Marc get his.

''Why don't you let your lawyer write to him?'' She still wasn't sure she was ready to face Marcus.

''I hate to do business like that. I'd go myself, but I think you can do a better sell job than me. I doubt he can say no to such a pretty face.''

She sighed. ''Uncle, you're asking him to leave his farm and his home and move to town. He might not be interested.''

Fritz stood and started for the door. ''We won't know unless we try, will we? Call me when you get back and let me know what he said.''

With a wave of his hand, he was gone, leaving Laura Leigh staring at the empty doorway with her mouth agape. Her uncle fully expected her to drop everything and go to Marc. She turned back to her typing machine. He would have to learn that she was a busy woman with a life of her own. She didn't have time to race off on a wild-goose chase. Especially after the man who'd broken her heart and left her alone with her memories.

For the next week, thoughts about Marcus haunted Laura Leigh. She pounded out her stories—serious journalism, not just the women's news—on her new typewriter. She'd wanted to be taken seriously as a journalist, and now her father had made it clear that she was in line to take over the newspaper when he retired.

She'd achieved her goal, and it hurt to think that she would deny Marc his dream.

Her mind made up, Laura Leigh contacted her uncle, who had his lawyer draw up the proper papers. Armed with a proposal only a fool would refuse, she boarded the afternoon train to Horsefly. The jitters in her stomach grew stronger with every mile the train clacked along the tracks. She wanted to see him; she didn't want to see him. She loved him; she hated him. She feared rejection; she didn't care.

Thoroughly confused, she disembarked from the train. As she'd done before, she rented a horse and buggy from the livery. Following the road, she drove toward the Lawrence place. Her heart raced as she turned down the narrow lane that led to the house. The homestead was much as she remembered it. The fence posts were in a straight line, the barn doors wide open.

In the distance she saw Marc walking behind a mule while plowing his field. Emotions overflowed her. She loved him. No doubt about it. No matter how he felt, she would still love him as she would never love another man. As she pulled the horse to a stop, she decided to show him how much she loved him. A plan formed in her mind.

Billy raced out and met her. "Miss Westbrook. Paw didn't say you were coming for a visit."

"He doesn't know. I wanted to surprise him." She climbed down from the buggy seat. Slipping her arm across his shoulder, she urged him into the house. "How are you getting along?"

The young man shrugged. "Okay, I guess. Paw explained what happened between him and my mother. She was too young to accept a husband, a farm, and a baby." A maturity far beyond his years gleamed in his green eyes that reminded her so much of Marc.

"I'm sure your father didn't mean to hurt you." Or me, for that matter, she reasoned.

"I know. But he's having a tough time. He seems so sad. Do you know we haven't had a decent meal since we came home? Paw quit cooking, and he hardly even eats. If he doesn't start canning, we won't have a thing to eat this winter."

Laura Leigh swallowed down her anxiety. Was it because he was still grieving, or was guilt gnawing at him? "I have some news that might help cheer him up." She tugged off her gloves and set them on the round table in the parlor. The house was neat and clean, but no luscious aromas wafted from the kitchen.

"I even went out and picked some blackberries, hoping he'd make a cobbler. He just told me to give them away. He doesn't feel like cooking."

"Where are the berries?" she asked, entering the kitchen. No pie cooled on the windowsill, and no stew simmered on the stove. Only a stale pot of coffee sat on the cold stove.

"On the counter. I ate some of them with sugar. I killed and cleaned a chicken. I figured if he didn't want to cook, I'd give it a try for supper. I'm getting tired of ham and stale bread."

Billy's helpfulness came as a surprise. It made her chore much easier. She glanced at the boy. If her plan was to have any chance of success, she needed to be alone with Marc. She didn't want his son caught in the cross fire between them. Digging into her handbag, she pulled out a notepad and some coins.

"Billy, can you do a special favor for me?" He nodded. "I want to send a telegram to my father. Will you be so kind as to drive the hired buggy into town and send it for me?"

"I'll have to ask Paw."

"I'll explain everything to your father." She scribbled a few words, telling her parents she would return the next day. If Marc threw her out, she would simply spend the night in town. "And you can stay a while and have a nice meal at the cafe. Visit with a friend. I'll take the blame if your father doesn't agree."

As if eager to get away from the farm for a few hours, Billy grabbed the note. Before he left, the boy added wood and lit a fire in the stove. Minutes later he was on his way to town.

Laura Leigh removed her hat and jacket. Tucking a cloth in the waistband of her skirt, she entered the foreign territory of a kitchen. Armed with Marc's cookbook, she searched for the necessary ingredients to prepare a decent meal.

Following the directions with his recipe, she put the chicken in a large pot. Taking the onions, carrots, and potatoes from the pantry, she did her best to peel them. The onions brought tears from her eyes, and by the time she finished the potatoes, they were half the size as before she began. Adding a few spoons of Marc's special spices, she put the pot on the stove to simmer. Just to make sure it would taste good, she added some of each of his special spice mixtures.

Sweat dampened her white blouse, now stained and dirty. Since the tour, she'd gained a new appreciation for women who cooked for their families. Next, she tackled the dessert. Thanks to Billy, she knew what to prepare. Besides, she'd watched Marcus bake a cobbler while they were on the tour. If she carefully followed the directions, she was sure to make it as good as his.

Marc had taken all he could. He stopped plowing his corn in the middle of the row and turned the mule toward the barn. With every step he took, he cursed himself a thousand times as a fool for letting Laura Leigh get away from him.

The past weeks had been the loneliest in his life. He'd lost his appetite and his desire even to prepare a decent meal for his son. After they'd returned home following the fire, he'd lost all interest in living. It was worse than after Serafina had left him years earlier. Then he at least had his parents and son to comfort him. Now he had nothing but his guilt to warm his bed and soothe his conscience.

As he loosed the mule from the plow, he made his plans. It was time to take the bull by the horns. No matter what Laura

Leigh had said, he knew she loved him. A woman of her upbringing and honesty wouldn't give herself so fully and passionately unless she cared deeply. And he loved her with all of his being. Without her he was a shell of a man, an empty vessel without a soul.

By the shadows, he guessed it to be about four o'clock. If he hurried, he could make the late train to San Antonio. If need be, he would pound on her door or camp out in her office until she listened to him. He left the barn and raced toward the house. A thin stream of smoke came from the stovepipe above the roofline. Billy must have gotten tired of eating cold food and was trying his hand at cooking.

Marc stopped at the pump for a minute. He tore off his shirt and stuck his head under the water. Quickly, he washed the dirt and grime from his arms. In too much of a hurry to heat water for a bath, he pulled off his overalls and boots, and washed his lower body. With the towel and soap he kept at the pump, he completed a bath. Wrapping the towel around his waist, he darted to the kitchen.

He flung open the door and yelled for his son. "Billy, get dressed. We're going to—" The words died on the air. His gaze fell on a nicely rounded female derriere poked in the air while the woman's head was almost in the oven.

She yelped, straightened, and dropped a baking pan on the table. Shocked, he lost his grip on the towel and caught it before it hit the floor.

"Laura Leigh?"

She stuck her finger into her mouth. "Marc, what . . . You're naked."

Guarding his nudity with the towel, he could only stare at her. "I know. I just washed up."

"Oh, my." Sucking on her finger, she studied him with those wide eyes that changed from light to dark as her gaze slid over his body. "You're looking much better."

The effect on his body was immediate and downright embarrassing. "I heal quickly. You look wonderful. I'll go dress, and we can talk."

She reached out as if to snatch away his meager covering. "Don't bother. I think you look rather fetching."

He jumped out of her reach. The fire that had begun in his gut raced up his chest and settled on his cheeks. "Where's Billy?"

"I sent him to town on an errand. He won't be back for a while."

So they were alone. And if his son ran into any of his friends, it would be nearly dark before he returned. "What are you doing here?"

She stepped back. Damp tendrils of her hair clung to her neck, and her once-white shirtwaist was splattered with spots. Her skirt was coated with flour, as was most of the kitchen. The heat in the kitchen had her face flushed. The woman was absolutely the most stunning creature he'd ever seen.

"I'm preparing your dinner."

He almost lost the towel again. For the first time, he noticed the pot simmering on the stove. In the baking pan, something black bubbled up from what looked like a large wad of dough. *"You're* cooking dinner?" The table was set with two plates and a small jar of daisies in the center.

She tossed her head. "Don't act so surprised, Mr. Lawrence. I had a very good teacher. And I followed the wonderful recipes to the letter."

"Are you planning to poison me?"

"Would I come all this way just to do you in?" She twined a finger in the burnished hair on his chest. Her gaze lowered to the front of the towel. "Do you think I should shed all these hot clothes and get comfortable?"

Quivers raced over him. "I'll slip on trousers so we can talk."

"That really isn't necessary."

The bulge in the front of the towel grew more humiliating with each moment. "Oh, yes, it is." He turned toward the parlor and the safety of his bedroom. At the door he turned and grinned, the first time he'd felt like smiling in weeks. "Don't go away."

"I won't." She fanned her face with her handkerchief. "By the way, where were you and Billy planning to go in such an all-fired hurry?"

"To San Antonio to convince the woman I love to love me back."

CHAPTER TWELVE

To convince the woman I love to love me back.

Laura Leigh sagged onto a chair and let his words sink into her heart. He said he loved her. She loved him. It should be so simple, but she was intelligent enough to understand that wasn't enough. Trust had to enter into the recipe if they were to ever have any kind of relationship.

Her gaze returned to the parlor and where he'd disappeared down the hallway. She was sorely tempted to follow him and join him before he covered that magnificent body with clothes. Since the moment he'd entered the kitchen, she'd been a quiver of nerves. It had taken all her self-control not to literally throw him to the floor and take advantage of his nudity.

The smell of scorched food drew her out of her reverie. Rushing to the stove, she lifted the lid off the pot. Something was burning; black smoke curled from the pot.

"Trying to burn down my house?" Marc snatched two large towels from the shelf and plucked the pot from the hot fire by the handles. He set it aside on the warming tray.

"I forgot to stir it. But I'm sure it won't be ruined."

He dipped a spoon into the pot, and took a sip of the broth. "Not bad. Let's let it cool while we talk." He wore a pair of canvas trousers, low on his hip, and his plaid shirt hung open. Damp hair clung to his forehead.

She shrugged. "It's way past time for talking." A knot slipped to the pit of her stomach. Moments ago, he'd said he loved her. Did he still love his wife, too?

"I know. Please sit down. You have to know what happened with Serafina." He gestured to a chair. After she sat, he turned another chair backward and straddled the seat. He crossed his arms over the chair back.

"I was eighteen when the Romany caravan came through the county. Every night the gypsies put on entertainment— dancing, singing, and fortune-telling. Serafina was barely sixteen, and I thought she was the most beautiful creature I'd ever seen. She had the grace of a young wildcat, uninhibited and free. I fell head over heels before I knew what hit me."

His gaze slipped over her shoulder, and she wondered if the memories were painful, or if he was living with regret or guilt. His face was unreadable. She bit her lip to refrain from asking him to stop. She didn't want to know how much he loved another woman.

"The Romany are a close-knit clan, but she slipped away from the camp and met me night after night. When it was time for them to move on, I begged her to stay, to marry me. When I approached her father, he threw me out. He would never allow his daughter to marry a *Gorgio*. She'd been promised to one of his cousins since she was twelve. Before they left, she found she was expecting my child. Her father threw her out of the clan and said he washed his hands of a daughter who disobeyed the laws of her people." His voice deepened, and his green eyes turned icy.

Laura Leigh shifted on the chair. As difficult as it was to hear the truth, it was necessary. He should have told her this weeks ago.

He cleared his throat and continued. "We married, and I

was delighted. But she was miserable. She hated the farm, she
hated my parents, and it wasn't long before she hated me. I
should have understood that a woman used to a nomadic life
couldn't settle down on a farm. Not long after Billy was born,
she ran away with another tribe of Romany who passed through.
When my parents died, I raised my son alone. It was easier
and less embarrassing to let everybody think she'd died. I never
saw her again until I ran into her at the fair.''

She dropped her gaze and studied the blister on her palm
from her carelessness while baking the cobbler. ''What did she
want of you?''

''In a word, money. She'd seen us together and thought
we were married. She threatened to expose me as a bigamist,
and to take my son away from me. I paid her all I had in my
pocket. Then I think it was she who set those hoodlums on
me.''

''How awful. They meant to kill you.''

''They tried. You saved my life.''

She dropped her hand on his crossed arms. ''Why didn't
you tell me the truth? Did you think I wouldn't understand?''
She swallowed down the lump in her throat and said what had
tormented her for weeks. ''Or did you think I wouldn't sleep
with you if I knew you were married?''

His head jerked up. ''I didn't once think about that. I didn't
tell you because I felt like such a fool. I hadn't meant to fall
in love with you.''

''Do you love me, Marc?''

He lifted her hand to his lips. ''Lady, these past weeks
have been the worst in my life. I was ready to go to San
Antonio and bang on your door until you listened to me.''
He turned in the chair and pulled her onto his lap. She
wrapped her arms around his neck. ''If you're so intent on
becoming a journalist, I'll leave the farm and take a restaurant
job. Anything you want, just so we can be together. I want
you to marry me.''

She shoved out of his arms and stood. He didn't know

how wonderful his words sounded. "Wait here." Racing into the parlor, she snatched a sheaf of papers from her portfolio.

When she returned, he'd shoved a spoon into the baking pan. "Do you mind telling me what this is?"

"Blackberry cobbler, silly. I followed your instructions to the letter."

He rubbed his chin. "I'd better take another look at those directions."

She swatted him with the legal document. "Sit down and take a look at this."

"If you'll sit on my lap."

Smiling, she propped herself on his knees and wrapped her arms around his neck. While he read, she couldn't resist tasting the skin under his ear. It was slightly salty and tasted better than his special strawberry-rhubarb pie.

"I can't read if you torment me like that."

"Then I'll explain what it says so we can get down to serious business. My uncle was greatly impressed with you. He wants to invest in a new business—a restaurant, with you as chef, manager, and partner."

He jumped to his feet, nearly tumbling her to the floor. He steadied her with his hands on her arms. "I don't take charity."

Her gaze locked with his. Stubborn green eyes met equally stubborn hazel ones. "I'm not offering charity. My uncle is a shrewd businessman. He doesn't give anything away. He only sponsored the tour because he knew it would be a profitable venture. It's the same with the restaurant. He's out to make money."

"Did you ask him to do this?" His hard voice chilled her to the soul.

"Of course not. Nobody tells Fritz Westbrook what to do any more than anybody can influence my father."

"I suppose that's where you got your determination."

"Yes. If you aren't interested in operating your own business, just say no. I love you and I only want you to be happy. We'll live out here if you want to farm your land. You can develop your recipes and I can start that great American novel I've always wanted to write.''

His gaze dropped to the papers scattered on the table. "Let's think about it over dinner. Looks like you slaved away all afternoon.''

"Oh.'' She covered her mouth with her hand. "I forgot to make the biscuits.''

"We'll do without.'' He picked up the dishes and filled both from the large pot. "Smells good. Where did you get the chicken? Don't tell me you killed and cleaned it yourself?''

She poured coffee into the cups. "Not exactly. Billy said he was getting tired of eating stale bread, so he killed the chicken and was planning to cook it himself. He also picked the black-berries.''

"So that's what they are.'' He flashed a smile that took her breath away.

"You knew all along. I followed your recipe.''

They settled at the table and began to eat. The chicken was overcooked and the potatoes and carrots mushy. Marc lifted a forkful and swallowed. "Good,'' he said. "But one thing is wrong.'' He shoved back his chair. "You're too far away from me. Come sit on my lap.''

Grinning, she jumped up and landed on his legs. "Other than that, is it okay?''

"More than okay, it's great.''

He took one bite and fed the next to her. The action was so intimate and personal that she had trouble swallowing. By the time his plate was empty, her skin was aflame and her knees weak. "Now for dessert,'' he said.

When she tried to rise, he tightened his grip on her. "Not that kind. I haven't had a kiss in so long, I might have forgotten how it's done.''

"A kiss? You call that dessert?''

"Sweetheart, your lips are sweeter than . . .'' He slid a glance toward the stove. "Blackberries.''

"With sugar on them?"

His lips touched the corner of her mouth, taking tiny sips at the skin. "Much sweeter."

She twisted her head to accept the full force of his kiss. He was right; it was sweeter than any dessert. His mouth covered hers in a kiss that was gentle and giving, offering a world of love and excitement. His body was hard and warm against hers. "If we don't stop, we won't get through the meal."

"The cobbler can wait." Without warning, he stood and lifted her high against his chest. "The dessert I want is better in the bedroom."

"Mr. Lawrence," she said, laughing. So much joy filled her heart that she couldn't stop grinning. "Are you going to compromise me?"

He growled and kicked open his bedroom door. Once inside, he shoved it shut with his elbow. "Good and proper. Then I'll shout it from the rooftop." Unceremoniously he dropped her in the middle of his wide bed and followed her down.

Some time later, Laura Leigh lay sated and feeling infinitely pleased in Marc's arms. Their lovemaking had been the glorious coming together of two souls meant for each other. She loved him so much, she couldn't bear the thought of ever being away from him.

"You're right. That was better than dessert." She nuzzled her mouth in the soft hair on his wide chest.

"Keep that thought," Marc said. He jumped off the bed and raced from the room.

She sat up and stared at his bare bottom until it disappeared into the parlor. Dumbfounded, she started to rise heedless of her state of complete nudity. Before she managed to swing her legs to the side of the bed, he returned, the baking pan in his hand.

"How can we fairly judge which is better unless we can

compare the two." He plopped back on the bed and set the pan on his lap. "Let's have a taste."

Sticking a spoon into the cobbler, he guided it to her mouth, then to his. "Good. But still not as good as your kisses," she said, her tongue swiping across her lips.

Smiling, he finished off the bite. "A little crisp around the edges, but it'll do for an amateur."

"Amateur?" She caught his face between her hands and planted a full, hard kiss on his lips. "What do you think of that?" she asked, pleased with herself.

"Excellent. But maybe you'd better forget cooking and stick to journalism. I read your stories. They were very good." He dropped a kiss to her bare shoulder. Tingles raced over her skin.

The compliment warmed her heart as the touch of his mouth heated her skin. His touch nearly robbed her of coherent thought. "Thank you. I'll expect a fine meal every evening after slaving at the paper."

"At the restaurant, love. I'll cook for you every day, but not at home."

She pulled back and saw her happiness reflected in his eyes. "You mean you'll accept Uncle Fritz's offer?"

He threw back his head and laughed. "Sweetheart, I may be a dumb farm boy, but I'm no fool. You've made me two offers I can't refuse." His mouth found hers and the kiss was so full of love and promise, she thought her heart would pop right out of her chest.

Abruptly, he ended the kiss. "You didn't agree to marry me. Are we expected to live in sin? Or will you indeed become the woman you pretended to be? Will you become Mrs. Lawrence before the whole world and your family? Or do I have to compromise you again?"

"Yes. What woman would refuse a man who can cook like the finest European chef and kiss like the greatest Latin lover? And yes, you can compromise me any time it pleases you."

"Looks like you expect a lot of me."

She stroked her fingertips down his chest. "I hope you can live up to my expectations."

"I'll try, sweetheart, I'll surely give it my all—in and out of the kitchen."

Marc's Quick-and-Easy Blackberry Cobbler

Pastry

½ cup sugar
1 cup biscuit & baking mix
¼ cup butter
¼ cup milk
¼ t vanilla

Heat oven to 375 degrees. Mix sugar and baking mix. Cut in butter. Mix in milk and vanilla. Shape into a ball and refrigerate 30 minutes.

Filling

½ cup sugar
1 t flour
1 quart ripe berries, cleaned

Grease 7x11 baking pan. Mix sugar, flour, and berries. Pour into pan. Heat in oven 10 minutes.

Roll chilled dough out on floured surface. Place over hot fruit. Cut slits for steam vents. Bake 25 minutes or until golden brown. Brush with melted butter. Sprinkle with sugar. Makes six to eight servings. Delicious served with ice cream.

Variations: Substitute 2 cans of fruit pie filling for berry mixture.

ROMANCE FROM FERN MICHAELS

DEAR EMILY   (0-8217-4952-8, $5.99)

WISH LIST   (0-8217-5228-6, $6.99)

AND IN HARDCOVER:

VEGAS RICH   (1-57566-057-1, $25.00)

YOU WON'T WANT TO READ
JUST ONE—KATHERINE STONE